The

Bogeyman

Chronicles

D1313022

TP

ThunderPoint Publishing Ltd

First Published in Great Britain in 2016 by
ThunderPoint Publishing Limited
Summit House
4-5 Mitchell Street
Edinburgh
Scotland EH6 7BD

ISBN: 978-1-910946-10-7 (Paperback)
ISBN: 978-1-910946-11-4 (eBook)

www.thunderpoint.scot

Dedication

For Shirley and Maisie

Book I

"About Perth there was the countrie
Sae waste, that wonder was to see;
For in well-great space thereby,
Was neither house left nor herbery.
Of deer there was then such profusion,
That they would near come to the town,
Sae great default was near that stead,
That mony were in hunger dead.
A churl they said was near thereby,
That would set traps commonly,
Children and women for to slay,
And swains that he might over-ta;
And ate them all that he get might;
Chwsten Cleek till name behight.
That sorry life continued he,
While waste but folk was the countrie."

Andrew Wyntoun, *The Orygynale Cronykil* (c 1420)

Chapter 1

"Of browneis and of bogillis full is this buke."

Gavin Douglas, *Eneados* (1553)

All Hallows Eve, 1326

The scratching rouses me from near sleep. The noise is close, perhaps from beneath the bed box where I lie. A claw against a hard surface. But slow and steady; not the scuffle or gnawing of a rat. Other sounds make themselves known – the thin, even snores of my younger brother and sister alongside; the fire spitting in the hearth beyond – but nothing comes to me louder than the tale of the madman who escapes his bonds and devours children, plucking out their eyes with fingernails long and curved like the blade of a sickle. I open my eyes but remain still, as though buried up to my neck in sand or floating in the river below the midsummer sun. The light of the moon outlines the shutters. The noise changes: softer, closer. Tap, tap, tap. TAP. A meat hook appears before my eyes, no farther away than the reach of my breath, rising up slowly from below the height of my pallet. A double hook, like a poised serpent, it drags long, pale fingers and a loosely sleeved arm behind it. I may be no more than eight years but I know enough of demons, ogres, brownies and boggarts. The cloaked head that follows the arm is all of those, none of those; it is a creature, a sequence of shifting creatures, first a fox then a wild hound, a boar, a bear, a leopard, a dragon.

'Boo!'

It is my father, grinning. He throws back his hood. When our eyes meet, he too is a child, though a guilty one caught with his

2

thumb in the honey pot. He has crawled into the room without my seeing it. He is sorry at affrighting me, but still smiles. It was a jest, while also a rebuke. He wags the meat hook. 'Andrew Christie, you were asked to paunch and hang the hare's fleshmeat many hours ago.' He whispers it: I am not insolent but must remember my duties in the future. He lays a sure hand on my chest. I am safe.

Chapter 2

*"Under his feet he mightily burst up a plank of
the chamber floor and therewithal covered him
again, and entered adown low beneath among the
ordure of the privy that was all of hard stone and
none window nor issue thereupon, save a little
square hole even at the side of the bottom of the
privy, that at the making thereof old time was
left open to cleanse and firm the said privy."*

John Shirley, *The Dethe of the Kynge of Scotis* (c 1440)

9th Day of October, 1327

The foul hole was as deep as a well and wide enough at its base
for young Brodie to spread his arms. At one time, he could lie
flat and stretch out his legs, though now he had to bend his
knees to fit in. But despite the passage of years, the drain at the
foot of the tower between the north and west walls of Edzell
Castle remained his fortified keep, where not even the warden
could reach. The tools of the gong scourer were not only for
dislodging compacted night soil: the coppiced hazel rod was his
lance, the broken floor tile his painted shield.

Brodie wrapped the ragged coverchief tightly around his
mouth and nose until it was as stout as any basinet helmet and
better able to withstand the stench of the foul hole. Handling
the floor tile as skillfully as a noble knight wields a hand axe, he
scooped the overnight ordure from the latrine chute and
emptied it into the basket outside, just below the square mouth
of the drain. He would normally dispatch his load without
tarrying, to the gong farmers cart by the east bailey wall, but it

4

was raining: the shit would turn to sludge, seep through the basket twines and run down his arms. Instead, he lay flat and scanned the courtyard through the drain opening. No enemies were in sight. The courtyard was bare and the heavy wooden gateway secure.

But something moved on the distant horizon. He strained his eyes. And saw movement again. Beyond the westernmost rampart. On the lower slopes of the Hill of Lundie, across the West Water. He was sure of it.

Brodie squeezed through the drain, one shoulder at a time since he had grown taller than a pole these past months. He ran barefoot across the wet grass of the deserted courtyard, crouching behind the sagging palm ball net, clutching lance and shield. The warden or one of the serjeants would be keeping watch at the gatehouse so he made for the north wall, clambering up the rope ladder behind the bakehouse, where the baxters were already at work. He scuttled along the parapet boards on all fours until he reached an arrow slit on the west wall. Sure enough, past the waterfall and now across the Pirn Brig, a wagon and escorts approached, though at such a distance Brodie was not certain from the banner that flew if they were friend or foe.

He crawled along the walkway until he was over the entrance gate. The wagon emerged from the screen of wych elms and jolted up the track. Two horsemen, iron hooded, cased in mail, followed behind. Brodie pulled his cloth visor farther up the bridge of his nose and gripped his makeshift lance tighter. A voice called out from the advancing party, though Brodie could not make out the words.

'Come, come,' shouted back the warden from the gatehouse.

Brodie watched through a small murder-hole in the walkway as the warden below moved with uncharacteristic haste to lift one end of the huge bolt from its metal lug and then the other, his hairless head passing back and forth like a palm ball batted from the glove of one player to another. The gate creaked open.

'Come,' repeated the warden. 'The way is clear.'

The horse hitched to the wagon trotted forward. 'I fly the royal standard of the King of Scots,' announced the driver, grey and bearded. 'Is this a house of the loyal Lindsays?'

'It is, sire – Lord Patrick de Lindsay of Edzell and Glenesk.'

'Then by good fate, you may serve your king.' The mounted party halted at the gate and the driver jerked his head back towards the load on his cart. 'I bring evil cheer. Prince John de Brus – your sovereign's infant son and brother to the throne's heir – has passed to God. To ease the king's mourning, I carry the child's bones to the Priory of Restenneth for proper burial among the faithful Augustinian brothers there. His casket is of fine beechwood and leather but was not assembled for a route as pockmarked as this. The lid has shifted and we must find a wright to make repairs. Do you have such a craftsman?'

'Of course, sire. But he is not here – he is at the Forest of Platir, cutting wood for our own building repairs.'

'I fear the prince's mortal dignity will be in jeopardy if more damage is done to his current resting place.'

The warden stepped forward so that Brodie could no longer see him through the murder-hole. Brodie stood up and stretched on his toes to peer over the top of the rampart.

'Then could you spare us a squire to assist our journey?' asked the driver.

A weak sun rose behind Brodie's head. The warden rubbed a hand on his bald crown and let out a slow laugh. He took two long strides forward. Standing on the shadow cast by Brodie's head, he turned and jabbed his finger. 'That churl can be your lock and key.' Though the sun was at his back, Brodie put his tile shield to his brow in meagre defiance. The warden switched his attention back to the wagon driver. 'The urchin is growing too tall to clear this castle's drains and cesspits much longer but his bony, orphaned arse will fit well on the lid of your casket. Do this, but I ask something in return – leave him in the cloisters when your work is done. He spends too much of his time here playing at games of war. Assuredly, he will make a better monk than scourer of turds.'

Before the sun had fully set, Brodie sat on a stone stool in the fading light of the garth at Restenneth Priory, a blunt razor scraping at his scalp. Master Robert stood behind him, cupping his chin in one hand and shaving with the other. The cloisters were no taller than the bathhouse at Edzell, but the strangeness of the place towered over him, shutting out the girth of the sky. Cloaked figures moved between the stone arches.

6

'What tasks did you have at the castle?' asked Master Robert.

'Scooped the night soil,' replied Brodie. He watched Master Robert take another clump of his copper hair and tuck it into a hide pouch on the ground.

'And anything else?'

'Tended beasts.'

'Then you may tend some more now that you are in the care of this priory.'

Brodie said nothing. The razor tugged at his cold skin.

'There…' said Master Robert, gliding a palm over Brodie's shaved pate. '…you have the tonsure.'

The master's hands were firm when they moved, but not cruel.

'You do not think of yourself as a servant of God? What age are you, child?'

'Seven years. Maybe more.' He suspected it might be less.

'You would rather be a soldier of a valiant lieutenant – yes?'

'I am bold enough to be a soldier,' huffed Brodie.

Robert moved around to kneel in front of Brodie, sliding a basin of water between them. He lifted Brodie's bare right foot and dipped it in the water. His hands were bigger than those of any farm labourer.

'I have seen many soldiers, some of them bold enough, most now no more than bones below the ground.' Robert bathed Brodie's other foot and then towelled them both dry. 'Have you ever read a word?' asked Robert, drying his own hands.

Brodie shook his head. He shuffled on the stool, the cheeks of his backside aching after a full day's journey in the wagon.

'Or written one?'

Brodie scowled.

'The driver of the wagon found this note below your seat, after you had left.' Robert pulled a scrap of parchment from the folds of his gown. 'So it is not yours?'

Brodie shrugged.

'Yet you sat on the lid of the prince's coffin, did you not?' Robert read the note silently then turned it towards Brodie. 'It seems to speak of you.'

About the size of a folio cut in three, the top and left edges were as straight as a parchmenter would fashion, the other two torn crudely. A riddle trailed from the initial red rubric like a

7

beast's tail, though Brodie was drawn to the illustration rather than the words. Along the top, a wolf with saliva – or perhaps blood – dripping from its mouth pounced towards the right-hand ragged edge. Its head ripped off, a serpent emerged from the wolf's loins as if a phallus. The top and left margins were woven with incongruously delicate, floriated scroll-work in violet and green.

'I am the master to scribes as well as novices at this house. If this is a message for you, then I must teach you the skills of the scribe – you should be able to prepare parchment from the hides of the beasts you tend, read it with your eyes and mark it with your hand.' Robert's smile was ample enough, though it barely creased his heavy features.

Brodie nodded but remained silent. As the sun dipped farther, he saw that the shadows in the cloisters were shorter than those cast by the castle bailey, the evening air sweeter.

Robert began to read aloud, in a coarser voice than the one he used to speak.

> *"When the mortcloth of a regal brother,*
> *Begins the Annals of Egglespether;*
> *First the prior's house will fall,*
> *To the overlord of Balliol.*
> *The wicked Norse wind usurps the west;*
> *Two grains from a seed of wheat, at best.*
> *Orphans of war; fiends in a den.*
> *Blood will fill the scribe's inkpot and pen."*

Book II

"At that time the whole of the adjacent land was to such a degree laid waste that there was almost no inhabited house left, but wild beasts and deer coming down from the mountains were often hunted around the town. So great then was the dearth and lack of provisions that the common folk were starving everywhere; and eating grass like sheep, they were found dead in pits. Nearby there lurked in a ruined building a certain peasant called Christy Cleke...[who] lay in wait for women, children and young people, and after strangling them like a wolf, lived on their flesh."

Walter Bower, *Scotichronicon* (1447)

Chapter 1

6th Day of December, 1335

Curled in the dirt like a dog booted in the ribs by its master, I watch as de Moray's men strip my father of his skin and divide it among themselves in small parts. I lie tethered to our standard: the Christies of Finzean, who forwent their obligation to join the army of de Moray in the battle at Culblean. If I turn and lift my head just off the ground, I can see it: my father's black, yellow and red pennon against the white clouds above, the pennon twitching one way, the clouds rushing the other. I breathe in dust, a fowl scratches and pecks loudly just beyond my ear. The burning house crackles as loud as a hundred pigs on a spit. The smoke mixes with the dust, the heat from the inferno dries my lips and burns at my eyelids. I close my eyes as my mother and sister are ravaged and beaten by one, two, five or ten men-at-arms. Peck, peck, peck. Scratch, peck. '...you fucking treacherous, cursed quean...' He squeals with pleasure, or laughter. Or is it a swine being slaughtered? '...suck on it, I command...you will be wide enough for a cat to hibernate for a year when the victorious army of de Moray has finished its business...' The other men say nothing. The fowl moves away.

Amid sobs, my mother screams: 'He made payment during peace! To commute service during war!' Over and over she shouts it. 'My husband made payment…he made payment…he made the wretched payment.' No-one responds. My sister moans and mumbles: something pathetic, not defiant. Heavy footsteps move close. I open my eyes. I have seen enough to know it is the squealer; he has a thick, broad-bladed knife in his right hand, hanging by his side. He is much bigger and more thickset than his giggly squeals suggested. He turns to say something to my mother/sister, a question of some sort: '…make a trumpet of his arse…you want me to?' He points the knife at me. Then swings it away. Then back again. Perhaps fearful where and when it will next come down, I follow the line of the blade. And beyond, behind Squealer, in the direction of the river, I see him! A small boy crouched in the reeds, gesturing wildly. My brother, who is not yet twelve years, is waving his arms madly, almost as though he wishes to be seen by the despoilers. His lips are wide, then pursed, again and again. He is mouthing my name: *An-drew! An-drew!* He half stands, clearly visible now, points at the river and pulls his arms to and fro, bending and straightening them. He is pleading, as though he has been waiting for this moment since we were woken by cries of 'Havoc!' before even dawn, as if willing his eyes to burst into a yell. My gaze travels farther. The boat: he is pointing at the logboat. The knife has moved closer; it is so close I can no longer see it without straining my neck. Squealer is standing over me. He follows my bulging stare. More fear-filled than at any moment since the first, I look back to my brother's hiding place. He has ducked down, hidden again. Squealer hacks at my bonds: two, three times, then a final sawing motion. He catches a finger. It is not greatly sore so difficult to tell which one, probably the small one on my left hand. But my hands are free. And now my feet. Squealer drags me into a standing position and hands me the knife. *Hands me the knife.* 'Son of the packsaddle – end your mother's pitiful drone,' he says, with no hint of a squeal. He holds a long-handled halberd confidently in his left hand. The curved axe head faces the ground, like a jester's open-mouthed, leering smile. I look at the knife in my fingers, at the men around the flaming scene: no more than a score, most handling spoil.

The woman still alive behind Squealer is my mother; the lifeless form is my young sister. A spear's throw to the right, my brother is climbing into the boat. I make a decision and fall to my knees. Squealer bends down to yank me upright. Before his grip has fully tightened, I spring to my feet and cleave his skull and brain, cutting down through him beyond his feet until the blade hits hard ground below and the handle shivers in two. I take the bare blade in my hand – it cuts into my palm – and bring it down between his legs, into his boneless flesh so that the thing will never swell again, in this life or the next. Then I run to the boat and my brother kicks off from the shore.

Chapter 2

*"The king of England had in a hostile manner
reduced with fire and sword everything beyond the
mountains …many souls who had fled to the
churches he had wiped out and completely
destroyed together with the churches themselves."*

Walter Bower, *Scotichronicon* (1447)

5th Day of August, 1336, until the 14th Day of the Same Month

The strong-armed force of knights arrived at the priory during the night in a clatter of destrier hooves and light steel. As modest as a visiting delegation of Carthusian monks, they refused to disturb the singing of matins and asked Prior Bernard simply for hospitality until morning.

At daybreak, their courtesy turned to hostility.

A din of wrathful shouts and the erratic ringing of the bell woke Brother Brodie. Unable to separate the truth of asleep from awake, he rose slowly. Sitting upright, Brodie saw the commotion: directly opposite, Brother Donald was on his knees, reaching between his scalp and the shadows around his bunk, as though unable to find his cowl; alongside, Brother Hector pleaded loudly with a soldier who was half through the trapdoor that led below; Finlay sat on the floor to Brodie's left, his back to the wall, picking at a crust from his nose; Brother Walter started towards the trapdoor, wailing. 'What storms of desolation do you devise for us?'

'No more words!' The soldier at the hatch brought the flat of his sword down on the floorboards with a fearsome crash. 'You will descend the ladder just as I say.'

Walter quieted.

Hector stared at the soldier a while longer, as if providing a final opportunity to revoke the order. Eventually, he turned to the others and, with a limp wave of his hand, beckoned them to follow him down the ladder.

Still sitting on his bunk, Brodie went to pull on his cowl, seeing only when he moved it what lay beneath: his belt and sheathed knife. Leaving the cowl, and with a glance upward, he carefully unfastened the sheath and withdrew the dressing knife. Fingers trembling, he flipped it inside his loose sleeve, so that he held the handle while the cold blade lay across his wrist and forearm.

Fearing any look would announce that he had a weapon concealed, Brodie kept his eyes from the soldier who herded the brethren from the dormitory into the church choir at the point of a sword. His gaze remained diverted from the two lancemen – one at the main entrance, the other at the night stair – who prevented them leaving the church.

Before anyone had taken their proper places, Prior Bernard ordered the brothers, lay and priestly alike, to lie prostrate and shrive themselves before the high altar, trusting that ritual worship would bring comfort. Brodie laid his cheek on the dusty floor, close to Brother Walter's feet, and joined Bernard in reciting the Confiteor. Walter's feet twitched and scuffed the floor in a way that caused Brodie more anxiety than the guards' steady grip on the shafts of their upright weapons.

A thump on the night stair door broke the thrum. Brodie and some of the brothers faltered; others raised their voices louder than before without interruption. The prior got to his feet, followed by Master Robert and Brother Hector, then Brother Hugh. Brodie remained prone but looked over his shoulder. The guard at the night stair moved to one side and the heaviest clad of all the knights they had seen – wearing azure and silver shoulder ailettes and decorated breastplate – pushed open the door and stepped into the chapel.

Bernard approached the knight. 'Are you the captain of this host?' The choir fell silent when the prior spoke. Brodie withheld a breath in the sudden stillness. The rumble of falling masonry and splintering of timbers could be heard outside.

'Who asks?'

'I am Bernard, prior here and father of these fearful brothers.' He swept an arm around the church. 'Why do you bring destruction to our house?'

Brodie raised himself onto one elbow to ease his own weight from his thudding heart.

The knight kicked shut the door. The clink of his mail chausses reached the ribs of the vaulted ceiling. 'I do not destroy, I build. Ruinous engines of war – a Bostour, mangonel catapults – to level fortifications in the surrounding lands. And since we strip timbers only from your own well-furnished quarters, it may also serve to remind you of your vow of poverty and austerity.'

Bernard hesitated for an instant before replying. 'I need no lessons in faith from one who preaches war rather than peace.'

'Then heed this lesson, peace-monger…' The captain leaned close to Prior Bernard, like one recalcitrant monk whispering to another in the choir stalls. '…The commonalty may have joined Moray to ensure Balliol suffered defeat at Culblean. But Balliol's overlord is on your soil now. And be sure that Edward – the King of England, Ireland, Wales and Aquitaine – will show no such frailty before the rabble. The machines of war that I build will reduce the lands to desolation, destroy freeholds and level each dwelling – houses of God too, if that is what is needed.' He leaned away from Bernard and raised his voice. 'Let it be known that I am Sir Henry de Bown, servant of King Edward.'

Bernard replied quickly, allowing no time for the declaration to reverberate through the church. 'Then you are of noble birth and the noble lion allows captive men to depart and spares the man who lays before him.' With a rippling motion of his hand, the prior indicated the brothers who were still prostrate on the floor. 'I beg that you spare this house of God and all within.' He bowed.

The captain moved a step closer. In the same motion, he thrust his forearm upwards, shovelling the heel of his gloved hand into Bernard's top lip and nose. The prior staggered backwards and slumped with a shudder into a sitting position.

The semblance of normality constructed by Bernard crumbled with the blow. Master Robert stepped out from behind the lectern at the western end of the choir and stood between de Bown and Bernard, who dabbed at his face and looked between the blood on his hand, his white surplice and the floor. Even without armour, Robert was a foot's length taller than the knight. 'By God's grace, let your sacrilegious hands take what they came for so that you may leave all the sooner.'

Robert spoke with equal measures of urgency and restraint, in a tone Brodie did not recognise as the scribe master's own.

In the silence that followed, Brother Archibald rose from his knees and stood just behind Robert. To the right of the small group, Brodie slid up onto his haunches and twisted his knife around so that just the tip of the blade poked from his sleeve. His fingers closed around the handle. Yet he could not muster the courage to raise his head and clasp so firmly to de Bown's stare. Still prone by the step leading to the sanctuary, Brother Peter carried on the Confiteor where Prior Bernard had left off.

The captain barged past Robert and seized a silver chalice jug from a shelf on the wall. He turned back to face Robert, brandishing the chalice like a club. 'If one with the cure for so many souls ordains that we should take what this monastery has to offer, who am I to refuse such bounty?' He kicked open the aumbry cupboard below the shelf and shouted to the two guards. 'These kindly men of God have offered us their silver vessels. Fill a sack with all that you can find!'

The first guard to the cupboard raked the contents onto the floor: a brass aquamanile pitcher; coloured altar cloths; white chalice cloths; the silver communion plate; a saintly image; a carved pyx for the Eucharist Host. The second guard picked his way quickly through the crowded church and gathered an armful of candlesticks from the altar. Climbing onto the freestone altar, he plucked a jewelled crucifix from the ledge of the middle of three lancet windows high on the east wall. The priory's missal skidded to the ground as he jumped back down.

'Books and worldly goods too!' shouted de Bown, seeing the liturgical book fall.

The guard by the altar kicked out at the nearest brother. The toecap of his boot caught Brother Peter's right ear. Peter gripped the side of his head, though his eyes remained downcast. Brother James rubbed his own face, as though that might somehow ease Peter's suffering.

16

'Tell me – where do you keep your moveables?' demanded the guard, while swiping a foot at Peter's shoulder. Peter responded with a stifled grunt.

Brodie looked around at the brothers, most now standing but some kneeling or prostrate; together, dazed and acquiescent.

The soldier dropped all but one of the candlesticks under his arm and hauled at Peter's tunic. Peter rolled onto his back without struggling. The guard raised the silver candlestick and brought it down heavily on Peter's knee, cracking first bone then flagstones. Peter let out a series of high-pitched shrieks and leaned forward to nurse his shattered leg.

'Please, please, please…' he whispered, rocking backwards and forwards. 'Take it, take it all, please, in there, in the book cupboard.' He pointed weakly at the entrance to the sacristy and library to his right.

'Enough!' Master Robert stood in the entrance Peter had indicated. 'Enough blood has been spilled.'

For a moment, his intervention appeared to have worked. De Bown nodded repeatedly, small nods as though counting in his head. Both guards looked to their captain.

His limbs stiff as planks, Brodie stood and edged towards Robert.

'And who are you to tell me enough blood has been spilled?' asked de Bown.

'I am Robert, master of scribes and novices and precentor in the chancel where we stand.'

Without a word, de Bown snatched the lance that stood propped against the shelf above the aumbry and ran past the choir stalls straight at Robert. Brother Hugh took a single step forward. Arms groped in de Bown's direction, in disbelief rather than meaningful attempts to block his charge. The lance pierced the scribe master below the ribs. De Bown continued to shove the lance deeper, first with both hands firm against the vamplate, then by thrusting behind the weight of his shoulder. Robert gasped, as though choking one breath in at the same time as he tried to force another out. The shaft of the lance bent close to breaking point as de Bown tried to lift Robert off the ground; he shifted it to a horizontal position and pushed the scribe master through the curtained entrance into the sacristy. After a final,

17

juddering heave, the lance passed through Robert's body and lifted his tunic at the back like a tent pole. De Bown lunged forward, past the tiny library cell, dragging Robert's body against Prince John's sarcophagus.

It had happened in a short space of time, but time enough for a thousand tragedies and a thousand triumphs elsewhere in the world. Brodie had not willed his feet to move but found that he stood behind de Bown, close enough to see blood welling in Robert's open mouth and demons gathering in his eyes. Brodie took a step backwards.

De Bown dropped the lance and spun round to face Brodie. 'Your Robert...' He spat out the name but otherwise spoke in a hushed voice. '...is master of no more than dust now. He should have submitted to his overlord, as his namesake Robert – the Steward of your wretched land – has to King Edward. To wit, it was your own High Steward who told us we could lay hands on metal and wooden riches at this house – and more than just that too.'

Brodie glanced over his shoulder. All eyes were fixed on the horror of what de Bown had done, but no-one appeared to have heard his last words.

Staring at Brodie, de Bown drew his arming sword and raised his voice. 'So, do we have another who thinks himself a soldier – at least, until I pierce him through with daylight?'

Still Brodie could not draw the knife from his sleeve.

'We have sacred relics...' called Bernard from across the church. '...Saint Curitan, who planted faith in the hearts of thirty six thousand converts and who witnessed the Law of the Innocents, which forbade even touching the hair of clerics. They are in the tower – take them and leave us in God's peace, I beg you.'

De Bown nodded rapidly, as he had done before, and told one of his men to check the tower. The soldier remained in the tower loft as long as it took his fellow lanceman to lift the lid from Prince John's tomb, put it through the painted glass window and tip out the dead infant's bones.

The first soldier descended the ladder with more caution than he had shown on the way up. He picked his way down the rungs with one hand; in the other, he balanced a small, wooden reliquary, ornately embossed with copper and silver.

'Then we now have all that we came for,' said de Bown, eyeing the reliquary. 'We should thank the good brothers for their generosity.' He bowed to Bernard and ordered the lancemen to pack up the communion vessels and library documents. He left the church with the relics under his arm.

Brodie was the first to Robert's side. His master's gaping stare was as still as a stone. Brodie drew Robert's eyes shut and tried to do the same with his slack mouth, though it fell open again. Brother James the infirmarian was next alongside, to check for signs of life. Prior Bernard had begun the Litany of the Dying even as he made his way across the church. "Go forth, O Christian soul, from this world..." On James's instructions, Brodie helped try to wrench the lance from Robert's body, which lurched heavily with every tug. The lance came some way but failed to withdraw fully. They gave up and slid the corpse onto the sacristy floor. Finally, Brodie drew his knife. He hacked the shaft where it entered Robert's abdomen and exited through his back, leaving a length of pole inside the body. The brethren gathered round. Brodie stood; he had the sensation of swaying, like a sapling yielding to the first squall of winter.

A single shout of 'Withdraw!' from outside announced the departure of the raiding party. Hearing the loud creak of heavily laden carts pulling away, Archibald told Brother Walter to fetch oil and water, Symon a winding sheet and Finlay a bucket of ashes. When they returned, Archibald scattered the ashes over the body – back and front – in the shape of a cross. Tilting his head back to prevent blood running into his mouth, Bernard sprinkled holy water and performed the last rites. The ministrations complete, he stood, sleeve held to his nose, while Archibald carefully wrapped the body in the winding sheet.

'How everlasting is the devil's envy?' said Bernard, shaking his head while he watched Archibald at work. For once, he seemed unable to find either a fitting sermon of his own making or an appropriate scripture. 'Master Robert will sup with Christ before this day is out and we must make preparations,' he added, recovering his authority. 'The Mass of the Dead will be sung after collation and night prayers – to be ready, our duties must change. Brother Archibald – you will take Master Robert's seat as precentor at collation and Brother Peter will take your place as sacrist.' He dipped his head apologetically at Peter. 'I can see you are lame, my son, but the bell must be rung for Master Robert before you visit the infirmary.'

Peter nodded his acceptance and, with assistance from Brother Hugh, hobbled towards the bell tower.

Bernard paused, holding a crooked forefinger loosely in the air. He hooked the finger on his top lip like a fleshy moustache. 'Brother Brodie…' He smiled, not from pleasure but as though he had recalled something elusive, '…since Brother Peter is now keeper of the bell and vessels, the librarian's duties pass to you. Is your hand able?'

'With God's will, Father.' Brodie's firm voice carried more certainty than his trembling hands.

'Very well. Master Robert's obituary will be read at collation. You must prepare the parchment and record our words of lamentation on the Mortuary Roll for the breviator to carry to the mother house and others, to request their prayers.' He went to turn away from Brodie but arrived at an afterthought. 'An inventory of library documents plundered and spared should also be compiled – include it among your assignments.' The prior clapped his hands three times in quick succession. 'Brothers who have not been handed tasks will place Master Robert's earthly remains on a platform before the high altar. There is much to do and time is against us. Do what must be done, as sure as we are Christ's garrison within these walls.'

Brodie had known death before, and on each occasion he had wondered only whether the liberated soul was on a journey to heaven, hell or purgatory. But he could not bring himself to think that Robert was in any of those places, or even pray that the scribe master would reach the bliss of heaven in due course. Master Robert should have been by Brodie's side, guiding him out of the church and along the goat's path that led to the low parchmenter's shack by the south shore of the loch. As it was, all that walked with him was the rustle of his own footsteps through the coarse heather.

Once inside the shack, Brodie set to work in the kind of trance afforded only to practised craftsmen. The sheepskins had been flayed, soaked in lime and urine, scraped on the beam and rinsed.

Now the drying frames stood upright in a large, open-topped crate beside the tool store. Brodie lifted out each wooden frame carefully and stroked the surface of the pale skins, back and front. The first three were as fine as sarcenet. The other two still had a glossy film on the hair side; Brodie reached for the curved knife on the shelf and gave them a last scrape. Unable to pull a blade in defence of his master's life, he now wielded one to do no more than prepare a parchment that would carry word of Robert's death. Brodie removed the skins from their frames, gently loosening each cord from its peg to avoid punctures or tears. He shaped two as scrolls and cut the remainder into folios.

Contrary afternoon winds had brought low slushy clouds from the north and the rain began to fall as Brodie left the shack. He sheltered the parchment under his forearm and quickened his step.

Brodie tried to keep his eyes from Robert's corpse as he walked back through the chapel, though the scribe master's pallid face was held in the light cast from the lancet windows above the altar. He allowed the movements and sounds of the others in the sanctuary to distract his attention: young Symon the novice on his knees, praying; Brothers Hugh and Finlay constructing the funeral bier; Archibald watching over them all, Robert's crucifix dangling from his fingers.

Brodie turned into the sacristy. Alone there for the first time, he drew the main curtain shut and took in the devastation. A neat, petal-shaped pool of blood remained where Robert had fallen. Elsewhere, the blood had been scuffed across the floor with the removal of Robert's body. The lid of Prince John's tomb had cracked in two when the lanceman went to hurl it through the window, leaving a small section still in place; it showed a lion curled around a child effigy's pointed poulaine toes. Fragments of bone, stone, wood and glass were strewn around the sacristy. The second curtain, which screened off the library cell from the rest of the room, had been pulled to the floor and the book cupboard emptied of its contents. The desk, however, appeared untouched; the writing tools were still in the shelf on the side and several texts sat neatly on the writing slope: copies of the Gospels and the Liturgy of the Hours, bound between wooden board covers. Beneath those volumes lay a fading bifolium folded between a pasteboard cover; written in archaic uncial script, it gave an account of the foundation of Restenneth – or, Egglespether, as it was termed – by Culdee priests in the eighth century. Brother James kept the Canon of Medicine, by Avicenna, and Bald's Leechbook in the infirmary so it was likely they too were safe.

Sitting down at the desk, Brodie reached into the cabinet behind the writing slope; his fingers touched wood. He pulled out a pine kist, then another, and another: separate kists for ecclesiastical scripts, indulgences, pension benefices, cellarers' accounts and notarial instruments. All neatly ordered by Master Robert.

Brodie glanced at the bloodstain on the floor. A memory of Robert alive stumbled over the reminder of his brutal death. He steadied himself by squeezing his eyes tight shut then stretching them wide open: twice, each time for more than just a moment.

He got up and dragged the fallen curtain over the bloodstain.

Brodie took a heavy breath and returned to his task. Mindful of the approach of collation, he worked with added haste, reading some documents in full but no more than glancing at most. He lifted a bundle from a tightly packed kist. Fingering through the papers, he found one common priory deed followed by another. As he returned a fistful of parchment to the kist, a seal flopped from among the scrolls. Unlike the others, the wax image of Saint Peter holding the keys to the kingdom of heaven in front of an inverted cross was elliptical rather than circular; and it was fixed to the document by a braid rather than stamped to a tongue of parchment. Brodie unravelled the scroll, an indenture of novitiate. The deed was written on a shortened length of parchment, with a jagged edge along the bottom where the document had been divided in two; the upper and lower halves would originally have been identical, one portion for each contracted party.

> "On the Feast of Saint Dionysius the Areopagite, in the year of Grace 1327, I Lord Patrick de Lindsay, of Edzell and Glenesk, without guile, place with you, the Prior and his brethren at St Peter's ecclesia, Restenneth, this oblate, whose worth as gong scourer has expired. The child is adjudged to be six years since his birth and is known as Brodie of the faithless

> *Afflecks, who received the incomprehensible but righteous judgement of God. He shall be bound continuously throughout his life in the Rule of Augustine, first as novice and, when of man's estate, he will take vows. Also, by this agreement, I promise to give, for expenses of bread, tunic, shelter and necessaries, two davochs of land at Monikie and Pitairlie belonging to the demesne at Monikie.*
>
> *Pledging all my goods, etc, renouncing the benefit of all laws, etc.*
>
> *To this, I Bernard, the Prior at Restenneth, receive the said Brodie and pledge to raise him in Holy fraternity to endure Christ's sacred wounds protected by the shield of faith and the helmet of salvation."*

A list of witnesses followed. The script was unfamiliar and did not carry the mark of Robert or Peter. The second copy of the document – what should have been Brodie's one – was missing. Brodie snatched at the kist with the charters. There were ten or more for that year but none contained the other copy or any further mention of Brodie or his family.

He scanned the indenture document again.

The first of three peals of the bell sounded from the nearby tower to summon the brothers for collation. Brodie's eyes returned to the same passages, as though they were illuminated in burnished gold and silver.

> *"Brodie of the faithless Afflecks…Whose worth as gong scourer has expired…The incomprehensible but righteous judgement of God."*

With the hum of the third bell still held between the priory walls, Brodie took his place at collation, in the unfamiliar seat of the scribe.

Brother Archibald rose from his place on the opposite bench, his sloping features sinking into a thin scowl. As precentor-designate, he led the obituaries: 'Today, Father, we should have the great bell rung.'

'For whom?' asked the prior.

'For our beloved Brother Robert, recently sub-prior, precentor and master to scribes and novices.'

Bernard bowed. 'May his soul and the souls of all the faithful, by the mercy of God, rest in peace.'

Despite being tiled, the low floor gave off an earthy chill. The only sound was Brodie's nib scratching mortuary roll parchment, his apprentice's hand struggling to keep up.

"Brodie of the faithless Afflecks…"

He rested his forearm on the makeshift writing desk – a table from the scullery – and rotated his wrist in a circle.

Bernard continued. 'Master Robert's soul has been freed from the chains of his body and departed to Christ, the author of true liberty….'

Unfamiliar with scribing in low light and too distant from the cresset lamps, Brodie edged closer to the window through to the dusky cloister. He squinted as he dipped his quill into the bone inkhorn.

'…We commend his soul to the Almighty by our psalms.' With open palms, the prior indicated a moment for personal prayer and contemplation.

"…The incomprehensible but righteous judgement of God."

Brodie blotted ink on the scroll and smudged it across the subsequent two lines with his drooping sleeve.

Collation closed with Prior Bernard reciting De Profundis. He thudded the arm of his chair three times and the brethren formed a line in age order along the north wall. Archibald, the eldest, pulled open the heavy oak door to leave. Brother Symon – excluded from the affairs of the house because of his status as a novice – stood meekly on the other side of the entrance, two steps up from the others, eyes lowered, hands together in prayer. Unmoving and enclosed by the concentric arches of the doorway, he had the appearance of a saintly icon mounted in a statue niche.

Surprised that his path was blocked, Archibald stuttered. 'Brother…son…what…?' Recovering with a tug of his cowl, he continued. 'Child, you await your superiors – what need do you have of us?'

'I have tidings, Master,' said Symon, still focused on the floor.

'Go on.' Archibald shifted sideways at the arrival alongside of

Prior Bernard's bulky presence.

'A messenger of the realm has arrived, Master...' – he nodded towards the prior – '...Father.'

'And what is the nature of his business? Speak up,' said Bernard.

'He brings news of a visit to our humble house – the High Steward of the realm himself, along with his consort, Lady Elizabeth Mure of Rowallan.'

'By my faith! When, child?' asked Bernard.

'He did not set a date, Father, but expected it would be within these first two weeks. The Steward is detained at Methven but will soon continue to the hunting park at Balmoral. The messenger is in guest quarters and has taken repast and drunk well of wine.'

The prior looked down the line of brethren until he fixed on Brother Hugh towards the rear. 'By the bond of our faith, brother, tell me it will be possible to rebuild my chambers and lodge guests there within two weeks.' He waved a hooded arm over his shoulder at the cracked arcading on the east wall of the chapter house, evidence of the damage de Bown and his knights had caused to the adjoining prior's house.

His face pitched at every angle – brow, cheeks, nose, chin – Hugh stared at the crumbling wall, as though assessing the task ahead through an open window. 'I cannot say for certain, Father. But every effort will be made.'

'Christ denies nothing to those who have brought him their greatest riches,' said Bernard. 'The Steward may not be our exiled and rightful boy-king but he is the sovereign's kin and of noble standing. Preparations must be made without delay. From cock-crow until the final hour of daylight all brethren should excuse themselves from any duties not devoted to the Divine Office and do as Brother Hugh bids, whether the task be small or large, in silence or with whatever tumult is necessary. With the ordinance of the Creator – and our prayers – a small stone may overturn a great wagon.'

Mention of the Steward's name – briefly from the lips of de Bown when the sun was high in the sky, at length now as it fell below the Whitehills – seemed to be following Brodie like a shadow. On neither occasion could he locate a response worthy of the royal subject matter. He remained mute and filed out of the chapter house, through the narrow parlour and into the church by the east processional door. Instead of taking his usual seat for night prayers, he passed beneath the painted cross on the rood screen that separated the lay conversi from the canons regular, stopping at the end of the choir stalls, before reaching the step up to the high altar. In the low candlelight, he could endure regarding Master Robert more closely. Without seeking permission, he stepped up into the sanctuary, towards the platform where the body lay. Brodie might have expected the amber glow and breezy movements of the candles to give the scribe master some appearance of life. All he saw were signs of death: a bruised outline where Robert's hands rested on the bier, his neck taut, eyelids stiff. Brodie made the sign of the cross. 'In the name of the Lord and indivisible Triune…' he said in a whisper. He kissed his trinity of three fingers and tapped a blessing on his master's cold forehead, lips and chest. '…Father, Son…'

Turning away, he glimpsed the contrasting expressions of Bernard and Archibald as he stepped down from the sanctuary. The prior sat in the recessed sedilla with bowed intensity. Next to him, Archibald was wide-eyed at the unorthodoxy of a lay brother entering the sanctuary without allowance.

*

During the novena of mourning, Brodie kept close custody of his tongue lest its overuse distract from the work of his heart – praying earnestly for the soul of Master Robert – and his hand, compiling an inventory of priory documents.

On the eighth day, he completed the inventory. But despite scouring the records, Brodie found no further sight of his own name among the lines of text.

On the ninth day of mourning, the Steward's baggage carriers arrived at Restenneth.

'Brother Brodie…' Malcolm the guest master intercepted Brodie as he waited in line to rinse his knife at the lavatorium.

'Master Malcolm.' He bowed.

'The Steward's courier brings papers in need of gathering and binding.'

26

'Papers?'

'The courier asks for Master Robert by name – such was his repute – but since he has ascended to higher enterprise than that of a lowly scribe, you must make the repairs. As haste is needed, you are excused from compline, though you must return to the choir chapel for Requiem. The papers await you in the library.'

'Might you know what is included among these papers?'

'I…I believe they are from the Steward's archive in Perth, though the contents are really neither my concern nor yours.'

'The Steward's archive?'

Master Malcolm sighed heavily. 'Brother, why so dim-witted? It is a simple task.'

Far from dim-witted, Brodie was performing a calculation, adding one thought to another. 'Of course, Master. I will see to it at once.'

Inside the sacristy, a wax-treated canvas covered the broken window. Master Robert's blood had long since been mopped up, though a stain remained on the floor.

Before even taking a seat, Brodie reached for the first of the pipe rolls that lay on the desk, the anticipation of accessing a new source of information taking the place of regret that the priory documents had provided no new discoveries.

The rolls consisted of two sheets of parchment attached head to head and joined with other documents from the same trysting place by a ridge of stitching along one side. All were from nearby locations: the royal residences at Methven, Scone, Glamis and Kindrochit; the religious houses at Coupar Angus, Arbroath, St Andrews, Perth. And Restenneth.

The priestly brothers shuffled into the adjacent choir for compline.

Fingers fumbling, Brodie smoothed the Restenneth pipe roll flat on the writing slope of his desk and thumbed through the papers: records of resident councils, parliaments and exchequer audits; tax writs, tailzies, grant confirmations, letters of protection and endowments.

Beyond the sacristy curtain, Archibald led the first of the three psalms.

Like the other papers, the endowments were in date order: one from 1333, two from 1330 and another from 1328.

The chapel fell silent; the darkness was complete beyond the shrouded window.

A moment later, Brother Archibald led the recital of psalm 133 – "Behold! How good and how pleasant it is for brethren to dwell together in unity" – and Brodie turned to the next sheet of parchment, dated 1327: the same year as the indenture of novitiate he had found. He grabbed at the next sheet, also from 1327, the worn stitching coming loose in his hands. He flattened the crisp parchment, already off-white, on the desk, breathing in the slightest waft of mildew as he did so.

> *"Our sovereign and most illustrious prince, King Robert the First, worthy by his valour to govern the empire of Rome, confers fitting endowments for prayers, soul masses and suffrages for his son, Prince John de Brus, now among God's chosen people in joy, pleasure and angel song, despite the ministerings of John the Barbour, learned in the Doctrine of Signatures. By sovereign command, the Prior and his brethren at St Peter's ecclesia, Restenneth, will also construct a Holy sacristy with window of lead and coloured glazing and right regal tomb of master mason's stone adorned with enamels. The Prior etc. will receive a sum of ten pounds and one tenth of the income from judicial procedures at Forfar, to be paid on the term days of Candlemas, Whitsun, Lammas and Martinmas. From this day, the ninth day of October in the year of our Lord, 1327, when Prince John de Brus was delivered from the castle at Edzell along with an oblate boy, this endowment shall include a weekly pittance of milk & almonds..."*

Brodie could remember little about his arrival at Restenneth – Master Robert removing his hair by the handful, a wearisome journey that threatened not to end until they reached England itself – and had been told nothing of his family. Now, in the space of ten days, access to the priory library and the Steward's archives had taught him something of both, but insufficient of either.

He left the endowment on the writing slope and lifted the kist with his indenture closer. He placed the two documents side-by-side as if they might fit together; they were cousins, but not in near degree. The indenture was written on parchment in unfamiliar italic, the endowment on vellum in chancery hand. Both documents made known a connection with the Lindsays of Edzell and Glenesk, though Brodie's fleeting recollections of those people and places shed as much light as a crack of distant lightning. The indenture gave him an age – of around fifteen years – perhaps a childhood home in the area of Monikie and Pitairlie, a family name – Affleck – and mention of a family itself, even if the description of their fate chilled him as thoroughly as a visitation from a ghoul. The endowment told him of the day he arrived at Restenneth nine winters before, in the same wagon as Prince John's coffin. He had sat by the dead royal's bones then, just as he did now.

Archibald preached in the distance. "...your adversary the devil is prowling round like a roaring lion, seeking for someone to devour..."

Brodie lifted the endowment and indenture – as carefully as he might proffer a Eucharist wafer – and put them on the lid of the kist. More hurriedly, he untied the knife sheath from the belt that drew together the drapes of his gown and opened the pocket at the front designed for a small blade. He eased out the fragment of parchment Robert had given him on that first day. Despite having committed the verse to memory, he read again the first line: *"When the mortcloth of a regal brother ... "*

Through in the chapel, Brother Archibald raised his voice for the benediction and lowered it again for the dismissal.

"Amen."

A heavy sludge displaced the weightlessness that had filled Brodie's head. He prayed silently for the merciful departure of Master Robert's faithful soul.

Chapter 3

"I therefore beg you and in begging order you to write a special and full account and record all these proceedings in fair writing indelibly in a book, that the memory of them be not lost by any length of time."

Henry III of England to Matthew Paris, a monk at St Albans (1247)

28th Day of August, 1336

Outwardly, repairs had been made in the weeks since the raid. Boards covered the broken sacristy window, lime and clay held together the cracked tomb of John the Brus.

But Master Robert's presence had been stripped from the library as thoroughly as the books from its shelves. Now it was Brodie's thumbprints that marked the lids of the wooden kists. New quills were cut by his hand. The draught wrapped around his ankles, chilled his knuckles.

Listening for approaching movement, Brodie wiped his fingers and placed a small piece of linen towel between the base of his hand and the writing surface, to ensure no sweat stained the parchment. The wind wheezed through gaps in the window boards. Thin arrows of light stabbed at the gloom, though reached no farther than the broken lid of Prince John's stone coffin. Brother Hugh hammered at a timber somewhere outside but the chapel was silent. Brodie picked a newly cut quill from the box shelf at the side of his desk, dipped the nib in the fresh batch of ink – momentarily pressing the tip against the rim to allow drools to fall back into the earthenware pot – and began writing.

*"The Feast of the First Fruits of August in the year
1336 began with great scarcity of food for the
common people due to ceaseless strife and
disturbance conducted between the armies of
Scotland and England. Such a famine has resulted
that those choosing not to flee their native soil eat
pods in the manner of pigs for want of food, swelling
up all over and ending their lives wretchedly. In the
fends and fights, our own priory at Restenneth was
put to the sword by knights of Edward de Windsor,
who spared no whit. Let my first words write that
Master Robert was bolder than a leopard in seeking
to protect his brothers from diverse tortures. Yet the
commander of the knights, who gave himself the
name Henry de Bown, feared neither God nor man,
for he desecrated the chapel by mercilessly poking the
valiant Master Robert with a spear until others
around were splashed with his blood and his soul
was parted from the burden of his flesh. The force of
knights went on to burn, slay and raise dragon,
busily ravaging the priory, scattering Prince John's
bones all about for crows to peck and seizing beams
from the prior's quarters to construct a war machine
they called The Bostour. Alas, they also plundered
the holy relics of Saint Curitan the Proselytizer and
took the library documents in a box. Let this not
be so, but de Bown avowed that the High Steward
had accepted the foreign king Edward as his
overlord and given instruction that sacred moveables
and great oak timbers were to be had at Restenneth.
Of a surety, the High Steward made no such
confession when he visited this house just five days
after the Solemnity of the Assumption of the Blessed
Virgin Mary, the prior's accommodation only just
habitable but with no partition between the upper
and lower floors. Neither did he broach any matters
of war and state – though his papers were bound
and sewn in readiness as requested – for no Council*

31

or assembly was held. The Steward favoured resting some days and carousing with Lady Elizabeth of Rowallan on others, until leaving one sunrise before this day, the twenty eighth day of the month of August, the Feast of our own Saint Augustine of Hippo ..."

No noise disturbed Brodie but some change in the light or shift in the air caused him to pull aside the library curtain, a replacement for the one torn down by de Bown and stained with Master Robert's blood. Brother Peter stood in the entrance to the sacristy, circator lamp swinging lightly in one hand. He saw that Brodie had been writing, took three long strides and snatched at the parchment on the desk. Peter's eyes scrolled down and up again, his lips moving wordlessly. He was as slow to lower the note as he was quick to thrust the lamp close to Brodie's nose.

'As sacrist, I am custodian of this library and all within it. Yet you scribe without my permission and do so with vile treachery,' said Peter with spitting fury. 'You corrupt your faith!' His top lip jutted more than normal.

'Brother, your wrath is out of place,' replied Brodie. 'With many previous records destroyed or seized during our recent misfortunes, Prior Bernard himself asked that I should prepare an inventory. This...that is no more than a note to those accounts.'

'By the milk and tears of Christ's mother, this is no note to the inventory! You seek to compose some kind of chronicle when you have neither the artfulness of mind nor the word from the prior to do so. And you produce this...' he sneered at the parchment in his hand. '...the annals of a country dweller.'

Brodie guessed he had the expression of a petty thief caught red-handed but only acknowledging the strength of the evidence the moment the assize declared his guilt. 'I had no intention of compiling the annals of...' Inadvertently, he had been about to use the words from the mysterious riddle tucked in his knife sheath. He corrected himself. 'Of our blessed Church of Saint Peter.'

Peter seized on Brodie's hesitance. 'And you put down such

falsehood on the strength of what? Tell me, why is it that your brothers have never uttered any knowledge of the Steward's supposed submission to Edward? Perhaps because it is not so?'

It was true that nothing had happened since to support de Bown's assertion. 'I suppose it is not so, though I can also be certain of what my own ears were told.'

'Ptrot! You perjure yourself. If the Steward wooed another sovereign, why would he make preparation for our own king to return from his chateau on the Seine?'

'The boy king David de Brus is readying to return?' Brodie dragged the exchange further from his own indiscretion.

'He is no longer a beardless boy – though still has few enough whiskers – but I am told he will come again to his kingdom before his eighteenth year.' Peter appeared to read doubt into Brodie's silence. 'I know it…' He lowered his lamp for the first time. 'Barbour, learned in the arts and physician to many living souls…' He waved the lamp in the direction of the tomb below the window without naming the dead prince as one of John the Barbour's former patients. '…said it as he asked me to describe word by word the exploits and deeds of King Robert de Brus – the rose of all chivalry – and his kin. And it will be no simple narrative – or chronicle. The Barbour said it is to be a great romance.' Peter shredded the note still in his hand and allowed the pieces to flutter to the floor.

Though there was barely a year between them, Brodie more than matched Peter in height and was already broader across the shoulders. He stood and faced Peter, close enough to offer confrontation without explicit threat.

Peter hesitated before nodding towards the shreds of parchment on the floor. 'And you should know that the early days of this month of August are dedicated to praising the Saints Dominic, Bernard and Bartholomew – not feasting in the name of the pagan gods and nature workers who pluck the first fruits from the field.'

His breath reeked of smoked eels.

With a slight but conspicuous toss of his head, Peter took a step backwards. His thin moustache twitched like a strand of yarn in the breeze. So too his chinstrap beard. His brow crinkled beneath a thatch of fringe. Brodie let the library curtain – less substantial than before and not yet dyed a rich hue – fall between them. Peter spoke through the fabric. 'Be sure of this – your deceitful words will find their way to Prior Bernard and Master Archibald.'

Brodie stood his ground until Peter's steps had receded, then sat back down at the desk, weary with forbidden resentment. He took a folio from the sheaf on his writing slope, folding it in half horizontally, then in half again to form an octavo no larger than a playing card. Rather than cut the creases to make individual pages, he gathered the fallen scraps of parchment from the floor, placing them in one of the pouches that had formed between the folds. Before hiding the octavo beneath Prince John's sarcophagus, he took his quill from the inkpot and wrote on the front cover in his finest cursive hand.

> *"The Annals of Egglespether – As put down by the hand of Brodie Affleck, in religion called Brother Brodie"*

Chapter 4

*"Under a slack shepherd, the wolf fouls the wool
and the flock is torn to pieces."*

Unknown poet (c 15th century)

Harvest, 1337

'Be in no doubt – the north wind blows harder now than the arses of all the cows and long-horned oxen in the whole of the earldom of Angus.' Fergus the Ward formed a line of three smooth white pebbles on the square Merelles board, which was carved into a slab by the open hearth. He removed one of Brother Brodie's pieces. 'Ah! I have you held fast.' Fergus rocked back from the smouldering new timbers into a bleary haze of smoke. He tossed Brodie's captured stone loosely across the woodrush mat where they sat cross-legged.

'But hear it again...' Brodie read from the fragment of parchment in his hand. *"The wicked Norse wind usurps the west."* He moved a pebble from a hole in the largest of the three concentric squares to the one nearer the middle but again failed to form a mill. 'Can the winds truly change so?'

The bullock bellowed and grunted in the byre at the far end of the toft, shuffling heavy hooves in the hay. An infant slurped at a breast or bowl somewhere behind the wattle screen. Mariota, still some growing to do but no longer a child, sat in the lee of the sparse light from the open shutters on the back wall. She focused on the twisting threads of the loom, her hair pinned back with a bone comb lest it should become entangled, her slender fingers moving easily.

'Since I have you bested...' Fergus gathered all the stones

from the board. '…I seize the spoil.' He smiled in a way that could not disguise his pleasure at winning the game. 'Now see this.' He lined up the stones in rows on the board, most at the corner by Brodie's right knee. 'In times past, some years before I came from the Letham Grange to guard your gate, most of the winds arrived from the south and west, though with boisterous gusts from the east and north too.' He swept his hand across the board, opening and closing his palm in each direction, as if scattering seed. Then he moved half of the pebbles diagonally across the board close to where he sat. 'These years past, the balance of elements has become disturbed. The winds have turned athwart, as if two opposites set against each other in a wheel. You must ask the Lord why.'

Isabel, the middle of Fergus's three granddaughters, tottered through from the cooking area. She leaned forward and beat the ground with a wooden spoon, as fiercely as though breaking clods with a mallet.

'But I have a question for you,' continued Fergus. 'Why do you ask this now if the verse has been in your pockets for so many years?' His eyes were on Isabel while he spoke.

'I thought it no more than a child's rhyme until we were ransacked by Edward's knights. How could other than a prophet know the prior's chambers would fall in such a way? Or that I would be asked to record events at Restenneth?'

'You were right to think it no more than a child's rhyme. Is it not most likely that you contrived these would-be annals to fit with your memory of the verse's lines?'

'Well…' Brodie's response waned as soon as it began.

'And I have seen enough of war to foretell that every house in the land will fall at this time or that.'

'What then of the prophecy that there would be only crumbs for bread?'

'The winter wheat was at times four grains – but not as miserly as two. We shall know of the spring oats and barley presently.'

Isabel poked the fire with her wooden spoon. Fergus took it from her hand. 'I could ask you what sense to make of saying blood will fill…' Fergus broke off. Isabel grinned, her hand hovering over the fire. 'Your mirth will turn to melancholy if you touch flames with fingers,' he scolded.

The child picked up a bracken frond from the floor, pulling it back over her shoulder in the opposite manner of a siege engine about to assail a creel.

'Longshanks will get you...' Fergus warned.

Isabel looked back, her eyes as fierce as sparks from a flint.

Mey had untied the bullock from the cobbled stand in the byre and appeared from behind the screen. Mariota smiled in the direction of her sister-in-law, though her attention was still on the loom. Wrapped tightly in a shawl, baby Elspet balanced on Mey's hip, sleeping like a bird on a bough. Mey nodded at Brodie and stopped to lean on the doorjamb. 'Isabel, come,' she said.

The toddler threw the bracken on the stones around the edge of the hearth and turned away, still with a stubborn countenance.

Mey yanked at the door grip. The light stumbled in as though it had been leaning impatiently on the closed door. The smoke and stale air went almost as quickly in the opposite direction. Mey led the procession outside: mother and dozing infant, harnessed bullock, three-year-old Mary, pouting Isabel and, hindmost, any number of bugs, beetles, ticks and fleas.

Fergus stood up, coughing in sharp, gouty spasms. He flexed his joints by lowering himself several times on creaking knees, like a leaky old boat rising and falling on waves lapping the jetty.

'Malise will be back from the nightwatch before much longer and I must scythe the harvest with him. Can you attend the gatehouse between prayers, friend?'

Brodie also got to his feet. 'Alas, my bread will be earned by moving the flock to grazings at Aberlemno after the singing of terce.'

'Is there an idle brother from your house who could do so without sundering the drawbridge?' Fergus headed towards the doorway.

'I will put it to Prior Bernard at chapter,' said Brodie, following Fergus out of the toft into the kind of dazzling, low glare common when the sun has not long moved into Virgo.

When Brodie emerged from chapter house and chapel after terce, threadbare clouds flitted high in the sky, as though carried along on a string. Eight hours later, as he prepared to leave the uplands at Turin Hill, the clouds had congealed in thick, grey clots. He stuffed the last of a straggly patch of wolf's claw into his pouch – Brother James would find it useful to treat Walter's excess of yellow bile – and looked around for the herding hound. It was nowhere close to the flock.

'Walk up!' Brodie called.

The dog gave a short yelp from somewhere behind the low wall of the ruined dun-fort.

Brodie stepped over the crumbling rampart and patted his thighs. 'Here!'

The hound refused to move as commanded.

'That'll do!'

Still it remained motionless. Brodie moved closer.

Timidly, the dog crouched low to the ground, withdrawing its paw from a fleshy heap in the long grass. Four, five steps on and Brodie saw it too: a severed sheep's head, neatly surrounded by a thin collar of blood, staring at the sky with hollowed out eye sockets.

'Be cursed!' Brodie looked at the heavens, as though hoping to see what had caught the creature's blind gaze. 'Forgive me Lord.' No bolt of lightning held him to account for his impiety; the curmudgeonly sky grumbled darkly but remained intact.

Brodie rolled the head to one side with his boot: a brown-faced Soay, not one of Brodie's flock but possibly from the priory grange at Nether Turin, large and probably male. Its curved horns had been hewn off and the flesh scraped from the neck to the base of the skull, leaving a flap of scraggy skin hanging loose. He hunched down. There was a clean incision down the length of the neck. No wolf tracks or hair, no signs of a struggle. Brodie stood. No gnawed limbs or smears of blood from a corpse dragged about the kill site.

The dog whimpered and stared up at Brodie.

Forgetting his surprise at the discovery, Brodie went as if to put the severed head on his own tonsured crown and bleated at the hound, which thudded its tail on the ground.

Brodie smiled. 'This time – walk up!'

The dog trotted towards the flock that grazed beyond the ruin. Following behind, Brodie knotted the loose neck skin to his belt and covered the sheep's head with his scapular. The flock skirted the earthen mound by the low cliffs and started down the gentle slope to the south-west. At the rear, Brodie swung his staff before him like a blind Dominican begging for alms.

The sheep reached the priory perimeter fence as the last light of dusk drained away. The dog flanked around to the right of the flock, to prevent it passing the drawbridge. Brodie languished some way behind, picking his way through the boggy ground by Lunanwell Burn. He slashed at an obstinate thicket of reeds in his path before finding firmer ground.

Drawing near, Brodie could see Fergus at the open west window of the gatehouse. He shouted up at the raised platform. 'Nightwatch after a full day in the fields – good fortune is not with you.'

'I am fortunate enough that the drawbridge is still whole after leaving it in the care of young Brother Symon,' answered Fergus.

Brodie was not close enough to see Fergus's smile but could hear the levity in his voice.

'Though I am weary enough to sleep until doom,' added Fergus.

Brodie caught up with the flock. 'How went harvest?' he asked.

'Wretched,' answered Fergus, letting down the drawbridge. 'Read me again that verse of yours – I fear great ruin looms.' A wide grin strained towards the unruly, rustic side-whiskers that tumbled down Fergus's cheeks. His hair, as thick as straw, looked as though it had been dropped on his head from a height. 'It will be songbirds for supper until day and night are again equal in length.'

The dog funnelled the sheep through the gate, driving them left to the open bucht without the need for a command from Brodie.

'Ale before compline, friend?' asked Fergus.

Brodie pulled aside his scapular to reveal the sheep's head.

'Devil's servant,' murmured Fergus. He raised his voice. 'Do we have wolves prowling in the uplands?'

'Only if they have two arms, two legs and a sharpened blade,' replied Brodie. 'I ought to notify Prior Bernard.'

'Tomorrow then.'

Brodie waved at Fergus with the back of his hand.

After bolting shut the sheep bucht gate with his staff, Brodie walked around the outside of the priory, passing the full length of the west and south ranges. The only light was shed from the beacon high in the tower and through the low arched window to the kitchen and storeroom. A pale goat loomed in the darkness, watching Brodie's movements, its eyes glinting red in the half-light. Brodie shooed it out of his path, though it barely budged. He saw Bernard before reaching the latrine block behind the east range. Dressed in a white surplice, the prior stood by the loch shore – so close the waves must have lapped at the hem of his vestments – his arms spread wide in supplication.

A shepherd without a staff, Brodie used the balls of his feet to poke at the rocky ground, feeling his way down the slope that led to the water's edge. No more than a quoit's throw from the loch, Brodie saw that the prior was not standing on the shore but in the water, beyond his knees, muttering an incantation. "…the pestilent breath of impurity…the Immaculate Lamb…" Caught between moving forwards and backwards, Brodie stood still. "…be our protection against the wickedness and snares of that cruel serpent and ancient, false gods…" The preliminary compline bell let out a single clang. Brodie flinched. Before the sound of the bell had bounced back across the water as an echo, Bernard turned to look over his shoulder, still mumbling "…the evil spirits who prowl about the world seeking the ruin of souls…" Brodie recognised the closing lines from the prayer to the archangel Michael.

The prior looked surprised but offered no explanation as to what he was doing or why he was wearing his surplice outside the chapel. He slowly lowered his arms. 'Your presence was missed – and noted – at vespers. I trust your absence was God's will.'

'I did not miss it in my heart, Father, though I was on an errand for the Lord.' Brodie pulled the sheep's head from his robes. 'For he guided me to this cursed beast.'

Bernard crossed himself and invoked the protection of the Blessed Virgin. 'As I surely knew, it is the work of those who worship the old gods on the hilltops.'

'The discovery was made in the area of the pagans' ritual sites, though their festival for dead souls is not for some weeks,' said Brodie. 'More certainty I cannot offer, but I venture this beast was damned for an altogether different purpose. Doubtless, it met its fate at the hands of man – perhaps by the blade of one who practises slaughter.'

Chapter 5

"If anyone, deceived by the devil, shall believe, as
is customary among pagans, that any man or
woman is a night-witch and eats men and on
that account burn that person to death."

Charlemagne, imposing Christianity on Saxony (789)

September, 1337, until the 24th Day of February, 1340

Still standing in the water, as conspicuous as Venus in the early
night sky, Prior Bernard ordered the sheep slaughter to be
entered in the inventory. Before the last of the leaves had fallen,
Brodie's quill was in his hand once again, this time to record the
disappearance of two hornless white-faces.

The following year, the business of lambing went ahead
unhindered. Two newborns died from skin over the nose, one
was abandoned by a ewe birthing for the first time and, in the
weeks that followed, another two perished when the temperature
dipped. However, the rest of the flock remained intact through
the summer months.

It was not until the days after the Feast of Saint Martin that
Brodie sat down to record another disappearance, this time a
long-horned ewe, again from grazings near Aberlemno. The
losses did not coincide directly with Samhainn or Yule. No
bonfires were seen at Pitscandly, Finavon or Turin on either
pagan festival. Not a rib bone or a scrap of hide turned up at the
ritual sites. Nevertheless, Prior Bernard suspected heathens and
so took the precaution of removing all the healthy ewes to the
larger and better protected Cistercian abbey at Coupar Angus.
The mature, lame and scabbed were slaughtered and salted. The

cattle were kept for their milk, the rams and wethers because they bore fine quality wool.

When the teind barn was plundered of a salted beef carcass and two vats of soused red herring in the third week of the first of the famine months of 1340, all moveable provender was taken indoors. As kitchener, Brother Walter offered to sleep by the stores, though his pallet was closer to the hearth than the larder. Brother Hugh raised the palisade higher than a pikestaff.

At his desk, Brodie scratched the latest stock amendments in the margin of the priory inventory: one vat of doukdrawis, soused herring being a favourite of Brother Peter's; twelve ewe carcasses salted and stored; four unfit and reserved to mix with fodder; three bolls of spring oats and one of wheat procured by the kitchen, five bushels of malted barley by the brewhouse.

There was a knock on the wooden shutters that had been fitted to the window. Brodie leaned closer.

Through a crack in the boards, Fergus pulled a face befitting a gargoyle. He shifted his mouth to the gap. 'You sit on your soft breeches while I hold the miscreants at bay, conversi,' he shouted.

'You keep your gate and I will keep mine, eldfather.'

'But can you keep the devil from the door of a common priory farmer and gateman and ensure me a swift voyage through purgatory?'

'I fear your layman's sins are too weighty for my young shoulders. But in exchange for a small endowment, I could surely offer intercessions and plead for the Lord's mercy.'

'A rogue such as you would run through my merks to fill your desolate library with scripts that tell the world more than it needs to know.'

Brodie jabbed two fingers through the gap in the boards and gave Fergus a reproachful poke on the temple. 'You have enough words in that head of yours to have no need of any more from books. Rid yourself of some by delivering whatever message brought you into my shadow.'

'A visitor awaits – he asks for you by name, though will say nothing of his business.'

'Does he have a name of his own?'

'Thomas of Ersildoune.'

Brodie recognised the name in a way that was just out of

reach. He ran through variations looking for more familiarity: Ersiltoun, Earlston, Erceldoun, Ercildoune. Each seemed more distant than the last.

He reached for the snuffer and extinguished the candle on his desk. Darkness gave way to light again when he opened the shutters. Brodie jumped through the window, though a fierce blast of wind almost knocked him backwards. He secured the shutters as he stood with Fergus.

'You know him?' asked Fergus.

'Ersildoune…'

The sun was low in the sky but shone with a confidence not seen since harvest. There was no need to seek out a path past the partially built nave to the gatehouse: the growth of the grass had been halted by winter and its height cut back by the appetite of the goats. To the right, in the rig extending from Fergus's toft, the early beans and spring cabbage were showing signs of health, though the sea-kale was slow and the peas appeared to be blighted. To their left, bluebells poked their first green barometers through the soil.

'…Ersildoune. No – a stranger to me,' Brodie concluded.

'Well this stranger certainly has a strange appearance – the clothes of a packman, hair of a wench and beard that would fit a grey old goat. He travels alone on a mule and carries little baggage. There is one more thing you should know – he wears a steel helmet despite being no soldier.'

Sure enough, though facing away while he hitched his sumpter to a pole, the visitor clearly wore a tarnished kettle-hat. He turned his head when Brodie and Fergus walked through the open front of the stable, though offered no greeting. Alyth walked in with a pail of water from the loch and passed between the three men to fill the trough.

'I will ask my daughter Mariota to fetch some fodder,' she said to the visitor.

'You are very generous,' replied Thomas.

Before leaving, Alyth switched her attention to her husband. 'Hector is back from market and waits for the drawbridge to be lowered,' she said to Fergus.

'Brother…Sire.' Fergus nodded once each at Brodie and Thomas. 'I must return to the gatehouse to allow Brother Hector entry.' He followed his wife out of the stable at an amble.

Thomas unbuckled his saddlebag and slung it over his shoulder.

'May I carry your bag, sire?' asked Brodie.

'Thank you, brother.' Thomas handed over the bag, which was heavier than it appeared.

Fergus's description of Thomas was reliable. He wore a shabby, pale surcoat that reached the straps of his boots. His head, face and chin were thick with knotted grey hair and he had fewer teeth than a toddling child. He carried the smell of the mule with him.

Brodie led Thomas out of the stable. 'Have you travelled far?'

'From beyond the Scottish Sea,' replied Thomas. 'Where many of the lands are held by the noble Lindsays,' he added, without further explanation.

'As they are here,' said Brodie, with some uncertainty.

'Yes.' Thomas prolonged the 's', giving it the sound of a hiss.

'I can have a guest bed prepared if you would accept our hospitality.'

'Excellent, though first I must ask if you have a foul hole. My buttocks are ready to burst.'

Brodie led Thomas directly to the latrine block at the far side of the priory, rather than drop off his bag at the nearby west range, where he would share a dormitory with the lay brothers.

'You asked for me by name, sire?'

'Indeed so – I have some business for you. You are a scribe?' He did not wait for an answer. 'And you can repair and bind parchment?' Brodie nodded. 'So, look in the bag.'

Brodie did as he was asked and pulled out three volumes: all bound in leather, all by the scholar Michael Scot. The tattiest of the three was his Physionomia. It had a bluish cover. Liber Introductorius and Liber Particularis, which were bound in black hide, made up the trilogy of renowned works.

'Mend the books for me and you may read them – or make copies for your library.'

Brodie riffled through the stiff pages of Physionomia.

'"God is the father who presents a child with an unused parchment for him to write down his teacher's utterances, for good or ill" – those words, or a variation, are in the book you hold. If you record events at this priory, you should remember them well. You will write truths that are called falsehoods...'

Brodie was reminded of Brother Peter's accusation on reading the first account in his annals.

'But a scribe worth the name must fill the blank page once he has started, whatever the dangers and accusations,' Thomas added.

Brodie accepted the teaching, without any sureness of its meaning. 'You are kind,' he said. 'And there is no limit on your stay at our house, though I fear I would not be able to mend the books any time soon. My foremost duty here is to tend the flock.'

They passed the outside of the refectory and the warming room then turned the corner towards the latrine. The light was fading, the wind gathering some force. Light, brisk waves brushed the shore.

The latrine door was wide open. Brodie showed Thomas in and went to close it from the outside.

'No, no, you must come inside with me,' insisted Thomas, beckoning with his hand. 'I will be gone soon but you may have what time you want with the books.'

Brodie stepped inside the block. Despite the open door, a stink lingered that would not have been out of place in the cow byre. Brodie pointed out the row of privies and backed away to lean on the door. Thomas took his seat in the nearest of the four stalls.

'A reiver troubles your flock, I see.' Thomas's shout bounced off the stone walls but soon deadened on the earthen floor.

'The thefts had stopped for some time,' Brodie called back. 'But how could you know we have again been plundered?'

Thomas spattered the lade below the privy and continued without answering. 'He will haunt you again – at the next full waxing of the moon – and with more grievous consequences than before.' He shuffled inside the stall. 'Do you have moss, or foliage, for me to rid myself of this turd?'

Brodie ducked into the adjoining stall, which was also empty of moss. He found a pile in the third stall and handed it in to Thomas.

'Thank you, brother.' He leaned forward and wiped his backside. A horn amulet swung loose from below his surcoat.

The charm dangled from a twine tied in seven knots in the pagan style. 'There are many places for danger to lurk on the road south of Monikie.'

'Monikie, you say?' The lands of Monikie and Pitairlie had come and gone from Brodie's thoughts since reading of them in his own indenture document.

'Yes,' hissed Thomas. 'It was once hazardous for those deprived of their lands, but will be known for different trespasses in the weeks to come. Be warned, great jeopardy awaits those who pursue the one you call a fiend.'

Thomas's apparent confirmation that lands around Monikie had been forfeited in the past, along with the sternness of his warning, caused a momentary instability in Brodie's humours; he imagined an initial surge of blood to his head, then black bile quickly filling his spleen. 'How…how can you know these things?' he stuttered.

'You ask many questions – the harder you press an eel, the more it slips away.' Thomas emerged from the stall. 'I will allow you one more then I must rest.'

'If you will not answer my previous questions, I will ask another. Why do you wear a soldier's helmet when there are no arrows to pierce your skull?'

'Mend and read the books, brother. The answers are all to be found in there. Mend and read.'

Chapter 6

"It was a mirk, mirk night, there was nae starlight,
They waded through red blood to the knee;
For a' the blood that's shed on the earth
Rins through the springs o' that countrie."

From the traditional *Ballad of Thomas the Rhymer*, unknown
author (c 13th century)

*25th Day of February, 1340, until the 15th Day of March in the Same
Year*

Thomas slept on – as silently as though death were watching
over him – when the lay brothers stumbled in the dark up the
night ladder after lauds.

He was gone from the dormitory by the time they arose for
prime.

Already wearing his breeches, warming vest, rough linen sark
and black tunic, Brodie had only to pull on his cowl, surplice and
night shoes to be ready for the second divine office. He took his
place behind Brother Hugh at the trapdoor opening. Just behind
Brodie, Brother Finlay snorted back a noseful of phlegm,
catching it in his throat with a rasp. He leaned past Brodie,
opened the shutters by Thomas's empty bunk and spat through
the narrow window with all the force needed to clear a choked
drain. By fortune rather than design, the crude construction of
the lay dormitory gave it added warmth in the winter, the heat
rising through the thin floorboards from the kitchen below and
becoming trapped by the low ceiling. Finlay's breath caught in
the cold, moonlit air that seeped in; it dispersed as quickly as
steam from coals laden with water. Outside, the light from a

single lantern glittered like a star below the horizon; Finlay closed the shutters before Brodie could tell whether it hung from the stables or gatehouse, though somebody was certainly at one or the other.

Brother Hugh was next to reach the trapdoor. Brodie followed behind. Peter was at the foot of the ladder, arm outstretched, holding his lamp high. In the glow, Brodie could see that the saddlebag was no longer by Thomas's bed.

'Hurry,' said Peter to Hugh. 'It is past time for me to ring the second bell.'

'Hold your impatient tongue and go to ring the bell if you must,' replied Hugh.

Peter said nothing more; the sound of fading footsteps and the disappearance of the light from his lamp announced his retreat. Hugh picked his way down the rungs into the shadows of the storeroom below.

Prime was cut short – no additional psalms, antiphons or versicles were sung or recited – with Prior Bernard announcing at chapter that he and Peter had to leave at the earliest possible hour to attend to important matters of the house and the realm in Forfar and St Andrews.

After chapter, Brodie pulled Brother Symon to one side in the parlour. 'Do you know if our guest Ersildoune is leaving the house?' he asked.

'Brother, I am a lowly chamberlain – not the guest master. I have been told nothing – you must speak to Master Malcolm.'

'Can I help my young brothers?' interrupted Malcolm. Still in the chapter house, standing two steps down from the parlour, he looked even shorter than usual.

'Master.' Brodie bowed respectfully, though also to stifle a smirk at the guest master's squat, dwarf-like appearance.

'Lift your cowl and speak freely,' said Malcolm through a hesitant, brittle smile.

'Thank you, Master,' said Brodie, raising his head and maintaining a solemn expression. 'I have books belonging to the guest called Thomas of Ersildoune. He said I could make copies, though I fear it would be ill-mannered not to offer to return them before he leaves.' In truth, their meeting the previous day had been as satisfactory as a half-finished sentence. Just as he would never extinguish his desk candle until his day's work was done, Brodie felt he had affairs to complete with the clapper-clawed old man, even if the precise nature of their business together remained elusive.

'Quite so,' said Malcolm after a pause.

'Can you say if he leaves our house?'

'I have been told nothing, though I am only the guest master – why would anyone trouble to tell me if a guest was preparing to leave?' Malcolm tried a more forceful smile, though it remained flat and unsure. 'But I saw that his mule was saddled before prime when I took alms of hard bread and cheese to the gatehouse for any beggars who might seek God's charity.'

Brodie nodded his thanks.

Malcolm stepped up into the parlour and put a hand on Symon's shoulder. 'It seems my young chamberlain has a bunk to attend to. Come child, I will assist.' Symon looked less than certain of the guest master's intentions. Malcolm turned to Brodie. 'Brother, I would be thankful if you could find the guest and bid that he waits until I can offer the Lord's blessing for his onward journey.'

'As you ask, Master,' said Brodie.

Malcolm ushered Symon from the parlour into the north cloister. Brodie should have followed them to the dormitory – to change into his outdoor boots and empty his piss pot – but instead went directly to the library to collect Thomas's books. Leaving the chapel, he peered over the low, unfinished north wall of the nave to try to catch sight of Thomas among the outbuildings. He saw only Mariota passing the forge in the distance, a shovel over her shoulder.

Brodie picked his way across the grass, each footprint crunching through the crust of frost and leaving its neat mark. He saw before reaching the stable block that Thomas's mule was still there, harnessed and fitted with riding gear.

Brodie called through the gloom. 'Sire?' He stepped into the barn and patted the brackish brown mule on the nose.

'Since when did your vows permit you to court mules, brother?'

The voice startled Brodie. He had expected an old and rusty response; this was as sprightly as a breeze. He twisted around. Mariota drifted towards him, slim hips swaying in defiance of her shapeless smock. The shovel was gone: now she carried halters and bridles around her neck and a saddle on each forearm.

Brodie gathered his wits. 'Better to court a mule than transform into one – you have enough leather on you for two beasts.'

'Ah! A brother who considers himself a jester.' Mariota brushed past Brodie and began to dress a walnut-coloured packhorse at the rear of the stable. She turned her back to Brodie. 'Or is it an ass I hear?'

Brodie could not see Mariota's expression, though her pitch carried as much animosity as the melody from a harp. He imagined her smiling at the sharpness of her own tongue. The approach of voices stalled the equally shrewd reply he had yet to hone. Bernard and Peter appeared over the low mound that led from the north shore, apparently arguing. Fragments of their conversation were audible when Bernard raised his voice. '…the Steward does no such thing!…the customs were collected by Carruthers – his own treasurer – for the benefit of the Steward's own pocket…. Blantyre and Keith are no better than he…' Bernard's words were clearer as he neared, so too the fact that the argument was one-sided. 'Taxation and rents should serve one purpose alone – the return of the king from France. They are not for the personal riches of any man, however noble his blood. The council at St Andrews – and God himself – will pass judgement.'

Peter, burdened by two saddlebags, was first into the stable. He seemed to be contriving different ways to agree with the prior. 'Just as you say, Father…To be sure, Father…It is as God wills it, Father.' Bernard held a third, smaller bag which had the bulging look of one put together by Donald the cook.

'Are the beasts ready, girl?' the prior asked Mariota.

'This one is, sire. It is no palfrey but has the smoothest gait of the two.'

'Very well. Give it here.' Mariota patted the horse's haunch to send it in the direction of Bernard's outstretched hand. The prior looked between the girl and Brodie, much as a hunter might weigh up whether to fix the hart or the hind in the sights of his crossbow. 'And you, brother, what brings you here? Do you seek some profane pleasure with this maiden?' He uttered the word 'maiden' with righteous anger held in check just long enough to receive a reply.

Mariota ducked shamefaced below the height of the second horse's withers, still grappling with its bridle.

'No such thing, Father! I would have no business with this girl.' It was not the gallant defence he had intended. Instead, he sounded cowardly and self-seeking. 'That it is to say, I would have no such intentions. My business lies elsewhere.'

'You have read the books so soon?' This time the voice whistled like a gust through the cloisters. Thomas emerged from the shadows by the stable entrance.

Bewildered by another unannounced arrival, Brodie stood dumbly.

'Those in your grasp, brother,' said Thomas.

'The books…Of course, sire. It is why I am here – to return them to you before you leave.'

'You have mended them already then?'

'I regret not, though I have had only the space of one day and one night to do so.'

'And I have said you may take as much time as you want – seven years and twice seven if needed. I will be back to retrieve them when the time comes.'

Bernard led his horse from the stable and Mariota handed the reins of the second mare to Peter, who followed at the prior's heels. Peter's gaze lingered on Thomas's amulet as he passed the old man. Bernard called back to Thomas. 'And where do you go in such haste?'

'I go in no more haste than you, prior, for I must journey alongside you and your canon.'

Bernard stopped with one foot in his rope stirrup, Peter bending to push him upwards into his saddle. 'And why must you travel with us? We have matters of church and state to attend to,' said Bernard.

'Prior, some do the work of king and realm – others prevent greater woe than is preordained. You set out to do your duty, I to do mine.'

*

51

Much passed as was customary on Saint Curitan's Day: Brodie slaughtered an ageing, fattened ram and two tender young geese for the feast; procession and High Mass were held with a solemnity befitting the occasion; the saint was venerated for his part in founding the priory more than five hundred years before, with a prayer of petition that his relics – a tooth, one kneecap and his foreskin – be recovered from the plundering Saxon king, Edward. And the moon fully waxed without fulfilment of Thomas's prediction that the reiver would return. A first read of the books left by Ersildoune told Brodie no more than he knew already: Michael Scot was an astrologer and alchemist, though others said a sorcerer who lost his shadow as a payment to the devil.

But everything that took place at the priory did so without Prior Bernard and Brother Peter, absent now for nineteen days and overdue for at least four.

The next morning, the waning moon still visible through clouds as slight as finespun gauze, Brodie collected the hide of the sheep he had slaughtered the night before and walked the short distance from the storeroom to the south shore. He passed by his parchmenter's cruck and waded through the long grass to the point where the Fithie River met Restenneth Loch; ten paces farther upstream, he reached the shallow, pink-pebbled bay where he would soak the sheepskin. He kneeled down and spread the hide below the water's surface, holding it with one hand while picking heavy stones to pin down the corners with his other. A swarm of tiny flies buzzed around his head, though he secured the skin before swatting them away. The gentle rise of a trout rippled the surface of the water no distance from his nose. Another left the water in a flash of silver to his right.

Then something else moved, though he could not say what or where: a shadow, perhaps, on the opposite riverbank.

Not a shadow but something dark: a hare, an otter, a crow?

It came into focus: blacker, bigger, by the water's edge, just beyond the eel-ark. A pile of battered rags, blackened timbers, a bull calf?

Brodie stood for a better view.

The thing moved, a leg emerging from a dark cloak or habit.

'Who lies there? Are you hurt?'

The thing – the person – did not answer, though Brodie imagined he heard a low moan over the gabble of the water. The river was deep at the eel trap and hardly narrowed before it reached the drawbridge. Unable to swim, Brodie gathered his tunic over his knees and ran back to the priory. No-one was in the storeroom or the kitchen so he hurried through to the cloisters. Masters Archibald and Malcolm stood in a slice of early sunshine by the north range, while Brother James bent down on one knee to tend the herbary in the middle of the cloister garth.

'Masters, brother.' He half kneeled and gave one nod for all three of them. 'A matter of urgency requires our attention outside the priory grounds.'

'It must be quite a calamity to bring you here in such unruly hot haste,' said Archibald.

'Forgive me, Master, though I fear it is indeed a matter of direst distress. A prone body lies on the far side of the river – smitten down or lame – and by the colour and nature of his clothing, I suspect it is an Augustinian brother, or possibly a Benedictine.'

'By the great martyr Saint Catherine! Lead the way, brother.' Archibald waved Brodie out of the west door. Malcolm followed behind.

'And I will fetch some healing remedies and cures,' shouted James the infirmarian after them.

Brodie was first across the drawbridge and round the bend in the river. Malcolm was not far behind and Archibald puffed at the rear, having slowed to walking pace by the time Brodie reached the huddled figure, who was completely covered, as though cowering under a blanket from some unseen apparition. Brodie went to shake what he imagined might be the figure's shoulder or arm; the handful of dirt-smeared cloth he took in his grip had the unmistakable rough woollen texture of an Augustinian's tunic.

Malcolm came alongside. 'Is it dead?'

Without answering, Brodie turned the figure so that a face with the pallor of death or fear emerged from cloak and cowl.

'By all the saints and the Lord himself it is Brother Peter Fenton!' Malcolm dropped to his knees in trembling prayer.

Brodie felt for the beat of Peter's heart and slapped him gently on the cheek.

Archibald caught up. 'Brother Peter…' He traced the sign of the cross three times across his chest. '…may God's sweet breath sustain him.' He fell to the ground and threw his arms around Peter's chest. The uncertain look of a novice in his eyes, he turned to Brodie. 'Does he live?'

Again, Brodie ignored his superior and tapped Peter on the cheek. 'Brother, you have reached your house. You are safe. Brother…' He tapped harder.

Peter blinked his eyes open: terrified, confused and relieved, one after another, all at the same time. He put a single arm around Archibald, who returned the embrace more wholeheartedly. 'Son, you are safe,' Archibald whispered.

'Are you hurt, or ill?' asked Brodie. He looked in all directions. 'Where are Prior Bernard and Thomas of Ersildoune?'

Peter groaned. 'My bones and flesh ail me…' He directed his answer at Archibald. '…though not to the degree my heart does.'

'Then you must tell us what happened,' said Archibald.

Peter fell out of his master's embrace. 'Our steadfast prior is dead – butchered by a bogle more evil than any hound from hell.'

Chapter 7

*"It is more barbaric...to tear apart through
torture and pain a living body which can still feel,
or to burn it alive by bits, to let it be gnawed and
chewed by dogs or pigs...Better to roast and eat
him after he is dead."*

Michael de Montaigne, *Essays* (1580)

15th Day of March, 1340

For a day, I tremble in damp shadows. For a night, I cast prayers
upwards into thin starlit air.

After trussing my brother's leg wound, and tending some
lesser injuries of my own, I face a choice: I can again feed us a
pottage of nettle leaves, bittercress, mugwort, darnel grass and
birch bark. Or I can return to the place of the fray.

On reaching the place of the fray, I find that the lamb is gone,
most likely scavenged by a night creature. The other body
remains where it lay, though a foot has been gnawed. The head
is nowhere around. The sight brings a memory: as boy thieves
we removed the heads of plundered beasts to ease our load. A
grim smile arises, flotsam from a wreck.

There is no need to lighten this load: I am able to push, roll
and drag it down the slope, over the bluff, along the bank and
into the birchwood.

The head already loosed, I remove the limbs, entrails and
virile organs. The flesh will be roasted so there is no need for
flaying. I skewer the tenderest parts – the ample haunches – and
rest the spit on props, over the fire. In my mind, I arrange the
other parts – salted and hanging from a row of pegs – in the

order they will be consumed: shoulders, spine, limbs, liver, kidney, heart, large bones to be broken open on a hammerstone.

Starved and feverish, my brother takes mouthfuls without a question.

I look straight up, beyond the mostly leafless trees. Geese flying south in formation, one skein closely followed by another, pass overhead. Light snow is beginning to fall, like blown ash, from crumpled clouds.

Christ took the bread, blessed it, broke it and gave it to them. And he told them: 'Take, eat – this is my body.'

I, Andrew Christie, eat.

Chapter 8

*"The blessed man raised his holy hand, while all
the rest, brethren as well as strangers, were
stupefied with terror, and, invoking the name of
God, formed the saving sign of the cross in the air,
and commanded the ferocious monster, saying,
'Thou shalt go no further, nor touch the man; go
back with all speed.' Then at the voice of the saint,
the monster was terrified, and fled more quickly
than if it had been pulled back with ropes."*

Adomnán of Iona, *Life of Columba* (c 690)

15th Day of March, 1340, until the 21th Day of the Same Month

'Though I swear by God's teeth he rose again as a saint,'
continued Peter, propping himself up on one elbow. 'As sure as
he was the Lord's cowled champion at Aberlemno, Dunninald
and twenty more places in this earthly life, our prior has taken
his seat among the saints beyond the gates of gold.'

'You speak no sense, brother,' said Archibald, replacing his
arm around Peter's shoulders. 'Truly, Prior Bernard was God's
deputy on earth but only the Supreme Pontiff Benedict the
Blessed can declare who will be exalted in heaven. What miracles
did you witness to say such a thing?'

Peter reached for a bundle held close to his body, behind
knees tucked up towards his chest. Brodie recognised it as the
food parcel packed by Donald the cook. Peter pulled open the
drawstring. As gently as though guddling for trout, he cupped a
hand into the base of the bag and lifted out the contents. Prior
Bernard's bloodless pate appeared first, then his stiff, white hair

and bulging eyes. A portion of his left ear lobe was missing, his full cheeks drawn in. Peter withdrew the severed head and the bag fell to the ground. Ragged flesh and skin from Bernard's neck poked between Peter's open fingers. Only the prior's closed mouth looked at peace.

Brodie rocked backwards. Archibald slipped his arm from Peter's shoulders.

Peter smiled at the head. 'I bathed it in a pool,' he said, as though in answer to questions not yet asked. 'See, his lips are as pure and blissful as a child's.' Peter thrust the head towards Archibald, who leaned away but remained on his knees. To Brodie's eyes, the prior's expression was far from meek; he looked furious, as if about to put a young brother under the rod for some breach of the rules of the house.

Archibald took Peter's hand. 'That may be so…' He shuffled closer. '…and his relics will be venerated in good time. But his tongue can no longer rehearse whatever mishaps and miracles have occurred. Only you can account for events these past days.'

Brodie detected impatience in Archibald's shallow brow.

'You must…' started Archibald, turning away at the sound of nimble feet.

In a moment, Brother James rounded the bend in the river. He arrived by their sides giddy and eager, carrying a basket of remedies.

'Brother Peter! Can it be you?' James looked at the gathered faces for an explanation. Strands of dark hair fell across his eyes; he blinked several times rather than brush them away.

Brodie shook his head.

James unhooked a small shoulder bag and gently laid it down; it clanged with the sound of metal instruments settling one on another. He kneeled by Peter, opposite Archibald, hesitating at first sight of the prior's severed head. Finally, he pushed the loose hair from his eyes. 'Chaste and fragrant Virgin,' he mumbled. In turn, he blessed himself, the patient and the head. James pulled the basket of herbs and potions closer. 'What affections do you have?' he asked Peter. 'Wounds, redness, swellings?'

Peter sat up. 'A monstrous army of them came upon us,' he said, ignoring James but at once alert. 'Thieves, set on plundering farm stock from our own priory grange at Monikie.'

Monikie: mention of the place again caused an unstableness to pass through Brodie, just as it had when Thomas said the name.

James twisted round to look at Brodie and nodded towards the empty pouch that had held Bernard's head. 'Water.' He spoke in a low tone, in a way that would not interrupt Peter.

Brodie got carefully to his feet. Returning from the riverbank with the pouch of water, he heard the pitch in Peter's voice rise. Closer still, Brodie saw Peter motion with his hands and arms as though describing something of great size.

'...the chiefest among the brigands was taller than a bear, with the horns of a boar and claws in place of hands.'

Brodie handed the water to Peter, who took a drink before continuing.

'Dauntless, Prior Bernard ordered the caitiffs to lay down the carcasses they had thieved.' Peter drank again. 'Only then would they be permitted to plead for God's mercy.'

'And so?' said Archibald.

'Believe this, rather than heed the good prior – who spoke only God's word – they beset us under a hail of stones and profaned the church for all its glory, saying it prospered while the common people ate grasses and suffered great dearth. Prior Bernard could withstand no such heresy and so spurred towards them, to relieve them of their insolent pride and make them repent. From nowhere, the beast who led them produced a weapon forged in the abyss – a whetted hook more curved than a Saracen's blade atop a wrought steel shaft as high as a house. In hazard of his life but not dismayed, our doughty prior continued his charge, drawing level with one of those who carried a slaughtered lamb.'

Peter broke off and sagged to the ground in a dramatic show of infirmity.

'More water,' he croaked.

James hurried to the river to fill the bag.

'Infamous rage! I cannot find the will or the words to describe what followed.'

'Yet, that is your duty,' said Archibald.

Peter tightened his grip on Bernard's head, which had fallen slack in his palm. 'Very well,' he said. Brodie helped him again into a sitting position. 'While our stout-hearted Bernard accosted the bandit with the lamb, the one wielding the infernal butcher's cleek prowled behind and cravenly sliced at the prior's neck, loosening his head from his shoulders with a single swipe.'

'The tyranny of the devil lies in the palm of your hands, my son,' said Archibald, shaking his head at length before continuing. 'But how could you have escaped unslain?'

'I can only say that my blade was drawn in an instant and uproar followed. Strokes were given and taken, though by mischance I was unhorsed in the affray. And here is the part of the tale I must tell more than any other. For I entered a blackness when I fell to the ground. But praise the Most High – Prior Bernard rose from his death to keep me from mine. One moment I was feeling blows and hearing curses, the next I knew only the prior's voice, scenting the air around like perfume.'

'And what were his words in this vision, Brother Peter? Tell us without hesitation.' Archibald leaned closer.

'He said his journey beyond life had taken him directly to Saint Curitan – as they were born into heaven on the same day, and at the same hour – but he had returned to offer protection to all Restenneth brothers. The ground then ruptured and the fiends fell back below to the hot core where they live. And when my eyes opened, the cruel multitude was gone, along with the bodies of those innocents they had slaughtered – our miraculous prior and the unblemished lamb, who both bled for the sins of the guilty. All that remained – cradled in my arms as gently as though it were a crown of thorns and thistles – was this redeeming relic.' He nodded at the prior's head.

'Did he say more?'

'Master Archibald, he said only one more thing – the name of the murderer. The blasphemous beast has the name Christie, though he is no child of Christ, or even of Adam's stock at all. This Christie with the Cleek is a wolf that crawled from its foul lair.'

Master Archibald stroked his nose at the point where the bones formed a ridge and stared from below his narrow crown.

'And what of Thomas of Ersildoune?' asked Brodie.

'The worthless old infidel disappeared like smoke in a storm,' answered Peter. 'Perchance he was leagued with the rogues. Certainly, he took flight at the first sign of steel.'

Brodie ignored the dismissive reply, though still wondered at the truth.

Reaching over, Archibald released Peter's grip on the prior's head, then swathed it in a bandage from James's basket. He hoisted his tall frame in stages: balanced on one knee with the severed head held heavenward; leaning to brush the grass from his tunic; upright with an arch of his back.

'Then the hunting dogs must be put on this wolf, so that he can learn of divine power and God's boundless love.' He scratched the brim of his generous nostrils, pinched a protruding hair and plucked it loose. 'First, a procession. To bear the relics of the venerable Prior Bernard – who had courage beyond measure, and even beyond good sense – into the church he adored.'

'We must do no less than you say, Master, for the everlasting beatitude of our prior and his saintly ways,' said James quickly. 'Yet the patient is weak and his temperament melancholic. He should take wine and spleenwort to put right the balance of his humours, but must also rest and be kept warm in the infirmary.' He turned his attention to Peter. 'Be sure to move between lying on your left and right sides in bed and avoid bathing for three days.'

James's rapid instructions, in his earnest southern brogue, put Brodie in mind of Prior Bernard chastising the infirmarian for reading scriptures at the table like a chattering blackbird. Brodie's memories of the prior did not fit exactly with Peter's rapturous visions.

Archibald tucked the severed head into the crook of his arm, facing forward. The others formed a column behind and they started back to the priory in solemn order.

*

They rode out on the trail of Prior Bernard's killer as a threesome – Fergus and Brodie on mules, Malise walking alongside – Brodie's task to record events while Peter ailed in the infirmary. Armed with broadswords, Fergus and Malise provided the soldiery. At Forfar – in exchange for hugman's loaves and four flagons of better ale – they were joined by two of the sheriff's deputies, who led the way to the spot described by Peter, a dip in the track narrowed by thick shrubs and deep enough so that no shadows were cast in its gloom.

One of the deputies dismounted and studied the ground by his feet, pulling aside stalks and stems with the point of his sword. Edging down the slope, he stopped and started at places that looked of no significance to Brodie. Before the dip reached its full depth, the deputy called out – though the sound of gushing water diluted his shout – and disappeared in a thicket of knotweed.

The others followed him into the undergrowth. Malise tethered the mules.

They all came to a halt by an abrupt rock face, black with seeping water. Out of sight, a burn hurried by beyond. They went no farther except one at a time, the deputies first, then Brodie.

Brodie heard a muffled shout from below as he scrambled down the slippery rock, flat against its surface and gripping weeds to prevent a fall.

The shout came again. 'We have something here!'

Brodie dropped the height of a man's waist through the air and came to land by the water's edge. Just downstream, the reckless charge of the burn was halted by a steep granite embankment. The water briefly jostled and churned before forming a serene pool, as if chastened by its encounter with the embankment. Behind Brodie, one of the deputies crouched below an overhang in the rock face. The other could not be seen.

Fergus landed beside Brodie with a grunt.

'Here! Come see.' The deputy in the mouth of the rocky recess addressed Fergus. Both he and Brodie hurried across.

The deputy was huddled over a makeshift fireplace. Rocks two deep – three on the north side where, on another day, the wind would scud down the linn – had been placed in a crude circle. The soil around had been trampled flat and there were signs of habitation: stacks of large logs, smaller branches and kindling; fine bones and scorched deadwood in the hearth; two sharpened poles on opposite sides, where a spit might have hung.

The deputy rubbed some ashes between his fingers. 'The fire is cold but this cave has lately been used as a dwelling place.' He gestured inside the crevice, which was low but deeper than it first appeared. A broad bed of flattened moss and foliage was tucked at the rear. Sheaves of burdock stems and nettle leaves lay in a corner beside a pile of bark Brodie recognised as silver birch. Rags scattered the ground. 'But it has been the den of only one fiend, or perhaps two – no more. With certainty, it was not the army you reckoned on.'

Malise came alongside after climbing down the rock face. 'Is this the place?' He looked about, bewildered.

Brodie envied the trace of disappointment on Malise's face, though would rather not confess to his relief there would be no sword-stirred skirmish that day.

'But this cannot...' Malise was interrupted by a shout, just audible over the teeming burn.

'Attention! Come to me!'

They followed the whistles and shouts of the second deputy as though they were tracks in the snow: upstream along the bank, then away from the burn, past alder clumps into woodland sparse with slender birches.

Attracted by the movement of his waving arm, they came upon the older of the two deputies standing in a sheltered clearing. He held a soil-stained human foot in his hand.

'It is a midden.' The deputy pointed at a disturbed patch of ground with the foot. 'And I would say it may hold the remains of a man.' He dropped the foot and slumped to his knees, grabbing at the dark earth with mittless hands. 'That was dragged a distance by a scavenger...' He nodded at the foot. '...and this midden has been rummaged too...though not fully...' he puffed. Even as he spoke, human ribs, blackened by fire, emerged from the dirt, as well as some assorted bones of other creatures – the skull of a rabbit or hare and larger bones of a sheep or boar – and strewn, muddied underclothes.

Brodie had never taken charge of such a ceremony before, though he knew the rite, and so blessed the emerging bones with all the reverence he could muster, stuttering only when the deputy exposed the clean incision in the spine that confirmed they belonged to Prior Bernard.

When no other human remains were to be found, the older deputy stood with an exaggerated stretch of his back. Malise fetched a saddlecloth and wrapped the foot along with the torso. Brodie completed the blessing by imitating the type of deep bow Master Robert had favoured when conducting a ritual.

Throughout it all, and on their return to the mules by a less parlous path, unwelcome notions struck Brodie like hailstones. The sight of the prior's skinless chest produced nothing sublime; in quick succession, it caused him to consider the fate of Master Robert, whose bones below the east cemetery topsoil would be long since stripped of flesh, and Thomas of Ersildoune, whose lot was still unknown. But more than anything, it brought to mind the prior's own counsel on banishing lewd and lustful thoughts by imagining the meat and fat inside a woman's skin as belonging to a corpse, stinking and rotting below the ground, consumed by maggots. Prior Bernard's teachings on Satan's bait had some effect when Brodie recalled Black Agnes guzzling him in her beer-soaked mouth, sucking as hard as though he were the brewhouse font. Not so when he conjured thoughts of Mariota: more likely he heard her living voice, saw her light smile.

They emerged from a tangle of bracken and briars, downhill from where they had entered the undergrowth.

'Should we search more for Thomas of Ersildoune?' Brodie asked Fergus.

'Ersildoune?' Fergus strained for a breath as they climbed farther up the slope, not the first sign of age Brodie had observed.

'Our visitor…' reminded Brodie, mounting his mule. 'He left Restenneth with the prior and Brother Peter. He too may lie in some nearby place.'

Fergus paused for a rest. 'Master Archibald gave instructions only to hunt those responsible for the death of the prior and retrieve what relics we could find.'

Malise helped Fergus into his saddle. 'I am grateful,' Fergus said to his son, before turning again to Brodie. 'I was told nothing of Ersildoune. Did he perish? Or escape?'

'Brother Peter believed he fled,' answered Brodie, riding ahead. 'I am not so certain.'

Fergus glanced up at the darkening sky. 'We will be fortunate to make it as far as Forfar before nightfall.'

Brodie said nothing until Fergus caught up. 'The fate of the prior grieves me but I speak up for Thomas because I had

stood where he had stopped, between th
infirmary, the papers from the library in

Barbour leaned towards Peter, not lay
but examining him closely; close enou
cheeks with wiry, black brows and hair a

'I have no doubt your pen writes with
to Peter. 'And the words you have writte
story even longer…' He broke off. In a
physician's authority, he instructed Pete
down on the bed. He pulled aside the
night shirt before continuing as before
change – The Brus, as I call it, is to be
rhyme in the manner of the trouveres o
require the hand of a makar rather than
be my task, rather than yours.'

Still lying on his front, Peter strai
shoulder, as if about to protest.

'Upright – on your arse,' ordered Bar

Peter turned and sat up as directed,
all others except Master Archibald, who
below the mounted crucifix.

Brodie could not be sure if Pete
precentor to petition for his merits as a p
Barbour's profanity.

Archibald tugged at his ear lobe.

'Your infirmarian…' Barbour offered
who lingered by his side – before swi
Archibald. '…Your infirmarian has at
diligently, succouring him with rest a
corrupting humours are deep enough
reached by such treatment alone. A
stagnated and his veins must be permitte
extended a flat palm towards his retainer

The aide rummaged in a bag on th
Barbour a small, bone lancet and a pewt

'Have you shit?' Barbour asked Pe
visible uncertainty.

Without waiting for an invitation, Ba
of the lancet's two blades into the un

thought it better to find someone alive than dead.'

Fergus shrugged and nodded at the same time.

Brodie had also hoped the indenture document that seemed to bind him to the area would somehow serve as a map to the territory, the simple reference to Monikie and Pitairlie leading him to further knowledge of his family and their fate. Yet the place was as unfamiliar as though he had disembarked from a boat and stepped on the shores of Flanders or crossed a dozen frontiers and arrived in the kingdom of Aragon.

'Do you know much of those who hold lands in these parts?' he asked Fergus.

'Merely the great houses – Lindsay, Ogilvie, Gordon and the Stewarts from Bonkle. I came to Restenneth after you, brother, and only then because the church gave me a place to plough for serving alongside the men of lord Bishop de Lamberton in the combats at the Bannock Burn, Carrickfergus, Endwillane and elsewhere. Why do you ask?'

'Then, you do not know anything of cadet branches? Perhaps the Afflecks?'

'Is this another of your riddles?'

The events of the day had borne Brodie along like a loose leaf in a tempest, allowing him no time to judge if they fitted with the verse discovered by Master Robert all those years before. 'I have found other words to perplex me since taking the scribe's duties,' he replied.

'Go on.'

'They are in library documents – an indenture binding me to the Rule of Augustine and an endowment describing my arrival at our priory. The indenture seems to give me the name Affleck, perhaps a home as a child in the area where we now ride…'

'Ahhh, I have it,' interrupted Fergus. 'And you would rather our search here continued long enough for you to find some remnant of this family? A parent? A brother? A grand manor with a privy of your own and serfs to work the land?'

Fergus's misplaced humour caused Brodie to turn away; he focused instead on the reins held loosely in his hand. 'I fear my parents have perished or suffered some other doom. It is most likely that my only brothers are those who share snores in the dormitory.'

Fergus pulled up his mule, causing
'Friend, I do not mean to be without p
with the breath of life in these lands.
many years ago. Your place to live and
Restenneth Loch now.' He smiled at Br
in Carrick and the Isles of Kintyre –
orphans…' He reached over and
shoulder. '…though my age is enough

Fergus dug his heels into the flanks

Brodie rode behind in the gloaming,
and steadings that had faltered, charred

*

Brother Peter lay in the infirmary for fi
fireplace and with the benefit of a
temperate east breeze, shutters closed
wind.

John the Barbour arrived without
Peter hailed the unexpected appearar
physician as a miracle, putting it down
Bernard's relics, now housed in an alta
Hugh and protected by a yellow sandst
promises made by Master Archibald, t
replaced by one of fine, carved alabaste
the miracle were needed, Barbour can
Benedict of Nursia, the patron of those
cured children of leprosy and even rais

Brodie paused at the infirmary do
writings on King Robert the Brus from
He considered knocking but judged
standing to enter unannounced.

'…you have been brought to my bed
martyr – and so, you are our first pilg
Barbour.

'Aye, so I am,' said Barbour with a l
Brodie's footsteps resounded below
Barbour halted him with a raised han
heavy cathedral robes. Brodie kneeled

forearm, just below the elbow.

Peter gulped a breath and quickly swallowed. Strands of blood trickled down either side of his arm into a bowl held by Barbour's aide.

'The malady must be released from your sinister side,' Barbour explained. 'Lent has not fully passed but it is Saint Benedict's Day – that will assist.'

Before the blood more than half filled the bowl, Barbour yanked Peter's arm vertical; some scarlet droplets ran onto the pale sheets, dilating deeper in colour than a cardinal's choir cassock. 'Clear the bowl and bring it back.' The retainer emptied the blood in the fireplace, careful not to pour it directly on the smouldering logs. Hurriedly, he brought it back to Peter's elbow.

'But I have another endeavour for you, at the request of no less than Robert the Steward, Guardian of the realm and heir to the throne itself,' continued Barbour. 'I arrive at your priory from Glamis, where I attended the birthing bed of the heir's spouse, Lady Elizabeth of Rowallan, who has borne a boy bairn after a wait of three years with only one daughter. In his joy, the Steward made it known that a great treatise should be prepared on the origins and flowering of the Stewarts, from their beginnings at the founding of the city of Nineveh to this present age.'

Peter's blood rapidly formed a spreading pool in the bowl.

Barbour glanced up at Archibald, silent beside the fireplace. 'Such a work on the merits of the Stewart line may find more favour now than at times past. Prior Bernard – may he rest with God and the stars above – was good and faithful, though he had little liking for the Steward.'

Brodie saw that Barbour narrowed one eye when choosing to stress a particular point.

'Yet the Steward has ruled as Guardian with a sage and steady hand since the boy king David fled his kingdom…' Barbour paused to take and inspect the bowl. Satisfied, he went on. 'And that must be known to history.'

All eyes were on the oozing blood as it neared the brim of the bowl.

'Will you undertake such a task?'

'Of course, but…' stuttered Peter.

'Excellent, so be it.' Moving briskly but with care, Barbour exchanged the bowlful of blood for a bandage held out by his aide. After binding Peter's arm, he raised his face, cheeks as ruddy as a rose, nose like a thorn. 'Shall I prepare for collation?'

Archibald took a step away from the fireplace and lifted his gown at the back to capture some heat. He bowed, still keeping a hold of his raised tunic. 'As a prelate of rank, you may gladly join our devotion to the saints.'

Peter spluttered. 'Then I too must join you in praise of the martyrs, as sure as I am as sacrist and succentor of this house.' He swung his legs to the floor.

'Can you be sure the healing has taken effect with such haste?' asked James. 'You have not put weight on your feet in a week.'

'I am sure,' Peter replied, wiping his brow. He got to his feet slowly and wrapped the top blanket around his shoulders.

Brodie stepped forward to hand the documents he had fetched to Peter but his way was obstructed by Barbour, who took the papers and passed them to the aide without a word.

Leaving the room, they had the bearing of a procession: Archibald and Barbour followed by James. Despite his unsteadiness, Peter shuffled across the floorboards with purpose, reaching the door to the dormitory a clear two strides before Brodie.

Canons and lay brothers crammed together in the scant warming room after collation. Master Archibald and Barbour retired to the prior's quarters with sweet malmsey wine and warming pans. By custom and good faith, the brethren gave proper regard to the announcement at collation that Barbour had taken the position of dean at the Cathedral of Saint Andrew in the town of the same name, from being precentor at Dunkeld. But their attention promptly turned to Brother Hector's tales from market.

'I heard it said that this Christie with the Cleek still prowls nearby in search of prey.' Hector wiped a dribble of ale from his beard. 'That he takes up quarters in caverns and feeds on forbidden beasts such as horses and, by Satan's bidding, now sets traps to slay women and children.'

'Brother Hector speaks the truth,' said Brother Finlay. Excitedly, he stood from his position on a stool by the door through to the chapter house. 'A travelling hammerman told me just this day that the savage wears the head of an infant on his thigh, fastened to his skin with stitches, as a symbol of his fealty to the devil. Like dogs, he and his beldame have grown coats of fur, snouts and ears on top of their heads.' Finlay snorted a small laugh into his tumbler.

Huddled by the fire, Peter spoke before Finlay could continue. 'Brother, the beast's allegiance to the archfiend is not in question – he eats flesh in blasphemous imitation of the Eucharist – but you should know that he does not travel alone with a witch. He leads a whole race of demons. I have seen it with my own eyes and felt the throb of their blows.'

'And I have seen with mine that his den was fit for only one or two,' interrupted Brodie.

Peter twisted around, his face flushed, as if in readiness to react harshly to Brodie's challenge. He held the position long enough for a silence to form.

Brother Walter broke the hush by calling on Donald the cook to fetch more ale.

Apparently choosing to ignore Brodie, Peter directed a still stare at the fire. He leaned from his seat and nudged a loose firebrand back towards the flames with a poker. 'Unlike all others here, I also saw with my own eyes Prior Bernard's martyrdom and the vigour of his saintly powers. God be blessed, his relics will keep our brotherhood at Restenneth free from harm, but what of all those not ensured his protection by the truth of my vision? I have spoken with Master Archibald and it is agreed that this priory should become a place of pilgrimage for all who seek the unutterable wisdom of the Divine Agency and God's good grace, which no man can withstand.'

Brother Donald pushed aside the curtain through from the refectory with his elbow, a dish of common cheese in one hand, pitcher of ale in the other; and the slack grin of one who had paid more attention to preparing the latter.

Donald laid the cheese plate on the floor in the middle of the room and kneeled to slice it into portions. Over his lowered head, Brodie's glance came together with Peter's glare.

Brodie stiffened. He resolved not to shirk the encounter, maintaining their look even as Donald slopped beer into his bowl.

Peter rubbed his arm at the place where the lancet had pierced his vein. In the same movement, he shrugged and turned to face the fire, as if a fitting response might lie in the ashes or among the fidgeting flames.

Chapter 9

"Give me my scallop-shell of quiet.
My staff of faith to walk upon,
My scrip of joy, immortal diet,
My bottle of salvation,
My gown of glory, hope's true gage,
And thus I'll take my pilgrimage."

Sir Walter Raleigh, *His Pilgrimage* (c 1603)

April, 1340, until the 28th Day of May, 1341

Pilgrims came to Restenneth, bringing with them ample offerings in return for badges and ampullae procured by Brother Peter, never in greater number than a year to the day after Prior Bernard's ascent but also throughout Eastertide until Whitsunday. With only two curtains between the library and the altar containing Bernard's remains, Brodie heard more than he saw of the worshippers: cries of the insane, moaning supplications and raised fiery tongues. Most were parish wrongdoers: villeins, soldiers, grassmen and herders footing it with staffs and scrips. Some lesser nobles and clergy arrived on horseback, few from afar. The only great man to pilgrimage did so on the Feast of Pentecost: Robert the Steward for one day and night on his way to Edinburgh for the homecoming of King David from France, exiled for a full seven years as protection against capture by hostile forces now in retreat. The Steward mostly played at tabula and dice with his men, who included his treasurer and chamberlain, David Carruthers; the Sheriff of Aberdeen, Robert Keith; and Walter Blantyre, a collector of customs from the same city. However, he also visited the altar, where he left a gold coin and two prayers: one for the cure of his infant son, who had suffered a mild apoplexy; another for the safe passage of Lady Elizabeth Mure, who remained at Balmoral with their son but was due to make the onward journey to Edinburgh by the end of the month.

Before heading south along with Archibald and Peter, the Steward also left a task for Brodie: to copy accounts of the recent parliaments at Scone and Dundee; and prepare the text in a way that was favourable to his guardianship. As Brodie understood, the Steward was hoarding power in advance of King David's return and the parliamentary records would be distributed selectively as evidence of his authority. Such assignments were no less dishonourable for being matters of strict instruction since Archibald's election as prior at Restenneth.

Brodie stood from his seat and opened the shutters, letting an effortless spring breeze into the sacristy and library. Had the dwindling flock not been moved indefinitely to Coupar Angus, he would be on the hills, leading the ewes and their newborns to higher pastures, rather than at his desk.

But it was not thoughts of tame beasts that most preoccupied Brodie.

The pilgrims brought more than coins and offerings: almost all had further tales to tell of Christie the Cleek. But the truth varied between them all. The Steward's man Fauside maintained that the cannibal had fled to the farthest point in the land and taken up in a subterraneous cavern of perpetual darkness at Bennane Head. A squire who attended the Earl of Mar heard that the intake of human flesh had frozen the fiend solid, so that he now stood in a ring of stones with his followers at the Hill of Fiddes. Huntsmen told how they came close to ensnaring a ferocious reiver who inhabited the glens of Doll and Clova. Oarsmen witnessed an aquatic leviathan rising from the waves, its serpentine neck arced the same as a butcher's cleek.

Not for the first time since the death of Bernard, Brodie reached for the books of Michael Scot, mindful of Thomas of Ersildoune's claim that they contained the answers to all questions. It was true that Brodie had made some discoveries among their brittle pages – coitus when a woman is menstruating will produce hunchbacks and lepers, drinking the milk of pigs and goats can make a person resemble the beasts – but another browse of Physionomia provided no answers that applied to Cleek's inhuman rampage.

Brodie lowered the book and turned to look beyond the open shutters. Despite a smirr of high cloud, the light of the sun lay as evenly on the grass as a covering of frost, the low slopes at Blackgate and curves of Pitscandly a charcoal blur against the haze. The steady beat of Brother Finlay's forge-hammer came from the direction of the workshops in the western grounds, its echo following close behind.

The rhythm was broken by a dull thump: beyond the sacristy and through the church, the main door from the nave banged open on its wooden stopper.

Brodie heard the tread of feet then recognised the put upon, pleading tones of Malcolm the guest master. A second voice had the pitch of youth. Among the whispered words, between the soft footfalls, a cripple's stick tapped deliberately on flagstones.

'Brother Brodie…are you at work?' Master Malcolm's inquiry from the adjoining chapel took the form of a hushed shout.

Brodie went to the sacristy entrance and pulled back the curtain. He tilted his head to indicate that Malcolm had his attention.

'We have pilgrims,' explained Malcolm. He was accompanied by a young girl, no more than nine years. Her jaw was buckled at one side. She leaned on a stick and dragged a useless foot behind. An old man walked alongside. He was bent low, not a hair on his head, his clothes marked with dirt. Malcolm guided him slowly by the elbow.

'This one appears to be mute, or at least has nothing to say, but the girl can speak,' Malcolm told Brodie.

The old man nodded.

'I have a sickness in my leg.' The girl's explanation was directed at the floor. 'And other places too.' She looked to Brodie and attempted a splintered smile.

Malcolm continued on her behalf. 'They bring no offerings but have travelled far, without shoes on their feet or beasts to carry them, in the faithful certainty that Bernard will work a miracle. Stay with them brother, I have much to attend to with Prior Archibald and Brother Peter absent for our king's homecoming.'

The old man tried to straighten his back and lift his head, presumably to acknowledge Malcolm's kindness. Struggling to do so, he offered a simple grunt instead.

Malcolm stooped towards the girl. 'God is alpha and omega. His providence sets all things in order and bestows all kinds of largesse on those faithful to him. Be humble with tears and follow the virtues of the saints,' he said.

The girl smiled again and Malcolm turned to leave.

As soon as the guest master disappeared through the night stair door, the old man dropped down and scuttled towards the altar on his knees, surprisingly agile. The girl hirpled behind. They stepped up into the sanctuary and adopted a position prostrate before the altar cavity. Both uttered a low moan.

'Do you need assistance?' asked Brodie.

The man waved a hand while still murmuring prayers and vigils.

His presence not required, Brodie returned to his desk, leaving open the curtains into both the sacristy and the library cell so that he could see the legs and feet of the prostrate pilgrims.

The crash that followed would have roused the whole priory – and anyone else within a mile – more easily than a thunderclap.

Brodie hurried through to the chapel. The stone cover protecting the relics lay on the ground in fragments and the old man was attempting to squeeze the girl, legs first, into the altar cavity alongside Bernard's bones.

'For Christ Jesus's sake!' shouted Brodie, stepping forward to restrain the old man, who was unexpectedly strong and determined. 'Why would you do such a thing?' The man was supporting the girl's head and neck so Brodie confined himself to preventing any further damage by holding them both in a sturdy, one-armed embrace.

Forgetting his own apparent dumbness, the man responded with a shout of his own. 'She must have healing bones next to her skin! It is the only way left.' His voice crackled with age.

'But you cannot do it this way. You are causing destruction,' Brodie reproved. 'And in a house of God,' he added, in the hope the man was a true devotee.

'No other ways remain. She is touched by the devil.'

Brodie laid the book he was still holding on the altar and let go of the man to support the girl, who was slipping from the cavity.

His arms free, the old man picked up Brodie's book. 'Then I will pour the balm of holy words on her cursed limbs.' His expression changed on opening the Michael Scot manuscript: he appeared to be staring into the far distance rather than in front of his own face.

Brodie grabbed the book but it fell at their feet.

The old man backed away from its landing place. 'That is no holy book...It is a book of magic...the devil's work...his demons crawl from the pages...'

The book lay open, face down, on the floor.

With the man at a distance, Brodie drew the girl from the altar cavity and set her on the tiles. Her face beamed with fervour.

Malcolm and Brother Symon appeared in the main doorway and made their way forward as far as the rood screen that separated the lay brothers' stalls from those set aside for the priests. They stood there, eyes and mouths agape. 'What is this ignominy?' managed Malcolm.

The old man picked up the girl's stick and used it to point at Brodie. 'You are no man of God – you are a servant of the devil. May the souls of unborn children smother you in your sleep.' He turned to the girl. 'Come, you will be crippled in more than your legs if you remain in this infected place.' He circled the book on the floor, grabbed the girl's hand and staggered down the steps into the chapel. 'The devil's imps are here!' he shouted hoarsely, barging past Malcolm and Symon. 'Soon they will be a swarm. Leave now, I warn you...'

The old man continued to issue other dire warnings, or perhaps threats, causing Malcolm and Symon to look troubled beyond measure. Gradually, the imprecations melted into the open spaces of the nave and then the outside air.

'Are the relics intact?' spluttered Master Malcolm, hastening towards Brodie.

At the same moment, Brother Hugh burst into the church.

Without heeding any proprieties, Symon ran past the others and kneeled by the altar to examine the cavity. 'Prior Bernard's relics are whole and have not been defiled,' he said, his breath and words coming shallow and fast.

'Though the stone cover is in need of repair.' Hugh had caught up. He held the two largest chunks of fractured sandstone, one in each hand.

'Has any other damage been caused?' asked Malcolm.

'Perhaps only the book,' said Brodie, bending to pick up Scot's Physionomia. 'It seems to be together,' he added, without looking closely.

'Very well. Brother Hugh – make what repairs are necessary to the altar. Brother Symon – sweep the tiles and assist in any other way. Brother Brodie, you will make good any damage to the library books. I will warn Fergus the Ward that a lunatic roams somewhere on our soil, if he has not already taken his feet elsewhere.'

Unable to fathom the old man's earlier hysteria but eager for a closer inspection of the book that caused him so much terror, Brodie slipped into the sacristy and drew the curtain shut.

Malcolm opened it again. 'Why did the pilgrim make those blasphemous remarks about you and this church, Brother Brodie?'

Brodie hesitated. 'I...I cannot say, Master. It must have been due to the temper of his mind.' He bowed and ducked into the library cell, allowing Malcolm to probe no further. Once at his desk, Brodie looked from one page to another, but saw nothing more than script, marginalia and a small number of miniatures.

A draught tugged at the pages.

Brodie leaned over, closed the shutters and lit a candle for light instead. He breathed deeply, causing the flame to flicker almost to the point of going out; it cast shades of light and shadow over the parchment.

And in that glow, he saw a flash of white on the fringe of the book's dark blue cover.

Brodie looked closer: the mark was a tear.

He lit a second candle and turned to the inside front cover: the tear was one edge of a flap. And sure enough, as the old man had avowed, an imp emerged from between a fold of hide cover and a layer of exposed pasteboard. But it was no fire-breathing emissary of the devil: the demon that so terrified the old pilgrim was nothing other than an illustration on a slip of parchment.

Brodie pulled the scrap loose. The parchment was bleached as white as the first snows on a peak. Above a verse, the imp came almost into full view, though the very top of its head had been torn off. The creature had lips, wide and full, the tail of a goat and fur, or hair, like smouldering ashes. Its glowing eyes gaped greedily down on a distressed baby in a bed of straw or heather and a spit of dismembered body parts: a crowned vulva and two arms. A halo of darkness floated above the infant. The words *"Packsaddle child"* were written below. The similarities with the riddle Master Robert found on Brodie's first day at the priory were unmistakable. The left edge had been cut straight and was decorated with corresponding myrtle and violet vegetal patterns. The verse was again written in the vernacular, in the same flowing hand and with similar metre and measure.

This time Brodie could read the words for himself.

> *"Hail the homebound king on rocky shores.*
> *As the queen of the morn is pricked like a whore.*
> *From the seed, a whelp will crawl,*
> *Stewarts, Christies; damnation all!*
> *But lend the brother a sanctuary bell,*
> *And Afflecks! Arise, eight depths from hell."*

He found himself rushing to the end before he had finished the mid-portion. He read the riddle again, more deliberately.

All knew the Stewarts and the head of that noble family, Robert the Steward, heir to the throne. And the name Christie had been heard throughout the kingdom as belonging to the cannibal. More difficult to guess was why the two names had been mentioned in the same bracket of words. But he had no time to think further on the question. The name that he saw brightest and boldest was his own. Affleck. The Afflecks: who, if the verse was to be understood and believed, could still rise from whatever place they held in hell.

Finally, Scot's books had yielded a discovery of consequence.

Brodie fumbled for his knife sheath and the fastener that opened the front pocket. He pulled out the older riddle; the parchment had yellowed slightly in fourteen years but remained lighter in colour than most documents of that age. But if the colour was not identical, all else matched: the vines and leaves of the painted creeper grew from one fragment to the other; the jagged edges where the parchment had been ripped fitted together precisely. And the small mark that Brodie had thought a smudge on the older fragment now formed the top of the imp's torn head. Pieced together, the creature bore the ears of a goat and the horns of a demon.

Chapter 10

*"The young king [David] despaired when he saw
the people of his kingdom…when he had heard
the complaints of these and others, he comforted
them the best he could and said that he would
avenge them or lose all that remained to him or
die in the attempt."*

Jean le Bel, *Chronique de Jean le Bel* (c 1350)

28th Day of May, 1341, until the 2nd Day of June in the Same Year

Brodie showed due contrition for failing to stay with the pilgrims in the chapel, confessing his wrongdoing before the brethren. Master Malcolm administered the sacrament of penance and imposed satisfaction: as well as fasting on the three Ember days that straddled the months of May and June, Brodie was to immerse himself to his waist in the Fithie River, while praying for God's grace to deliver him from the guilt of sin.

Arms outstretched in the shape of a cross, weighted sconces of brass with lighted candles in each hand, he took up position in the Fithie one, two and three times.

"God, the eternal king, my heart is contrite for I detest my sins above every other evil…"

Yet, even as he recited the Act of Contrition, the lines of the riddle crept between the words.

"And Afflecks! Arise, eight depths from hell."

"…because I dread the loss of heaven and the pains of hell…"

Always the end of the riddle came to him first, followed shortly by its beginning.

"Hail the homebound king on rocky shores."

"…who are all good and deserving…"

"As the queen of the morn is pricked like a whore."

Distracted, he stopped praying and waded to the shore, his sodden tunic slapping against his knees.

Brodie's outlook on the riddle had followed the worsening mood of the weather. He had been as bright as the sun after first reading of the Afflecks and their potential redemption from unknown sins. But unease gathered force with the winds that brought gruel-grey clouds to Restenneth the day Lady Elizabeth Mure's expected arrival became an unexplained absence. Now that the dark sky had set to a firm sludge, the verse – and particularly its first foreboding lines – clogged his thinking. After all, Lady Elizabeth, spouse of the heir to the throne, was apparently absent at precisely the time King David was due to return to his kingdom. The under-meaning of the riddle was plain enough: Elizabeth Mure of Rowallan would suffer some vile embrace at any day. Yet no names said as much. And his concerns about Lady Elizabeth's lateness had already been dismissed by Malcolm at chapter.

Brodie took to the water once again, his hem rising in the current, and resumed his penance.

"…to confess my sins, to do penance…"

He had completed as many recitations as there were apostles when he saw Mariota approaching to his right, on the opposite riverbank. A flurry smothered his bald crown and pinched the tops of his ears, the water dragged more heavily at his legs, river moss oozed between his toes. Brodie hurried to finish his prayers before she drew level.

'Brother Brodie, there are easier ways to extinguish candles than to lower them in the water with such ceremony.' Mariota, who was carrying a privy bucket, gave him a spry smile.

"…and to amend my life. Amen." Brodie blew out the candles and hooked the brass holders onto his belt. He shouted over the flow of the water. 'We must all do penance for our sins – which ones have you committed to be put in charge of the soil bucket?'

'If you have such an interest in the bucket, I will happily tip it at your feet for a closer look.' She motioned as if to hurl the contents in his direction.

Brodie splashed to the shore in imitation of a retreat, though any real haste was impossible in his waterlogged woollens.

'Fear not, Brother Brodie, this is reserved for the fishes and toads. Wring yourself dry while I take it beyond the eel trap.'

As Mariota passed by, Brodie saw that her hair was twisted in a strand like a rope.

Brodie trudged from the river and slumped down on a knot of grass. The pebbles around his feet stained dark with dripping water. He shivered. Mariota came back into view. Brodie wrung some water from his tunic, splashing his dry boots. 'May the Lord confound...' He squeezed his damp feet into the boots and stood to greet Mariota.

She called across the river but her words were lost in the gathering wind.

Brodie cupped his hand to his ear to show he had not heard.

Mariota shouted louder, stressing every word. 'Are... you... clean?'

Unsure of her meaning, or even if he had heard her correctly, Brodie shrugged.

Mariota edged closer to the water's edge. 'OF YOUR SINS!' She stood with one hand on her hip, privy bucket swaying in the other.

A few thin drops of rain broke the surface of the river. Then Brodie felt it on his crown, his nose. He looked up; billowing clouds had formed a vengeful sky. Before he had time to reply, heavy droplets pitted the boulders around the bank. The deluge began an instant later, the rain slashing through the air and splattering the river. Without another word, Brodie and Mariota picked up their pace and hurried along opposite riverbanks. Cutting across the heather mounds, Brodie saw young Mary and Isabel scampering back to the tofthouse from harvesting scallion in the rig. Isabel still clung to a small, limp bunch of what looked from a distance like daisies or stitchwort. Brodie bypassed the toft, hurrying instead for the gatehouse. He reached the shelter of the gatehouse porch before Mariota was in sight beyond the palisade.

Brodie heard the trapdoor above open with a thud. Fergus's grinning face appeared through the opening. 'Come up the ladder and warm yourself by some coals,' he said.

'A moment,' replied Brodie. He blinked water from his eyes.

Mariota rounded the palisade and clattered over the drawbridge.

Brodie wiped his fringe with one hand and used the other to hold the door open for Mariota. She bustled in, scattering dewy drops and filling the bare porch with quick breaths. She took in Brodie's sodden appearance. 'And so my question is answered – you are not yet cleansed and the Lord sent a storm to help with your ablutions.' She laid a hand on his elbow. 'Do you have other sins you are not confessing, Brother Brodie?' Smiling, she reached for the plait of hair behind her head and brought it over her shoulder. She wrung it out as though it were a shirt on washing day. Mariota smoothed the rest of her hair away from her forehead and started up the ladder to the watchtower, where her father and Malise waited.

The fire in the brazier was small enough that its sparks would not cause a hazard in the wooden tower loft, but it gave sufficient heat to dry their toes and hands. Fergus and Malise shifted to the floor and gave a stool each to Brodie and Mariota. Fergus's gaze lingered on Brodie in a way that, for once, gave him the expression of an elder. Brodie shifted his backside on the seat.

Fergus stoked the fire. 'Another forenoon has passed without the arrival of the Lady Elizabeth. Did you ask Master Malcolm if he would consider a search?'

'I did,' answered Brodie. 'But he will not spare Malise or any others, saying the priory has to carry out its own work and is already short of brothers and laymen.'

'More likely he sees his own wilted boughs and prefers to look at something young and green,' said Malise.

Brodie said nothing.

'I have seen his amorous blinking too,' agreed Mariota.

Heedful of his vow of obedience, Brodie simply nodded.

Still cross-legged on the floor, Fergus leaned backwards. 'You two need more warming,' he said, scooping a skillet into an open beer barrel against the wall. He ladled in honey from a pot and, sitting forwards again, rested the pan on the fire.

But before any steam had risen from the mixture, Fergus stood sharply. The watchtower loft was only three strides across in each direction; Fergus seemed to reach the small window on the west wall in a single bound, Malise at his heels. Fergus threw open the shutters and held Brodie and Mariota quiet with an open palm while surveying the carse beyond the Fithie River. The wind growled at the shutters that remained fastened.

Matching his previous haste, Fergus then moved to the south window. When it opened, a gust swirled through the loft, yanking the flames in the grate one way then another.

'A horseman arrives at speed,' concluded Fergus after a brief period of silence. 'Perhaps bringing news of Lady Elizabeth.'

Mariota jumped up and stood beside her father. Brodie went to the west window and peered into the mirk of the storm along with Malise.

The pound of galloping hooves reached Brodie's ears before his eyes saw the approaching horse. The mounted messenger drew up his grey palfrey opposite the watchtower. The horse breathed mist and a ball of mucus from its nostrils. 'I bring vital word of your king,' the messenger shouted.

'Then you must come inside,' replied Fergus. Without further hesitation, he unwound the lifting rope from the drum, lowering the drawbridge to a horizontal position. Fergus was first down the ladder, followed by the others.

The messenger guided his palfrey across the drawbridge and dismounted. He continued when they had all assembled below the gatehouse archway. 'Beacons must be lit and others told. On its return from France, the king's ship became weather bound and could not anchor at Edinburgh. The winds have forced it north, though no-one can say for certain where it will land.' Mariota took the reins from the messenger. 'I have travelled all the distance from Edinburgh, half through the night, stopping near Stirling and at Perth – my horse can go no farther. A separate messenger has gone from Dundee to the Tironensian house at Arbroath so that a fire can be lit in the great tower at that place. But my instruction is that the vice chancellor at the cathedral in Brechin and the families of Maule and Lindsay of Brechin, Edzell and Invermark must be told to form a landing party farther north at Montrose, should the king's barge put in there. The black friars in the town can prepare hospitality.'

Since that first day at Restenneth, each reference to Brodie's infant days had added a further shade to his few, uncertain memories: rain coming down on one bank of the burn while sun shone on the other; making spears from rushes; a nearby hill that must have reached higher than any other; a gate; snow; a thick crack in an icebound pond, like a frozen ripple; a huge, wet cow turd. But there were more things he did not see or know. Had he his mother's full features? Or the colour of his father's hair? He never imagined brothers or sisters but did he truly have none? The messenger's naming of Edzell – the only place other than Restenneth referred to in both his indenture and endowment documents – brought its own unbidden image: the warden at the castle there, bald on his head but with hair covering his face, hurrying to and fro while Brodie furtively played at soldiers.

'You have ridden long and far, sire – you should rest while I go.' In his eagerness to keep hold of the connection to Edzell, Brodie spoke with more urgency than intended. He adopted a more careless tone. 'I can manage a horse well enough and know the road.'

'Brother, you ride better than you wield a sword – Malise must escort you.' Fergus looked to his son, who nodded. 'That way, he will get to join a search after all, even if it is for a king rather than a consort. And Master Malcolm will want to ride along to receive the king, if it happens that he finds a landing place nearby.' Fergus went as if to lead the messenger in the direction of the priory but turned back to Brodie to add an afterthought. 'You can ask at places along the way if they have seen or heard of Lady Elizabeth.' It lay somewhere between a question and a request.

The mention of Edzell had taken Brodie once again to the end of the riddle he had found in the cover of Scot's Physionomia, with its lure of redemption for the Afflecks. He returned to the opening lines.

"...*queen of the morn...pricked like a whore...*"

'Beyond doubt, her fate is also our concern.'

*

The priory horses were more suited to bearing a plough collar than an urgent message. However, spurred on by the prick of their riders' heels, they made good ground, reaching Brechin Cathedral before vespers and Montrose for compline, though only brief prayers were said at both places. At Brechin, the Lord William Maule-Lindsay sent out couriers to make known the king's fate, agreeing that they would also ask for news of Lady Elizabeth along the route. On reaching Montrose, Malise and Lord William's squire attempted to light a fire by Scurdie Ness but the storm was blowing such quantities of wind and sand that the delegation decided instead to move north of the dunes. Throughout the journey, Brodie searched for a moment to ask the squire questions about Edzell but he attended his master too closely to allow an approach.

The group did not draw rein again until they reached the Hill of Morphie. From there, what appeared to be the king's barge was visible as a smudge, just closer than the grimy horizon. With the ship in sight, they began building a beacon below a brief scarp, east of the crest. A small pyre amassed but the slopes were mostly treeless so Brodie and Malise went to fetch more branches from an aspen spinney to the north. When they returned, others had arrived: the churchmen from Brechin Cathedral, a tutor with the name Mortimer, who claimed to have the favour of the Brus family, and some merchants of middling stature. The black friars from Montrose came soon after, picking their way carefully through the gorse and rocks due to wearing only flimsy shoes on their feet. They immediately took up position below the signal fire. Facing out to sea, they sang the Benedicite harmoniously then fell prostrate, fingering beads as they prayed for the salvation of souls. Master Malcolm belatedly joined them and urged the seculars from the cathedral to do likewise. Lord William, his squire and the merchants took shelter below an old yew, its splayed branches like bony limbs. Although the distant barge seemed anchored on a bank, Brodie, Malise and the tutor Mortimer excused themselves from prayers, saying a watch should be kept on any progress the king might make. They stood close enough to the fire so that its flames were neither too hot on their right side, nor the wind too cold on their exposed left. As they watched, the grey twilight thickened to the black of nightfall.

And with darkness, the gale eased: until the rain was as light as mist from a waterfall. Now and then, the moon, just past full, appeared through cracks in the clouds. The sea glowed brighter than the dark sky or the shadows on the ground, allowing Brodie to see that two escort vessels accompanied the king's barge. He was straining to count the number of masts they carried when Mortimer shouted out.

'It moves!' He was pointing a finger seaward. 'The king's ship is on the move!'

The friars fell silent. Burning logs sputtered and spat. With little wind to drag the flames, sparks from the fire flew high in the air. Lord William and Master Malcolm came alongside Brodie and the others. The tutor's still outstretched arm took the place of any words.

For a moment, it seemed as though Mortimer had detected nothing more than the motion of distant waves. But it was soon clear that the bobbing lanterns of the convoy vessels were moving, in a northerly direction, towards the shore.

In the downhill pursuit that followed, the draught horses reached as fast as a canter. Such was the pace, Brodie briefly feared the frantic whirl of his mare's hooves would cause the beast to tumble over itself, like a child charging downslope. However, they kept up the speed all along the rocky coast from Milton Ness to Inverbervie, slowing only when the king's flotilla turned sharply towards shore, then stopping on a clifftop at Bervie Brow, where they watched the king's barge furl its square mainsail.

Breathless, Lord William ordered his squire to tie up the horses. Master Malcolm nodded at Malise to do likewise.

'The king must be berthing in the haven below,' said Lord William. 'We will go down the crag on foot. Those following behind can join us in good time.'

Brodie dismounted but kept hold of his reins. 'I will tether the horses,' he said to Malise. 'Your strength may be needed to help Master Malcolm down the precipice.'

'You believe his wilted boughs are ready to crack?' muttered Malise with a grin.

With the others scrambling down the steep slope, Brodie finally had time alone with the squire.

'May I ask you – do you know much of the Lindsay place at Edzell?'

The squire adopted the indignant expression of a superior. 'I travel all these lands in the service of Lord William and know each person of standing.'

Clarions sounded out at sea, losing pitch in the swell. Brodie guessed the king was transferring to one of the smaller, single-masted vessels. The barge took in its triangular foresail.

After securing the horses, Brodie and the squire started down the slope.

'I read that Patrick de Lindsay was once Lord of Edzell and Glenesk. Is that still so?'

'He is as a flower among knights and as bold and doughty as he ever was. Why do you ask?' The squire's severe fringe, hanging as heavily as an altar cloth, flopped with each footstep.

'I may have known him once before…' Brodie skidded on some shingle. 'And do those with the name Affleck serve him or his kin?'

'I know of no Afflecks of any rank.' The slope steepened so that it was almost sheer. They clung to rough dune grasses, which jabbed Brodie's wrists beneath the sleeves of his habit, dry from the river but now damp with sweat. At the foot of the bluff, they slid down, then trudged through a bank of soft sand. The squire seemed to have thought further on the previous question, though he answered more to himself than Brodie. 'Or could it be that the Afflecks held their lands from the Umfravilles, supporters of the disloyal Balliol and Beaumont and rightly disinherited of territory and title for failing to enter the king's peace?'

The truth of it snatched a breath, caused Brodie to miss a pace.

His family had owed allegiance to the traitor Balliol and the invading King of England. And, given the punishment inflicted on the disinherited for their treachery, they had almost certainly lost their lives as well as their lands. He felt the impact of the realisation as straightly as though he had been dealt a heavy blow to the chest. And the fate of his parents would have been confirmed by the wax seal of the king whose standard fluttered ever closer to the shore.

A natural path, sloping comfortably downward, took them

through the thigh-high grasses to the level of the cove. Driven by a sharp sea breeze, surface sand skidded along the ground, pricking Brodie's ankles. Behind, and for some distance to the north, windblown arches and hollows in the rock had the smooth look of sculptures started but left unfinished. Almost directly ahead, the king's convoy moved towards a narrow fisherman's jetty. The lead boat lowered its sail and took to oars.

His steps heavy in the loose sand then firm where waves had washed ashore, Brodie followed some distance behind the squire, not choosing a particular direction himself. He heard the trumpets announce the arrival of the king but the squire's words about the Afflecks played louder. Picking his way through storm debris and stepping onto the wooden jetty, Brodie saw the steersman angle the rudder oar so that the royal boat drew alongside, but his attention was fixed on some point beyond the horizon.

'Brother...Brother!' The squire was shouting at Brodie. The king's boat was mooring and the squire had already tied a line from midships to the only cleat on the jetty. 'The bowline...' He was pointing impatiently at a deckhand who was poised to hurl a mooring line to where Brodie stood. 'Find a place to secure the bowline!'

At the shout, Brodie was instantly back in the cloisters: receiving and obeying an instruction. He gathered the line and attached it to a pillar.

In time for the king's disembarkation, they formed a line on the jetty, Lord William at the head, followed by Master Malcolm. Mortimer had arrived – if not yet the merchants or the friars – so he took his place next. The squire, Brodie and Malise made up the remainder of the meagre welcoming party.

They kneeled and bowed their heads, meaning Brodie saw little. Rather, he felt the king step back onto the unsteady ground of his realm through a lurch and sway of the planks beneath their feet.

Further movements of the jetty and the sound of more voices suggested others were stepping ashore, and then that the king was moving down the line. Brodie could not hear much of what was being said over the noisy slop of waves below the pier. He measured the king's progress by the thud of approaching footsteps.

Feet and legs clad in high boots stepped into Brodie's vision, stopping in front of the squire.

'Fount of all honour,' said the squire, bowing his head even more deeply.

A woman stood just behind King David. Judging by the rich velvet pinsons she wore, it was Queen Joan of the Tower. Despite the obvious finery, Brodie could not help but notice that their shoes had been spattered by some foul liquid.

The king shuffled to the side, so that he was directly before Brodie.

'And you are a brother at the Restenneth house of Augustinians along with Master Malcolm, who greets me in place of your prior?'

'I am, Sir King.'

Brodie lifted his head just enough to look at King David's hands, as if he might be able to tell if they were capable of carrying out, or ordering, one or more executions. A broadsword hung loosely by the king's side.

'You may stand when you address your king. Or he addresses you.'

Brodie stood. He raised his eyes in their sockets, if not his head in its hood.

'My brother, the prince John, lies buried at your church. He was no more than an infant at death but he carried the same blood as mine in his veins. I should visit his tomb. Is it well tended?'

'I sit by it in the library, Sir King. It has suffered some damage in the wars but also been given repairs and prayers.'

'A library, you say? Then you must be a scribe. And a scribe can tell the whole world of my return, for the world is not here to see the occasion for itself.' He swept an arm around the empty beach. 'Perhaps you should include the story in a great chronicle – one that goes on to describe the victories that will assuredly be mine at the castles of Roxburgh and Stirling a short time before Balliol and England's Edward are finally expelled from my land. There is much to be told of King David the Brus.' Whether deliberately or not – Brodie could not say – the king pronounced his own name with a guttural French 'r'. Likewise, he had no way of telling if the request for a chronicle was sincere or intended to be humorous.

'Another arrives, spurring fast!' shouted one of the boat's crewmen. King David turned first to where the boatman pointed at a horse splashing through the shallow surf.

'And so there is one less who must read your tale to know what happened this night,' the king said to Brodie with a smile.

Brodie fought back an inclination towards the king's sly charm. Could he smile just as easily when he sealed a death warrant? He certainly seemed capable of contradiction. After all, an unsheathed sword glinted in his hand yet there were no enemies in sight. In other ways too: fair curls fell cheerfully on slender features but the same hairs were matted with sea spray and salt from the hardship of the crossing; his tabard carried the royal crest and he wore a trimmed mantle of woven brocade clasped by a ruby brooch but his hose – one red leg, the other yellow – bore the dirt of the ship and the lustre had gone from his mail coif; he was a king with a queen – though she looked less than stable on her feet – but no golden crown on his head.

The horseman came almost upon them, dismounting with an expansive swing of his leg. Not even bothering to secure his horse, the rider ran towards Lord William. Seeing the king, he fell to his knees before the royal party. 'Sovereign nobleness, forgive my ill manners. But I have a message that must be delivered with the utmost haste.'

'You may stand to speak,' said the king.

The rider stood but kept his head bowed. 'The tidings come all the distance from Lord William's keep at Invermark.' He gave a sideways glance in his lord's direction. 'The courier carrying news of the royal barge's misfortunes asked also for word of Lady Elizabeth Mure of Rowallan. On hearing the name, the bailiff for those lands immediately spoke up, saying he had come across a wandering handmaid who was without a mistress. She used Lady Elizabeth's name but her story was so fanciful that he took her to be feeble-minded, or at least muddled.'

'However muddled or fanciful, you have come to tell us this story and so you must,' said the king.

'My lord king, I cannot know if her tongue is treacherous or truthful – for we believed that the creature she described had fled to the most distant corner of the realm – but the servant girl said Lady Elizabeth was carried off to some unknown place. Not by any common sinner, but in the grip of the flesh-eating monster they call Christie Cleek.'

The king swung his sword gently backwards and forwards so that the crossguard brushed his hip. He showed no surprise at the message.

'The handmaid was only spared so she could report that a ransom must be left at an appointed time and place.' The courier finished the dispatch in a hurry, as if by doing so he would avoid any wrath it might provoke.

The king looked over his shoulder at Lord William. 'I have heard the names both of the brute that prowls my kingdom and my kinsman's spouse, Lady Elizabeth, even if I had little time to know her before leaving for France. Can we go to your keep at Invermark this night?'

'Sire, it is difficult ground to travel at night. I have a stronghold at Brechin, though that is also a tiresome ride. The closest place that befits a royal visitor belongs to my kinsman, Lord Patrick de Lindsay – at Edzell.'

'Then Edzell it shall be.' He sheathed his sword. 'To prepare for the king's justice, as soon as we see morning light.'

Chapter 11

"But still, at the darksome hour of night
When lurid phantoms fly,
A hapless bride in weeds of white
Illumes the lake and sky."

Traditional rhyme about Craig Maskeldie's Bride's Bed
crags, included by Andrew Jervise in *The History and
Traditions of the Land of the Lindsays in Angus and Mearns* (1882)

4th Day of June, 1341

The new-found cavern is midway up the eastern slope of Craig
Maskeldie, just before the cliffs become steep, the narrow
entrance half concealed by rent rocks. The dregs of twilight shed
a mild gloom. Inside, the cave is long and low, thick with smoke
but mostly dry. The roof lifts only at one place, in the centre, as
if to make way for a huge boulder that sits there. My brother lies
along the back wall, covered by the dead churchman's robes.
Since our escape from Finzean, he fears that every flame
pursues him from the underworld, and so he stays as far from
the fire as possible, a vair fur over his face to keep the smoke
from his nose. The woman captive is pressed against the damp
south wall, the only place where some water leaks in. After an
initial frenzy on being seized, she now lies still, sleeping with tiny
sighs that together seem less substantial than breathing. The
braying wind and coughs of my brother help to keep me from
dreams that are likely to bear me again to the day de Moray's
men came, savaging with flame and steel until the grass around
my family's Finzean farmstead grew red with blood. Instead of
sleep, I sit by the fire and weigh my sins against my misfortunes.

My brother cries out in his sleep, in a way that could be any tongue or none, either due to a night terror or the injury he received in the encounter with the churchman.

Some kind of madness grows in my gut like a worm: it stirs at the sudden and unexpected noise from my brother and rises as an ill-tempered qualm.

So I go to the back of the cave, crouch down and, to ease my irritable heart, clamp a palm over my brother's mouth. He grinds his teeth. I can feel his jaw moving through the fur, beneath the skin of his cheeks. The top of his visible ear twitches, he snorts through his nostrils.

What timber am I made from if I choose to silence rather than comfort my brother?

'And what of my cold?' It is the woman captive. She has not spoken in a day at least and the sound of her voice takes me abruptly to my feet. I strike my shoulder against an angle of the cave wall and stifle a yelp.

She sits up. 'You prefer it by the fire. Could it be that you have no need of the fur around your shoulders?'

Until now, she has repeated boldly that she is Lady Elizabeth Mure of Rowallan, the gentlewoman of Robert the Steward himself, and we will be hanged high and drawn at the tails of horses for daring to take her captive. All of this may or may not be so, but she is certainly of sufficient rank to earn a ransom that is handsome enough to keep us from living a life like starved beasts. But she makes this new request with all the hesitancy of a child. And in that moment, my anger and fear are gone. I slide the pelt from my neck and kneel down. Up close, she has amiable eyes and wooing lips. I go to cover her bony arms.

And she grabs at the horn amulet around my neck, twisting the twine with all her force.

I am turned almost onto my side so that I can barely move except to reach over my shoulder and try to loosen her grip on the amulet. She is strong and a deathly creak comes from my choking throat. I prise up one of her fingers, then another.

The twine snaps.

I fall forward but she is on me before I can turn onto my back. She stabs me with the sharpened horn amulet: on my back, shoulders, neck, the arms I use for protection. Again and again.

I cannot say if I cry out from the blows – they merely spread a coldness – or if she makes any noise, but my brother wakes with a roar and a wail. Perhaps it distracts her: I am quickly able to take hold of her wrist and push her arm away. The amulet pitches into the darkness. I feel a wetness on my neck and cheek. My blood? Her spittle? My brother is still screaming, though the sound seems to travel a long distance. I tear off the fur I gave her and she squeals in fear. And then I see it: I see in her white, thrashing eyes that she has been sent to me by God, or the devil. Her husband once ruled the realm and so commanded the same wayward forces that slew my family without pity while collecting pillage. I am no longer in the cave: I am in a narrow tunnel without end; I am back in the farmstead, more than filled with – how many? – years of brimming rage. There is a monster on my back, a beast in my stomach. My mother and sister are being eaten by leprosy, while I can only look on. My brother still shouts in the distance. I strike the captive across the face to stifle her squeals. I tear at more than the fur. I tear at her gown, her chemise, her breast girdle. She squeals louder. And through the squeals, I hear laughter. She is standing over my mother and sister, laughing. I search for a weapon and find it below the folds of my rags, a half-forgotten stiffness that swells to more than a handful. I will prick her just as Squealer and the others pricked my mother and sister. I will bring her to hard perplexity, just as I did Squealer. I hold some piece of clothing tightly against her neck with one hand and use the other to reach below her kirtle. And when she is bare, I fasten her in a foul embrace of the flesh, to desecrate her just as Eve desecrated the faithful tree, just as Squealer lewdly violated my mother and sister. I stab for every wound suffered by the Christies of Finzean.

And then, a moment or an hour later, it is done.

I am back in the cavern. The captive lies still. She is no longer squealing. She is not the commander of the forces that ravaged my family, bloodying their swords to the hilt at Finzean. She is not Squealer. She is Lady Elizabeth of Rowallan, who has done no wrong other than attempt to escape from me.

And I am Andrew Christie, Christie of the Cleek, a most wretched and hideous thing, a half-life. A bogle-man.

Chapter 12

*"An outcast from pity, a robber, a sacrilegious
man, an incendiary and a homicide, a man more
cruel than the cruelty of Herod, and more insane
than the fury of Nero…I say, this man of Belial,
after his innumerable wickednesses, was at last
taken prisoner by the king's servants, as the king
ordained that he should be formally tried."*

Westminster Abbey monk, *Flores Historiarum* (c 1307)

23rd Day of August, 1341

'Andrew Christie…'

Christie barely responded to the justiciar's summons. He remained on his knees by the central pillar of the Arbroath Abbey chapter house, head drooping loosely. Amid the rise and fall of the shouts and murmurs that followed the opening of proceedings, Brodie noticed the mid-morning sun settling into the centre of the large circular window on the east gable, like some great conjunction of God and man.

The king's justiciar leaned forward to read the indictment. His hair, long and limp at the back and sides, hung as straight as the carved lines of the high-backed abbot's chair that cramped his fleshy limbs. "…Also known by the name Christie of the Cleek. Put to the horn as an outlaw, you are placed beyond the laws of this realm and so excluded from all manner of answer or plea to the crimes charged against you – murder, robbery and diverse felonies and degradations."

'And a slave of the devil with a taste for the flesh of Christians!'

Brodie looked up from his writing slope, quill still in hand.

No-one claimed the shout but the stares of the senior men on the bench at the front, along with those standing in a crowd behind, assigned it to Robert the Steward. Others called out in agreement. To Brodie's right, one of the monks on the stone bench around the wall began a low chant, unprompted by any superior. The Steward's chamberlain, Carruthers, emerged from the throng and aimed a kick at Christie, though his foot only glanced the prisoner's back before making contact with an edge of the octagonal pillar. Further enraged, Carruthers hauled at Christie's rags, clubbing him with fists, forearms, elbows and knees before being pulled off by two serjeants and a monk.

'This is a court of the king!' shouted the justiciar, though it did not fully restore order. He got up from the abbot's chair so that he stood alongside the other justices. 'His peace must be held!'

Gradually, the crowd quieted. Unable to gain further distance from Carruthers because of his restraints, Christie hugged the tiles. The red sandstone arches of the vaulted ceiling sprouted from the central pillar, which was of the same quarry, giving the impression that he cowered below rich, spreading boughs. Elsewhere, the stonework had been rendered bright white with limewater and chalk. Behind Brodie, on the centre of the north wall, hung the arms of the justiciar of Scotia, Lauder of Quarrelwood: a scarlet drape bearing a silver griffin. Flanking it were the banners of the other justices: Sir Alexander Seton; Roger de Balnebrich; Adam, Bishop of Brechin; and Abbot Geoffrey.

Lauder raised his voice over what babble remained. 'If justice is to be done, the crimes must be recited to these wise lords, my assessors and counsellors in this matter.' He motioned at the justices before turning again to the crowd. An imploring open palm replaced his clenched fist. 'Earls, barons, prelates – allow it to happen.'

Finally, the chapter house neared silence and Lauder read again from the bill of indictment. "By common repute, did Andrew Christie, leading fellows unknown, take and slaughter stock from lands and holdings at Monikie, Guthrie, Dunnichen, Restenneth, Aberlemno…"

Brodie watched as the sun fell directly on the prisoner's

bruised brow. Christie, still not full grown, forced shut his swollen eyes. Blood smudged his cheek. Clumps were missing from his haggard hair. Turning onto his side, Christie held tightly to his left leg, bare because he wore no breeks beneath his ragged tunic. Everyone gathered there could see that he bore some resemblance to a wild beast. But to Brodie's eye, he scarcely fitted the monstrous depiction contained in the indictment.

"…according to the testimony of Brother Peter Fenton, sacrist at Saint Peter's ecclesia, Restenneth, the prisoner and his multitude feloniously and eagerly attacked and wounded the said Brother Peter Fenton and his prior, who had the name Bernard, also losing the head of Prior Bernard, cutting him up piecemeal, devouring the parts that lay around and drinking his blood as if it were wine…"

Despite expecting some exaggeration in Peter's account, Brodie still paused his quill at the description of Bernard's death. Peter had made no previous mention of further mutilation of the prior's body. And the charred remains that Brodie blessed at the ravine appeared to have been roasted over a fire rather than consumed where the attack took place.

The justiciar continued, in a voice that was louder than Brodie had ever heard in a house of God, except when men joined together in praise. "…By the word of the same Brother Peter Fenton, who travelled with our Lord Robert the Steward to record events, the prisoner persevered with his wickedness, leading his accursed host from the place now commonly known as the Den of Fiends to a cavern called Gryp's Chamber at Craig Maskeldie. Therein, the Steward's armed force found the bones of thirty or more travellers, including those of women and children, with some limbs hung to dry and others left in salt…"

The search parties had been formed after a night that roused reluctant memories for Brodie: the malicious creases on the face of the Edzell warden; the stench from the tower drain; the chill off the floor of the great hall, where he once again slept alongside the castle attendants. But the stay at Edzell did no more than that: none of the servants' faces was familiar and those he asked knew nothing of the name Affleck. Soon after morning light arrived, Brodie had been woken and assigned to a search party led by the Sheriff of Forfar, to record Christie's inevitable capture in a chronicle, as requested by King David on the beach at Inverbervie. It was true that Robert the Steward's troop had reached Gryp's Chamber first. But Brodie arrived just one day later and saw none of the gruesome evidence described in the indictment.

Lauder finished reading with a reminder that no witnesses would be called or pleading permitted. When he leaned back in his chair and Sir Alexander Seton promptly produced a document of his own, it seemed there would be no deliberation among the justices either.

Standing to Lauder's right, Seton coughed. Taking in a breath of the hot, heavy air, he pronounced the sentence. "For these manifest crimes, it is decided that Andrew Christie…" Christie let out a moan, rolled onto his front and began to beat his head on the hard ground. Seton glanced up but hardly hesitated. "…also called Christie Cleek, is judicially condemned to be drawn on a hurdle from this abbey, through the west gate and beyond the dell to the Gallowden, where he shall be hanged high. Also for his felonies, he shall be taken down and cut open, his heart, liver, lungs and bowels put in the fire and burned for his injuries to the church. As an outlaw, his hands, feet and lustful parts shall be cut from his body and, before empty of blood, his head will be removed. To put dread in all who behold, his body shall be divided into four quarters and taken to each corner of the realm for display. Thus severed, his head shall be hung on a gibbet from this abbey's gatehouse to warn all who inhabit the boglands that the place beyond king and church is the Demon's Dale."

The horse that pulled Christie – stripped naked, face down on the wicker hurdle – led the parade through the streets and out of the town. Brodie stayed at the rear, to avoid the barbarous spectacle as much as the shit, spittle and cudgel strokes aimed at the condemned man. They crossed the Brothock at the point where the banks were steep and walked in procession towards Keptie Hill, Christie howling at severe jolts of the hurdle and otherwise uttering high and low sobs like a nursling. A mature greenwood of broad elm trees and some of the common kind of oak enclosed the path that swept around the northern slope of the hill. As they passed under the thickest of the branches, two boys ran past Brodie, in the opposite direction from everyone else, one chasing the other. The one in pursuit chanted a rhyme:

> *"Christiecleek! Christiecleek! He's efter you and I;*
> *Boil our brains, bake us in a pie."*

They circled round Brodie and headed once again towards the front of the column. An instant before he was caught, the boy being chased shouted over his shoulder.

> *"Halter oan his neck, hingin' from a tree;*
> *Now the bogle-man can no' get me."*

The two fell to the ground in a tangle of limbs, yelps and giggles. Only then noticing that they had almost reached their destination, the boys leapt to their feet and pelted hiddy giddy down the track leading out of the wood to the foot of Keptie Hill, on its sheltered west side. When Brodie emerged from the cover of trees, he saw that the gallows stood directly at the foot of the hill. A tumble of rocks had settled on the lowest portion of the slope, forming a makeshift gallery that overlooked the gallows. Beyond the height of the scaffold, where the hill lost some steepness, the rocks were fewer but larger, the tussock grass dense and deep. The two boys sat on the rocks nearest the hangman's ladder.

Royal proclamations and the Holy Writ made much of justice and judgement, wrath and righteousness. But where, Brodie could only wonder, did Christie's hasty trial and impending execution fit with the will of God and the laws of kings? He searched the scriptures for guidance. Mark the Evangelist showed the ways of both cruelty – the beheading of John the Baptist by Herod Antipas – and mercy: sparing Barabbas from crucifixion even though an insurrectionist and murderer. Reminded of the Gospel, Brodie looked on from afar, just as Mary Magdalene and Mary, mother of James the Less, had at Golgotha.

Below, the natural gallery had almost filled. Some others stood close to the scaffold. Christie seemed unable to stand so the hangman dragged him closer to the rope. The crowd jeered.

Above, the sky quickly darkened. A breeze rippled through the trees, fluttering their leaves like a thousand tiny birds.

After a struggle, the noose was fitted around Christie's neck and the doomster read out a summary of the indictment.

Almost as soon as the clouds arrived, a summer downpour pounded groundward, as though released by a trapdoor. Brodie edged farther into the trees. One leaf, then another and another, twitched as they were struck by heavy drops of rain. Behind the clouds, the sun began its descent.

Brodie turned away from the gallows and made his way back through the woods. After a dozen or ten steps, he heard the clatter of the trestle being kicked away. The crowd cheered.

By the word of King David, he was to provide a full account of the trial and punishment, but Brodie trusted in the brevity of Mark the Evangelist. He settled on what he would write of the execution in the king's chronicle.

"Past the sixth hour, they executed him. And he did not cry out."

Chapter 13

*"For when the deed was done, this foul and base
wretch fled to sanctuary at St Cross, and I, as
you may think, after him with all the posse."*

Arthur Conan Doyle, *The White Company* (1891)

25th Day of August, 1341

A spluttering north-easterly carried the summer rains past Restenneth, allowing the barley harvest at the priory to continue uninterrupted since beginning two days before the Feast of Saint Bartholomew the Apostle.

At dawn on the fourth day of harvest, Brodie stood outside the brewhouse along with the farm workers and other lay brothers, cradling their dewcups of ale before starting work. The clear sky promised sunshine but the early morning, late August air contained as much chill as Brodie's freshly drawn drink.

Brother Hector formed them into teams and handed out the tools: a long-handled scythe for Brodie, a whetstone and lengths of binding twine for Fergus.

In the croplands, the villeins who owed a tenth part of their labours to the church were lounging around a cart, waiting for the priory workers. Twins from Mid Dod – as tall and thin as the stalks they were about to cut – joined Brodie's team. Brodie and the twins would reap while Fergus followed behind, gathering and binding.

Occupied with the harvest since returning from Arbroath, Brodie had found no time to write a word of King David's chronicle. But at work in the field, thoughts came to him with the regularity of his swinging blade. Some were beyond certainty:

death, the harvester of all souls, had taken Christie and he would now be suffering terrible torments for his sins. Other questions left Brodie with doubt: why had deceits been told at the trial – and with casual ease, in a house of God – if Christie's guilt was so assured? And why did the proceedings inexplicably contain no mention of Lady Elizabeth of Rowallan, even if she had been freed, apparently unharmed, within a week of her capture by Christie? Brodie could no more change history than pluck a star from the heavens. But he could at least hope to find truths to put in the king's chronicle.

Brodie stopped working to wipe a trickle of sweat from his eye.

Over to his left, Fergus rebuked one of the twins. 'Watch your blade! You have it covered in soil!' The boy held up his sickle and shrugged. 'Not so close to the ground,' added Fergus more gently, marching towards the boy. 'Like this...' He imitated a cutting motion to show what height to reap the barley. 'Your blades need sharpened in any case – give them here.' Fergus took the tools from the twins and shouted over to Brodie. 'Does your mower need sharpened?'

Brodie looked down and saw that he had been hacking at the barley stems rather than cutting them cleanly. He nodded over at Fergus, who rustled through the barley in his direction, sending up a flurry of small brown birds. Brodie sat down among the tall grasses – as if their still stems might offer some shade – and blew a cleg from his nose with a sharp puff of breath. His sleeves already rolled up, he tucked the hem of his heavy tunic into his belt to give more relief from the coarse-spun wool. He wished for a return to the cool of dawn.

'The sun is heavy on your head, friend? Alyth says I will soon have the tonsure myself.' Fergus rubbed his naturally thinning hair.

'Heavy enough to grind me into the soil,' replied Brodie. 'How much longer can it be until the mealtime bell?'

'See there – the toun women are readying to claim their glean.' Fergus broke off from sharpening the scythe to point over Brodie's shoulder; a pair of women sat below the shallow shade of a young ash tree near the end of the east track, waiting for the bell to ring, the signal that they could begin collecting the fallen grain.

Despite his impatience to hear the noonday bell, Brodie startled when its peal came less than a moment later. In the still air, the clang rippled outwards and dispersed in all directions, like a pail of water tipped in a pool.

'Then your prayers are answered before even saying sext,' said Fergus, handing the scythe back to Brodie.

The peasant women were among the barley stubble before the priory workers had left the field. Already without shawls, they shamelessly stripped off their kirtles so that they wore only light smocks and slats of wood strapped to their feet. A knotted coverchief held the hair of the older woman, who bared arms as stiff as oars. Age had hauled down the creases of her jowls and corners of her tight frown. Not so the more youthful of the two, still a growing girl. Brodie could only guess at the form below her loose smock. But he saw enough – legs to the knee, fine wrists, neck unveiled below her throat – to think she might have been cast in a mould.

Fergus recognised Brodie's gaze. 'Prior Archibald would have you beaten three times around the church for such cravings,' he said, louder than necessary.

The older woman stood upright and gave Brodie the long, unflinching stare of a sorceress casting a curse.

'The prior…yes…' muttered Brodie, quickly leading Fergus and the other priory workers away from the field. 'He will be pleased with the yield.' His attempt at digression was as hopeless as smothering a blush.

'A priory is not the place for a young hinny,' continued Fergus. 'Unless she prefers to choose between lechery and celibacy.'

Brodie could not be sure whether he was being mocked or offered sympathy. Or worse, that Fergus had a punishment of his own in mind. Could he have seen Brodie resting a greedy eye on Mariota? Surely he would not consider taking her away from this place? One thought came before the previous one had reached a conclusion. He cast a sideways look, and another: still he could not read the mood of his friend, the first time he remembered such a confusion.

'You think it no place for toun girls?' stuttered Brodie,

watching the ground passing below his feet as they walked. 'Or…others?'

'Malise…' Fergus trailed off.

'Malise?' Brodie's confusion deepened.

'Malise!' This time Fergus shouted out his son's name.

Fergus changed his pace into a run without another word.

Brodie looked up and saw what had caught Fergus's attention: up the slight slope and just around the corner, Malise grappling with a stranger at the gatehouse porch.

Brodie joined Fergus in a run.

On reaching the drawbridge, it was clear that Malise was not in any difficulty; he sat astride the stranger, who was curled tightly beneath, face pressed against the ground, silent but half-heartedly trying to shrug a shoulder or elbow free now and then.

'He has no rights to the glean,' said Fergus, breathing heavily.

'It is not the rights to the glean he is after. He demands only his right to sanctuary. Yet he will not give his name so that the oath can be taken. He offers no blows but tries to enter the priory when released.' Malise appeared perplexed at such behaviour.

Fergus went down on one knee and spoke close to the stranger's ear. 'You need only cross the drawbridge to take refuge here. But first you must give the clerk of the chapter your name so that an oath can be taken.'

Fergus looked over at Brother Hector, who gave Brodie a nod, to indicate that he should fetch the priory records and a writing board.

Brodie edged through the lay brothers who had gathered on their way back from the fields. When he returned from the library, the small crowd had mostly dispersed to take midday prayers; only Fergus, Malise and Hector remained. The stranger was still on the ground but now sitting up, without restraint. Immediately, Brodie recognised a familiarity. But it was one he could not place. A drover or herder he had met on the hills? A face among the common people at Mass? Perhaps he had encountered the stranger while on an errand for the prior, or the king?

Behind the mangy whiskers, the fugitive must have been around the same age as Brodie. His dirt-crusted hair, a shade

105

between brown and red, grew outwards rather than downwards. The skin was tight across his cheeks and forehead, limbs jutted through scraps of hide clothing. But he was broad enough across the shoulders to suggest he might once have been stout and strong.

'...blessed by the contagion of holiness but only if you repent your sins,' Hector was saying. 'And even then you must not bear any pointed instruments or venture beyond the priory precinct before sunset or after sunrise.' He saw that Brodie had returned and told the fugitive to stand. 'Let him take the oath and I will tell the prior of his arrival,' he said to Brodie.

Hector left scratching his beard.

Brodie had only administered the oath twice before: to a debtor and a robber, both fugitives from Forfar. But both occasions had occurred since Pasche, so he needed no reminding how to proceed.

'Lay your hand on the church book.' The fugitive did as Brodie instructed. 'Take heed on your oath. You shall be true and faithful to Prior Archibald, the canons of this church and the mother house at Saint Mary's, Jedburgh. And so may God and his holy judgement help you. Kiss this book and describe your name and crimes.'

The fugitive pressed his lips to the book and closed his eyes. 'I ask for my right to ring the sanctuary bell. On oath, I am the brother of the one called Christie who was hanged, drawn and reaved of life for crimes many and hideous.'

The man said it so plainly and simply that Brodie experienced no surprise at the declaration. He lowered himself to the ground and leaned his quill on the writing board. In cold ink on cartulary parchment, the words were as sober as a notarial clause.

And yet as full of consequence as a king's pardon.

Brodie's letters had none of the elegance of most other scribes. And he could only write one word for every ten spoken. But those on the page before him could have been lifted from the riddle he found in Scot's book: *"Christie...brother...sanctuary bell..."*

Fergus muttered a curse. He took a breath that swelled his chest.

When the fugitive opened his eyes, Brodie detected in his

heavy, beseeching lids a likeness with the creature bound in fetters at Arbroath Abbey. His foggy stare might have stretched back a hundred years, or might endure for a century more.

The fugitive continued. His voice veered little from a single, low tone. 'On the day of judgement, may God award me what I deserve for my wickedness, for it has been abundant. But let it first be said that my brother has paid his debt to nature. I beg mercy for his departed soul. I beg too that, whatever region he inhabits, he will forgive my cravenness – I fled the law enforcers when I should have stood by his side, I cowered when I should have shared his fate. But by the terrible sword of correction, I should hang higher than any other and spill out my guts before I breathe out my life because I also have the blood of the churchman on my conscience…'

He adopted a position of prayer. Brodie saw that one of his fingers was no more than a stump.

'…even if he was only killed in defence when he came at us with a blade. And, as God will judge me, I ate his flesh but only because we neared death by starvation – the lamb we took fell and had been scavenged when I returned to the place of the fray. We could go no farther to find morsels because of injuries suffered at the hands of the churchman. But one more thing must be known. I stood on the hill at the Gallowden and can say that our crimes are not those described by the doomster.'

The man's attention momentarily retreated, as though all his effort was needed just to locate a breath in his throat.

Brodie checked how much ink was in his pot.

The fugitive recovered, his dark gaze again on Brodie. 'We took no more human life than that – none of the thirty travellers declared in the enrolled indictment. And we led no horde of vile curs. We were only two brothers, driven to sin for want of nourishment and a place to dwell. But for the falsehoods of the doomster, I ask to be submitted to the judgement and sanctuary of God rather than the justice of man.'

He kneeled and bowed his head until it rested on the ground.

Brodie could not find any words to say and so wrote the fugitive's instead, taking time over the sweep and flick of the letters' ascenders and descenders, concentrating on their consistency.

'And what name is given to this brother of the Cleek?' Still standing, Fergus spat the question out, as though the man's explanation tasted as bitter as wormwood.

The fugitive stretched to look up at Fergus from his kneeling position. Again distracted, he paused as if struggling to recollect his own name 'Duncan,' he said finally. White, stringy beads of saliva caught in the corners of his lips.

Fergus folded his arms across his chest.

"Duncan". The name looked curiously flat on the page. 'Duncan,' said Brodie. 'Duncan Christie – cross into the precinct of the priory and, as is the custom, take your sanctuary.'

*

Brodie lay flat on his stomach, straddling the doorway between the refectory and the warming room, arms and legs outstretched on the floor. His crotch and left shoulder were crammed against the cheeks of the entrance, his forehead hard on the cold flagstones of the warming room and nose pressed so flat that it dripped mucus. He raised his lips from the ground but still breathed in dirt. He could smell, but not see, that the brethren ate pottage. And from the rich tang, he guessed it contained boiled meat.

Brother Symon stuttered to the end of the day's reading some time after the scraping of dishes had finished. Prior Archibald allowed the silence to settle before ringing the small bell that indicated the brothers should wash their spoons. Brodie recognised from the boot heels that stepped over his prostrate body on the way to the lavatorium that Symon and Brother Donald had remained in the refectory – as expected of the reader and server – along with Archibald.

Lances of sunlight slanted through the plughole windows high on the south wall. Amid dust-spangled air, Prior Archibald's feet came to rest by Brodie's cheek. 'The rule commands you to hate your own will. Every occasion of presumption is to be avoided in the monastery without the instruction of the prior.' Brodie heard the crackle of knee joints as Archibald bent close to his ear. 'Yet you, a clerk, a lay brother, could not confine yourself to taking the oath. Without seeking an instruction, you granted sanctuary to this beast – a sin-sick beast who feasted on the flesh of our own Prior Bernard as though taking the very body of Christ. Why would you be so contemptuous of your seniors?'

Brodie knew to observe a silence rather than murmur a response.

Archibald stood. His voice had lost its proximity when he spoke again. 'This savage called Christie has been given fresh hay to lie among tame beasts in the stable – that is enough sanctuary from this house. He has not taken abjuration or satisfied the church by his penance and so no immunity will be given. Let him be handed over to the jurisdiction of Robert the Steward, who captured his black-hearted brother.' Archibald stepped over Brodie. 'Lest one diseased sheep contaminate the flock, you will be excluded from the common table and the saying of prayers with the brethren. You will make satisfaction by lying prone in the doorway to the refectory and the church, at the feet of all those who come and go. And you will take your food alone, after your brothers…' He paused as though forgetting his own mind. '…And it will not be blessed. Now, go to work in the fields and consider your penitential sorrow.'

In concerning himself with the fate of one ill-omened Christie, then another, Brodie wondered if he had suffered an injustice of his own. Like the fugitive in the stable, he was given only bread and water at prandium, and now at supper. And like the fugitive, he was excluded from the company of others. Yet Brodie would not swing from a rope for his faults, as the Cleek had done. Neither would he lose the sanctuary of the priory, as Prior Archibald intended for Christie's brother. At worst, he would receive a dozen strokes from the birch rod.

Voices astir in the adjoining warming room announced the arrival of a newcomer. Through the door to the kitchen at the other end of the refectory, Donald the cook, presumably also aware of the arrival, replied with a clatter of pans.

High and haughty tones identified the newcomer as Brother Peter, even if only some words were distinct.

'…Christie's trumpery… roused to wrath…'

Brodie turned in the direction of the kitchen at the sound of shuffling footsteps; Brother Donald appeared, his head lost in his cowl. He moved slowly through the refectory, a chafing-dish with eggs and cheese held in hands covered by a cloth. Despite walking directly by, he gave no sign of noticing Brodie's presence.

Donald nudged open the curtain, holding it there with his backside as he laid the chafing-dish on the floor. He uncovered his head, bent over and prodded at the contents of the dish.

Brodie could see through the doorway that Peter stood in the middle of the warming room floor. With the curtain open, his words were as clear as his paunch, though the latter seemed accidental on his slight frame.

'I should see this fugitive for myself before the Steward puts him to the multitude for the destruction of his flesh so that his spirit might yet be saved in the day of the Lord.' Peter's clasped hands were tucked modestly below his jutting belly but still he had the bold look of an abbot on a dais.

Brother Finlay was first to break the expectant silence that followed. 'They will blast his limbs.'

And Brodie came to a decision.

He wrapped the remainder of his bread in his cloth, hurried through the empty kitchen and out the storeroom shutters into the western grounds.

Duncan Christie lay curled on the ground at the back of the stables, a safe distance from restless hooves. His legs were buried in the hay so that he looked like only half a man. He took in thin breaths of dry, pungent air and let out thick snores.

Brodie crouched down and shook the shoulder of the sleeping figure, who was quickly alert and upright.

'You must leave this place if you want to keep your life. Can you swim?' Christie nodded. 'Then find your way to the riverbank behind these stables, stay hidden as you move downstream and cross the water beyond the bend, before it spreads itself into the loch. From there, follow the stars and the sun south. Take this…' – Brodie handed over the bundle of bread – 'and seek sanctuary in the farthest house from here. The Cistercians have places at Dundrennan and Glenluce in the south-west debatable lands. They follow a strict rule and so offer a potent blessing.'

'But I have sanctuary here.' Christie swatted loose straws from his cheek.

'You are to be turned over to the Steward, who will put you

to the mob. I cannot say when your sanctuary will be breached – perhaps by morning – but I can be sure it will happen. Do as I say and leave.'

Christie stood, not bothering to brush away the hay still fastened to his rags. 'You will be punished for this,' he said.

Brodie had imagined that Prior Archibald might devise some new, weightier punishment to cast at his feet. With that in mind, he turned to the rule so often cited by Archibald. 'To bear persecution for justice's sake is an instrument of good works.'

'God thank you.'

'You can do something in return.'

'Anything you ask.'

'I have been to all the places around here that people might know the name Affleck and found nothing. I believe its discovery is tied in some way to you obtaining refuge. Look and listen for the same name wherever you ring a sanctuary bell. And bring word of anything you find back to me. Will you do that?'

'I will find a way.' His attention already elsewhere, Christie shifted his eyes around the stable block. He bent low to pass the horses and mules, so that his hands almost touched the ground as well as his feet.

And, quiet as a thought, he was gone.

Brodie remained where he sat as long as it took to watch Christie go, contemplate his own likely fate and recite his night psalms. Leaving the stable, he repeated a line of the Kyrie Eleison with each step he took towards the western range.

"…Lord have mercy. Christ have mercy. Lord have mercy…"

Brodie settled on his bunk ahead of the brethren, before the great silence.

Book III

*"The following year there was great dearth and
scarcity of provisions in Scotland; and it is said
that some took up their quarters in caves and fed
on forbidden beasts, like dogs; and even on
children and women, as for instance in the case of
one, Criste Cleik by name, who, with his beldame,
killed and ate many children and women. But in
the end they died, being publicly handed over to
justice and put to an ignominious death."*

Maurice Buchanan, *Liber Pluscardensis* (1461)

Chapter 1

"Histories do not hold consistent language, either one way or the other...certain chronicles are entirely perverted, corrupted, violated, and, very often, indiscreetly so changed that the assertion of one chapter seems to annul the purport of the next."

John of Fordun, *Chronica gentis Scotorum* (c 1360)

August, 1341, until September, 1349

"Pity us! The kinbrother of Cleek the Butcher tread his diabolical feet on Restenneth's Holy soil. Pity us more! This Duncan of the abominable Christies fled before the most high and most excellent Robert the Steward could slit his nose and brain, out of reverence for the passion of our Lord."

Peter Fenton, *The Stewartis Oryginale* (August, 1341)

"Holding Council here at Restenneth since the fifteenth day of the month of June in the year 1342, the most gracious prince King David discerned the attention given to Prince John's tomb and granted a sum of twenty pounds from the customs at Dundee to provide soul masses for his infant-dead brother. After the bestowal, the King recounted how the walls of the castle at Roxburgh had been surmounted with ladders by Alexander Ramsay of Dalhousie and the great keep at Stirling taken after many months of siege, in

despite of fire issuing from iron pots like hail. He favoured those who had a part in returning the full kingdom to his dominion, the office of Sheriff of Teviotdale being conferred on Ramsay of Dalhousie, while the faithful Malcolm Fleming was clothed with furred cap and cloak. It is to be noted that records found in a tower for muniments at Stirling – by sad sorrow none of our own – told of some noble men who had shared their allegiance with Balliol and England's Edward. Yet the King showed his mercy, confirming the lands of Patrick Dunbar, Earl of March, the Earls of Fife and Strathearn and the Murrays of Tullibardine, despite their follies. Most lands and titles of Robert the Steward were in like manner confirmed, though the Baronies of Bathgate and Ratho were withheld due to his particular vacillation between the seigniory of rightful and wrongful kings, as avowed in this priory by the trespassing knight Henry de Bown, and once included among the words of these annals."

Brodie Affleck, *The Annals of Egglespether* (June, 1342)

"The whole tale is tedious and I should be cumbered to tell it all but, according to the king's say, a rose of the Steward's chaplet had fallen. Lord be thanked, Robert the Steward does not desire baronies and earldoms, but only virtue, glory and licence to loyally serve his sovereign nobleness. And so, he prosecutes the king's command in Liddesdale and the borderlands while others run the tilt and banquet with harpists and buffoons. He keeps the peace with Sir William Douglas, the Flail of the English, while the king, astride a charger sent from France, crosses the border on the advice of young men and flatterers to raid and spoil, not one but five times, most lately in this tenth month of the year of the Incarnation of the Lord, 1342."

Peter Fenton, *The Stewartis Oryginale* (October, 1342)

> *"Two times in the same number of years, the Steward's gentlewoman, Lady Elizabeth of Rowallan, has had births. And by Saint Juliana, one is a boy."*

Peter Fenton, *The Steartis Oryginale* (February, 1343)

> *"Sad happenings have come to replace fortunate events in the kingdom. A pestilence among fowls in the year before this one caused so many to be smitten with a kind of leprosy that almost every cock and hen perished. And at the seventh hour on the day after the Lord's Passion in this year, the higher heavenly bodies of Saturn, Mars and Jupiter came together in Aquarius, which scholars from antiquity forewarned would, with other eclipses, lead to the death of kingdoms, a deadly corruption of the surrounding air and great mortality."*

Brodie Affleck, *The Annals of Egglespether* (March, 1345)

> *"Believing all the chivalry of England to be waging war in France with Edward, the gracious King David made his summons for an army to enter the defenceless void. But the Archbishop of York, the Lord Neville and the Lord Percy called together men from all parts of that land, who took up their stations for a fight close to Durham on the seventeenth day of the month of October in this year. The monks from that town, who watched and prayed from a mound called Maiden's Bower, said the Scots issued many strokes with heavy axes but the archers of the English were too fierce. There was a lamentable slaughter and the Steward took to flight when the first arrows reached his ranks, allowing the Englishmen to obtain the place and the victory. King*

*David fought valiantly and loosened two teeth from
the mouth of his captor, a Northumberland squire
with the name John de Coupland."*

Brodie Affleck, *The Annals of Egglespether* (November, 1346)

*"The king allowed the prompting of young and
impetuous men to prevail over expert counsel, which
advised that the appearance of Saint Cuthbert in a
vision should cause him to turn his horse from
Durham and start the warlike expedition afresh
another time. And for that misreckoning, he was
shackled to a black courser and led through streets
to the strong tower of London. But a good ending
shall follow this beginning, for the worthy and noble
Robert the Steward, very expert in the art of war,
took wise advice and did an about turn, to return
north and give himself over to energetically protecting
the interests of the kingdom. On the third day of this
month, the chief men not slain nor taken in battle
returned him to the position of Guardian, deeming
him most powerful in the king's absence."*

Peter Fenton, *The Stewartis Oryginale* (May, 1347)

Brodie stroked an ink-stained thumb across the page of The
Stewartis that described the Battle of Durham and its
consequences.

He and Brother Peter had chronicled the same span of years,
yet their accounts were as opposite as the land and the sky.
Brodie had concerned himself with king and commonwealth,
which latterly included David's downfall; Peter took notice only
of events that involved Robert the Steward, who was once again
in the ascent.

Half standing from his seat, Brodie stretched to lift his Annals
from the library shelf. He put one book beside the other on his
desk.

More than just the contents varied between Peter's chronicle
and his own. Brodie's book was smaller in size – written on

priory parchment shaped as quartos rather than folios – with only his own plain ink drawings for decoration. In contrast, the latest volume of The Stewartis had been put down on the fine new kind of paper from Vicenza and illustrated at the St Andrews scriptorium. The pages were rich with all the colours of nature, including even the rare blue of lapis lazuli.

But Brodie's eye did not follow the neat flow of the text or linger on the sparkle of the shell gold illuminations. It rested instead on two small notes scribbled on the final page. The first was below a passage about Pope Clement endorsing the legitimacy of the Steward's offspring as potential heirs, should that question arise because of the king's indefinite captivity in England. The undersized text, which Brodie first took to be a gloss or proverb in an otherwise pristine margin, did not resemble Brother Peter's hand and so likely belonged to a transcriber at St Andrews. Brodie strained to read the brief note.

> *"Guided by God's avenging hand, a ship from Normandy has brought with it a foul cargo to the port at the burgh of Dundee in this month of July AD 1349. Immortal, have mercy on us."*

The second scrawl might have been an annotation, tagged as it was at the end of the final passage, a scornful dismissal of attempts to remove the Steward as Guardian over the lack of progress in negotiations for David's release.

Again, Brodie squinted to read the dwarfish text.

> *"A dreadful judgement has descended upon us. A first seaman from the infected French ship died a terrible and unwonted death days after arrival. And since then, three more and even a monk from Arbroath have succumbed. In this fourth week of September, a pilgrim arrived here – to seek healing from the bones and tooth of Saint Andrew the Apostle – his skin puffed out and swollen and black."*

Chapter 2

*"In men and women alike it first betrayed itself
by the emergence of certain tumours in the groin
or the armpits, some of which grew as large as a
common apple, others as an egg, some more, some
less, which the common folk called gavoccioli.
From the two said parts of the body this deadly
gavocciolo soon began to propagate and spread
itself in all directions indifferently."*

Giovanni Boccaccio, *Il Decamerone* (1353)

12th Day of October, 1349

'Malise has boils, brother. My sturdy son has boils.' Fergus
pulled Brodie aside from the brothers returning to their
dormitory after prime. Standing in the shadows of the
storeroom, at the foot of the lay brothers' ladder, he wore the
pleading, defeated look of a beggar at his own gate. 'In the
places they say – under his arms, his thighs, and has pains in his
limbs, and there is something like blood in his piss.' He stopped
to take a breath. And let out a slow, controlled sigh. 'But there
has been no fever.' His last words might have been conceived
as hopeful but they carried mostly desperation.

'Can you be sure they are…' Brodie held back from mention
of the plague, as if the word itself might carry a contagion.
'…that they are boils and not some other kind of blister?'

'If they are blisters, they are like none I have ever seen. Does
Brother James have a remedy for this new infection?'

'Some say drinking ale brings relief, others that blood should
be let out by a blade or leeches.'

Fergus tottered to the side and leaned on a hogshead. Instinctively, Brodie reached out a steadying hand. 'Come.' He led Fergus through the kitchen and outside. Drizzle fell from a silted sky.

'I have heard it said that the infected last barely two days. Or fall over and die even while talking. Is that the truth?'

Over the years, Fergus's side-whiskers had crept towards his chin, gradually forming a beard that grew at the same rate as hairs disappeared from his crown. The overall impression was that his hair was slowly slipping from his face.

'Many have died – I would not tell you a lie. But others have not.' Brodie tried a stiff, reassuring smile. 'I will fetch James. You should attend to Malise. I have read that this pestilence travels on winds from the south but might also be the exhalations of the kind of marshes and ponds that lie to our north. Let Malise breathe air but only when the wind is from the other directions.'

'Say him a prayer, brother,' added Fergus.

'I will.' Clouds of their breath caught together in a drifting miasma.

Brodie had hoped the plague might pass by Restenneth on a bluster. Or, if it must arrive, it would keep its distance: let across the threshold by a pilgrim who could be ushered to Bernard's shrine and then out again; brought from the parishes by one of the ministering canons, who would soon recover in a soft infirmary bed; perhaps a brother already in old age might become enfeebled and die, before being buried with due ceremony below the chapter house floor.

In reality, it had arrived with the stealth and spite of a phantom.

Brodie saw Brother James – striding away briskly along the north cloister – before he had time to think where he should look for the infirmarian.

'Brother!' Brodie called out more noisily than was permitted, his voice resounding louder still in the narrow cloister.

James turned, but in surprise rather than disapproval. He gave a shallow, hurried bow. 'Brother Brodie.'

'I fear the plague is upon us.' Brodie spoke in little more than a whisper. 'Malise the gatekeeper has boils. And other signs.'

James invoked Saint Ninian and the Fourteen Holy Helpers.

'I said he should rest and take some air,' added Brodie.

'Then let us go and see how he ails.'

The two brothers walked to the tofthouse in silence. The rain had stopped but each of the surrounding hills now wore a hood of mist.

The door was open just enough for James to reach a hand in and push it agape. A mild easterly breeze puffed at their backs. Inside, grey morning light oozed through cracks in the turf and timbers, though mostly the house was lit by the shifting glow and spark of flames from the hearth and kitchen, the only movements and sounds in the room.

Fergus's head appeared around the wattle screen. 'He is sleeping but close to awake. There is still no fever.'

Brodie and James stepped behind the screen. The kitchen was stuffy and at the same time a chill lingered as if the house itself had the fever. Malise lay on a mat on the floor by the brazier, uncovered by any blankets, head and shoulders propped on a bale. Fergus stood by his side. With a relief he had not anticipated, Brodie saw that Mariota was in neither the kitchen nor the byre beyond. Or anywhere else in the clammy house.

'When did the first sign appear?' asked James.

'He was restless with coughs and sneezes in the night but I thought it no more than a common sickness. Before daybreak, he woke with complaints of pains in his arms and legs. And there was blood when he first pissed in the bucket, though there has been none since.'

Fergus looked to James for an immediate response but instead the infirmarian crouched to pull up Malise's night shirt, slipping the patient's left arm from its loose sleeve until he lay naked except for the folds of linen gathered across his chest like a baldric. Gently, James raised Malise's bare arm to look at where it joined his body and then pulled apart his legs to examine his groin. In both places, lumps like hen's eggs stretched his skin taut.

'That…' Fergus leaned close to inspect Malise's armpit. '…might have grown some since the day began…' He pointed at the boil. 'Or could it be the light in here?' He looked around in all directions, as if measuring the shapes and shadows elsewhere in the house.

'The tumours seem to match the plague,' announced James.

Fergus's chin dropped to his chest.

'But there are no lurid spots or markings. And he has no fever.' James pulled Malise's night shirt back down and stood. 'Keep him in this way but do not allow his liver to overheat. Let him sleep only in moderation but avoid the air spirit that will travel from his eyes when awake. I will arrange for his blood to be drawn.' He turned to Brodie. 'Brother, can you assist? There should be no delay.'

Brodie's gaze was on Fergus, who had yet to lift his head. 'We should get the treatment started,' said Brodie, laying a hand on Fergus's back.

Fergus nodded his downcast head.

'Brother Brodie…' James was already at the door, waiting.

'He is strong.' His throat tight, it was all Brodie could manage.

Outside, a step behind James, he took a long breath.

James slowed, allowing Brodie to catch him. 'I will take his blood and give him a vinegar tonic but it is likely he will die in one day or seven. Already, half the clergy at St Andrews and Arbroath have fallen and more in other churches and towns, just as they did in England and France. In truth, we cannot know how this malady moves from one person to the next. To keep others from the same fate, the afflicted gatekeeper should spend those days alone, the door and windows fastened shut.'

Chapter 3

"*So, so, break off this last lamenting kiss,*
Which sucks two souls, and vapours both away.
Turn thou ghost that way, and let me turn this,
And let ourselves benight our happiest day,
We ask none leave to love; nor will we owe
Any so cheap a death as saying, 'Go.'"

John Donne, *The Expiration* (1609)

October, 1349, until the 21st Day of December in the Same Year

With each week that tipped autumn further into winter, Brodie added one name or more to the priory records. Malise, the first on the mortuary roll, dragged out his life for a full nine days. Through a delirium, it was long enough to witness his wife, Mey, and twelve-year-old daughter Elspet fall prey to the infection, which in the last throes turned their toes and fingers black. A week later and then another, Brother Hector and Brother Walter became death-sick. James the infirmarian suffered contagion but recovered by drinking his own potion of crushed river pearls added to wine and herbs. Brother Finlay showed signs of fever and developed dark spots across his body but returned to health after vomiting blood.

Rain came the morning after the third Sunday of Advent following a week and a day of still snow. Brodie woke abruptly to the sound of the downpour clattering like pebbles on the dormitory roof. Before leaving his bunk, or even sitting upright, he groped his neck, armpits and groin, just as if he might be measuring dimensions for his own grave cut. On finding no signs of boils, he lay back and waited for the bell that signalled prime.

The plague had brought its decay to more than just mortal flesh, as Brodie was reminded when he led the sheep from the priory to graze on the carse mulch after chapter. With fewer hands to gather the harvest, cabbage and turnip rotted in the rig. Two of the apple trees stood askew, branches hanging limply, not yet staked or pruned. Fallen fruit perished on the ground among the slush. Beyond the orchard, the wood-store was less than half-filled with logs.

And beyond the wood-store, the gate that Fergus had kept so tightly shut stood open to the world.

Brodie hurried his pace and commanded the herding dog to drive the flock.

Fergus was neither working outside the tofthouse nor on guard in the unattended watchtower.

Before Brodie had fully crossed the drawbridge, the old man came into sight, struggling up the greasy slope from the field with a handcart. Mouth open, he panted great puffs of breath in the rain-steeped air.

'Let me help,' Brodie shouted.

Fergus looked up but did not stop. Brodie came alongside and took one of the cart's wooden shafts. He nodded back at the heavy load. 'Why strain yourself? The fieldstone can stay where it is until we next plough and harrow.'

'The field is not my concern.'

Brodie recognised his friend's many hardships. 'I could cut the logs,' he offered. 'Or salt the meat. Whatever tasks need done.'

'If the meat is not salted, there will be less food on the prior's table. If the wood is not chopped, there will be fewer flames in the canons' hearth.' Fergus stopped at the top of the slope and set down his shaft of the cart. Brodie did likewise when the weight lurched to one side. 'Brother, I do not mean to vent this on you.' Fergus remained untouched by the plague but he had a weariness that seemed to sink him into the mud. 'The farm is not my concern, at least for now. Why tend crops and beasts for a brotherhood that consigns my son and his family to a pit on the carse with all the other unfortunates, rather than find them a patch of consecrated ground alongside brothers Hector and Walter?'

Brodie had no answer. Fergus picked up one shaft of the cart, then Brodie the other.

'My concerns are with the living and the dead. For the sake of the dead, I will use these stones…' Puffing again, Fergus jerked his head over his shoulder at the load on the cart, '…to mark their final place with the sign of the cross.'

By Prior Archibald's decree, lay and priestly duties were strictly divided. However, given Archibald's seclusion since the outbreak, Brodie could only wonder if his writ extended any further than the locked door of the prior's quarters.

'I will bless the stones and make the ground holy,' said Brodie.

Fergus nodded slowly, in time with his stride. 'Brother, you said the pestilence might rise from marshes and swamps – do the scholars yet know if that is true?'

'It is one possibility.'

'Could it be that the bodies of the dead are sweating vapours that seep through where the ground is softest?'

'That could be true.' Brodie had never heard the idea put forward.

'Some of those dead were put there by my own hand, brother. My task as a youthful soldier under Bishop de Lamberton's command was to finish off the dying and pile the parts of bodies high. Could it be that those avenging corpses of war are bringing my punishment?'

'Friend, you have prayed devoutly, said Mass and given alms many times since then – any sins of yours have been corrected by penance. Your soul is clean.'

They stopped alongside a patch of recently turned earth. Fergus tipped up the cart. Stones clanked and crashed together as they slid to the ground.

'This place has too many swamps and marshes,' said Fergus 'And too many corpses. For the sake of the living, I must find a new place to live.'

Brodie heard the words but found himself staring at Fergus rather than offering a reply. Fergus had recently lost a front tooth, he noticed. The old man's thick skin buckled where it met his eyes and cheekbones. 'You are leaving?'

'If I die there will be no man left to watch the gate and bring in the crops. A church that allows its servants to pass from life with no more account than a dead goat would soon enough turn the women out of our house for a man to take their place. I have a debt to pay here – and can pray for my soul in the nave – but Mariota and the hinnies do not. And so, my decision is that they shall go to the Isles of Kintyre, where the air is cleaner. They will be in the charity of my kin and can find themselves a home. I know you have affections for her, brother, and I am sorry for that but do this for me – ask the prior at chapter if he will assign a church labourer to watch the gate until I return. There is little work to be done on the farm over Yule and the first famine month – we should leave without delay.'

*

At the times and places he looked, Brodie could find nothing of Mariota. On his return to the sheep enclosure, she was neither in the stables nor at the river collecting water. After chapter – where Prior Archibald granted Fergus's request, though with an expression more suited to taking a mouthful of putrid meat – Brodie found time to go to the byre, which was as full of odours as it was empty of people. Expecting her to be at the loom, he visited Fergus between none and vespers, but only Alyth was in the house.

His ears noticed her presence before his eyes: the same moment he walked into the candlelit sacristy after evensong she made herself known with a quick, firm rap on the window. All Brodie could see in the darkness beyond the coloured glass was the silhouette of a slight figure. Given that the fine new window – funded by King David's bestowal from the customs at Dundee – could not open as the old shutters had done, Brodie took up a position somewhere below the genuflecting image of Saint Peter and spoke in a hushed voice through the glass. 'Is it you? Mariota?'

'Brother Brodie?'

'Have you been waiting?'

'Not long.'

'Should I come outside?'

'I have the bull.'

Unsure of the significance of the bull, Brodie hesitated. 'And you need to return it to the byre?'

'Soon. But it is showing signs of upset. Can you help?'

Only then, the bull snorted. A sudden jangle of its chain suggested it had yanked its head abruptly.

'Wait there. Or bring it to the church door.'

Brodie hurried from the sacristy and through the church to the entrance. 'Mariota?' Outside, his urgent whisper seemed to fall to the ground along with the fine droplets of dense rain.

'Here.' She emerged from the shadows on the north side of the nave, the bull following behind on its chain. 'It will not keep its head up,' she explained. 'Take the staff.'

'I will hold the chain – you take the staff.'

Mariota complied with Brodie's suggestion without a word, handing over the chain before taking the bull-staff and carefully walking round to the other side of the beast. Brodie gave the chain a firm tug.

The only light was from dim clouds above so they walked some steps through the long, wet grass in silence, paying close attention to the ground for divots and rocks.

'Your father should be leading the bull to the byre,' said Brodie as they neared the path that ran alongside the outbuildings and workshops. His eyes had adjusted to the dark; Mariota appeared to nod in agreement.

'Can we go somewhere before the byre?' asked Mariota.

Before Brodie could answer, she had guided the bull to the right, away from the tofthouse and byre, towards the forge.

'Did you come to the window because of the bull?'

Mariota peered over her shoulder before turning her pale face towards him. 'Brother Brodie, you should know – my father says I must leave. With Isabel and Mary. To his kith and kin in the south.'

'When?' For reasons he could only estimate, Brodie feigned surprise. 'And why?' He asked the second question as they passed below the awning of the forge. A block anvil was mounted on a broad tree stump in the centre of the forge. A small smelter stood upright against the wall by the river. Brodie looped the bull chain around the anvil and leaned against the stone smelter, cold now for weeks. Mariota clapped the bull's glossy flank.

'He thinks there will be no plague there, and promises that I will not suffer the same fate as Malise.'

'I named your brother in my prayers today. And Mey and Elspet – for God to refresh their souls.' Brodie folded each hand inside the opposite sleeve of his gown. He realised too late that it was the same pose Prior Archibald assumed when attempting to appear particularly pious and humble.

Mariota stepped forward and pulled his arms free, so that they hung awkwardly by his side. She took his hands in hers, from below, as if lifting the handles of a barrow, and stroked the back of his left wrist with her thumb. A thread from his throat, through his gut to his groin, pulled as tight as a bow string.

'He says too that I will need guidance and governance. He thinks man is a woman's head.' She smiled for the first time. The bull scraped a hoof on the earthen floor and tossed its head, rattling the chain. 'There are husbandmen there who will give me a ring and the girls a home.' She tried another smile, let go of Brodie's hands and stretched out her arms. 'We go at the earliest morning.'

He must previously have imagined such an embrace because he recognised his surprise at finding her slender but firm to hold, rather than frail and brittle. Her hair smelled of damp leaves and wood smoke. She squeezed her arms in a way that no onlooker would have seen, but felt to him as tight as a buckle. Brodie could have said she was every turn in the weather, every purl of the river. Instead, he withdrew his hands and folded them inside the wide sleeves of his gown.

Chapter 4

"Thus took the nightingale her leave of me.
I pray to god, he always with her be."

Sir John Clanvowe, *The Book of Cupid, God of Love* (c 1380s)

December, 1349, until the 1st Day of July, 1350

The teachings of Prior Archibald – and Bernard before him – would describe the condition suffered by Brodie after Mariota's departure as a divisive attack of lust. His spirit was engaged in a war with his flesh, they would say. But Brodie was gathering reasons to think his prior's words doubtful. Could Jews truly be agents of the plague, as Archibald declared? They were so few and there was little distinction between Jew or Greek, Scotsman or Englishman. Likewise, there was nothing in the way the pestilence chose its victims to suppose any connection with dancing, wrestling, unseemly sports, disobedient children or men who dressed in inappropriately tight and buttoned-up clothing. Why should Brodie believe that common people who suffered a sudden death would pollute the churchyard? After blessing the trench that contained the bodies of Malise, Mey and Elspet, he had found nothing in the church statutes to support such an assertion. And if Archibald could misjudge so much about the plague, could he not see corrupt affections where godly ones existed? Or might that be the truth? Perhaps Brodie had mistaken his own poisonous temptation for sweet appetite. Either way, did he act with strength and wisdom by restraining his urge or weakness and folly in letting it pass?

Brodie was given the answer to another question when Fergus returned in the last week of January: even though there had been no further plague deaths at Restenneth, Mariota had found a place with the Fergussons of Kilkerran and so was unlikely to be back.

Fergus recounted the hardship of the journey: southbound, a ferocious cold and two nights with no shelter or sleep, huddled together for warmth. And he described the spread of the plague: bloated, pale corpses dumped in the Molendinar Burn in Glasgow yet clearer air once they took to a boat at the port of Inverayr. But he said little of anything else. One day he would watch from his tower with an absent gaze. On another, he would lead the oxen with new-found intensity, his eyes fixed on the ground, as if expecting the ploughshare to turn up the bones of long-dead foes along with the sod. Excused from all but the major canonical hours to assume Malise's tasks, Brodie took his place alongside Fergus in the watchtower and fields. Sharing the old man's melancholy, he had just as few words to offer.

The second outbreak arrived before the plough-irons had fully combed the fields, only this time, its black breath drifted through the door of the canons' dormitory. Master Malcolm and Brother Symon – the eldest and youngest in the choir stalls – died on the same day in April. James the infirmarian was next, his self-medication not effective a second time. Among the lay brothers, Hugh was infected, though recovered, just as Brother Finlay had five months earlier. When it became apparent with Brother Donald's death that there were insufficient hands to prepare for the Solemnity of Saints Peter and Paul, Prior Archibald called the remaining brothers together.

'Our own Augustine, Bishop of Hippo, preached that the Apostles Peter and Paul were one, even though their martyrdom occurred on different days. In the same way, devout canons from this church were called on different days after a foul blast of the wind but now dwell together in unity in that place where prayer is everlasting. May their souls and the souls of all the faithful, by the mercy of God, rest in peace.' After a moment of prayer, Archibald put one hand, then the other, inside the opposite sleeves of his gown. He lifted his head. 'Let us now speak about the affairs of our house.' He looked around the chapter house, picking out each brother with a stare, as if counting their number. The few present could have fitted on the same bench. 'A vigil will be held for the saints and the Creed recited for the resurrection of the dead. But it will be the last such observance at Restenneth.'

Brother Peter, alone on the north side of the chapter house, made a show of nodding in agreement, while maintaining a look of regret on his face. Archibald nodded once in return before continuing. 'Pagans, Jews, Arabs, eternal associates of the devil – together they build a foetid nest of disease throughout Christendom. But no evil doing can prevail against the Lord, whose army in heaven grows stronger with the passing of every chosen soul. Brothers, our souls will follow when bidden, though first we must do God's work in this earthly life. But look around for yourselves – we no longer have the numbers to do that work here. And so, fortified by the sign of the cross, we will take our holy merits to other places, farther from the plague, where the church walls are thicker, to again feel the heat of divine love.'

The unforeseen prospect of leaving the priory filled Brodie with a turbulent sense of anticipation. Restenneth was all he had known since a boy, even if he had not chosen it for himself. But it had been less of a refuge ever since the death of Master Robert and less homelike again with the arrival of plague. The departure of plague victims, dead and alive, had further eroded his regard for the place.

'Only the farmer and his gudwife will remain,' Archibald added. 'To collect what harvest they can and secure the priory buildings.'

Immediately, guilt replaced desire; in savouring his own future, Brodie had given no thought to Fergus's fate. He rebuked himself. Hands clasped, he picked with one thumb at a scab on the other, just where the skin met the nail: his own small, private penance. A tiny bloom of blood formed. He gouged harder.

Archibald cleared his throat with a hoarse growl. 'Just as the more noble men withdraw to northern parts to be able to continue governing the kingdom, our community will move in the same direction. Bishop de Deyn of Aberdeen, that good friend of Robert the Steward, is ailing and requires senior churchmen to assist with the administration of his diocese. It is decided that I will serve as dean of that place and our trusted sacrist, Brother Peter, will take the position of treasurer. In that way, he will maintain guardianship of our vessels and the venerable Bernard's relics, ensuring their safe-keeping behind locked doors in the Cathedral of Saint Machar.' Archibald turned to the lay bench on the south side of the chapter house. 'The cathedral chancellor has lost scribes to the plague and so you will be of some use in that office, Brother Brodie, though first you must assist the farmer. You will remain here at Restenneth until the crop is harvested. Brother Hugh, Brother Finlay – the Steward has found places for you at the Augustinian Priory of Monymusk, which is in need of repairs to the western tower and chancel arch.'

Archibald poked his finger in his ear and scratched with small, circular motions. Brother Hugh looked ahead, showing no response. He might have been listening keenly to the prior, or just as easily admiring his own masonry work on the wall behind. Finlay stared at his feet.

'Very well. If there are no proclamations or accusations…?'

Brother Peter sat upright as if about to speak but seemed to receive a surreptitious sign from the prior, and slouched back down.

'Then we should pray for guidance on our journey.'

Aberdeen was no Restenneth. Brodie had hastily formed a notion of moving to a quiet monastery with a full library and a just rule; a place in the south-west, closer to Mariota's home so that he might test his urges once again, the destination of the fugitive who fled carrying a promise to ask for word of the Afflecks. Aberdeen was in the opposite direction, towards the north-east; a burgh where three thousand people – as many Flemish as Scots – crammed into four streets, where the stone buildings were as grey as the dead Northern Ocean.

*

The morning after the saints' feast, the brothers' stomachs were heavy with scorched mutton. A further day and their heads were light with immoderate helpings of ale. Prior Archibald and Brother Peter left with some ceremony after prime, as soon as the sheriff's escort arrived.

Brothers Hugh and Finlay took more time, first collecting their spare garments and then readying their own mules. Brodie met the departing brothers at the stables. 'I have filled a bag with loaves, cheese and meats,' he said, handing the parcel to Brother Hugh.

'Brother Brodie...' Uncharacteristically, Hugh laid a hand on Brodie's shoulder. 'Archibald is a pox-bitten cunt. As is his baggage carrier, Peter Fenton. Put what distance you can from them.'

Disarmed by Hugh's plain speaking, Brodie busied himself with tightening the saddlebag. The brothers mounted their mules and shook the reins.

'Your advice is useful,' Brodie finally shouted after them.

Just beyond the turn in the path, Brother Finlay looked back over his shoulder. 'Farewell, Prior Brodie,' he cackled. He loosened his grip on the reins and held his hands together in mock prayer. 'At last you are a shepherd of more than sheep – but now you have no flock.'

The draught horse in the stable champed on meal. Swallows swooped and darted, stirring the air.

*

Either side of Alyth serving up barley bere, Brodie and Fergus laboured with their weeding tongs, pulling corn cockles and marigolds, thistles and dead-nettles. Resuming where they left off the previous day, they worked from opposite ends towards the centre of the oat field, rather than side-by-side, only occasionally coming close enough to call out a greeting. At intervals, Brodie found himself listening for a bell, though of course none sounded. He worked through sext and none until he guessed from the height of the sun that vespers neared, or might already have passed. He rested his hands and chin on the long handle of the weeding tongs and waited.

'I should light a lamp in the church,' he said when Fergus came closer.

Fergus stood upright and stretched his back with a grunt. 'Is it that time?' he asked.

'The sun says so.' Brodie tried a blithe tone.

'You go. I will wait until darkness is closer.'

Brodie picked up his basket of weeds.

'Will you eat with us again – at supper?' added Fergus.

'My hand has slit the throat of sheep and goats often enough but is less practised at turning bare joints into food on a plate. Set aside a bowl for me.' Encouraged by his friend's offer, Brodie allowed himself a smile. He plucked at stray weeds as he left the field.

In church after dumping the weeds at the midden, Brodie lit lamps on the sills of two of the three trefoil windows. As Archibald and Peter had taken most of the candles, he moved one from the third window onto the bare altar. Stripped of its linen cloths and damask frontal, the altar looked no more than a common block of stone. Fragments of masonry lay among trampled wisps of dust on the ochre and saffron sanctuary tiles, damage caused during the removal of Bernard's relics. The vessels and crucifixes were also gone from the niches, aumbry and lancet windows. Even the ewer and towel were missing from the lavabo.

Brodie took his customary place beyond the rood screen rather than occupy the empty choir stalls. With no precentor to lead the psalms, hymns and versicle, he confined himself to his own private prayer and silent recital of the Pater Noster.

Directly after his abridged observance of vespers, Brodie went to the library.

Startled by the spectacle that greeted him, he made it no farther than the sacristy doorway.

Only in midsummer, late on a bright evening, did the sun reach a place that allowed it to cast its light through the painted sacristy window. Brodie had seen the effect before, but never had it glowed with such intensity. Through a hundred different shapes of cut-glass, a sliver of sun glittered on the wall like a procession of orbs. On the window itself, the figure of Saint Peter bowing to receive the keys of heaven from Christ took on a new radiance.

Without thinking further, Brodie took the two verses of riddle from his knife sheath and moved over to the window. He held the pieces of parchment high above his head. Perhaps the vibrant light would illuminate their precise meaning. So much of what they said had proved to be true: his own arrival at the priory, violent events of war, even changes in the seasons and the harvest. Other parts, however, were more obscure. He could see that a connection had been established between the Stewarts and the Christies due to Cleek's capture of Robert the Steward's wife, Lady Elizabeth Mure. But why were the families together doomed to damnation, as the second riddle forewarned? Also, no mention was made of it at Cleek's trial, yet the verse suggested Lady Elizabeth had been deflowered like a whore, hinting as well that the coupling would produce some kind of bestial offspring. Of more frustration – and despite looking at the final lines of the riddle from every direction – Brodie could still only guess that the salvation of the Afflecks somehow rested with Duncan Christie finding sanctuary.

Brodie lowered his arms and went to his desk. Rather than write a passage or shape a quill, he fitted the two scraps of parchment together. Now that he was alone in the priory, Brodie studied the illustrations without the need to look over his shoulder. Images of a wolf and a child appeared to correspond with words in the text but the other decorations offered no obvious meaning.

After a time, the fading filter of sunlight to Brodie's right told him that supper would soon be served. About to fold the riddles into his sheath, he stopped himself. Instead of doing so, he smoothed the pieces flat, fitted them together precisely and left them where they lay.

Despite the closeness of dusk, Fergus had yet to return from the fields when Brodie walked through the door of the toft. Passing beyond the wattle screen, he saw that Alyth was braising leftover mutton on the fire. He appraised her the way he did everyone he had not seen for a day. Had her manner or mood changed? Was there anything about her features that signified the plague? She moved with her usual short steps and splayed feet.

'You are still eating scraps from the feast table too?' Brodie gestured at the meat cooking on the brazier.

'Was your prior trying to empty the teind barn and storeroom before he left? That feast could have fed all the people of Forfar.'

Alyth did not know it, but Archibald truly had instructed that all unsalted meat, green vegetables and cheese should be put on the table. Remembering Brother Hugh's words, Brodie sought to keep a distance from the prior's decision. 'Other advice was given about provisions,' he muttered. Even before he had finished saying it, Brodie felt guilt at breaching the confidence of chapter. He took a seat on a turned up pail and changed the topic. 'Fergus is late back from the fields.'

Alyth put a lid on the cooking pan. 'He blames his sins for the plague on our house and thinks the toil a penance.' She added a handful of spindly branches to the subdued fire. A dry leaf sizzled. Small flames flickered around a whorl. 'He speaks of nothing except our misfortunes and his part in bringing them upon us.'

'He has little to say to me at all – in the fields and at the gatehouse. He puts his silence down to aching teeth.'

Alyth turned to look directly at Brodie, holding her ladle upright like a cudgel. She had a slight squint in her right eye. 'The ache is from inside his heart, not his mouth.' She patted the hand with the ladle on her chest.

'You have enough reasons to leave this place. You might find happiness at Kilkerran, with Mariota and the girls. Unless they have plans to return?' Brodie added the question as an afterthought. He focused on Alyth's left eye.

She held onto his inquiring gaze longer than was comfortable. 'I cannot say that she will be back. And my husband has his penance to do here, remember.' Alyth fetched three bowls from a crate and rested them close to the fire. 'And what of you, brother – should you go elsewhere to find happiness?'

It was as though her skewed stare had found a passage to his thoughts. If so, she would see his lustful urges. And know of his preoccupation with not only Mariota, but also the fate of the Afflecks. Her eyes might even detect that the increasingly unjust ways of the church were giving him reasons to doubt his vow of obedience.

He looked away, mumbling articles of the rule in witless response. 'It is not for me to seek happiness….or become attached to any pleasures…or want to fulfil desires…'

Mercifully, Fergus walked through the door, allowing him to fall silent.

He stood beside Brodie and clumsily took off his boots with dirt-stained fingers.

'Did you finish the field?' Brodie asked, seizing on the distraction.

'And started on the second,' said Fergus, red-faced, sitting down on a stool with a burdened sigh. 'Is it mutton?' he asked his wife.

Alyth went to bend over the brazier; stopping, she pushed white curls first behind one ear, then the other. 'And green vegetables.' She opened the lid of the pan and ladled in a small amount of water.

Brodie's nose and eyes were filled with a heady billow of steam and the sight of grey meat in a mixture topped by a glaze of floating fat.

No animals had died from a black death at the priory but there were stories of it happening elsewhere. Brodie thought it an unlikely possibility, though it was one he had never entirely dismissed. On seeing the pan of food, he made a further connection: his own hand wrote of a pestilence that made men utterly shrink from eating unclean fowl in the years after the king returned from France. He leaned away from the brazier, turning his head to the side.

Alyth served up the stew.

Fergus lit a tallow lamp on the back wall. The sweet, rancid smoke from the peeled rush wick drifted across the room.

Brodie chewed dryly on a chunk of mutton.

Chapter 5

"You shall never leave with my permission, but you shall remain here and die."

Saint Dunstan, to runaway monk Brother Edward (11th century)

July, 1350, until the 28th Day of August in the Same Year

The silence in the deserted priory was unlike that enforced on the community during meals, processions, study and repose. Brodie regarded it like hide on a parchment drying frame: stretched to more than its usual length and width, taut and easily punctured. Each room had new sounds. Empty of brothers' snores, the lay dormitory was filled instead with the creak of timbers. In the rain, water dripped through the chapter house roof. With only his own spoon scraping a bowl or a pan in the refectory or kitchen, Brodie could make out hoodiecrows squabbling in the fields beyond. Winds whined in the church tower. He had made discoveries in forbidden places too. The steady flow of the lade was audible only from the beds on the east side of the canons' dormitory and infirmary; rock doves nested in the roof above the lesser chamber of the prior's quarters.

Absent from all the places, along with the parlour chatter of the brothers, was the voice of God.

And so, judging that the divine would be loudest at the priory on the feast day of Augustine, Brodie climbed the ladder to the bell tower early on the last Saturday of August. He stopped on the second gallery and pulled the rope. The doctrines said the great bell uttered God's very words; all Brodie heard was his personal sequence of rings – one long, five short – which until two months ago summoned him to his superiors.

Brodie let go of the rope and shuffled the ladder into place below the belfry trapdoor. Through cobwebs that clung to his hair and tunic like goosegrass, he climbed into the roof space, as close to the heavens as the ladder would take him. The sun struggled through gaps between huge, swelling clouds. Squeezing past the great bell, Brodie leaned on the sill of the west window arch. Neither Fergus nor Alyth were in sight. He could descend the ladder, walk through the open gate and cross the drawbridge without anyone knowing he had gone. He had a notion of simply travelling the opposite way to that directed by Prior Archibald, holding on to no more than the unlikely prospect of finding a home with Mariota or earning salvation through Duncan Christie. But even if nobody saw him leave, a writ for his capture as an apostate would soon enough follow his spoor. Prior Archibald would permit nothing less. And soon after, he would face excommunication for spurning his habit. Beyond that were disgrace and the likelihood of countless other miseries.

Unable to comprehend God's will, Brodie went to retreat back down the ladder. Edging past the bell, he caught sight of Fergus leaving the barn in the western grounds, a grain-flail over his shoulder, the swingle end swaying loosely.

Brodie stopped and shouted. 'Threshing already?'

Fergus walked on without hearing.

Brodie took the metal clapper in his hand and banged it against the side of the bell.

This time, Fergus looked up. He veered towards the church.

'You are threshing already?' Brodie shouted again.

Fergus peered upwards, shading his eyes with his free hand. 'And you can help – after whatever feast you must have in the name of the founder of your order.'

'After I have led myself in prayer and held chapter alone.' He smiled.

'Three of us working will fill ten sacks for market. After chapter then, brother.' Fergus turned towards the toft with a wave of the flail handle.

Brodie counted the days. All monies made by the priory had

to reach Brother Peter before the final term day of the year. To accomplish that, the flock and surplus grain would have to be sold at Forfar before Michaelmas: thirty two days. The primestock market was held on the second Saturday of the month: fourteen days. The grain should be sold at the earliest date: two or, at most, four days.

From the belfry, parts of the market town were visible. To the south of the gatehouse, through the Whitehills, smoke drifted from the grange at Gowanbank. Beyond that, the steeple of the parish church stood taller than any other structure. In imagining a lifetime away from the priory, Brodie had given no heed to the day and night he would spend alone among seculars carrying out the cellarer's harvest market duties in place of Brother Hector. It was a return to the world, of sorts, without the need to abandon his habit.

Chapter 6

*"He beat himself so hard that the scourge broke
into three bits and the points flew against the
wall. He stood there bleeding and gazed at
himself. It was such a wretched sight that he was
reminded in many ways of the appearance of the
beloved Christ, when he was fearfully beaten.
Out of pity for himself he began to weep bitterly.
And he knelt down, naked and covered in blood,
in the frosty air, and prayed to God to wipe out
his sins from before his gentle eyes."*

Description of a friar's self-flagellation (14th century)

1st Day of September, 1350, until the 6th Day of the Same Month

'By this celestial letter…carried by Peter the Hermit…' The
master of the flagellants waited for the boast of the letter's
provenance to silence the pedlars' drums and bring the crowd at
the Forfar mercat cross to a complete hush. A short distance to
the east, at the foot of the steps up to the parish church, Brodie
made out only the words that were shouted. "…an angel
delivered the word of God…marble tablet descended…glowing
with heavenly light…" He unloaded the two unsold sacks of
grain from the cart and carried them one at a time up the steep
steps to the church storehouse. Weighted by coins, his belt
pouch nudged his thigh with every step. Brodie guessed from
the pitch and roll of the flagellant master's voice that he had
begun reading the letter.

Once the grain was secure and the cart had been pushed tight
against the wall, Brodie emptied the earnings on the table in the

church sacristy. The pile of silver looked more than a pouch could hold. Left on the altar by pilgrims, coins appeared little different from scraps of metal cast in the dirt of the forge. Up close, no bigger than buttons in his fingers, they took on a new refinement: the stiff engraving of a youthful King David with sceptre, hammered lines of a long cross, intricate Latin inscriptions and markings that, he guessed, identified the time and place of mintage. Brodie could admire the artisanship, if not understand the allure that led people to swindle and slay just to possess such treasures. He supposed he could not expect to understand: a cloistered life might demand obedience, poverty and chastity but it brought a ready supply of provisions in the teind barn and logs to burn in the grate.

Unfamiliar with handling the English and Scots pennies – and even twelve French deniers – Brodie counted the takings twice, hurrying to finish when he heard the steps of someone entering the church. He stuffed the pouch in the safe place below the sacristy floorboards before moving through to the chancel, where a hunched figure settled down to pray at the altar. The devotee must have heard the rustle of Brodie's heavy gown but he remained absorbed in prayer.

Outside, there was a warmth in the air, even though a new month had arrived. Brodie watched from the churchyard's elevated position as the flagellants formed a circle around the master and two lieutenants, who stood on the steps of the slender mercat cross. The lieutenants held banners of violet and red above their heads, the master brandished a simple wooden staff. The followers had taken off their shoes and stripped to the waist; the leaders wore hair shirts. All kept on their long, felt hoods.

Brodie picked his way down the mossy steps. Drawing closer to the gathered crowd, the dust of the street turned to mud churned with mule dung and scraps of discarded produce. Closer still, Brodie could hear the master clearly.

'Mankind has clung to grievous sins – vulgar pride and greed, usury of money and victuals, failure to observe the Sabbath.' Brodie took a place farthest from the mercat cross, at the back of the crowd, which was five deep in places. Behind him, a boy stood in each of the weigh-beam pans, balanced in a way that allowed both to see over the heads of the adults. A single huckster continued moving from person to person, selling tallow candles and cloths from a basket, but even she whispered her pitch. Otherwise, the crowd was still.

The master stepped down from the mercat cross steps and walked from one follower to the next. Halfway around the circle, he doubled up and screamed aloud, as though pained by a blow. 'May they pay a teind to hell! For chief among the sinners are unchaste priests and those nuns who pollute the virgin's habit.' He scanned the onlookers as if able to detect such sins from a distance. Brodie lowered his head.

'Heretics,' breathed a stranger close to Brodie's ear.

Brodie only glanced to his right but saw enough to know that the man who spoke was a cleric: shorn of hair from ear to ear and wearing a buttoned, black cassock. 'Father,' Brodie acknowledged.

'His Holiness Clement of Avignon has ordered that these penitents be excluded from communion for their heresy,' the cleric explained. He added a phrase in Latin that Brodie understood as: "Beneath an appearance of piety, they set their hands to cruel and impious works."

In the circle, the flagellant master slapped the face of a follower, who threw himself to the ground and lay face down. The master addressed the unmoving figure. 'Only the Blessed Virgin has saved you from destruction for your unworthy conduct. And only then because you have chosen to join the Brethren of the Holy Tawse for the number of days that Christ lived as years.' He lashed at the prone follower's buttocks, back and legs with his staff. The man lifted his head from the mud and began reciting the Ave Maria, a strain in his voice but managing to no more than flinch at the repeated blows.

On finishing a third Ave Maria and also a Pater Noster, the man on the ground pulled a three-tailed thong from his belt and began to whip his own back, still face down, muttering quietly. 'Holy Virgin. Mother of Sorrows. Show mercy.' As soon as he did so, another follower was pulled from the circle and beaten by the master. After reciting the same prayers, he too began to flog himself with a heavy leather scourge, though he lay on his side and held up three fingers with his spare hand. He shouted loudly. 'Spare us Lord Christ! And our penance will spare mankind from destruction!'

'Why do they behave differently?' Brodie whispered to the cleric.

'The one on his side confesses sins of perjury, the other is an adulterer.'

Blood quickly appeared on the backs of the flagellants. Looking closely, Brodie could see that their knotted scourges were tipped with sharp metal spikes.

Others joined the ritual until a dozen whipped themselves and cried out.

The master yelled over the commotion. 'The blood they shed is a garment to be worn for their wedding feast with God. Sinners, step forward and mingle your own blood with Christ.' One onlooker, then another three – all men – did so, mumbling confessions that Brodie could not hear. The master ordered them to lie on the ground. 'Have the sacraments of the church...' He punctuated his sermon with strokes to the bodies of the penitents. '...saved you from plague?'

Someone in the crowd called out in agreement. 'Dens of thieves! Cast them from their pulpits!'

The master continued, alternately exhorting the onlookers and lashing the prostrate penitents. 'The true nature...of the deceivers...will be revealed...by the beast of the apocalypse... Christ has shown...His wounds to us...the Brethren of the Holy Tawse...Join with us...and find redemption...in the suffering and sacrifice...of the Great Tribulation.'

The adulterer summoned his strength and aimed a particularly fearsome swipe between his own shoulders; his flesh ripped and he roared in pain. He dropped the scourge and slowly folded his knees beneath his body until he crouched on all fours.

A gaunt young woman with dark eyes barged through the crowd and ran towards him. She caught his dripping blood with a rag and smeared it on her cheeks. 'Oh, miraculous blood,' she wailed. Mouth and eyes wide, her hollow face took on the appearance of a skull.

'Tiny-fisted tantrums,' spat the cleric next to Brodie, not bothering to lower his voice.

'There has been no plague since their processions began,'

countered a man in front, half turning around. From the stains on his bare, folded arms, he looked to be a dyer.

'That is true. But there was no plague at all on this island until they brought their processions from Perugia,' replied the cleric.

The dyer said nothing.

'Yet now the gates of cities from Thuringia to Picardy are closed to them,' continued the cleric. 'Why might that be – if their intercessions are so persuasive?' The hair the priest retained was coloured like a starling, black with flecks of white. It stretched in any number of directions and distances across his scalp and even beyond his neck. High eyebrows that almost met in the middle gave him an expression of near constant surprise. A fiery mark spilled from temple to cheek.

The dyer did not answer, his attention now fixed on the raised arms of the master and the lighted torches held high by the lieutenants. The repeated thud of leather subsided along with the moans of the flagellants. Through gasps, they formed a column three abreast in front of the master, who retook his earlier position on the uppermost step of the mercat cross.

'These brothers make a living sacrifice for your redemption,' he reminded the crowd. 'Render your thank offerings – sit them at your supper table, let the blood of their sacrifice stain your straw bedding.' He lowered his arms and prodded inconsequentially at the ground with his staff. 'After morning praises, our holy troupe makes the procession to the toun at the Kirrie Muir. Put your marching feet next to ours and be baptised in blessed blood.'

The cleric snorted with derision. 'Aye, take your place – for a fee of just four silver pennies.'

Brodie swithered between intrigue at the extent of the cleric's knowledge and concern at the anger his comments might provoke.

The cleric seemed to read one, or both, thoughts. 'You appear worried, brother. It is in the scriptures – God loves a glad giver.' A wide smile pinned back his cheeks. He closed his bright green eyes and tilted his head forward. 'Priest John, from Fordun.'

Fordun waved a dismissive hand in the direction of the flagellants at the same time as he turned to head towards the church.

'Priest John,' replied Brodie absently. He followed Fordun, sidestepping awkwardly to avoid splashing into a mirky puddle.

'Of Fordun. Chancery priest.' As they walked, Fordun pinched the sleeve of Brodie's dark Augustinian gown and rubbed the rough fabric between his fingers. 'You are a Black Austin. There are few of your order in the northern provinces. Might I suppose you are from the parish's mother church at Restenneth? Perhaps you are the scribe who inhabits that priory alone?'

'I am,' said Brodie with hesitation, muddled by Fordun's abrupt arrival at such close truths.

'Brother, I am no Merlin the Seer.' Fordun stopped at the foot of the steps up to the parish church. 'I am on a journey for the chancellor in Aberdeen and one of my next visiting-places is your priory at Restenneth – to fetch you from your desk and take you to the great cathedral where you are to work.'

'I am to leave for Aberdeen?' Brodie's muddlement deepened. 'But I have companions at Restenneth...Books need collected from the library...'

'Books, you say? Time will be made for leave-taking with your companions. For now – come with me.' Fordun beckoned Brodie to follow him beyond the entrance to the parish church and down the steep, grassy slope of the western graveyard to the chaplain's house.

Inside, the chaplain's house was as big as the priory refectory. A fireplace and smaller oven, both unlit, were set into the stone wall facing the entrance. Two bed boxes with canopy frames but no curtains attached had been fitted awkwardly into the space behind the door to their right. Other than a cross chiselled on a white sandstone panel above the fireplace, the house had no decorations or hangings. The few furnishings included a squat press between the beds and a large table that stretched from wall to wall below the south gable, form benches on either side.

Fordun jammed the door shut with a post and kneeled by the nearest bed. He slid back a wooden side panel from the bedstead and dragged out a shallow wooden chest. His hand hovered over the strap that held the chest shut. 'I have collected more than just stray scribes on my journey. Look for yourself.' He opened the lid to reveal neat stacks and scrolls of papers. 'The ancient chronicles of the Picts of Scythia and the Scots have been plundered since the first year of this century and before. My purpose is to recover what has been lost and compile a history since Queen Margaret. See...' He reached into the chest and lifted out a sheaf of documents. 'You asked about the penitents at the marketplace – these dispatches contain the same papal bull that proscribed their processions.' He sifted the bulls and briefs enthusiastically, taking one from the bundle. Fordun pointed close to the pope's monogram, where the leaden seal was fixed by a hemp cord. 'See there – issued on the feast day of our own Bishop of Whithorn, Saint Acca, ten full months ago.'

Brodie saw the date clearly enough. But more vivid, in that bull and others handed over by Fordun, was the fate of the apostate. Many religious, it seemed, had taken leadership of the flagellant movement. In return, they might face arrest, loss of benefices, excommunication. Worse, the edicts and decrees carried murmurs that sham monks and friars would encounter persecution, beatings, even torture.

'Is this the life of an apostate?' He directed the question at the papers in his hand.

'More end up as farm labourers or beggars than carry a scourge and join the bleating brethren,' Fordun answered. He leaned forward, as if about to deliver a harangue, but then stopped and settled back on his knees. 'There are ways for a monk to wander without relinquishing the habit. Any scribe from the chancellor's office who made it his task as well as mine to recover these records would travel to towns and cities, in this nation and neighbouring lands.' Fordun replaced the papal documents in Brodie's hand with another batch. 'Look where I have journeyed in just these past two months – Kinghorn, Dirleton, Ercildoune, Melrose, your own mother house at Jedburgh. And my next destination is the Priory of Restenneth, where I am told a lay brother using the name Brodie writes a chronicle for the king himself. No doubts he would make a worthy attendant on any such travels.'

Fordun's nostrils flared. He smiled at his own self-satisfaction.

Rather than dwell on Fordun's expression, Brodie retraced his words, coming to rest on one in particular: Ercildoune. It was a close enough match to a name Brodie had not heard in a full ten years, even if he had thought it often. Thomas of Ersildoune, who had given him Michael Scot's mysterious books and then disappeared during the fray that led to Prior Bernard's death at the hands of Cleek. Brodie read the topmost letter, a noncommittal reply from Pope Clement to earlier correspondence from King David. Below that was the king's original supplication to the pontiff, a plea to support David's position in negotiations for his release from captivity in England. Brodie glanced hastily through the letter but saw no mention of Thomas. He checked the signatures of witnesses at the end: Haliburton, de Leon, others he could not make out. No Ersildoune or Ercildoune.

'An annalist for the king would need documents such as this to fulfil his obligations to his royal master, no?' offered Fordun.

Since the capture of his royal patron at the Battle of Durham, Brodie had recorded the arrival, return and retreat of the Great Plague but little else. In the face of such mortality, few other events seemed worthy of description. But a returning king would demand a more complete account of his reign.

Brodie began to read the correspondence again, more studiously, comprehending the contents. King David was prepared to meet a number of onerous conditions to secure his freedom from the Tower: acceptance of Edward or his son as heir presumptive to the throne of Scotland; attendance at the same king's parliaments and great councils; a commitment to support England in times of war; English possession of all Scottish castles and fortresses. And most unlikely of all: restoration of lands to the disinherited, the disloyal faction that included the Afflecks. *"...Those banished and proscribed from Scotland for their demerits, and their heirs, whose goods were long ago confiscated...should recover their pristine status and their goods..."* A list of names followed: Walter Comyn, Richard Talbot, Henry de Ferrers, Macdougall of Lorn, the MacDowells, McCans and Mowbrays. Last on the list of great names was Umfraville, liege lords of the Afflecks. No lesser folk were identified by name but removing the stain from the Umfravilles would surely do likewise for their vassals. His search for one name – Thomas of Ersildoune – had led him closer to another: his own.

'How could you come across the king's personal dispatches?'

asked Brodie, affecting a scholarly interest.

'It is only a copy,' replied Fordun with equally contrived modesty. 'More in my library is written by the first hand.'

'Do you have other reports of these negotiations?' Brodie curbed his inclination to ask a dozen more questions.

Fordun laughed, a single grunt. 'Nothing since that in your hand was dispatched from the papal palace only a month ago.'

'Of course.' Brodie passed the correspondence back to Fordun. Supposing he had been upbraided for presumptuousness, Brodie asked a different question. 'Do you know anyone who uses the name Thomas of Ersildoune?'

'Ersildoune, Ercildoune…Whatever name he uses – there is one who truly believes he is Merlin the magician.' Fordun's eyes bulged with mirth. He pointed at a florid *"TT"* written in fern-green ink at the bottom of the letter from the pope. 'It is his mark on this dispatch. He is the transcriber.'

Brodie must have looked puzzled because Fordun continued with some impatience. 'True Thomas…' Brodie had heard the name, of course, but never made any connection. 'Thomas the Rhymer,' Fordun pressed. 'The old greybeard is known by many names but not often Thomas of Ersildoune.' Fordun packed the papers back in the chest. 'You could give him whatever name you chose if you met him.' He closed the lid. 'So, will you join me?'

*

The new sun had not yet climbed above Cunning Hill when Fordun and Brodie parted at the parish church steps. The chancery priest turned south towards the slopes of Balmashanner, beyond which he would reach the road to Dundee. After a night there, he would journey on to the earldom of Fife, where he had an appointment with the Great Register of the Priory of St Andrews. Brodie guided his draught horse and cart east towards Restenneth.

Fergus was on the far side of the third priory field, having put away his grain-flail and taken out a long-handled scythe to harvest the spring barley.

Brodie drew rein and stood on the front edge of the cart. He attracted Fergus's attention with a noisy jangle of his money pouch and an extravagant, sweeping wave at the empty cart. 'All gone,' he shouted. 'Enough grain to feed all the men of Moray – exchanged for just these puny coins.'

Fergus formed his fingers into a tight bunch and tapped them against his lips in a gesture that invited Brodie to eat. 'Later,' he called.

Brodie bent to pick up one of the two redware flagons on the cart. He hoisted it above his head and mimicked pouring the contents into his mouth from a height. 'Then I will bring the church-ale.'

After stabling the horse and cart, Brodie swept and scoured the priory buildings, mindful that he should complete as many of his duties as possible before Fordun returned from St Andrews to fetch him to Aberdeen. Drifts of dust had accumulated since he last cleaned the church, chapter house and prior's quarters. The wax from guttered candles stuck firmly to the sills of the trefoil windows. Greasy, black spills surrounded the tallow lamps in the refectory and warming room. A blanched weed had forced itself through a crack in the storeroom wall and grown as tall as a child.

On his knees in the chapter house, sweeping around the prior's chair, he was disturbed by a voice from behind.

'Your prior demands excessive obedience if you must bow before his empty chair.'

Brodie turned to see Fergus in the warming room doorway. 'As you are senior here now, perhaps you should sit in the prior's chair to hear my confession and give your blessing,' he added lightly. Only in saying the words did Brodie realise their truth.

'It is after noon – we should eat,' suggested Fergus.

Brodie bowed. 'As you say, Father.'

Fearing his friend's new, cloudless mood might darken in a blink, Brodie said nothing of his imminent departure or the encounter with Fordun. Instead, during the amble from church to toft and again between mouthfuls of church-ale, red berries and Alyth's salted bannocks, he told other tales from Forfar: the spectacle of the flagellants, his own clumsiness in money matters, the din of the market.

After luncheon, Brodie went to each of the places he knew

149

best: the two beds he had used in the dormitory, as a novice and then lay brother; his common seats in church, chapter and refectory; the patch of grass in the garth where he sat on his first day, the pillars of the cloister arches looming as tall as the tower of Parma; the north range that trapped the summer sun during novice lessons with Master Robert; the location of the same master's murder at the entrance to the sacristy; the desk Brodie had inherited from Brother Peter not an hour later.

He sat at the desk and looked vaguely between the writing slope and shelves, empty of books but for a psalter, lectionary and collectary; at Saint Peter on the painted window, keys in hand; towards the cracked tomb of Prince John; at the tiled floor, plain walls, timber roof.

Eventually, he snatched his pen-knife and a batch of goose feathers from the desk's box shelf. He imagined shedding memories with each stroke that shaped the plucked feathers. He counted them as he worked: one, two, three…five…seven new quills.

Only one storage kist still contained any documents: Brodie's Annals of Egglespether; the two enigmatic verses of riddle; bifolia of text discarded by Peter as unworthy of inclusion in his Stewartis; Michael Scot's books; his own indenture document slipped between the covers of Liber Introductorius; and an account of the plague by Friar John Clyn of Kilkenny, which had been left by a pilgrim. Peter and Prior Archibald had taken everything else.

Brodie stretched to take the liturgical books and the priory records from the shelf. He accounted for the takings at market on the single, short scroll that contained the few records logged since the departure of the other brothers. He rolled up the scroll and put it in the wooden kist along with the liturgical books. Lastly, he emptied in the coins from his pouch. Without further thought, he closed the lid and returned the kist to the cabinet behind the desk.

Eager to help Fergus in the barley field before sundown, Brodie shortened the already abbreviated version of vespers he had made his own, stopping at the altar to say a single Pater Noster but otherwise praying silently as he passed through the church. He stepped outside into unexpectedly bright sunshine mumbling the Songs of Ascents. "Those who sow in tears shall reap in joy…he that goes and weeps…shall return rejoicing, bearing sheaves."

Before Brodie's eyes had adjusted to the direct glare of the sun, Fergus emerged from the shadow cast by the kitchen block. Taken by surprise, Brodie spluttered a question. 'The barley is all harvested?'

'Almost,' replied Fergus. He held up one of the flagons of church-ale Brodie had brought from Forfar. 'My mind is on the fruits of last year's harvest.'

Brodie squinted and shielded his eyes. 'I could swing a sickle – if you would rather rest?'

'Rest your own arse – while the sun is still high. Come…' He beckoned Brodie to follow. 'We should sit by the river.'

Fergus led the way to a grassy lip overhanging a dent in the riverbank, where the current settled briefly then hurried on. He slipped off his boots and dangled his feet in the water. Brodie did likewise.

Fergus took a long drink from the flagon. He closed his eyes and lay back in the long grass with a groan, holding one hand to his ribs.

'You are pained?' asked Brodie, taking the flagon.

'One day it is my back.' Fergus kneaded his back then moved his hand to his hip. 'The next day my haunch. Or a knee, or a shoulder. But I am better here.' He tapped his head with his forefinger.

'You need rest.' Brodie sipped at the ale.

'It is not rest I need, it is work. I have a penance to do – to guard against my sins passing to my daughter.'

'Friend, you have made satisfaction for any sins – I am sure of it.'

'I may have avoided the plague – even if I wish it had taken me rather than others – but there is one debt that no man can escape. What will happen to Mariota and the young hinnies then? And Alyth too? On their account, I must pay my arrears while I still occupy this body.' He spoke with a sigh in his voice.

Dabs of clouds trailed across the sky like stepping stones. A magpie on the opposite bank let out a prolonged cackle.

'Your profit would be greater if you left this place to live with the rest of your family.'

Fergus shook his head and reached for the ale.

'My time has come to leave,' blurted Brodie, into a silence that had not fully established. 'I am to travel with Priest John of Fordun. I will find Mariota. And care for all of them if you are not here.'

Fergus sat up, smiling in a way Brodie recognised from before the plague. 'Friend, you are concerned – there is no need, at least not on my behalf.' He reached into the bag on his belt and brought out a bundle of charcoal sticks. 'I knew your time was coming, if not as soon as this, so I brought you these from the willow wood, for whatever books are put in your fist to decorate. Do as you say, and go. Use one of these sticks to draw me a picture when you find her.' His younger smile appeared again, like a new flame licking around an old coal.

*

Four days later, Brodie was gone from Restenneth. He took his night shoes, surplice, change of tunic and the kist in a sack; he left behind a promise to seek dispensation to return for spring ploughing.

Chapter 7

*"The Scots answered with one assent and one
voice, that whilst they wished to ransom their
king, they would never submit to the king of
England, so King David returned to the Tower."*

Henry Knighton, *Knighton's Chronicle* (1337-1396)

Springtide, 1351, until the 19th Day of June, 1355

Brodie returned to Restenneth for five ploughing seasons and
four harvests. Each year, Fergus seemed more infected by age,
bodily at least. Alyth too was in decline, encumbered by the
burden of maintaining the priory. Brodie might have been
contaminated by their creeping decrepitude: he had a new
slackness about his gut, the beginnings of a stoop in his
shoulders. Weariness lurked when he rose for the night office
and, on some recent occasions, he had to piss before the
morning office. Greying hairs clung to the blade when a razor
last scraped his crown. Beyond those unwelcome happenings,
he was niggled by a near ever-present uncertainty with the
secular world. In Aberdeen, he spent some nights and days at
the Trinitarian friary where he borrowed a bed and a desk.
Other times, he would work through the hours at the Cathedral
of Saint Machar, updating court estreats or sewing together
sections of exchequer scroll. But he never remained in
Aberdeen longer than a month before Fordun summoned him
on another journey. And so he spent more time on the back of
an ass than at a familiar desk or pew. Rather than tread his feet
on the boards and tiles of the same dormitory, chapel, chapter
house, sacristy and refectory, a new week would bring a new

monastery scriptorium, church library or fortress muniment room. He clerked at the Dundee parliament where King David tabled terms for his own release from English custody – including restoration of the disinherited – and heard the reasons for their emphatic rejection at Scone nine months later. He met more seculars in a week with Fordun than he had in a year at Restenneth. He purchased goods with money, visited taverns and slept for two nights in a flock-filled bed with matching bolster. However, despite travelling to corners east and west, Brodie had yet to reach farther south than Paisley Abbey and was therefore no closer to finding Mariota or Duncan Christie. Or Thomas of Ersildoune, and whatever he might know of the Afflecks and Umfravilles. But, excepting his personal disorientation, the greatest uncertainty of all was the direction in which his devotion lay. He had tried to make a gift of himself to God but, for reasons beyond comprehension, remained unable to surrender his every breath. Searching for the divine in books only added to his confusion: emerging scholarship told him to question orthodoxy; volumes of established church doctrine demanded its acceptance. In the absence of an obvious alternative, Brodie read on. And scribed and transcribed, bound and repaired, sewed and decorated.

Anticipating the easy familiarity of Fergus's company, Brodie requested dispensation to assist the Restenneth harvest for a fifth year. Before the first thistles were cut on the Nativity of Saint John the Baptist, he received his answer.

'The chancellor is to refuse,' said Fordun.

Brodie remained at the door of Fordun's manse, modest beside those of the other residentiary canons in the chaplain's court. 'Does he say why?'

Fordun stepped outside and closed the door behind him. He fastened the padlock with a thick copper key. 'You are needed elsewhere – on the order of the king.'

'The king?'

'Negotiations for his release are due to commence again. He has read your chronicle of the years leading to his capture and the plague that occurred since and believes your hand will write a fair account of proceedings. You once asked to read more reports of these discussions – now you can write them for

154

yourself. You are to be one of his courtly scribes, for some time at least.'

They walked on in morning shadows gripped between the chanonry houses and the steep wall that enclosed the cathedral grounds, Brodie taking in Fordun's unexpected declaration. On their right, the scorched upper façade of the bishop's palace and the three corner towers not destroyed in the wars with England's Edward were visible over the wall. A multitude of pigeons cooed from an unseen dovecot. Turning left towards the cathedral, Brodie saw Brother Peter up ahead, also walking in the direction of the church, alongside two chapter priests: no doubt making it known – as he had to many others, even before the novena of mourning raised de Rait to the nine choirs of angels – that John the Barbour was chosen as the new diocesan archdeacon.

'Where are these proceedings? And when will they happen?'

Fordun ushered Brodie into the churchyard between grey watchtowers, stiff and many-sided like basalt columns. 'Come to the library and I will show you the order. It has been put down by a skilled hand, and even adorned.'

Brodie stepped from the south porch into the chapel, disordered with masons at work amid random stacks of building materials. He looked upwards at the central tower through a fog of stone dust. The new granite stonework reached at least six cubits. Sheets of lead had replaced some of the timbers.

'The steeple will resemble the papal tiara when it is completed,' remarked Fordun. 'And contain a peal of fourteen tuneable bells.'

The library was off the passage beyond the presbytery. Five desks were crammed into the tight space. Leather satchels of documents hung from pegs. Waxen tablets had been stacked against the wall through to the treasury. Brodie breathed in the same still, dry air that had filled his tiny library cell at Restenneth.

Fordun went to the farthest desk, close to a square window on the south wall, and lifted a sheet from the writing slope. He affected the tones of a herald issuing an announcement. "King David of Scots, by the grace of God, to his scribe, in religion Brother Brodie, of the Augustinians at Restenneth, and Brothers Laurence and Gilbert, red friars from the Order of Trinitarians at Aberdeen, dedicated to the Holy Trinity and the ransom of captives…" Losing interest, he trailed off.

Fordun urged Brodie to move closer. 'But see the penwork.' He brought the document closer to his face, while also holding it slightly to the side for Brodie.

Brodie scanned the introduction Fordun had just read. 'Where is your name in the preface?'

Fordun waved away Brodie's question. 'No other leave is allowed until our new archdeacon has been installed – may the onward soul of the Most Reverend John de Rait rest in peace – and the Barbour is not expected to return from an audience with His Holiness Innocent the Sixth in Avignon until next week or later. You will travel without any delay, in the company of the Trinitarians.'

He resumed marvelling at the artistry of the dispatch, nodding his head in admiration. 'Formal cursive in the vernacular, flushed right, generous margins, wide spacing. And these garlands have been coloured with…'

Before Brodie could ask another question, Brother Peter interrupted from the open doorway. 'The new archdeacon is a patron of letters and a wise head.' The timeliness of his intervention gave the impression he had been following their conversation through the treasury wall. 'We will all serve the cathedral in new ways from the day he is installed.'

'…verdigris,' concluded Fordun, ignoring Peter. 'The garland has been filled with verdigris.' Finally, he looked up at Peter. 'The Barbour is a fine poet, that is true. And less of a historian.'

Brodie recognised a smile behind Fordun's rigid expression.

Peter responded after a hesitation. 'For certain, he appreciates the merit in creating words of his own rather than journeying hence and thence collecting the words of others.'

'Yet at the moment the Barbour arrives, your Brother Brodie will be travelling hence and thence, first to…' Fordun glanced down at the letter. '…to beyond Glasgow, where he will be joined by the cleric, Robert Dumbarton, and the king's Galloway confessor, Adam de Brechin, before going to Odiham in the very distant south. Along the way, he will be both making words of his own and collecting those of others. Is that not so, Brother Brodie?'

The king's order said it better than Brodie could: he was

finally bound for the far south, eventually England but first Glasgow and perhaps Galloway: the location of Dundrennan and Glenluce, the abbeys he had commended to Duncan Christie those many years before.

'It must be so,' mumbled Brodie.

Fordun read on, seeming to take pleasure in Peter's silent indignation at such rejection of Barbour's methods. "…Do my will, carry out the service of God, and deal in peace without delay or interference."

Abruptly, he stopped reading.

His relish gone, he continued in more measured tones. "Or alas, tomorrow will bring a calamity and a misery! A blast that shall exceed all those yet heard – that shall strike the whole nation with amazement, confound those who hear it, humble what is lofty and level to the ground what is unbending. Safe and secure conduct is granted to all to whom this letter comes. May God deliver you from the power of the king's enemies – witches and wicked women, wolf's heads and wolves. Borrow from brothers the sanctuary bell. Once again, hail your homebound king from foreign shores."

A lull followed.

'So, your frivolous ways rebound to your soul's danger – beg the Lord to have you in his keeping on this journey, brother.' Peter used the fraternal address, but with disdain, in a way that was some distance from the spirit of the gospels.

The closing lines of the letter did not rhyme like Brodie's scraps of riddle, yet the wording was as close as a rainbow and the rain. Equally conspicuous was the *"TT"* transcriber's mark in the left margin: True Thomas of Ersildoune.

Chapter 8

*"When cruelty and injustice are armed with
power, and determined on oppression, the
strongest pleas of innocence are preferred in
vain... 'Six months ago,' says the Wolf, 'you
vilely slandered me.' 'Impossible,' returns the
Lamb, 'for I was not born then.' 'No matter, it
was your father, then, or some of your relations.'
And immediately seizing the innocent Lamb, he
tore him to pieces."*

Aesop, *The Wolf and the Lamb* (c 6th century BC)

23rd Day of June, 1355

One page, then another and another, I cast my childish Book of
Nurture into the bonefire. Behest after behest, virtue after
virtue: do not wipe your nose on the cloth or let clear drops fall;
neither claw your flesh, lean against a post nor lumpishly let
down your head; keep from casting bones on the floor or
picking your ears, nostrils and teeth at meal-time; never lick the
dust out of your dish, which is for cats and dogs to do; spit not
in the basin, packsaddle son, that thou washest in; avoid being
too riotous, revelling or rage too rudely; make obeisance to your
lord. Learn or be lewd.

The pages flicker and flare in little more than an instant, rather
than smouldering the way parchment does. As with my young
days, I cannot rid myself of them quickly enough. Until
tomorrow arrives, I remain cup-bearer to my senior brother,
ordered to attend him with reverent regard and dutiful
obedience, gaining nothing under him but growth. In the

morning, during the fourth month of my thirteenth year, on the day of Saint John – who divined a baptism in fire – I am to be confirmed into the Holy Spirit of the church: a soldier of Christ. No longer of tender age, I will hunt and hawk as becomes the son of a noble man, rather than study courtesies and letters like a beggar's brat.

'Bairn!' The shout is from my father, Lord Robert, Steward and Guardian of the kingdom. Through the darkness, the light from the fire shows that he is casting stones at a mark with other great men. They drink the good beer that comes from Ely and eat biscuits spiced with cloves. Squires and grooms hold candles and other lamps. 'Are you to stare into the flames of the wakefire until dawn?' He laughs in a way that invites others to take heed of the words he has just spoken.

'Or do you hug the fire because you fear that the bogle-man waits in the darkness?' The mocking mouth belongs to the young whoreson of Strathearn.

My father turns and silences the cackles that follow with a look I can imagine but not see. Then his eyes rest on me. 'Since it is your last day as an innocent, come and help with these.' He lifts up a sack, which I recognise as the one holding the cats caught in the vennels of Perth. I go over, at an easy pace, shoulders and head held up. He slides a wooden crate close to me with his boot, then hands over the sack. I understand his intentions. One, two, three, I put the cats into the crate. Two browns and a grey with dark stripes. A groom slides a pole through the crate, between the slats. I take one end of the pole, my father the other. Balancing the crate between us, we move to be beside the warmth of the fire.

Beyond the flames, beneath a bright moon, the Loch of Clunie is as still as a fresh fall of snow. The fortress on the hill behind is less than a shadow in the blackness.

'Up! As high as you can reach, my shaveling boy.' He demonstrates that he means I should lift the pole above my head.

The chatter of the men, and not a few women, quietens.

I need no further instructions.

In two strides or three, I have walked around the fire so that the pole has nowhere else to go but directly over the tallest flames. The cats in the crate are briefly silent, then screech in a frenzy. A roar of glee goes up from the gathering. The wails of the caged creatures grow louder.

To my ears, the rough music has something of a melody.

Before the cats are still and silent, or the wood has scorched through, we set the crate on the grass. Two cats tumble out, singed of fur and near lifeless. It is no longer possible to tell between the browns and the grey. Young men and boys jostle to prod and stab them with blades and boots.

The third cat darts from the crate, also blackened but still with some vigour.

'Go on!' my father yells. 'After it!'

The wretched demon in disguise has cheated its fate, escaped the midsummer rite that I was chosen to perform.

I give chase, up the slope, away from the water's edge, but fall to my knees at the first lunge. Bellows and shrieks come from around the fire. I reach out again: what fur is left on the beast slides off in my fingers, as easily as a skate on ice. But it slows enough for me to trap its tail with my foot. I put the other foot on its midsection, near its neck. And lean, and lean, then with two feet. It would die another day, if not this one. I rock back and forth on my soles, shifting my weight. It screaks, like metal on metal.

And then bursts open like a ripe fruit.

I lift the limp creature by the tail and carry it back down the hill in the direction of the fire, aloft.

'Your pride has turned to pleasure at seizing the prey – it says so in your face,' calls my father, himself pleased. I am close enough to see his wide, intoxicated eyes. He snorts a laugh and moves even closer, until his sour breath falls on my cheek and he speaks to me alone. 'Not yet, but soon enough, all the verts of Badenoch and others in Moray will be yours to hunt and chase as you please. But your head should not only turn at the snap of a twig under the hoof of a stag. You must also take aim whenever you hear the name Christie. Listen keenly for it Alexander Stewart, my bastard son – the boy-wolf.'

Book IV

*"There was such a miserable dearth, both
through England and Scotland, that the people
were driven to eat the flesh of horses, dogs, cats,
and such like unused kinds of meats, to susteine
their languishing lives withall, yea, insomuch that
(as is said) there was a Scotishman, an
uplandish felow named Tristicloke, spared not to
steale children, and to kill women, on whose flesh
he fed, as if he had bene a wolfe."*

Raphael Holinshed, *Chronicles of England, Scotland and Ireland*
(c 1577)

Chapter 1

*"In cloisters, where the brothers are reading, what
is the point of this ridiculous monstrosity, this
shapely misshapenness, this misshapen
shapeliness? What is the point of those unclean
apes, fierce lions, monstrous centaurs, half-men,
striped tigers, fighting soldiers and hunters
blowing their horns?...In short, so many and so
marvellous are the various shapes surrounding us
that it is more pleasant to read the marble than
the books."*

Abbot Bernard of Clairvaux, Cistercian criticism of Cluniac
excesses (1125)

3rd Day of October, 1357, until the 14th Day of the Same Month

Freed from eleven years of captivity by the treaty signed in
Berwick, King David issued his first wish and command before
putting a foot in his own realm: no great ceremony should
celebrate his return; all endeavour must go towards restoring
governance and administration to the kingdom. Besides wearing
fine new robes tailored in Southampton, the king left all else
behind in England: his queen and falcons at Odiham, in the
protection of that castle's keeper; the red friars, Gilbert and
Laurence, as a condition of the ransom agreement. So it was that
King David crossed the border accompanied by a retinue that
included just six knights, with their squires and valets, alongside
de Brechin, Dumbarton, Brodie and two other clerks. Great
men and prelates were arrayed beyond the walls of Berwick, but
they remained there only long enough to ensure the king and his
closest counsel were mounted on the most nimble horses, so

that the royal chancery could be convened at Edinburgh's castle without delay. All others were told to return to their parishes. Unlike the other clerks, Brodie was given no order to scribe at the Edinburgh deliberations and so he finally turned his rein in the direction of the Galloway abbeys – bypassed on the way south but again now within range – travelling in company with Robert Dumbarton as far as Roxburgh and Adam de Brechin, the Galloway confessor, the whole distance to Dundrennan.

Between the hills of Barend and Fagra, at a place where the burn turned abruptly east, the abbey church came into sight, its grey ashlar walls bringing more than just the promise of clean blankets to lie beneath, warm vegetables at supper and fresh hay for his weary mule. Still more alluring than those long overdue comforts was access to the cartulary records and with that the prospect of finding the name and fate of the fugitive Duncan Christie.

'What is your business at Dundrennan, brother?' De Brechin had not spoken since around when they crossed the Kirkgunzeon. He stopped, allowing his own retainer to pass by and Brodie to catch up.

Startled by the sudden amiability, Brodie stuttered half an answer. 'As you know sire, I am a scribe.'

'You are here to see the books from Ireland?'

'The books from Ireland?'

'This place has a fine collection, perhaps the finest. Some boats sail to Kintyre believing they follow the tread of the Dove of the Church and so there are books there too – illuminated copies of the Albanic Duan and the Annals of Tighernac at Saddell Abbey and others at the chapel dedicated to Saint Columba – but the monks here are entrusted with the greatest scholarly riches from Ireland.'

Kintyre: Mariota's destination at the outbreak of plague. His understanding of the territory was so scant that Brodie committed this scrap of knowledge to memory for safekeeping. 'Truly, great riches,' he replied, reluctant to share either his thoughts or the true purpose of his search.

De Brechin grinned like a beef-witted child. 'The account of Brandan the Navigator tells of faraway people with dog legs and swine heads.'

'Saint Brandan witnessed many wonders on his voyage to the Isle of the Blessed,' said Brodie, unsure how else to respond to de Brechin's amusement.

De Brechin urged his hackney on. Brodie followed his lead and they rounded the northern limits of the abbey grounds, marked by a stone wall heavily patched with clay.

Approaching the gate on the west side, de Brechin recovered some of his knightly bearing, though with a leftover smirk that called attention to his undershot jaw and sagging eyes. 'What other documents interest you?'

'Any that are of importance to the monastery,' said Brodie, still vague. 'Charters, mandates, quit-claims.'

'You will find all of those here but more at the daughter house of Luce in Glenluce.'

'Does that community receive many sanctuary petitions?' Brodie asked with as much indifference as he could feign.

'A royal scribe should know it – the Abbey of Luce has rights of sanctuary granted in a charter from the king, in the way of the great English churches.'

Brodie was reminded of his recent visits to York, Westminster, St Martin le Grand, Beaulieu and Durham. 'Even treason can be forgiven there?'

'Both petty and high.' De Brechin pulled up his horse at the abbey gatehouse. 'Fetch the porter,' he ordered his retainer.

Despite his relative youth, the retainer had puffed out cheeks that betrayed an absence of teeth. He dismounted and searched for a place to knock or sound a bell.

'There are books at Glenluce too,' added de Brechin. 'Some say a complete library of sorcery lies below the ground, buried there when the librarian Michael Scot lured a plague into a vault and sealed the entrance. Others prefer to think he occupied the devil by challenging him to spin ropes from sand at Ringdoo Point. Either way, the scholar Scot is still esteemed there for saving the brethren from the certainty of death.'

The Cistercians received Brodie and de Brechin at Dundrennan with strict adherence to the Rule of Benedict. The porter was prompt, meek and full of the fear of God. Abbot Giles knelt before his guests in prayer, as if they were Christ himself, and exchanged the kiss of peace. The divine law was read, their feet were washed, food was served without a murmur. The greatest care was shown and every brother who passed by kept close custody of his eyes and mouth.

Due to the exactness of their observance of the rule, the order also held that ownership of any possessions was a vice to be cut out by the root. And so the porter impounded their belongings before the visitors had even passed through the gate, allowing Brodie no occasion to open the Michael Scot books in his saddlebag since de Brechin had mentioned the scholar's name.

It was not until he stood by his bunk in the guest house after compline that Brodie again saw the saddlebag. With no brothers present to enforce the great silence, de Brechin drank ale and played at cards with a gentleman pilgrim who lapsed into a rasping, unfamiliar tongue.

Brodie emptied the saddlebag of its contents.

He had studied Scot's texts closely enough to know where there was no mention of Glenluce and so looked in less familiar places. If not the first page he turned, it was close to where his hand fell: among the front matter of Liber Particularis, a tribute to the author, written in the vernacular rather than Latin.

> *"Master Michael Scot, of the Province of Scotland, son of Balwearie, father of Luce; mathematician, anatomist, illustrious doctor; scholar at Oxford, Paris, Bologna, Salerno; theologist worthy of praise and honour; translator of Toledo, instructed in Hebrew and Arabic; servant of Honorius and Gregory, Bishops of Rome; astrologer to the Lord Emperor Frederick."*

Just as the snake is blind to all but the charmer, Brodie had seen only Scot's words and none of the marginal notes added by later hands. Now his eyes were fixed to the page: at first, on the reference to Luce; then the illustration directly above. He had passed it by a hundred times, like a familiar feature of the landscape, a scree path or patch of marshy ground he knew to avoid: the simple line drawing of a ragged figure before a church, beneath a procession of stars. He saw it now as though every stroke of the pen were his own: the letters *"L" "U" "C" "E"* on each point of the steeple crucifix; the missing finger on one hand of the praying figure; the smudged name above the illustration, which he had taken to be *"Christus"*.

No calamity had befallen Brodie and the others during their two years in England, as cautioned in the dispatch transcribed by Thomas of Ersildoune, though they had closely followed the instruction to stay in places of sanctuary and also visited shrines of fervent prayer. But the truth in Thomas's distant promise that answers would be found in Michael Scot's books was plain the moment the second riddle slipped from the covers of Physionomia. Now the frontispiece of Liber Particularis seemed to provide an answer of its own. The missing finger of the figure matched the one absent from Duncan Christie's hand the day he sought sanctuary at Restenneth. And, looking as keenly as though he were threading a needle, Brodie could not say for certain if the blurred name above was *"Christus"*, as he had supposed, or if it might in truth be *"Christie"*.

*

Rousing from sleep, Brodie sensed that his dreams held some significance. But they slipped from his grasp with every moment of awakening, hastened on their way by the hollow peal of the prime bell. In their place, he had a recollection of Michael Scot writing that dreams while not digesting food foretold the future. The lightness in his gut reminded him that the Cistercians had provided no supper.

After prime, with thoughts of Scot still on his mind, Brodie browsed the Dundrennan library. Before the arrival of terce, he had established that the abbey archive contained no separate sanctuary register. And other than the Irish books, which indeed filled a shelf, there was little else of interest.

Eager to thumb instead the pages of the Glenluce cartulary, Brodie strapped his saddlebag to a fresh mule. He left the abbey, without de Brechin, while the brethren gathered in good order to enter the church for sext.

A ruddy twilight had come and almost gone by the time he drew rein at Carsluith. Despite the gloom, the ferrymaster agreed to take him across the bay in exchange for a penny and a prayer.

Brodie was given a pallet at the old Church of Saint Machutus on the hill at Wigtown.

The next day, Brodie followed the route the ferryman had described: west across the Machars; north on reaching the shore, where the waterfall like a mare's tail fell through the hills; inland just before the Mull of Sinniness formed cliffs at Auchenmalg. A league farther and he came to a stone cross where the track went in four directions. The inscription *"SANCTUARIUM"* identified the cross as a marker of the Glenluce sanctuary girth. Brodie took the path closest to where it stood, which led north and west from the crossway. The course of one narrow burn and then a broad river brought him to a mound overlooking Glenluce.

The monastery might itself have existed in a dream. Water flowed on every side, the land all around had been laid out as either field or orchard and two chapel towers rather than one rose above the cloisters. Through sunlight diluted by the season, the trees alongside the monastery seemed closer to autumn than winter. The tall beeches on the brae where Brodie stood were parched brown, the rowans shedding yellow leaves. Closer to the abbey, some branches of the birches on the downslope were in winter, others in autumn. Closer still, an elm casting its shadow over the gatehouse remained as green as a fir.

Beyond the gatehouse, Brodie found that the Glenluce community cultivated no such bounty inside church and chapter. The walls and ceilings had been painted, but the colour of a rain cloud. There were no polishings, hanging lamps or wrought candleholders. In the narrow library, a stern wind shifted through open shutters high on the east wall.

'Which entries do you need?' If the complexion of the librarian's bushy brows and sparse hair were a direct match for his white Cistercian habit, his brawny tone was the opposite of his feeble, stooped frame.

'Serving the king has taken me to places of special immunity in England – the shrines of Saint Cuthbert, Edward the Confessor and Saint Thomas Becket among many others.' Brodie was hopeful that the mention of such potent saints would find favour with the monk. 'But only on returning do I learn that your own house, here in my native land, was granted sanctuary privileges in foundation charter.'

'Anyone doing business for the king should know that is so.'

'Forgive my vulgar ignorance.' He bowed. 'Perhaps you could instruct my mind and guide me to any such petitions.'

The old man grunted and moved to a waist-high rack below the window. He flipped open the clasp on a whitewood box and struggled to lift out a bulky scroll. Brodie went to help, taking one of two handles bundled with parchment.

'Put it in the cradle,' directed the librarian.

Brodie placed the handle he held on a large copper hook at the side of the box. The librarian did the same at the other side, and then began to scroll the parchment between the handles. The cartulary appeared to be confusingly organised, with leaves bound together in a single roll, separated in some parts by blank folios, arranged both geographically and by topic. 'There are many. Do any in particular interest you?'

'Those involving treason would demonstrate this house's special privileges.'

'All these pages speak of our nearness to godliness.' The librarian stopped here and there, twisting his neck to examine an entry. 'There are fewer involving felons but still a number. These records date to King Alexander and the son of Alexander. How many years do you need?'

'Perhaps since around the time our present king first returned from exile – fifteen or sixteen years before this one.'

The librarian muttered an indistinct complaint. Turning past a succession of land leases, he stopped. 'Here is one at that time. Though not a traitor.' He spoke as he read, using his finger to pinpoint the words on the page. 'A slayer. Granted sanctuary.'

'When precisely was this?' Brodie edged closer.

'The year of God thirteen hundred and forty one, just as you asked.' The librarian answered without the need to search for a date on the page. 'Night theft of victuals from monastery kitchen,' he continued. 'Privileges of sanctuary forfeit. Put under the rod. Flogged until death of the body.'

'He is dead?' Brodie did little to contain the shock in his voice.

'The sanctuary seeker was not a man but a woman – a mother who spitted her own weanlings on a prong.'

Learning that the fugitive was a woman and had died, Brodie faced the prospect that his journey's end lay first with one unexpected change of direction, then another.

'Were there any others who rang the sanctuary bell?'

The old librarian read on without answering. He scrolled past another entry. 'No other felons sought sanctuary here until...' He twisted his handle again. '...until two years after the king returned from his Normandy chateau. A violator of women.'

'But others did ring the sanctuary bell?' In repeating the same question, Brodie heard his own desperation. He added another for variation. 'That is, did any others do so in the year of the king's return?'

'Brother, if you seek an exact petition, you would be wise to ask for it.'

'The king seeks to restore governance – and so must know all types of villainy that have escaped his justice.' It was some kind of a truth.

Caught between showing his vexation with a lingering sigh or an exaggerated shake of the head, the librarian tried both. But at least he did so while returning to the sanctuary register.

'During Eastertide, two tolled the bell. One had driven away sheep. The other had stolen a fattened cow... In the days after the Feast of Saint Brioc, a tapster asked for sanctuary, giving the reason that he had made an assault...Then the slayer came, as I have described.' He continued to twist the scroll. 'No more took the oath for the remainder of that year.'

Brodie stared at the parchment. He had thought it a simple calculation: his own recommendation that Christie should flee to the Galloway abbeys; the illustration in Scot's book that matched the appearance of the fugitive; the reference to Glenluce on the same page. But, added together, the separate parts did not match the sum he had expected. The sanctuary register contained nothing of Christie.

'Brother, if lengthy study is to be undertaken, you must do it alone. I have other duties.'

'Of course. I am most grateful.'

The librarian turned the scroll handle once more to reveal a list of names. 'Sanctuary petitions for the year after the king's return follow this register of others who visited our monastery.'

'Others who visited?' Brodie asked it as a question that did not require an answer.

'Take care of what you touch,' ordered the librarian, slowly starting to shuffle out of the room.

Brodie moved his eye quickly down the list of monastery visitors, seeing descriptions of pilgrim monks, domestics of the faith, travellers, the poor, the sick. Arriving at the place in time Christie had fled from Restenneth, he slowed to read the entries.

Knowing that the fugitive Christie would likely have taken some weeks to reach Galloway, Brodie looked still more carefully at arrivals the next month, September in the year 1341. There were fewer names listed there, but no matter: he had need of only one.

'This entry makes mention of a stranger who was given a bed in the third week of the month of September – but no name is attached.' Brodie spluttered it in an unseemly flurry.

The librarian backtracked slowly, moving as though his bent shoulders burdened under a yolk.

'Those entries have been put down by a fair and able hand – my own. Which one has you in a dither?' He glared where Brodie pointed, longer than was needed simply to read the passage.

'Ahhh…' he murmured, remembering a thing part forgotten. 'The devil had poured madness into that one's ears – to make him have no memory of a name, or much else besides. Since his mind was hindered by sickness, we assigned him a room and treated him patiently. As with other insane, he was shaved of hair so that no demons could hide there. And a burr hole was put in his skull to remove the stone of madness. Even then he only said as many words as days that passed.'

'What became of him?'

'He bore good heart to all around and became a servant of the church, entering into the life of the farm and fighting fires of thatch with a pole and hook. Every Sunday for a year, he presented himself at the church door for castigation, feet bare, draped in a sheet.'

'And his name?'

'He never found his own so this church gave him one of our choosing – David, that great ruler of Israel, and Maxwell, in the way of many nearby families.'

'Did he remain close by?'

'Brother, if this was the knowledge you sought, you should

have asked for it in one question rather than many. He is David Maxwell, now burgess and hide merchant in Kirkcudbright. And still a good servant of this church.' The old man laid a finger on Brodie's chest. 'You should know another truth, brother – the abbot will hear of your superfluous demands and falsifications about an errand for the king.' The librarian began his painstaking retreat from the library for a second time.

Chapter 2

*"A young lass of one year old…was saved and
brought to Dundee, where she was fostered and
brought up. But, when she came to a woman's
years, she was condemned and burnt quick for the
same crime her father and mother were convicted
of…eating of man's and woman's flesh."*

Robert Lindsay, *The Historie and Cronicles of Scotland* (c 1579)

15th Day of October, 1357

Even though morning fell on the Christian Sabbath, Brodie was put out of the abbey directly after chapter for his failure to observe the whole discipline of the rule. Concerned less with the punishment than reaching Kirkcudbright before nightfall, Brodie rode his mule harder than it would have preferred, raising it to a trot around and beyond Wigtown Bay.

The ringing of curfew guided him the final distance to Kirkcudbright, the directions of a returning fieldman, along with the reek of the tannery, to where someone might know of a hide merchant such as David Maxwell. Across the River Dee, the foul odour was more than just a reminder of his own parchmenter's cruck at Restenneth. It brought breaths filled all at once with dung, piss, ripe sod, scorched clay and rancid, sweet spices.

With darkness blotting the sky, Brodie moved away from the burn – little more than a dribbling leak from higher ground – towards the glow of a fire among the tannery buildings. The outlines of tanning pits were visible through the mirk beyond the open front of a long wooden structure. Four or more pigs foraged among fallen leaves in the yard outside.

Brodie dismounted, leaving his mule untethered.

Closer, he could see that the firelight came not from the main building, but a louvre-board shed set just apart. Through the open doorway, a dim figure raked smoking ashes.

Brodie stepped inside.

Such was the intensity of the stench, he was instantly taken back to a time before he fashioned parchment in a cruck by the shores of Restenneth, to the airless privy at Edzell Castle he scoured as a boy. Instinctively, he put a hand over his nose and mouth and twisted his head to be nearer the outside air.

'It is no rosewater, but it helps.' Brodie turned to the man, standing upright now, wagging a cloth in his outstretched hand. 'Vinegar,' he explained.

The vinegar-soaked rag covered Brodie's mouth and nose but nothing obstructed his eyes, which saw more than a man with spreading features, trimmed beard and rounded shoulders. They saw too a wretch with puckered brow and a sorrow that filled all his garments. And they saw a fugitive with a beseeching stare and only four fingers on one hand.

'I am here to find…' he stumbled, unsure whether to use the name Christie or Maxwell. '…the hide merchant called David Maxwell.'

'Then your search is over.'

The odour of the drying shed had settled on Brodie, clinging like a new skin. He took the rag from his face. 'And is my search for Duncan Christie also over?'

Chapter 3

"Thou shalt go on thy way with this prevision;
If by my murmuring thou hast been deceived,
True things hereafter will declare it to thee."

Dante Alighieri, *La Divina Commedia* (1308-1321)

15th Day of October, 1357, until the 21st Day of the Same Month

The man took his share of recognition, but slowly, in the way a waxed moon emerges from behind dawdling clouds.

'You are the brother…' His knees folded so that he squatted by the fire. He sighed, uneven and drawn out. 'And I am Christie, just as you say.'

Brodie already knew as much but hearing the words layered one relief on another.

Christie picked up a stick and prodded at the embers. 'Are you here to make satisfaction for your sin of letting me free?' Slumped and staring into the ashes, he seemed to bear the weight of whatever load Brodie had unburdened as a result of their meeting.

'I am here to ask a question.' Christie said nothing and so Brodie continued. 'Many years ago, you agreed to look and listen for the name Affleck. Have you found or heard it?'

'Brother, for a time after fleeing your priory, some kind of poison flowed into my mind. I did not know my own name let alone any others.'

'The monks at Glenluce said the same – but I believe there is a connection between our names.' In a tangle of overeager fingers, Brodie opened his belt sheath and drew out his knife.

Christie got to his feet, backing off.

174

'No, no.' Brodie dropped the knife and reached deeper into the sheath. 'This is all I have.' He held the two scraps of riddle high, one in each hand.

Christie nodded, reassured.

Brodie rolled a smouldering log from the edge of the fire into the centre. A flame twisted up one side. He added a second log and then kneeled by the sprouting flames, spreading the riddles flat on the ground. Carefully, he pieced them together where the illustrations of one fitted with those of the other.

Christie unhooked a lantern from the wall and crouched to look closer.

'Can you read?' Brodie asked.

'Most words, all those taught by the Glenluce monks.'

'Then read this – see, it uses your name,' said Brodie. *"Stewarts, Christies – damnation all"*…Followed soon after by my own – Affleck. And the two names appear connected by a brother who seeks sanctuary – perhaps you, the brother of Cleek.'

But Christie's eyes were not on the words; despite Brodie's promptings, they gaped only at the illustration of the pouncing wolf along the top edge. 'Brother, there is something I should show you.'

He led Brodie out of the shed and along a muddy track to a small, square dwelling behind the main tannery building. A haar of smoke hung over and around the house. Christie tapped the lintel above the doorway on the far gable, indicating that Brodie should duck to avoid the low frame. Inside, the place was thick with wood smoke. A woman sat by the hearth, rocking a baby on her lap. Before anyone could speak, she put her finger to her mouth. 'Hush.' She nodded at the baby. *Just asleep*, she mouthed.

As he weaved through a clutter of crates and baskets, tools and utensils, pans and bowls, Christie gestured with an open, upright palm for Brodie to remain by the door. Stopping beyond the fire, Christie pushed aside a bulky string of onions and reached into the blackened rafters. He held whatever he then retrieved in a closed fist and turned back towards the door.

'Have you penned the pigs?' the woman whispered.

'I will now,' he whispered back.

Christie closed the door gently behind him.

'My wife, Agnes,' he explained to Brodie outside. 'Infant

Margaret has not yet been born two months.' They walked some steps in silence. 'Brother, I am David Maxwell now – tanner, lesser merchant, husband, father to Margaret and Jean. Must you tell them that I left another name behind at your priory?'

'Rest yourself content, I have an interest in only one name – Affleck.' Brodie followed Christie back into the drying shed. The light inside had grown with the flourishing flames.

'Do others know I am here?'

'No-one.'

Christie sat next to the fire. 'Put the verses down,' he told Brodie.

Between curiosity and confusion, Brodie laid the riddles on the ground as he had done previously.

'Brother, before I show you this, there are some truths I should tell you. It is no lie that I forgot my own mind when I first came to Glenluce. By God's great mercy, I was permitted to serve the Cistercian brothers, rearing and slaughtering beasts on their farm without remembering my sins, for a time at least. When better able, I took up as a labourer here in the burgh for a year and a day. With so few left alive after the plague, my wife's father provided me with boots, clothes, drink and food, as a journeyman skinner. He lived through the plague but was weakened by it. All of this...' He swept his hand around. '...was his – I hold it only by my marriage.' He leaned back, scuffing the dusty ground with the toe of his boot. 'And perhaps because no others would scoop the dung and collect the piss pots for fear of infection.' He opened his palm to reveal a tiny scroll, not tied but rolled tight. 'My wife's father was eaten up by lice and died an ill death two years ago...'

'May his soul rest in peace.'

'He made his confessions and even uttered some words of a prayer.' Appearing to recall the scene, Christie remained in a dwam. Emerging with a small shake of his head, he continued. 'He also left many possessions – almost all to his daughter. But he put one in my hand – this.'

To flatten the scroll, Christie unrolled it one way, verso facing outward. Then he folded it back on itself, so that penwork was visible between his moving fingers. With as much care as Brodie had shown, he placed the scrap of parchment directly alongside the one discovered by Master Robert. The top edge of the two fragments formed an unbroken line; the torn inside edges fitted as neatly as a dove's tail joint. The partial illustration of the phallus-serpent was now complete, its jaws stretching open to reveal a dripping, forked tongue. The verse below took the same form as Brodie's riddles.

> *"Seven depths, six depths, five depths, four;*
> *Three depths, two depths, one depth more.*
> *Son of Affleck, who followed the bell,*
> *David the tanner of Maccus Well;*
> *Three leagues west to the Eildon Tree,*
> *Names once lost will return to thee.*
> *But from a whelp, the wolf will grow.*
> *Packsaddle child, full grown foe."*

'All by the same hand…' exhaled Brodie.

Christie brushed the portion he had just unravelled with his finger. 'It uses your name, and mine…I took that to be the reason the old man made it a gift…and it could have some meaning…' He straightened his legs but remained bent over, hands on his knees, still examining the text. 'But is it not more likely that these are just lyrics on a page?'

Brodie crouched over the riddle. 'Yet so much of what it says has shown to be true.' He pointed at the upper portion of parchment. 'See here – the prior's house at Restenneth fell just as it describes. And it foresees changes that occurred in the winds and crop yields.' Brodie read Christie's verse again. 'This appears to know that we have both lost family names – and even suggests where we might find them again.' Brodie stood. 'I have passed by the hills at Eildon on the way to Saint Mary's of Jedburgh, but do you know these exact places?'

Christie picked up the riddle. 'The Maccus Well is said to be the first place that any of the Maxwell kin held land, though it is little more than a haugh by the Tweed River. The tree must be close to the hills that share its name.' He handed Brodie the fragments of parchment, including his own. 'If I had believed it to contain any truth, I would have found a way to pass it to you. It is yours now.'

Brodie recognised an apology. 'You have my gratitude. If there is a place where I could rest my head, I will be gone in the morning,' he said, already contemplating a night with the odour of the drying shed as his blanket.

Christie latched onto Brodie's wandering gaze.

And Brodie met a new expression, one that contained a flaw behind the glaze of Christie's eye.

'I see my brother in different places,' he said, clutching Brodie's arm. 'From afar, I see the Steward's men lead him limping from the cavern, willingly it seems, he might even be exchanging a smile with one of his captors, while I tremble behind a rock clutching a puny troutlet that will never now touch his lips.' Christie spoke in a tumble of words, with the desperate haste of a penitent making a long overdue confession. 'From my place among the grasses on the hill at the Gallowden, I see him dragged through the trees, blackened and bloodied. I see the noose fitted precisely around his neck, knot at the side to prevent his neck breaking in the fall. I see his skin turning to blue, the fluids spilling from his body, the point of the blade on his flesh. I hear it too – his sucking wounds and small groans that do not match the magnitude of his death. And in each sight and sound, what I do is worse than nothing. Why? Because I feel an elation – an elation that the captor's fist is not on my shoulder and it is not my living bowels that are bundled onto the brazier.' He let go of Brodie's arm. 'Tell me, brother – what tariff would a confessor's manual put on those sins? How many years of penance for a half-man such as me?'

'The cock bird has lost a tailfeather.' The small voice came from the doorway.

They both twisted around in surprise.

The girl, who must have been around four years, held a single dark feather upright. Her brow was creased in a scowl, her pert shoulders held tight.

Christie did not move, hand still hovering where it had fallen from Brodie's arm. After a moment of silent searching, he located a lighter expression 'She thinks the fowls her companions,' he turned back to explain. Brodie saw for the first time how his face might look with a smile, though beneath his new countenance he could also have been wondering how long

178

his daughter had been standing at the door.

'Come over, my Jean.'

The girl did as she was asked. A step or two from her father, she stretched both arms out and up.

He picked her up. Balancing her on his hip, he took the feather. 'You can put this with the others.'

She nuzzled a weary head into his neck.

'Or...' Christie said it with the brightness of an idea just arrived at, a new thought plucked from an old memory. 'This monk might show you how to make it into a pen – he is a scribe.'

Other than the young girls at Restenneth, Brodie had had few dealings with children. 'Of course...yes, I could do that,' he stuttered.

Jean did not look up.

'It is late now – perhaps in the morning. Are the birds safe from the foxes?' Using two fingers, Christie prised his daughter's chin away from his shoulder.

She seemed to muster whatever exertions had not been accounted for during her waking hours, and put them all into a single, emphatic nod. Lids sagging almost shut, she flopped back down on her father.

'Then I will do the same with the pigs. But tomorrow they will need a new keeper because I must go on a journey. Could that be your task, along with caring for the chickens?'

'Where must you go?' Her face still pressed against her father, Brodie discerned the question as much by the girl's plaintive tone as the actual words.

'Tomorrow, only as far as the toun.' Christie glanced up at Brodie. 'After that – perhaps farther.'

*

Keen to escape the stench of the drying shed, Brodie seized the offer of a sleeping place in the dwelling house. With thick pelts over and beneath him, he curled around the fire, which was banked high with greenwood. The Christies lay together on the opposite side of the hearth. Such was the density of smoke, sleep was disturbed by one cough after another; it was ended by gulls bickering above the roof and daylight leaching through the

179

wattle walls.

Christie broke his night fast with a wedge of cheat-bread sopped in ale, but for sustenance rather than out of gluttony; the burgh business that took him into Kirkcudbright would provide no further opportunity to eat until well after noon. Before leaving, he made an oath to return in no more than two days and then travel on to Eildon with Brodie.

'He goes into the toun to attend the Michaelmas head court with the other worthy burgesses.' Until Agnes spoke, the room had been filled with a kind of rhythm: her grinding oats with a quern-stone, Brodie whittling Jean's feather with his pen-knife. 'But he has not said why he must then journey to Eildon.' It was not phrased as a question but Brodie knew it to be one.

'Your husband is good enough to show a churchman a place he does not know.'

'A travelling brother would surely know a region with so many great churches and monasteries?'

Brodie detected a shrewdness that would not be easily appeased. He dallied on eyes that were never far from a smile. 'The religious houses, yes. But your husband knows more precise places – the Maxwell lands at Maccus Well and others.'

Agnes paused to feed some more grain into the quern. On her lap, Margaret wheezed and waved a hand at hair that had fallen from the grip of her mother's comb. Agnes used a finger to brush the loose hair behind an ear and then continued grinding. 'I have blood relations at Maxwellheugh and can promise that all you will find at the Maccus Well, however favourable, is wholesome air and fruitful fields.'

Brodie leaned his head closer to his hands. With tiny, exact strokes, he shaped the nib of Jean's pen. 'And what might I find at the Eildon Tree?'

Agnes spluttered a laugh, her eyes instantaneously wide with surprise then tight with mirth. 'You will need all good fortune just to find the tree itself – because no such thing exists.'

Between her mother's smirks, Jean walked in the door, hopping over the clutter towards the fire.

Brodie must have looked abashed because Agnes continued more tenderly. 'The hills with the same name are real enough but the tree is an invention in stories and songs.'

Jean stopped by Brodie's shoulder. Chin tilted to her chest, she stared between Brodie and the feather.

'Jeanie, tell the monk about the Eildon Tree.'

She shook her head.

'Jean…' Her mother's prompt carried a mild warning.

Her delivery hushed and halting, she began to recite a rhyme, mumbling at first so that Brodie could not hear the opening line.

'Speak up,' Agnes urged.

She raised her voice louder than necessary.

> "…A ferlie he spied wi' his ee,
> And there he saw a lady bright,
> Come riding down by the Eildon Tree…"

'That will do, Jeanie,' said her mother, disapproving of the girl's defiant tone.

Jean had remained by Brodie's shoulder throughout the exchange. 'Is it a pen yet?' she asked, nodding at the feather.

'Almost,' answered Brodie, switching his attention back to the task of cutting her a quill. He supported the nib on his left thumbnail and used the point of his blade to remove the last shavings from the tip of the feather's shaft. 'Perhaps when I return, I could make some ink and show you how to put down your name?' He looked to Agnes for the authority to make such an offer.

She directed her response at Jean. 'The words, or picture, would last till doom – not like drawing in soil or sand with a stick,' Agnes said approvingly. 'You could do it between chores.'

Satisfied at the prospect, Jean went to skip back out of the house.

'Have you gathered heather for the floor yet?' Agnes raised her voice to make herself heard before Jean disappeared.

'After fetching the eggs,' she called back.

'Close the door!' Agnes shouted in vain. She tutted. 'The vapours from the hides fill the air as soon as it is left open,' she explained to Brodie, emptying the milled oats into a bowl.

Brodie jumped up to pull it shut.

'See that…' Agnes was pointing over Brodie's shoulder. 'The horns of the moon are turned up – it will hold the rains. The weather will be good for your journey to the Eildon Tree.' She smiled.

Outside, through the doorway, the new moon was low in the morning sky, a faint inverted arch behind an even smear of cloud.

*

Two nights later, Christie brought back accounts of the kind expected of a burgess returning from head court: four bailies, all good and sufficient men, had been chosen from among their number; every burgess was allocated some days and nights to keep watch and ward; rents and customs were collected; fealty was sworn to the king. But he brought other reports too. A dispatch from the royal exchequer had requested that all persons, whatever estate or sex, give a sum of their choosing towards the ransom of the king. And it was further proclaimed that binding fiscal decrees and trade pronouncements would be issued before the month's end, perhaps at the head courts in Lanark or Peebles.

'But it is more likely to be at Roxburgh – in five days,' explained Christie. 'That is in the direction of the Maccus Well.' He spoke in short bursts, between mouthfuls of salted beef. 'As a merchant, I should attend.' He snatched another chunk of meat from his trencher and chewed hungrily. 'Can Eildon wait until after the meeting?'

'Some few days will add little to a wait of years,' said Brodie.

*

Dusk became day and the sun rose soft in the sky, just as Agnes had forecast.

Christie was first to work, moving the saturated hides from the floater pits into the layer pits and others from the layer pits into the drying shed.

Brodie built up the fire, as he had each morning, adding the driest of the heather from the floor onto the hottest of the coals. He constructed a cone of kindling on top and placed alongside the single scorched log that amounted to more than simply embers.

He cast around for more firewood but found only Agnes's

still stare. She sat on a stool to his left, Margaret feeding at her breast. Brodie caught the slight motion of the child's head, the sounds of her breathing, heavy through her nose while she gulped down milk. Disconcertingly, the suckling child's proximity to her mother seemed to put Brodie at a closer distance too, in a way that caused him to imagine Agnes's touch.

'I should fetch some logs,' he said turning his eyes away.

'Brother, I do not mean to speak out of place but my husband guards his past so closely that you are the first proof I have seen of its existence. He confesses to have been undone by the wars but will say no more. Wherever your journey takes you, I beg it is not in the direction of his younger years. Can you give such an assurance?'

For four days, Brodie had watched her with the curiosity of a hill herder tracking the movements and moods of the clouds. But only in braving this gaze did he arrive at the realisation he had been assessing her because in all features – aside perhaps from the point of her nose – she looked as Mariota might now, eight years after leaving Restenneth.

Before Brodie could answer, Christie walked back in, his hands and forearms smirched brown from immersion in tanning mixture. 'Your mule should rest. I have harnessed horses for us both,' he said.

Unsure whether to respond to wife or husband, Brodie said nothing. Instead, he attempted a bow that at least proffered God's good grace. It emerged as a single, stuttering nod aimed somewhere between Christie in the doorway and Agnes on the stool by the fire.

*

Conditions remained fair almost the complete distance to Roxburgh, wind and rain appearing only briefly on the final approach: a blustery shower that flashed through morning sunlight.

The rain stopped as abruptly as it had started, allowing spirals of smoke to resume their upward drift beyond the roofs of the burgh houses. Travellers, most footing it but some mounted, gathered in number as they neared the toun. At the west tollgate, the crowd was such that Brodie and Christie had to slow their pace to cross the narrow bridge over the fosse, which was half-filled with a sludge of ordure and cooking pot dregs.

As a condition of their truce, the kings of Scots and England shared an uneasy occupation of the disputed burgh. On this morning, soldiers from the English garrison took up a place beyond the substantial stone houses, where the road forked sharply right towards the castle. Scottish men-at-arms lined the market street and guarded all points around the marketplace. Proceedings would be led by the warden of the Scottish marches but with Sir John de Coupland – captor of King David at the Battle of Durham and now keeper of Roxburgh Castle – by his side.

'Fire hooks are to stand at four places around the burgh and beaters must be ready with water…' Marching sunwise around a large ash tree towards the south of the marketplace, the crier bellowed out one ordinance after another. 'No man may play at bowls or dice within the burgh walls…Fleshers should not cast the entrails of animals or pails of blood or filth into the king's street during the sitting of head court…Past the third hour, pelterers are forbidden from scouring furs…If a man leaves a horse standing in sight of any justices, he is to be brought before the court at the first fault and punished.'

'We should tether the horses,' said Christie, dismounting. As he did so, one boy followed by another ran from the crowd, taking different routes between traders carrying loads and pushing handcarts.

'A stable for your horse!' one shouted, his voice pitched high among all the others that filled the marketplace. He came alongside and gripped the bridle of Christie's horse. 'It has hay and good meal.' The urchin, scraps of leather on his feet and a scrawl of black hair, noticed Brodie's presence. 'Just a silver penny for both beasts,' he added.

The second boy arrived. 'We have a watchman and a dog to guard against thieves,' he pointed out.

'But which of you knows where the head court will sit? Is it by the mercat cross?' Christie pointed at a squat wooden cross on a mound of earth.

'Under the tree!' spluttered the first urchin. 'The court meets under the tree!' His pleasure at the quickness of his tongue was evident, apparently causing him to elaborate. 'It gathers at nine rings of the bell.'

'Very well. Since you answered first and fullest, the horses will go to your stable.'

Brodie slid from his saddle and handed his reins to the boy.

'But you will get no more than a cut halfpenny,' Christie went on. 'And only when I return.'

A deal done, the boy shrugged and led the horses in the direction of the eastern approach to the marketplace.

The bell began to toll as Brodie and Christie crossed the square, hurrying them – and others – to join those already around the ash tree. A flurry of its drab yellow leaves fell to the ground as if disturbed by the trampling and shuffling of so many feet. The crier nailed the list of ordinances to the tree, ceremoniously timing each blow to coincide with the chimes of the bell. More autumn leaves fluttered down with each strike of his mallet. Christie and Brodie nudged their way among the onlookers. Like a choir taking its lead from the precentor, the crowd quieted only after the bell of Saint James's Church had done so.

The crier made a further announcement in the near silence. 'The lords William of Douglas and John de Coupland; the justices from Lauderdale, Tweeddale and Teviotdale; the justice clerk.'

Heads turned to a slow procession emerging from the arched courtyard of the tolbooth, two storeys tall with a solar and shallow shingle roof.

In contrast to a monastery procession, the youngest of the men – Douglas and de Coupland, who looked not to have yet reached Brodie's age – led the way, clearing a path through the crowd. The justices following behind were at least two score years. Trailing them, at a pace of his own keeping, the clerk was most senior of all. Slight and grey, he struggled with bulky bundles under each arm.

Emerging through the throng, de Coupland arranged the liripipe tail of his hood so that it wrapped around his neck and hung down the front of his doublet. At such a close distance, the splendour of his attire was apparent. His buttoned doublet of blue and yellow was trimmed with gilt-silver and embroidered with images of parrots and fowls. By contrast, Douglas wore a modest dark gown that reached his ankles, decorated only by a heart-shaped badge attached to a gold livery collar. The justices at his heel also dressed soberly, each wearing a vermilion mantle and coif cap. On reaching the tree, all five squeezed behind a folding table and onto a west-facing wooden bench intended for no more than four. Partially screened by branches, the justice clerk spoke briefly to the crier and then scuttled back in the direction of the tolbooth, Brodie guessed to fetch more seating.

The crier again began to circle the tree. 'Hear this! May God reward our most gracious lords, the sovereigns of Scotland and England, for what is publicly proclaimed and expressly granted here today. For they have agreed and assented that trade between these two realms, after an absence of years due to strife and discord, is once again to be permitted.' Seeming to emphasise the significance of the announcement, the crier performed one circuit of the tree in silence.

'God be thanked,' muttered Christie. He held a position staring at his feet.

The crier continued. 'Also by agreement, the coinage of the kingdoms will be equal in value.'

Christie nodded his approval.

'And so...' The crier paused to unravel and read from a scroll. "Since these decrees will bring much prosperity and harmony, the consent and deliverance of the communities is sought for an assessment by inquisitors of the value of all harvest-time lands, goods and sheepherds for taxation and customs."

All around Brodie, onlookers groaned.

The crier went on to announce a series of other measures intended to raise revenue for King David's ransom or extend crown control in some other way. Wool and woolfells would be requisitioned at cost price and resold at a profit, all decisions made by lieutenants during the king's captivity were to be reviewed, justice ayres would be increased in number to inspire terror in delinquents.

'This is approved by the great seals.' He held up the scroll from which he read, flourishing the oversized seals of both kingdoms – each as big as a hand – green for the exchequer of

Scotland, red for the chancery of England. 'God speed you and give you good day.' The crier completed his proclamation with four bows, one in each cardinal direction. Douglas, de Coupland and the justices stood to leave without having uttered a word.

Christie turned away, shaking his head, as the justices departed into the crowd. 'So, I am permitted to sell my hides in Carlisle and Alnwick but the king's cofferer will take for himself whatever surplus I make.'

'Less despair!' The justice clerk stood right there facing Christie, as close as the sea comes to the shore. 'There will also be a revocation of crown wards and lands alienated during the king's minority and captivity – and even the return of some disinherited before his reign began, Christies and Afflecks among them.'

Startled, Christie took half a step backwards, jolting like a skittish colt.

The clerk tugged at his frayed russet robe and doffed his battered kettle-hat. 'True Thomas. Of Ersildoune, some say Ercildoune.' He set his helmet on again. 'You have arrived sooner than I expected.'

Chapter 4

"Then cheer up Scots, cast from you care and sloth,
And pray believe what Thomas says is truth."

Blind Harry, *The Wallace* (c 1477)

21st Day of October, 1357

'You have read the books of Michael Scot, yes?'

Brodie was borne back to another day, when Thomas asked the same question. Then, they were together in the stables at Restenneth, Mariota readying horses for Prior Bernard and Brother Peter; now, he faced Thomas across a broad writing table in the low-lit garret of Roxburgh tolbooth, Christie at his shoulder.

And despite the passage of years, Thomas might not have aged a day.

'The books you asked me to bind and repair?' Brodie sought an answer of sorts: verification that he spoke to the same Thomas as before and not a younger but otherwise identical relative.

'And gave for you to read and make copies – of course those books.' The hiss in his voice, as well as the kettle-hat – which remained on his head still – certainly matched the earlier Thomas.

'You…you did not die in the affray with Cleek?'

Thomas neither shook nor nodded his head but moved it in a way that could have been either or neither.

With some effort, Brodie returned his muddled thoughts to the books. 'The verse in the cover of Physionomia, the illustration that helped lead me to the abbey at Glenluce – were those for me to read?'

'Do you know why I have the name True Thomas, brother?'

He laid his palms flat on the table, bony fingers splayed.

Brodie resisted frustration at Thomas's evasion. 'I have heard it said you foresaw the death of one king and the birth of another.'

'I cannot say or write a word of a lie – that is why. And it is no lie that peace between kingdoms north and south will only endure when lands strewn with dead men's bones are returned to their owners.' Thomas cast his eyes around, examining every dusty corner of the garret. 'Where might it be?' he said, perplexed, though the room was almost entirely empty of possessions.

Brodie and Christie exchanged a look of mutual bemusement.

Thomas began rummaging among the only papers in the room, the same scrolls he had carried to and from the head court sitting, now on the floor behind the writing table. 'No...no...' He tossed aside one, then two more. Finally, he held up a loosely rolled parchment, managing an expression that combined both triumph and defeat. 'The decree revoking alienated lands and wards,' Thomas explained. 'Not all the seals are yet affixed – and so no announcement was made at head court – but many great names are included here.' He laid the scroll on the table and arranged the seals that hung loose on cords into a ragged row.

Brodie and Christie shuffled closer. At such a distance, tufts of white hair were visible sprouting from Thomas's ears and below the neck of his robe. His skin was as rough as a plank.

Moving his finger from left to right, Thomas pointed at selected seals. 'The earls of Mar and Sutherland, Ramsay of Colluthie – soon to be Earl of Fife – Bishop de Landellis of St Andrews...The Steward has yet to append. So too the Earl of March...But these here belong to the sheriff of Fife, the bishops of Glasgow and Brechin, the knights William Livingston and Robert Erskine.' He lingered on a large brown seal picturing an armour-clad figure on horseback, hunting falcon perched on his outstretched arm. 'Others would go even further than revocation to secure a lasting peace.' He rested the seal in his palm and read out the Latin inscription. '"*The seal of Lindsay of Ersildoune and Wauchopedale*" – my own kin since Lord William de Lindsay took those titles from that great prince, David of Huntingdon. And see these other Lindsay seals – Crawford, the Byres, Glenesk. I have made it my business to counsel these great men that lands unjustly acquired from the disinherited should be returned to their owners – for the necessary sakes of peace and justice.'

'And these nobles have given some heed to your counsel?' asked Christie.

'Would you heed an old man who cannot tell a lie?' Thomas smiled. 'It helped that Sir Philip of the Lindsays saw the same truth when Cuthbert of Lindisfarne appeared plainly to him in a vision.'

'And the king too would restore the disinherited,' Brodie declared 'I read it in a letter transcribed by your hand.'

'You read correctly, brother – I also act on his instructions. And already he has given John MacDougall of Lorn and the MacDowells repossession of their lands,' agreed Thomas. 'Though I fear the king's interest lies increasingly in weakening his enemies rather than strengthening the kingdom.' Content to allow a silence, Thomas looked between Brodie and Christie, head cocked like a jackdaw.

One then the other: a gash of sunlight appeared through the window behind Thomas; a breeze twisted up the narrow staircase. Caught in both, a strand of web hanging from the rafters wafted across the table in Brodie's direction.

'In the marketplace you said the lands of the Afflecks and Christies would be among those returned – is that so?'

'Not all the territory once owned but some – four oxgangs of freehold tenure farmed by the Afflecks north of the Broom Well, by Monikie, and all the Finzean lands from the Feugh to the A'an. Lord Lindsay of Glenesk is in agreement, though the grants are not yet confirmed. Receiving the king's seal and the assent of the three estates may take some years. I say again – you are earlier than I expected.' Thomas gathered the seals in both hands, careful not to pull any loose, and put the scroll back on the floor behind his chair.

The cobweb drifted close to Brodie's face. He swatted it away.

'It does not take a prophet to know what you will ask next,' said Thomas, replacing his hands flat on the table.

In his mind, Brodie had formed the question many times, in different ways; uttering it aloud for the first time, to someone who may provide an answer, he found a new way again to present the words, their full meaning at a distance. 'And the

Afflecks – what of them?'

'Some cousins in degrees removed remain alive. No others survived the destitution. Apologies, brother, but you must know it.'

He had anticipated that hearing the truth spoken would cause a disturbance, a swell he had tracked from the horizon finally making landfall. His family was dead. He would never see a face, hear a voice, touch the hand of a mother or a brother. But the truth of it caused no great turbulence. True Thomas, the man who could not tell a lie, had it right: Brodie knew the fate of his family, had known it for as many years as he could remember.

Thomas seemed to guess at Brodie's thoughts. 'But restoring the land will restore the name of your family. There will be no more disgrace attached to the Affleck kin.' He dipped his helmeted head at Christie. 'Fellow, I need not tell you that it will take more than a title deed to restore the Christie name. But reclaiming the land would give some measure of deliverance.'

Christie's eyes were elsewhere.

'I will send word when the time is come.' Thomas jerked upright, causing his kettle-hat to slip forwards on his head. He pushed it back. 'For now, I must prepare a message for the king, to inform him that taxes have been levied at head court.'

'You are to be thanked for your endeavours and should now be left to your business.' Christie bowed. He hitched up his hose as a sign he was readying to leave.

'Wait a moment.' Thomas's behest held Christie still. 'Brother Brodie, your itinerary next takes you north – is that so?'

Brodie was given no time to reply.

'Very well – you should carry my message to the king's council at Scone, which is to be held in the days around the Feast of All Souls. But take this warning with you – it is said that the king has new favourites. You should remind him that you have diligently chronicled his reign since the day he arrived back on our rocky shores.'

Again, Christie made to go. 'I should visit the pelterers' guildsmen,' he said, '…and also have spices to buy…' He left the garret with head low, muttering weak farewells and a vague arrangement to meet Brodie at the mercat cross.

A time later, Brodie also left, the message from Thomas in his grip, a baffling assertion that they would tryst again – but at the non-existent Eildon Tree – in his ear. Outside, a group of children played hoodman blind in the tolbooth courtyard. Brodie steered a way between their darting runs and bold feints. Beyond, the marketplace was busy with traders and visitors, though Christie was not among those who loitered at the mercat cross. Rather than tarry, Brodie opted to visit the only place he knew would gladly receive his confusion. Kneeling on a cold church floor, he would say one prayer for the dead, to shelter the souls of his long-departed family, and another of thanksgiving at the prospect of restoring their name. He followed the street that led south, towards the Church of the Holy Sepulchre on the banks of the Teviot. Before reaching its rounded walls, the sext bell rang at the Franciscan friary a short distance to the east, inviting him there instead. The clouds had lowered and darkened when Brodie emerged from chapel. On leaving the shelter of the friary's high precinct walls, the wind gusted with new vigour on his face and ankles. Gratefully, he recognised that the rhythm of the prayers had at least becalmed the mood of his mind.

Passing by the ash tree – the bench still in place but the table now gone – Brodie had picked out his own piebald hackney in the crowded marketplace before he saw Christie. Closer, both horses came into view, several paces apart. As there was no tether stake nearby, their front legs had been hobbled with a rope. Christie was crouched over a cloth spread with goods just bought. Brodie made out a bundle of nails, a string of lampreys bled from the mouth, small mounds of powdered spices that might have been pepper and nutmeg or mace, along with cinnamon quills and red sugar.

'Did you check that the pepper was not damp and swollen?' Since travelling from town to town, Brodie had come to know many of the wiles used by traders.

'Agnes wanted the spices.' It was the only answer Christie managed before he began packing away his goods. He wrapped the lampreys, secured the powders and sugar in small pouches of their own then bundled all the goods into a sack. 'We should go,' he said.

'You will reach no farther than the wood of Carterhaugh

before nightfall. Would it not be better to allow your horse a full day of rest and leave in the morning?' suggested Brodie. 'There is a place for us at the friary – I have asked the guest master.'

'We would have reached beyond the Ettrick Forest if you had been at the cross earlier.' An anger deepened the creases and darkened the shadows around Christie's eyes.

Brodie felt a flush in his own cheeks. Christie's ill temper brought him more abruptly to what he had to say. 'So, will you reclaim the lands?'

'Neither of us will – you are a churchman who has taken a vow of poverty and I am an outcast who must hide his past even from his wife. The lands will remain with the Lindsays, whatever True Thomas says.'

'Perhaps, but there would be no loss in returning when Ersildoune sends word – to learn what offer is to be made.'

Christie strapped the sack to his horse with a needlessly forceful yank and turned to face Brodie. 'Brother, a clerk for the king knows I am no David Maxwell, as do you, even if I cannot fathom how my past name arrived on both your tongues all at once. Is it more likely that I would lose my head or gain a title if I ever returned to another court of the king?'

Brodie said nothing. He had considered the impossibility of his taking ownership of Affleck land while in holy orders, yet given no thought to Christie's difficulties.

'I should put as much distance as possible between this place and my own – and hope no others know that the tanner David Maxwell is in truth the brother of the beast executed as Christie of the Cleek, the bogle-man whose name uttered by a nursemaid silences every crying child. Whose name I cannot endure spoken by my own wife to my own children.' Christie mounted his horse. 'Rest here if you choose but do so without me alongside your friary bed.'

'Forgive me, I had given no heed to the dangers you might face. Do as you think is right and be assured that I will keep my quiet about your new name.' Brodie unfastened the hobble from his horse's legs. 'You should be thanked. Our account – if such a thing ever existed – is settled. But I beg one final kindness. To be sure I arrive at the king's council in advance of All Souls, I should leave from here rather than return first to Kirkcudbright.

Can I be allowed to ride this horse to Scone and onwards, to deliver Thomas's message?'

'Brother, five merks will buy me a new hackney – my concerns are more costly than simple silver coins.' Christie tried a smile. It remained flat and weary, without sufficient purpose to raise his bearded jowls.

Chapter 5

*"His Majesty began first to touch for the evil.
According to custom, thus: his Majesty sitting
under his state in the banqueting house, the
chirurgeons cause the sick to be brought, or led, up
to the throne, where they kneeling, the King strokes
their faces, or cheeks with both his hands at once."*

John Evelyn, *The Diary of John Evelyn* (1660)

*22nd Day of October, 1357, until the 8th Day of November in the Same
Year*

From singing the invitatory in the darkness of the friary chapel
the next morning until dismissal at nightfall, Brodie observed
the liturgy of the hours completely, the first time he had done
so since King David insisted on properly venerating the holy
cross at the Priory of Lindisfarne.

And during the Office of the Dead, he might even have heard
a whisper of consolation from God.

His heels firm against the flanks of the sturdy piebald, Brodie
reached Scone in the early morning of the Feast of Simon the
Zealot, a full five days before All Souls and ahead even of the
king's harbinger. Since he had no way of knowing precisely when
council would convene, Brodie entrusted Thomas's message to
the abbot at the Augustinian house by the Moot Hill.

With the day lapsing from its beginning to its end, Brodie
drew comfort from his final approach to Restenneth: workaday
familiarity at a distance of enough months to form years.
Pitscandly's looming brow, the churning Fithie River in spate,
the heavenward reach of the church tower. The scents of the

mixed wood and the carse: dry leaves and fallen seed cones, green mosses and brown, mouldering bracken fronds.

But alongside such familiarity, the changes that had occurred took on more prominence, as if caught in their own glint. The trees were taller, the main track broader, more rutted, and the croplands had encroached on grazing ground to the west of the priory. Not only had the fields grown in size, they were also laid out in a new arrangement of strips. Reaching the principal boundary ditch, Brodie saw too that the winter crops had been more neatly cultivated than at any time since the plague.

The shrill yelp of a pig stopped Brodie on the track up the slope to the priory. His horse's hooves silent, between the sobbing calls of a bird, he heard the tiny rustle of brittle leaves falling to the ground.

Then, from the beechwood at Fledmyre, repeated snorts and a shout: noises and a place that tallied with the priory herd pannaging for nuts and mast.

A short way towards the commotion, a huge hog crashed through the ferns to Brodie's right and began rooting around a broad oak. Another followed. Behind both came a call that he recognised: the persistent trill whistle that Fergus resorted to whenever a farm animal failed to heed his instructions. His friend still unseen, Brodie shouted through the branches. 'You would do better herding a shoal of mackerel than those pigs!'

Fergus emerged in parts: ruddy cheeks below eyes straining through branches; body bent to avoid a low bough; a waving arm of acknowledgement.

Although Brodie had called out a quip, Fergus offered nothing playful in return. He pointed at the shallow dell separating them. 'The rains have made it a bog.' He shaped his hand like an arrowhead and aimed it east. 'A hundred strides back the way I have come, the track is firm – it will better suit the horse. Join me and these wretched swine.'

Brodie forded the marsh at the place described – boards had been laid across the soft ground since he last entered the woods – and rounded the dell to join Fergus.

Taking the reins in one hand to dismount, Brodie tried another light remark. 'A one-time soldier of de Lamberton – taking pigs to pannage? How can that be so?'

Again, Fergus resisted. 'Truly, it cheers me to look so closely on the features of an old friend but I will not lose this sour temper until the pigs are returned to their enclosure.'

Remaining in his saddle, Brodie used the horse like a longboard to keep the pigs from straying into the underbrush. Fergus walked up ahead, whistling constantly, rattling a bucket of nuts and swatting his stick at pigs that foraged too long or nibbled each other's tails.

'The prior thinks me no more than a swineherd,' declared Fergus, between closing the sty door and fastening the enclosure gate.

Having matched Fergus's previous silence with one of his own, Brodie was unprepared when his friend finally spoke, and so spluttered a question as a reply. 'Prior Archibald?'

'Which other? Since Lammas, he says I am no longer to work in the fields.'

'But you have harrowed the topsoil to a fine tilth. I saw it for myself.' Even as he spoke, Brodie noticed signs of neglect in the rig: the peascods had not yet been gathered; the broad beans were brown, beginning to blacken.

'The cropland is leased to toun men. The prior would rather collect rent from them than leave harvest in the care of an old man.'

Fergus stopped and bid Brodie do the same by laying a soft hand on his chest. Up close and still, Brodie saw his friend anew, but diminished. Fergus had lost two spans in height and one in width. His outstretched hand trembled; the skin around his eyes folded in layers.

'Brother, it is not just my age that restricts me to the sty and the rig. Alyth has a sickness and needs keeping.' He took his hand away. 'Come – you should see her.'

Stepping through the door of the tofthouse, Fergus's lour lifted in an instant. Plainly surprised, it was as though he had poured a sour brew and tasted sweet perry.

'You are well enough not to need rest?' His question was directed at Alyth's nether end, all that was visible beyond the wattle divider screening off the cooking area.

Brodie caught the odour of an unemptied soil bucket.

'She mostly sleeps,' Fergus added, turning to Brodie.

Alyth half-stood from whatever pot she had been stirring, spoon still in hand, and peered around the screen. 'But look – Brother Brodie!'

If the years had enfeebled Fergus, they had reduced Alyth by many more degrees. No amount of sewing and seamwork could conceal that the same overgown and apron hung from a frame that had long since shed its bulk. The impression from the parts not covered – sunken sockets, cheekbones casting shadows, hands all knuckles – was that her flesh had begun to draw inwards. Even in the favourable glow of the fire, her skin was pale, her scalp visible through thin, patchy hair.

It was only when Alyth fully emerged from behind the screen that she brought the thick, dark crust on the side of her neck into view.

Alyth caught Brodie's stare. She pointed at her own neck. 'This grows while I wither on the bough. That is your thought, yes?'

His actual thought, as his eyes adjusted to the dim, was that the sore – the pattern of various sores – seemed to possess the texture of bark.

He looked from her neck to the dirt floor. He tightened his belt. 'Has it...' Brodie found her gaze once more. 'Have you been treated?'

'A travelling apothecary administered an elm poultice,' said Fergus. 'Your Prior Archibald said a barber-surgeon would attend, though not until the planets are in order, not until Mars has come and gone from Taurus.'

Brodie tried the calculation. 'But...that will not be until Lent, at least.'

'In this year it occurs after Martinmas, according to the word of your prior.'

'But a scrofula such as this should be treated without any delay.'

'It causes no pain,' added Alyth. 'Though does bring weariness. And some fevers.'

'Has it seeped?' asked Brodie.

Alyth put an uncertain hand to her neck, as if the possibility that the sore might rupture had only just occurred to her with Brodie making the suggestion. 'Should it seep?'

Fergus continued on his wife's behalf. 'The apothecary said

the king provides a better remedy than any elm poultice – his royal touch on a coin then worn as an amulet. You scribe for the king – could you make that so, brother? Could you ask for that touch?'

'The king has shown little interest in my scribings since before we left England but…'

'Brother, do not trouble yourself,' interrupted Alyth. 'Such miraculous cures are for God in his mercy alone. I will add pond lily root to the salve – that is more likely to ease the swelling. Offer a word for me when next you pray. There are saints who take a special interest in this curse?' She returned to her pot, bending with difficulty.

'Saint Marcouf of Nantus has healing powers.'

'Then petition him rather than the king. And in return, I will fill your bowl for supper.' She smiled, showing warmth despite her suffering, grateful to be providing hospitality rather than dwelling on her miseries.

Fergus made a move towards the door. 'The fire needs wood. Brother, will you help?'

Brodie responded to the prompt by following his steps.

Alyth called after them 'He will try to persuade…' Some of her words went astray behind the closed door. '…laying on of the king's hands…no attention to his ungodly superstitions…'

Outside, the darkening sky was frayed pink in patches and streaks.

'Brother, there is truth in what Alyth says – I have heard enough vouch for the king's touch to believe it a miraculous cure.' He stopped at the muddy entrance to the woodshed. 'But as much as the touch of a king, she needs the touch of an only daughter. Mariota has not been back since the day she left – and I can no more retrieve her than the first days of winter can follow the last days of spring.' His eyes had a haziness, like grease cooling in a pan. 'Brother, I fear the divine physician will visit Alyth before the barber-surgeon ever does. As well as petitioning the king, can you bring Mariota to her mother?'

Mariota: the name had visited Brodie less frequently with every passing month. The image he held had obscured too. Were her eyes brown or green? Or some combination of both? How did her height compare to his? He tried to judge by using their single embrace as a measuring tool. That day in the forge, had she reached his nose? His chin? As part of a new home in the Isles of Kintyre, she was now likely married, perhaps with children. Only at that thought did he consider, it seemed belatedly, the possibility that she might not even still be living. On leaving Restenneth, she may have eluded the plague, but childbirth – or grief at the loss of any number of infants – could have taken her with almost as much ease.

'Do you know where she is? If she is well?'

Combining gestures of frustration and resignation in one motion, Fergus flung up his arms and then let them fall to his sides. 'I have not travelled farther than Forfar since Alyth's sickness and before that never reached even half the distance to Kintyre.'

He stepped into the woodshed, across a mat of trodden shavings, breathing air that was dense and damp with savours of cut timber.

Brodie lingered, aware that he had yet to respond to Fergus's request to fetch Mariota. He must have taken ten hundred thousand steps since leaving Restenneth and not one of those had led him within reach of her name. A myriad more might take him no closer. And now he asked himself if Mariota was even a name his ears still strained to hear.

Inside the shed, Fergus was bent over, groping for the driest of the logs, rejecting one, throwing another onto a pile behind his feet.

No matter his perplexities about Mariota, Brodie was certain that he could do nothing and go nowhere until he learned how he was next to be deployed by Fordun, or perhaps the king. 'I will go to Aberdeen first, and then do whatever can be done.' Falling into place behind Fergus, he kneeled to gather the firewood.

*

Working with the haste required of a scribe already past the day he should have returned to his patron, Brodie twisted loose the vetches and the peas, cut back the vines and planted out the spring cabbage. He gathered wild crowberries and plucked ripe orchard apples. When the rain came on the fourth day – untroubled by wind, it fell directly and unceasingly from sky to ground – he unbolted the priory door. Intent on ensuring the chapter house and prior's accommodation were fit to receive any lordly guests in need of quarters, he discovered that, despite ailing, Alyth had resolutely maintained their condition. On the tenth day, he slaughtered the largest of the hogs and salted the carcass. Between the tasks, on All Saints and All Souls, they said prayers of obligation, built up the fire and prepared a list of the departed to place before the bare church altar. Even without a dry new log to brighten the room, Fergus's face was as easy to read as the words on the page: by next All Souls, Alyth would likely be added to the list, groaning in purgatory with the rest of her kin.

'A plot of Affleck land is mine, if I choose to take it.' Brodie had found no other occasion to make the announcement and so did it now, as he shovelled his horse's dung into a barrow.

Fergus grunted but paid more attention to fitting the bridle over the piebald's head. 'Affleck land?'

'North of the Broom Well. By Monikie. Four oxgangs of freehold were farmed by the Afflecks.' The prospect still so distant from his grasp, Brodie used Thomas's words rather than search for his own.

Fergus slid two fingers below the noseband to check it was not too tight. He patted the horse's neck and turned to Brodie, head tipped sympathetically to one side. 'And what of the family you lost as a child? Your search was for the farmers not their farmland.'

Brodie returned to his shovel. 'None close survived the destitution, as I knew must be true.' Again, he borrowed from Thomas.

Fergus stood alongside. 'Brother orphan, even if you know such a thing as a certainty, there is still sorrow in hearing it said.'

'But disgrace will no more be attached to the Affleck name if the land is restored,' Brodie added quickly.

'Who told you this?'

'Thomas of Ersildoune.'

'Is he…?' Fergus clutched his jaw and moved it from side to side, a habit that had formed after so many years of aching teeth.

'He is a justice clerk for the king.'

'Then it may be so. But you should not be sure – kings and clerks can change their outlook.'

Brodie's shovel scraped hard ground. Arriving at a conclusion, he stopped and leaned on the handle. 'I am sure of this and this – with the fields leased, you are no longer secure here at Restenneth, and the Affleck land cannot be mine as long as my vows oblige me to contribute all goods and property to the common life. And so, the land should be assigned to you. Fergus the Ward – gallant soldier, loyal watchman, Monikie farmer and freeholder.' Finally finding his own words, Brodie finished with a flourish, like a marketplace conjurer presenting a trick for the scrutiny of the crowd.

Blinking back at Brodie, Fergus played the part of the beguiled onlooker. 'But there is Alyth…the church…I could not manage such a tract.'

'It could be let for rent, just as the fields are here.'

'It would not be permitted.'

'Do not dismiss it so easily.' Brodie planted the shovel in the barrow of dung. 'I have access to laws and statutes made in assembly and issued under the great seal. I will read those for precedent. Fordun has the writings of Aristotle. And Thomas of Aquino. I will ask the chancery clerks how it could be done. Better, I will ask the king himself when I kneel three times and beg for his touch on a medal to hang around Alyth's neck.'

Fergus sniffed. He scanned the stable in all directions until his gaze finally snagged back on Brodie. 'Your offer is kind and do what you will. But I would rather you found a way to make Alyth well again.'

Chapter 6

"Follow thy fair sun, unhappy shadow!
Though thou be black as night,
And she made all of light,
Yet follow thy fair sun, unhappy shadow!"

Thomas Campion, *Follow Thy Fair Sun* (1601)

10th Day of November, 1357, until the 29th Day of April, 1358

Despite the late hour, Fordun worked on in the cathedral library. After collecting and conferring sufficient texts, he had devoted himself to a new pursuit: writing his great national chronicle. He sat at two desks pushed together, the south window at his back. One of the desks was clear of all but his writing materials. Source books were stacked on the other. Straddling both, a copy of Aelred's Genealogia lay open.

Even though it was well after night prayers, Fordun was not alone in the library.

Brodie acknowledged the figure hunched over a desk by the door. 'Brother Peter.' He bowed. Additional care would need to be taken over the words he was about to deliver.

Fordun looked up, pen poised in ink-smudged fingers.

Brodie was struck by the realisation that Fordun wrote with his left rather than right hand. Distracted, he offered no greeting.

'A word for your patron, brother?'

Brodie found his wits. 'Father.' He bowed again, stiffly.

'Have you rested since your return?'

'And prayed devoutly in thanks for my safe passage.'

'Very well. It is late now but there is much work to do from the earliest morning.' He scribbled his quill in the air to indicate that Brodie's scheduled tasks involved writing.

'Not just transcribing Priest John's work – mine also.' Peter sat upright.

'Brother Brodie, your hand is the most able in this library,' Fordun explained. A falter in his otherwise steady stare suggested a mild apology that Brodie was also to be Peter's assistant. 'You will only work when we cannot do so ourselves.'

He had intended to speak truthfully to Fordun: could he be granted an absence to locate a Restenneth Priory farmhand – there would be no lie if he made no mention of gender – at the behest of an old man and his dying wife? Given that his destination was Kintyre, Brodie had a notion of how he might lure Fordun into agreeing to his request. Due to Peter's presence, he moved directly to the inducement. 'Father, you said when I returned yesterday that your intention is to extend your history to include the deeds of Malcolm Canmore and Margaret of Wessex.' He waited for confirmation.

Fordun nodded.

'It occurs to me – Adam de Brechin, the Galloway confessor, told me of great books that provide accounts of the reign of King Malcolm. Books that I believe are not included in your collection.' He waved an upturned hand between the documents on the desk and the floor.

'Go on.'

'The Albanic Duan, recited at the coronation of King Malcolm, and also the scholarly Annals of Tigernach. They are housed in the library at Saddell Abbey. In Kintyre,' he added hesitantly. 'Perhaps I should make copies.'

'I know where to find the Abbey of Saddell,' replied Fordun with some impatience.

'Kintyre!' Brodie wheeled around to see Brother Peter shaking his head disdainfully. 'There is little there other than a boat to Ulster. Archdeacon Barbour will not allow it.'

Brodie turned back to face Fordun. The priest's lingering look contained first a calculation, then recognition of half a truth; trust that Brodie's real purpose involved good works; and, finally, an offer of regret.

Fordun stroked the fiery mark on his cheek. 'Those are worthy sources, just as you advise. But your work for now is here, transcribing in this library rather than any other – this history of mine and Brother Peter's chronicle of the Stewarts.'

'As you wish.' He backed towards the door, past Peter's desk, bending low to conceal what must have been disappointment on his face.

Still shaking his head, Peter loaded his quill with fresh ink and returned to work. 'Could there be other reasons for a journey to Kintyre?' He said it in an undertone, though loud enough to pass through the library.

*

Before the last leaf of the year had fallen, Brodie began transcribing an account of Walter fitz Alan's bravery at the Battle of the Standard. He had finished recounting the crusading deeds of Alan fitz Walter by the time the first bud of the next year appeared.

'Brother Peter's mockeries and miseries can smart like jabs from a scorpion,' observed Fordun. Following another peevish exchange in the library, Peter's sulking steps disappeared from the passage outside into the presbytery beyond. 'But you should remember that a scorpion's sting issues from its arse.'

Brodie grinned. And for a moment, they were boys playing a Hocktide prank.

Fordun laid down one quill and picked up another, dipping it in a pot of red ink. He began colouring a rubric. 'Have you yet received a missive summoning you to scribe for the king?'

Reminded of his apparent loss of royal favour, Brodie's smile sagged.

'King David has held two councils in Edinburgh since the Feast of the Conversion of Saint Paul and is now on the move,' Fordun continued. 'My history should know if he is able to meet the first instalment of his ransom to England's Edward. If you do not scribe for the king, you should do it for me. I will write a letter of appointment for you.'

'What of the transcribing here?'

'Your studious hand deserves a new task. My history can wait. So too can Brother Peter's.' Fordun peered over his nose. 'Archdeacon Barbour cannot enforce arrogant edicts while he is studying canon law and theology in Oxford. If he is not carousing with courtiers and poets, that is.'

Brodie allowed the scoff at Barbour to pass by.

Fordun went on. 'The king is due to convene again within the week, at Perth. Then he will travel elsewhere. It is said he may have business to conduct with Cunningham of Kilmaurs, whose seat is close to where the Inverayr boat sails to the Isles of Kintyre. Perhaps you will find an occasion to visit Saddell Abbey and copy those books that provide valuable accounts of King Malcolm's reign.' His raised brows conveyed words left unsaid.

'I will find and retrieve what is most desirable,' replied Brodie, his thoughts more on Mariota than the Saddell library.

*

Mars came and went from Taurus, and still the barber-surgeon did not attend Alyth; the planet had long since moved into Gemini when Brodie crossed the drawbridge at Restenneth on his way south. Anticipating the absence of surgical treatment, Brodie had filled a pouch with lard from a grass-fed sow and the flesh of a she-ass. No wolf parts were available – even from the backlands' counters – though stealth and silence yielded a slice of dog's liver from the infirmary at the red friary.

But the sight that greeted Brodie was no patient in need of a remedy. Although far from a recovery, Alyth had refused to submit to the worst of her condition. She passed more time awake than asleep. And while her bearing remained mostly slow and deliberate, some movements had sharpened along with the appearance of her bones. He watched the precision with which she tied a new broom, chopped the syboes, swatted a hornet.

Relieved, he shrugged and handed Alyth the pouch. 'The ancients prescribed it. Take it in a broth.'

Alyth responded with instructions of her own, all of them known to Brodie: follow waterways all the distance to Perth – the Dean, Isla, then Tay; travel to St Andrews in daylight and only on roads cleared on both sides to avoid the cruelties of brigands and footpads; fill your costrel with water at every lavatorium; if you must do so due to an absence of nearby churches, request the charity of an honest merchant rather than risk lodging at an inn-house.

Fergus too offered advice, some in conflict with his wife: apply fat and honey to the piebald if it wearies; south of Kilmaurs, east of Turnberry Bay, visit a lesser branch of the Fergussons of Kilkerran to learn Mariota's precise location in Kintyre; a tavern with cloths on the tables – and pipes of Rhenish – will be safe enough for lodgings.

*

Fordun's letter of appointment furnished Brodie with a seat on the clerk's bench at the councils in Perth and St Andrews, followed by a stool and trestle table at the investiture of William Cunningham of Kilmaurs to the earldom of Carrick. Brother Godfrey, one of the senior chancery clerks who scribed during the negotiations in England, welcomed Brodie with a teetering smile and an airy sigh. There was something of an apology about all that the Holyrood Augustinian said and did, Brodie was reminded. No others, King David included, offered even that cursory recognition of his presence.

Brodie wrote of the subject most discussed among the noblemen at repast: Ramsay of Colluthie's elevation to the earldom of Fife, as foretold by True Thomas in the Roxburgh tolbooth garret. He said nothing of the subject most discussed in the kitchens and stable blocks: Queen Joan's departure from the court and request to join the Franciscan nuns. The matter of King David's ransom payment to Edward, it was decreed, would be considered at the Dumbarton assembly in six days. The span of time was insufficient for a crossing to Kintyre but would likely allow him to reach Kilkerran and ask Mariota's mainland kin of her precise dwelling place in the isles. On good tracks, unhindered by heavy rains, it might even be possible to make the journey in five days.

*

Four mornings before the end of April, with the sun rising into as clear a sky as spring permitted, Brodie followed the Carmel Water south from Kilmaurs. Such was the meandering route, he travelled farther east than west – and hardly south at all – towards a bed at Mauchline Priory rather than the Dominican friary at Inverayr as intended. The sky empty of all but spills and splashes of cloud, Brodie made better ground the next day along the well-trodden banks of the Rivers Ayr and Doon, though still he failed to reach the lands of the Fergussons of Kilkerran. On the third morning, mist still hugging the ground, the dew on the tended grass glinting like hoarfrost, he saddled the piebald with a haste that betrayed a growing unease at his slow progress. By this day he should have been turning his rein north and making his way to Dumbarton; instead, he was still heading south. Every step he took felt like two in the wrong direction.

Leaving Crossraguel Abbey, Brodie climbed the gentle slope of Knockbrake, then found the low ground on the far side of the Hill of Kildoon, finally rejoining the Water of Girvan at Carsloe. To avoid the steep banks and thick woodland on the west side, he crossed at a bridge just to the north before resuming southward. Other than a shepherd guiding his flock and foresters entering the distant Glenshalloch Woods, Brodie had seen no-one on the journey. He heard rather than saw the next presence: what sounded like a chorus of mouth music, just as he rounded a loop in the river. Almost immediately, the rhythmic sound faded. Perhaps it had only existed in his imagination, or been carried off on a wayward wind.

Some steps farther along the track, he heard the melody again: this time a lone woman's voice, singing a verse. Then a number of others responding with a chorus. He followed their chants to a place where the trees thinned to form a gaping maw. Beyond, the river bulged broadly from bank to bank. Kneeling by the edge of a stone-strewn bay, a row of ten or twelve women scoured and beat at laundry, each slop and slap of the water matching a lull or lift in the tune.

A heavy woman, the only one standing, broke away from the others and walked towards Brodie. As she neared, Brodie saw that the bulk she carried was not flesh at all, but heaps of laundry on each shoulder. And she was no more than half a woman in age.

She smiled and began laying items of clothing on a holly bush jutting into the sunshine.

'God gives you a good day,' said Brodie.

The girl looked up long enough for Brodie to know she had a coy expression.

'I go to the Fergussons of Kilkerran – how do I take my way there?'

She giggled. 'You seem to know it for yourself – the Fergussons of Kilkerran are at the township of Kilkerran.'

Stifling his impatience, Brodie dismounted. He led the piebald closer to the girl.

When she had found a place in the sun for the last of the wet clothes, the girl began to move restlessly, from one foot to the other, unable to find a place for her arms. Eventually, she crossed one ankle over the other and settled her hands on her hips. Her waist was so slim that her fingers almost met at her navel. She cocked her head. 'And what other names might these Fergussons have?'

'A maiden. Or a wife. Mariota the Ward. Though she might have taken a husband's name. And she is in Kintyre rather than here.' Brodie recognised that he was bumbling, as though he had borrowed some of the washer girl's restiveness.

Her small, dark eyes and thin lips spread wide when she grinned. 'There is a Mary Fergusson. And there was once an Etta. But I know of no Mariota.'

'I take my way to all the Fergussons – to ask their guidance – not any one in particular.'

Her eyes flitted this way and that, like a meadow bird searching for a sturdy perch among buckled stems. 'You will find Kilkerran half a league farther on. The men will be at work in the fields, the women at the river – just as we are.' She jerked her head at her companions.

The men would have been with their crops or beasts every morning since before the calends of April. 'But how can you know it is washing day for the women?'

She pointed at the sun, shading her eyes. 'God has delivered a day that deserves nothing less.'

Brodie measured the distance by the steps of his horse and skill of his eye. By his judgement, the chatter of more washerwomen reached his ears almost exactly half a league downstream, their place marked by sheets hung to dry on the wooden bridge where they worked. Concerned at the safety of the rotting structure, Brodie tethered his horse to a sturdy trunk and stepped warily onto the bridge deck. After four or five steps, he saw the women below, through a void in the boards. 'Dames and damoiselles, have I found my way to the Fergussons of Kilkerran?'

The woman directly under his feet – he could see no others – looked up, straining her head back to see upwards through the gap. 'Who asks?'

'An Augustinian brother.' Given the distorted angle of her head and neck, it was difficult to judge her age. However, Brodie guessed she must be among the senior women and so added an afterthought. 'Who carries a message from a mother and father.'

'Fergusson women are here.' She ducked her head and there was a hushed exchange.

One of the women scrambled from under the bridge. She snatched at a clump of weeds for support. Black laundry soap had stained her arms grey. Emerging onto flat ground, she dried her hands on her apron, front and back, then rolled down her sleeves. Her homespun clothes were stippled with sunlight squeezing between branches and early leaves. She straightened and stared up at Brodie. 'I am Mary Fergusson.'

At whatever angle, it was no Fergusson woman standing in the shadows of the bridge trusses and alder trees; it was Mariota the girl, daughter of Alyth and Fergus the Ward.

Chapter 7

Thomas Campion, *Follow Thy Fair Sun* (1601)

29th Day of April, 1358

In less time than it took to complete a breath, Brodie saw all that he did not recognise as belonging to Mariota: married woman's headdress; drawn brow; sagging shoulders; grey-brown, undyed tunic; wooden shoes; small, tight hands folding over and around one another.

'He is my priest,' she said to the other washerwoman, falsely. 'A priest from the monastery where I lived with my family.'

Even her voice had an unfamiliarity, though Brodie could not place what made it so. Her pitch might have been higher. Or there was a difference in the way she intoned this word or that.

'He was confessor to many parishioners. Even to the brides of Christ at the nunnery of Elcho.' One bewildering lie followed another.

After a pause, the splash of water told Brodie that the washerwomen had returned to work.

'And why is an Angus confessor wandering the lanes of Carrick?' Through the gap in the bridge, Brodie caught the last flicker of a glance upwards from the senior of the women. When he looked back to Mariota, her eyes were wide. The tiniest nod of her head implored Brodie to collaborate with her lies.

'I journey between churches and religious houses preserving

211

some records and composing others. I have come from the Abbey of Crossraguel and had intended making the crossing to Saddell in Kintyre,' said Brodie, remaining mostly truthful.

'Then I hope you are not the helmsman guiding the way because you are travelling in the wrong direction for a sailing to Kintyre – the boat leaves from Inverayr.'

Brodie fiddled with his sleeves, straightening one then the other. 'I…go to other places,' he said feebly. 'Of devotion…'

'If so, you must tie a cloot and say a prayer at the well of Saint Ninian,' interrupted Mariota. 'It is the source of the headstream in the woods behind Kilkerran. The apostle's intervention is said to have cleansed two lepers there. The Culdees built a white stone chapel nearby. And I should make confession to you, the spiritual father of my girlhood, who has most care and cure of my soul. Before Pentecost. When do you leave?' She blurted it all with a new intensity.

Brodie recognised her desperation. 'I leave soon, but should visit such a place.'

Mariota again wiped her hands on her apron, though they must have been dry. 'Very well.' She closed her eyes, gathering herself. 'We will lead you there when the washing is done, yes?' She raised her brows in a gesture that sealed the agreement. With a final nod, she scrambled over the rocks to rejoin the other women.

Unsettled by the unlikely reunion, Brodie remained where he stood, gripping the handrail, staring into the deep growth on the far side of the bridge.

'Do you hear the confession of many or only one?'

He could no longer make out anyone below the boards but guessed the question, and the suspicions it contained, belonged to the senior woman. She could not have deemed from his appearance that he was a lay brother who had no authority to hear confession. Yet her tone carried a confidence in her own judgement.

Unable to frame another near-truth that was likely to satisfy the woman, Brodie lied. 'I have suffered for the faith and will plead for any who has sins to confess.'

*

The women rinsed. Brodie led the piebald to graze on speargrass and flowering cow parsley. A huge bank of grey clouds formed, sliding overhead and shutting out the sun like a grave slab.

The laundry was loaded onto the piebald in two batches, one to the rear of the saddle and one to the fore. The two women who left the track at Ruglen took the stack of garments over the horse's shoulders. Another turned off at Tradunnock with nothing in her hands. The senior woman – older than she had looked in the gloom below the bridge, the skin that was taut when she strained her neck to speak now hung in folds under her chin – along with Mariota and a silent younger girl continued all the way to the woods at Kilkerran. They stopped in a clearing – the tiny, square chapel on the far side – and unloaded the sheets. The senior woman advised that any who attended for confession would likely do so around the eleventh hour. Mariota lingered behind the others to whisper that she would return by evensong.

The inward walls of the chapel had long since been skimmed by a trowel and showed mostly stonework below the tattered plaster. Yet the altar recess, not much broader than Brodie's outstretched arms, had been neatly dusted and brushed. And the altar itself was adorned with a clean fair-linen, embroidered crosses prominent on the front edge and corners.

Brodie sat on the bench along the north wall. It was so narrow that it might have been intended as a shelf rather than a pew. He leaned forward, elbows on his knees, and tried to unpick the confusion of the morning. His search for Mariota had ended, yet come to no conclusions. The woman he had unexpectedly found bore only some resemblance to the girl that had left Restenneth. Even the name she used was no longer the same. What, other than the passing of years, had brought about so much change? Why was she in Carrick rather than Kintyre? Did the wimple she wore on her head signify the status of a wife? Or perhaps a widow?

After noonday prayers at the altar, Brodie broke his fast with oaten loaf. As he ate, he tethered the piebald at a place where it could drink from the burn and feed on soft rushes.

More questions came to Brodie as he followed Mariota's directions deeper into the woods towards Saint Ninian's shrine.

Would another day and night in Carrick leave time for a return to Dumbarton before the king's council convened? How many church decrees would a lay brother breach if he administered the sacrament of confession and penance to the people of Kilkerran? Would the confessional seal, however sham, provide sufficient proximity and seclusion to let him hear just Mariota's voice, allow him to rest a gaze on her altered features?

On the approach to the shrine, grubby rags and garments that had been dipped in the holy water hung from trees and bushes like grotesque hazel and goat willow catkins. Brodie stopped by the well itself – more exactly, it was a spring bubbling from among rocks coated with a mucus of green algae – and petitioned for both Mariota's fate and his own, even throwing a bent tack from his saddle into the water as a votive offering.

But although venerated for his promptness – being the earliest to travel from Rome and Tours to convert the southern Picts – Saint Ninian made no intervention to ensure Mariota attended with any haste: the sunshine dimmed with each successive break in the clouds, the shadows of leafless branches lengthened.

Brodie sat on the chapel doorstep to wait.

Aside from the brief, stop-start shuffle of what he took to be a tree squirrel or a blackbird in the undergrowth, there were no sounds of approach until the sun tilted its light upwards, away from the woodland floor towards the canopy, just catching the ridge of the chapel's western gable.

A branch snapped; leaves rustled under feet. 'Brother…' Mariota said it with a hesitancy that almost reduced the greeting to a question. She emerged through the shrubs to Brodie's left.

He stood up, smoothing down his tunic.

'Others might come,' she said.

'Mariota…' He moved towards her. 'You know I cannot hear confession of your sins or those of others.'

'We should go inside.' Head bowed, she walked past him into the chapel.

They went to sit along the north wall but, unable to position themselves comfortably on the narrow pew, moved to the floor.

'Apologies for my lies at the river.' Chin low, Mariota cast only her eyes upwards.

Brodie nodded his acceptance of her remorse. 'Of course.'

'You appeared like a sprite from the deep,' she explained with a small smile. 'I was contriving a reason to see you alone – those words were the first words that came to my mouth. Though others arrived in my thoughts.'

She hesitated, folding her hands – red and blistered, Brodie noticed – as she had at the river.

'Seeing you on the bridge, in your robes, made me think it – I am in need of a churchman, though not a priest or confessor.'

'Go on,' he said, bemused.

'As a scribe, you know the church laws – that is so, is it not?'

'I am no theologian but I know the canons of the apostles. And most later decretals.'

Mariota folded her arms across her chest. 'And what protections do they offer for those who are treated cruelly?'

An ire roused in Brodie. 'Who is treated cruelly?'

Mariota ignored his question and repeated her own. 'Are there protections?'

'A transgressor of church laws might be put to the whip, or required to make offerings. Or face other punishments.'

'Cruelty is not grounds for an annulment of marriage?'

Brodie's ire re-formed as exasperation. He stood. 'Tell me – are you the sufferer of this cruelty? Or Mary? Young Isabel?'

'Brodie, sit back down.' Mariota tugged lightly on his sleeve. 'What do you know about obtaining an annulment?'

Brodie retook his place on the floor, legs crossed in reflection of Mariota's pose. He controlled a sigh. 'A priest would know better, but I can say that judgements of separation are mostly delivered when it is shown that an earlier betrothal has been promised.'

'But other grounds exist?' A quickening in her eye movements betrayed the arrival of disappointment.

'There are other impediments – nonage, affinity, servile status – but marriage is a sacrament and should not be dissolved while a man and wife remain alive.'

'I have heard it said that force and fear is also an impediment.'

'Only if it prevents the original consent from being freely exchanged. Mariota, if I am to give my advice, you will have to tell me more about this marriage. The crueldoer is your husband, yes?'

Her head drooped. She nodded over and over, like a splintered bough bobbing in a gust.

'What form does his cruelty take?'

'It is not only his cruelty – also his mother's. He uses an open hand. Hers is always closed. They will say it is for railing or chiding or scolding. Or because I have used a rough hand to comb his hair. Or worn a furred hood.' She shrugged. 'More likely it is because my seed has clotted and my womb is cold. God be praised, the girls suffer little.'

Brodie leaned back.

Mariota might have seen some instability in his expression because she took his hand in hers, as though he were the one in need of comfort. He anticipated a stroke of her thumb – as she had done in the forge at Restenneth – but none came. Instead, she squeezed his fingers, her palms rough and damp.

'The bishop's court can show mercy in cases of excessive cruelty.' Brodie did not say it, but he was far from sure the court would consider that the treatment described by Mariota amounted to excessive cruelty. 'But the process is burdensome. It would involve a journey, perhaps some distance…'

'Whithorn,' interrupted Mariota. 'The consistory court is in Whithorn, I have learned as much.'

'You could not go alone. Footing it would take four days. Through backwoods and blindways visited by outlaws. You would need to ride in the company of others – witnesses prepared to support your testimony, if you know of such fain and faithful souls.'

She shrugged, as if to suggest that may, but also may not, be possible. 'What of the proceedings?'

'They are in the manner of Daniel questioning the elders. The factions, along with their witnesses and any proctors, attest before a commissary, who examines the testimonies and proclaims a judgement. But presenting a libel is costly. Could you meet that?'

She looked at the ground. 'My hopes are ill-founded – is that the truth?'

With less hesitation than he expected of himself, and all the ease of a secular, Brodie reached for her free hand. 'I am no consistory clerk, or proctor, but I have come to know a justice clerk of renown. I will ask him your question and return with an answer.' Only at the thought of True Thomas was Brodie reminded of the changes in his own fortunes, all of which he had intended making known to Mariota: the abandonment of the priory, his work for Fordun and the king, the discovery of his parents' fate and the promised restoration of Affleck lands. 'Your father may soon come to possess lands that will earn an income – that could meet the cost of a libel.'

Mariota raised her eyes. 'The church is granting him land as reward for his service?'

'His loyalty is due to be rewarded.' Despite not being a complete answer, the words were true enough. Saying them reminded Brodie of another truth. 'Mariota, your mother has a sickness.'

She let go of his hands. 'A sickness? Is it baneful?'

'She has a scrofula. You might know it as the king's evil.'

'I know of scrofula.'

If Mariota knew of scrofula, there was no need for Brodie to describe its consequences. Without the need for the words he had rehearsed, Brodie regarded her attentively in the thin grey light of the chapel. The sight that met him was not the picture that, one distant day on the banks of the Fithie, he had promised to draw for Fergus. Those many years before, she had been on the cusp of beauty; now he saw the shadow of it passing by.

'Could you find a way to visit your mother?'

'In seven years of marriage – to a husband who prefers I use Mary of Nazareth's name, on account of her being both bountiful and chaste – I have yet to be given leave to journey north or east of Carrick. The dead will rise before I receive dispensation to travel to Restenneth.' Mariota went to tuck loose hair below her wimple, though none was showing. Standing, she yanked down her sleeves so they reached beyond her wrists. 'I must go.'

Off balance because one leg was numb from sitting in a cramped position, Brodie stood unsteadily and followed Mariota out of the chapel. At the opening and closing of the door, a dozen finches rose from the branches of a sapling. They twisted and veered, only flying off when they all faced directly into the breeze. A larger bird clattered unseen in the treetops.

'You should leave,' said Mariota. 'If you would rather not hear the confessions of the Kilkerran women, that is. Does enough light remain to reach lodgings?'

Bats rather than birds would be in flight by the time Brodie reached Crossraguel. 'I can find a sheltered place.'

'Do all you can for my mother, Brother Brodie.'

'If the left hand is adversity, the right is prosperity.' The attempt at reassurance sounded as glib from Brodie's mouth as it had seemed sage when uttered by Fordun across a desk in the Saint Machar library. 'I mean to say, I will do all I can for you. And your family. Be sure of it.'

Mariota turned her head away. 'Perhaps better that I do not hope for overmuch.'

'I will return.' He put a hand over the crucifix around his neck. 'You have my oath.'

'Then I pray your solemn word is good.'

Mariota went westways into the woods. Brodie saddled the piebald and travelled north. Above, clouds the colour of sweet whey ambled across a near-black sky.

Chapter 8

*"It is called the Slough of Despond; for still, as
the sinner is awakened about his lost condition,
there arise in his soul many fears and doubts,
and discouraging apprehensions, which all of
them get together, and settle in this place: and
this is the reason of the badness of this ground."*

John Bunyan, *The Pilgrim's Progress* (1684)

April, 1358, until Summer, 1361

Brodie wrote for Fordun and Brother Peter: transcribing their
chronicles and putting down accounts of the king's assemblies.
He read for Fergus and Mariota: statutes and decretals that
described how to reassign land and dissolve lovelorn marriages.

His writings from council and parliament testified to a king
who had successfully made payment of the first instalment of his
ransom to Edward – despite returning late to Dumbarton,
Brodie had been among the first to know it would happen – but
at considerable expense to the community of the realm. Taxes
of six pennies were exacted at a meeting of the estates in the
month of the November, only to be further raised following a
miserly exchequer audit five months later. Yet, in spite of his
difficulties collecting sufficient monies for the second
instalment, the king took the road to London for the Feast of
Saint Thomas Becket, a generous retinue in his company, at a
cost of a thousand merks. And he returned north with an offer
of revised terms: Edward of England would forgo further
ransom payments but only if the kingship passed to him or his
heirs should David remain childless, a greater likelihood since

Queen Joan's estrangement and exile from court. The proposition provoked such a clamour – led by Robert the Steward who, as heir presumptive, anticipated the loss of his succession to the throne – that the king was forced to wield the ceremonial mace at the Scone parliament of October in the year 1359.

The king that Brodie first met on the sands at Inverbervie had a new kind of slyness about him.

Brodie's readings had revealed much too, though little of it gave reason to be hopeful about the legal causes of Fergus and Mariota. As long as Brodie wore the habit, any Affleck land he inherited would pass directly to the Restenneth Augustinians and their nominal superior, Prior Archibald. By custom and decree, any attempt to transfer title by quitclaim would be considered theft from the church. The land could only become the property of Fergus if his name rather than Brodie's was confirmed in deeds of title under the seal of Lindsay of Glenesk. And, as far as Brodie could judge, Mariota was more likely to obtain a marriage annulment if her husband – he conjured an image of him as a short, swag-bellied brute – was struck by leprosy or a madness than on the grounds of the cruelty she had described.

But despite failing to put the law to use on behalf of Fergus or Mariota, Brodie remained bound to his solemn pledge. If he could not find persuasive precedent in statutes and decrees, he would turn directly to their authors for answers: the clerks of episcopacy, consistory and chancery. Perhaps also the justice clerk of renown he had described to Mariota. With good fortune, he would one day soon seek the counsel of Thomas of Ersildoune.

Chapter 9

"My little dripping pen travels
Across the plain of shining books,
Without ceasing for the wealth of the great –
Whence my hand is weary with writing."

Poem ascribed to Columcille the Scribe (c 6th century)

7th Day of May, 1361

> *"The tumult at Scone was founded upon the*
> *granting, by our lord king David, of the earldom of*
> *Moray to the High Steward of England, Henry de*
> *Grosmont – to wit Duke of Lancaster, Knight of*
> *the Garter, crusader among the Prussians and*
> *holder of lesser titles – which great men from all*
> *parts of Scotland complained was damaging and*
> *dangerous to the sovereignty of the kingdom."*

'My Brother Brodie – how could the king's doings be
dangerous to his own realm?' Rather than await an answer,
Brother Godfrey resumed reading aloud from Brodie's writings.

> *"In this year of 1359, the ambassadors Robert*
> *Erskine and Norman Leslie returned bounteous*
> *from the Apostolic See, with papal bulls granting*
> *David, King of Scotland, a tenth of the income and*
> *rents of the whole church to assist with payment of*
> *the ransom due to the king of England. The*
> *clergymen made a strong stand against these*
> *directions. Their response was expressly given: the*

Sitting on a stool in the chaplain's court at Saint Machar's Cathedral, in the light of a sun some few hours risen but not yet beyond the height of the wall to the bishop's garden, Brother Godfrey flicked through the papers in his hands. A basin of cloudy water and a sodden towel were on a second stool. Brodie stood behind, razor in hand, renewing the chancery clerk's tonsure. He had hoped that the common lave would provide an opportunity to seek Godfrey's learned counsel on matters of law.

But the clerk had questions of his own to ask. He pointed at another page. 'And here you describe a squabble over the purchase of Italian silks and Flemish jewellery from a king's deposit secured at Stirling Castle, as set down in the ledger of the clerk of the wardrobe.' He sighed. 'A rift with the church, whispers about the royal purse – why would you write such seditions?'

Brodie guided the razor with short, close strokes. 'I put down only what others utter in assembly.'

'But brother...' Such was Godfrey's vexation, he ran short of words. 'If those utterances provoked treason – would you put them down still?'

Brodie almost spluttered a laugh. 'Be assured, I am no abettor of treason.' He dabbed the blade around the rim of Godfrey's tonsure. 'Where did you get these accounts?'

Ignoring the question, Godfrey flushed. Against pale skin, through fair, shorn hair, the redness rose to where Brodie's fingers gripped his scalp. 'The kingdom is not so far from rebellion,' he offered.

'Those made to contribute more taxes to the exchequer and others whose land is transferred to royal favourites such as Lord Henry maintain that wiser government and fairer lordship would allow no cause for rebellion.' Brodie said it mostly to measure the current dimensions of Godfrey's temper, which he remembered as short but shallow from their travels in England.

Godfrey's shoulder flinched, though he kept his head still under the blade in Brodie's hand. 'Strong men are needed in Moray. And Mar. Better the ways of men such as Lord Henry de Grosmont than the lawlessness of the Steward and his unruly bastard sons. You must know it, brother – they design to bend the king to their will. And they interfere with the revenues of the church.'

'I know it,' said Brodie, yielding to sincerity. He wrung out the towel and wiped Brother Godfrey's pate. 'Your tonsure is done.'

Godfrey stood, handing over the papers, which consisted of passages from the accounts Brodie had produced for Fordun's history, written in a familiar hand. Brodie took his place on the stool. 'These belong to Priest John of Fordun. How have they arrived in your possession?'

'Words that describe the king, belong to the king. And are available to his scribes,' Godfrey added quickly. He drew a palm across Brodie's scalp. 'Have you not shaven within the past three weeks as prescribed?'

Brodie paid no heed to his diversion. 'I am a scribe of the king – do the words not belong to me?'

Godfrey wetted Brodie's crown. 'You once scribed for the king – no longer.'

It had never been put so plainly to Brodie. 'Is that so?'

'Just so. Before, as now, your writings displease him.' Godfrey began shaving Brodie's tonsure, his fingers moving quickly.

'But…how could that be?' The razor nicked Brodie above his ear. He winced, though the slight pain sharpened his thoughts. 'The king showed no displeasure with the volume that described events leading to his captivity and the great mortality that followed.'

'And after that time?'

'After then I wrote of many things – the abandonment of my own priory, the rituals of the flagellant brothers, my journeys with Priest John – none of them insolent towards the king.' A dribble of watery blood ran down Brodie's cheek and dripped on his lap. 'He described my hand as fair,' Brodie recalled.

'It was what you did not write that caused him displeasure.' Godfrey rubbed Brodie's crown and mopped the trickle of blood with the damp towel. He moved from behind the stool so that he stood in front of Brodie. His eyes fluttered nervously into a heavy blink.

'Your accounts of the negotiations in England were…' He searched for the word. 'Lacking.'

'Lacking?'

'You wrote nothing of the king's pilgrimage with sixteen horsemen to Saint Thomas's tomb at Canterbury in the year of his release. Or how he distributed pennies to the crowds and gifted alms at the cathedral church. And you said nothing of his successes in the Smithfield tilt yard while the kings of both England and France looked on.'

'That is why I have lost his favour? Because I made no mention of his charitable giving and knightly tilts?' Brodie weighed it up with a shake of his head.

'There were other omissions — his veneration of the feasts of Luke, Matthew and Michael; King Edward's esteem for his counsel, even enlarging the castle at Windsor on account of his urgings; his hawking with the prince...'

'Did the Aberdeen cathedral scribe Peter Fenton supply these copies?' Brodie waved the papers in his hand.

'That is not your concern.' Godfrey snatched them back without answering, though his shifting expression revealed that Brodie had arrived at the truth. 'If you — and your patron, Priest John of Fordun — would rather not be associated with those who hatch plots, write your every word with care, at today's council and on each day that follows.'

Attending council in the gloomy great hall of the bishop's palace — makeshift red deal timbers, slung low over their heads, had yet to be replaced by vaulted stonework — Brodie carefully noted the appointment of the shire's sheriff and confirmation of the rights of the burgh's Carmelite friars. With exactitude, he followed the wording of the king's announcement that insufficient monies had been raised to meet the next instalment of the ransom due to Edward. Uncertain how to document the council discussions about the four-fold increase in the annual cost of the royal household, as gleaned from the exchequer rolls by the Steward, Brodie left his pen in the inkpot. Later, alone in the library, he scratched in the margin the figures from this year and last.

Chapter 10

*"From caterans and robbers, from wolves and
evil creatures, Lord deliver us."*

Prayer from *The Litany of Dunkeld* (c 14th century)

18th Day of July, 1361

Guided by the Mead Moon, we lift the flocks, herds and
plenishings from the slopes of Cnoc Chalmac, the fields at
Tornahaish and the barns all around Corgarff. Day is closer than
night when we cross the bridge at the Luib and approach the
walls of the stronghold west of Corgarff.

The men of Clann Donnchaidh have obtained their spoil,
three score and ten head of stock. Now I claim mine: the bended
knee of the cowering community.

'Friends and fellows of Corgarff.' I shout it in the direction of
the huddle of torches where the castle palisade spans the gate.
'Open the gate and welcome your new lord.'

'Gilbert Glencairnie is our lord,' a bold one shouts back. The
helm and habergeon he wears shimmer in the reflected light of
his torch.

'Glencairnie has resigned his claim.' At the prick of my blade.
'Under heritable title, his lands and offices are mine.' Lest the
occupants look more closely at defying my lordship, I direct the
Donnchaidh men to fetch the cart containing the remains of the
last destroyed shieling. The roof timbers are uncommonly
sturdy and will burn well. The men begin to stack them at the
main castle gate. Once more, I offer my truce. 'Come – receive
the protection of Alexander Stewart, lord of estates in
Badenoch and Moray.'

'What protection is it when you destroy our homes and plunder our cattle?' It is the one with the latten armour again, though now his boldness is giving way to insolence.

'Better a letter of protection from Alexander Stewart, sure to put the mightiest of foes to flight, than one issued under the seal of Glencairnie. This feeble palisade he raised for your defence would burn at the first spark of a flint.' I ride close to the men building the woodpile. And I see fear fixed on the faces of those who peer down from the palisade. 'A lord must receive payment from his tenants.'

One of the Donnchaidh produces a coal from its wrapping of sage leaves. He blows on a tinder nest; small flames form.

There is no need for harsh threats: the fiery perils that will result from resistance are clear. After some little time, the people of Corgarff begin to issue from the postern at the side of the main gate. The bold, insolent one is among the first to emerge. Mac Anndra, the leader of the Donnchaidh – expert in equal measures with a sword in his hand or goshawk on his arm – orders each Corgarff man to discard his weapons, even hidden knives and cleavers.

I call the bold one towards me. 'Who is it that hesitates to enter into my peace?'

He removes his helm and holds it in the crook of his arm. He bows but does not bend his knee. 'I am the constable here, instructed to defend these walls.'

'Kneel before your liege lord, vassal.'

The force of my words takes him to his knees. The tinder fire behind his back spits into life. He glances at it over his shoulder. Comprehending that he has erred in withholding his allegiance to my dominion, he bends his head. 'I seek only to be faithful in my duty,' he says.

'Then you will deliver the keys of this place to my lap.'

More sticks are added to the tinder fire; its smoke passes his nostrils and he is cowed. 'As you bid, my lord, though I beg that this stronghold comes to no harm.'

'What is your name, constable?'

'Murdoch, my lord.' His head is turned a degree to the side, as though he is anxious to observe if the tinder is being put to the woodpile but dares not avert his eyes from mine. 'Murdoch of the Christies.'

Christie: the loathsome swarm detested by my father, Lord Robert the Steward, due to their association with the capture of my mother.

In response to hearing a name so offensive to virtuous ears, I spur straight at him, so that he sways and stumbles to avoid a trampling. 'Remove your mail vest,' I tell him.

'Sire...' There is the pleading of a milksop concealed in the single word.

Without the need for an instruction, four Donnchaidh men are on the Christie insect. They remove his habergeon, toss it aside and look to me for further orders. 'And his other garments,' I say. He struggles, but not with conviction, until he is stripped. The men hold him down, one at each limb. 'Secure the postern,' I call out to mac Anndra. He replies that the place has not yet emptied of the old and the slow. 'Secure the doorway,' I repeat.

I dismount and swipe at the naked creature: three, four times with my blade. Blood rushes from his swelling gut.

He clenches his teeth in an attempt to withhold the cries, but cannot remain silent; there is a sputter from behind his gums, a rattle in his throat.

At my command, a stake is taken from the woodpile and driven into the ground beside the quivering figure. I bend over him. 'Do other Christies dwell in this colony?'

'None other...only me,' he says, though I can read the lie in the frantic movements of his eyes. I pull him up onto his knees, seize a flap of skin from among his injuries and fix it to the post with a nail.

He grunts, teeth still gritted, and sprays spit.

'Light the woodpile,' I say to the Donnchaidh men at the gate. Turning back to the constable, leaning close to his ear, I add: 'In my generosity, I lend you a choice. As the defender of these walls, you may extinguish the flames – I give you leave to do so. Life, limb and all goods within the castle will be unscathed, though you will lose your skin. Or, you may keep your skin – but the Christie insects, and others, who remain inside will burn while the red cock crows.'

He pleads, bawls, grasps at the dirt.

Eventually, he crawls towards the burning gate. Amid roars that reach beyond this dawn to the one just past and the one still to come, his skin uncoils like yarn from a spool.

Chapter 11

"*A fairer pair were never seen*
To meet beneath the hawthorn green."

Sir Walter Scott, *The Lay of the Last Minstrel* (1805)

June, 1361, until the 30th Day of July in the Same Year

In losing the king's favour, apparently beyond reprieve, Brodie gained a new purpose. Alongside loyally scribing for Fordun, he would finally and without falter commit to easing the ailments and afflictions suffered by the Wards.

Despite arousing royal displeasure with his writings, Brodie determined first to request the king's touch for the evil tormenting Alyth, though the approach he made when the court baited at Inverbervie on the journey south from Aberdeen received short shrift. The knight Sir Roger Mortimer, who came to the entrance of the royal tent, dismissed Brodie's petition with a sneer, saying that the king's head ached overmuch for him to attend to such trifles.

Reassured by Brother Godfrey's assertion that King David was likely to hold all discourses until the next Ember fasts in private chamber – due to the magnates being close to rebellion and ransom negotiations with Edward in a delicate condition – Brodie turned off the coastal track at Montrose, leaving behind the belligerence of the royal court for the benevolence of Fergus and Alyth's tofthouse. He greeted Alyth with a bagful of curative meats from the red friary – if not a coin touched by the king – though found that her condition had deteriorated sorely. Since she required near constant rest and repose due to greatly swollen ankles and a melancholic temperament, Brodie remained only the number of days it took to repair winter damage to the tofthouse.

Clouds of all shapes and shades were high and low in the late morning sky when he directed the piebald away from the priory, towards a mysterious old greybeard whose last words to Brodie promised they would next meet below a tree that was held to exist only in rhyme and song.

*

The sky that rose up behind Black Hill, filled the heavens and fell back below Eildon's triple peak might have followed Brodie all the distance and days from Restenneth; the evening cloud forms remained as haphazard as good fortune or ill, possessing all the gravity and lightness of foreboding and promise.

Brodie asked at habitations along the Tweed for Thomas of Ersildoune's whereabouts but learned only of one who resembled his description: an old scribe named Thomas Learmont who occupied a tower house near to Earlston, which Brodie had passed on the road to Eildon. The inhabitants advised that on a good evening Learmont might be found watching the sun settle at a favoured waterside location nearby. One set of directions followed another, leading Brodie east and south of Melrose Abbey, past the brae where a long dead thief or other wrongdoer still twisted on a rope, attracting flies.

Brodie took the higher of two roads out of the town, passing the ruins of a fort once under the sway of Rome. Initially paved, the track became rutted and broken as the slope steepened. The flagstones disappeared altogether when Brodie entered a neat but dense oakwood. Through the wood, he came to a crude tollgate, the barrier formed by a fallen trunk with most but not all branches removed.

'Gatekeeper?' Brodie waited and watched for the window or door of the tollbooth shack to swing open.

No reply came back.

Brodie dismounted and guided the piebald around the barrier, past its jutting branches. Beginning to doubt the reliability of the directions he had been given, Brodie followed the trail only a short way, stopping at its highest point. To his right, Eildon's three peaks were arrayed like a row of knuckles, the sun coming to rest in a cleft between the two most prominent points. On the left, the trail gave way sharply to form a steep-sided gully. He hobbled the piebald and shuffled towards the edge, peering over. At the foot, white water swirled in a pool. Such was the foaming turbulence, Brodie could not immediately tell whether the burn flowed east or west. Due to the tilt of the surrounding land, it appeared to run directly below the ridge where he stood into the cold depths of the hills, though nature would surely expect it to travel in the opposite direction. He went farther along the track to reach a place where he could better judge the burn's course, seeing then that it scurried down from the hills, as it surely must.

Brodie scanned the landscape: greensward on one bank, a fringe of mountain ash and downy birch on the other.

And a glint of steel directly ahead, where the burn kinked to the north.

Brodie strained his eyes, but saw only shades of light and dark on a shallow grass embankment.

As he wavered between continuing his search for Learmont and ending it before dusk fell, the piebald scratched at the ground and tossed its head. Brodie returned to its side and loosened the hobble. 'At ease, at ease.' He led the horse to thick undergrowth, where it munched hungrily on flowering lion's teeth. Brodie clapped its ribs. 'If there must be time for you to eat, then there is time enough for me to return before you have filled your gut.'

Brodie scrambled down the scarp and made his way along the near-treeless south bank, wading through tall grasses. Before he could be sure what had caught the light of the sun, a voice called out indistinctly. There was movement from below a squat, tangled hawthorn tree, white bloom still as thick as snow despite the nearness of August. A man sat up, resting on his elbows. He tipped back his steel kettle hat. True Thomas, Thomas the Rhymer and now Thomas Learmont of Earlston, the old man below the hawthorn tree answered to any number of names, though Brodie knew him by yet another: Thomas of Ersildoune.

'Lie alongside me, Brother Brodie Affleck,' said Thomas. 'Beneath the boughs of the Eildon Tree.'

During Brodie's hesitation, a cuckoo called out from among the branches of the tree: asking, answering.

Brodie moved under the hawthorn's awning, the heavy scent of its blossom at once as sweet as honey and as foul as the odour of the tannery or parchmenter's cruck. 'I was assured no such tree as this existed,' he said.

'You can see it for yourself.' Thomas waved loosely at the hawthorn overhead.

'I have questions about your foretellings,' continued Brodie.

'Come lie here,' repeated Thomas.

'There is an urgency.' Brodie remained standing.

Thomas patted the grass by his side. 'I will answer your questions with as much urgency as a fading summer sun allows.' He pointed towards the hills. 'See how it turns that great stone silver?'

Brodie turned. Just below the summit of the middle peak, a large column of rock – tall and pale but otherwise unremarkable – gleamed in the sinking sunlight.

'It can only be observed during the mid-months, from precisely this place,' added Thomas. 'And even then only for the moments before the sun falls.'

True enough, the tall stone faded to grey as quickly as it had brightened, and then became indiscernible from the surrounding rock and scree.

Seemingly satisfied by having witnessed the spectacle, Thomas lay back, hands behind his head. With some reluctance, Brodie sat on the ground next to him. No new lines seemed to have formed on Thomas's face, Brodie noticed, though the old man might have drained of some colour. White hairs now outnumbered grey, his face and hands were pale, his eyes peered through a fog.

'Your questions – what do they concern?' asked Thomas.

'Return of the Affleck lands,' Brodie replied. 'And another matter.'

'The lands will soon be disclaimed by Lord Lindsay of Glenesk – the seals of the nobles are affixed and the deeds await only the king's consent and confirmation, though you will know that the assemblies where he could make such a decree are nowadays few in number, given the many troubles that beset his realm.'

'I am grateful for your efforts but fear I will not be permitted to reclaim the land.'

Thomas considered Brodie by way of a sidewards gaze. 'Is it the king you fear? He makes many poor judgements, sadly, but would not refuse confirmation, whatever your minor folly. Lord Lindsay sits at the king's right hand – his wishes will not be overturned.'

Brodie withheld an answer while he paused for thought.

'Did you cross him? Perhaps when the moon was full? The arrowhead lodged in his skull makes him severe at such times.'

Putting aside the likelihood that the July moon had been full when Brodie was refused an audience at Inverbervie, Thomas's assessment, for once, was wrong. 'It is not the king's confirmation that causes me concern – at least, I had not considered so until now – it is the habit around my shoulders…' He tugged at the front of his tunic. 'This and my vows prevent me from inheriting, or even transferring, title…'

'Ha!' interrupted Thomas. 'Before you say more, describe the other matter that troubles you.' He sat upright, back against the tree trunk, eager as a jay.

'A farmhand – she is treated cruelly by her husband and seeks a separation. I had hoped your knowledge of the consistory courts would find a way to annul…'

'I see it now!' Again, Thomas interrupted. He clapped his hands in excitement. 'As clear as the waters of the Bogle Burn that flow past our feet.' His cheeks briefly flushed the colour of spindle fruit.

'See what?'

He laughed gleefully. 'You are struck by the dart of love!'

'I seek to do good works…'

'But have found no way to turn the law towards your affections?'

'It is the truth that I have read nothing gainful in a multitude of statutes and ordinances and decretals.'

Thomas stood, hands on his bony hips. 'Have you read the constitutions of your own Augustinian order?'

'Why would I read constitutions that concern themselves with the administration of monasteries and observance of the divine office?'

'Because they contain much more besides.' Thomas stretched his back. 'Such as the ways the religious enter and leave a community.'

In the moments that Brodie took to assess Thomas's meaning, the boughs of the hawthorn tree groaned in the slightest of dusk's passing breezes.

Brodie stood to face the old man, uncertain that he had comprehended Thomas's true meaning. 'Do you advise me to consider leaving my community? If so, I would wander in apostasy.'

'If there was no profession, there can be no apostasy. Were you expressly professed on serving a year of probation?'

'My profession was tacit – I made my mark with the sign of the cross, my tunic was blessed. Prior Archibald said it more than once – a lay brother's profession need not be solemnized in the manner of a priest.'

'At what age did you enter the priory, brother?'

'I have an indenture document that says it was six.'

'Then read the constitution for Augustinians issued by the pontiff Benedict in the year 1339. While you read, remind yourself – if there is no apostasy, there need be no abandonment of your faith, or excommunication from the church, and you may inherit or transfer the Broom Well lands as you choose.'

Brodie recognised some of the possibilities in Thomas's unlikely proposal, but could see no advantage for Mariota. 'What of the marriage annulment? How would casting off my habit bring that to a conclusion?'

'Go to her as a secular and find out for yourself.'

Brodie was about to ask for an explanation but Thomas had entered a reverie.

The old man began to circle the tree, in the same direction as the sun travels across the sky. He moved stiffly, in what might have been a dance of fits and starts, merrily chanting what might have been a tuneless song.

"A nut-shell seem a gilded barge,
A shieling seem a palace large,
And youth seem age, and age seem youth:
All was delusion, nought was truth."

Chapter 12

"We, who support your order, ask you to consider what honour there is for you in keeping this boy, a boy so clearly underage in the year of probation, a boy who is illiterate or nearly so."

A father's letter to the bishop of Worcester (1327)

30th Day of July, 1361, until the 11th Day of August in the Same Year

"Since lesser ages are lacking in holy heart and incapable of glorying in the fellowship of brothers, admission to the monastery below the age of seven is forbidden, with profession not to take place until 15 years. And since evil can make a plank out of a splinter, profession following one year of probation must be express and not tacit. Profession should be made in like ways for those who entered the monastery in tender youth before this present year, one thousand three hundred and thirty nine years after the Bountiful Virgin gave birth. Before God and his saints, the novice will swear stability, moral conversion and obedience to the Rule of Augustine and promise to live without goods and in chastity until death."

The book of Augustinian ordinances in the generously shelved library at Melrose Abbey described it more plainly than Thomas had managed: youthful admission to the order should in no circumstances take place under seven years; and, if any doubt of age existed for brothers who already walked the cloisters, profession must be expressly rather than tacitly made at some time beyond fifteen years. Yet the indenture of novitiate Brodie discovered on taking up the Restenneth librarian's duties gave him an age of only six on admission as an oblate boy. And since Archibald's election as prior in the months following the reforming Augustinian constitution of 1339, nothing had been done to ensure all brethren were expressly professed.

By deed and law, Brodie could request release from his religious vows without attracting the odour of apostasy.

*

On a return journey that involved crossing many thresholds – uplands to lowlands, July into August, the southern shore of the Scottish Sea to the northern, the boundary of the earldoms of Fife and Angus – Brodie considered his own possible move from one existence to another, examining his faith alongside the rule that bound him to the Order of Saint Augustine.

The opening commandment did not require scrutiny: Brodie had no cause to doubt that his chief purpose was to love God before all else, even if the divine voice had remained mostly silent since Restenneth's abandonment, and perhaps as long ago as Master Robert's killing.

But he regarded the precepts that followed with less certainty. Despite sharing a guest bed at the red friary in Aberdeen, he could hardly be said to live harmoniously with a community of brothers in oneness of mind and heart. And, due to travelling from place to place as a cathedral scribe, he owed more obedience to Fordun than his own house superior, Prior Archibald. Aside from his indenture document and the scraps of riddle he hid in his sheath, Brodie took only common property and called nothing his own; yet the very reason he now considered seeking dispensation from his vows was to inherit four oxgangs of farmland at Monikie. His chastity, too, had been sullied: as a youth, accepting hand gifts from Black Agnes, in adulthood, by fixing a wanton eye on Mariota.

Fittingly, Brodie concluded his self-examination on the feast day of Dominic, zealous inquisitor of heretics and apostates. Uncertain how to explain his decision to Fergus and Alyth, he hurried directly to Aberdeen, passing by Restenneth.

Light rain followed a day of bright sunshine, causing scents of the soil to rise from the canons' gardens and dovecot green in the cathedral precincts. In the still evening, Brodie passed along the deserted chanonry as silently as a draw-latch in the night, stopping when he arrived at Fordun's manse. He dropped to his knees as the door opened. 'Priest John, my thoughts give me reason to make confession – will you hear it?'

'To your feet, Brother Brodie – I am not your lord.'

Brodie did as instructed.

Fordun sighed wearily. 'Is there such an urgency for this confession?'

'I would rather say it now.'

'Then you can do so here rather than in the oratory, to spare me putting on my boots.'

Fordun waved Brodie inside, to a stool by the fire, and shovelled some coals on the dark embers. He slid a chair from below a desk at the other side of the hearth and sat opposite Brodie. 'So, make your confession.'

Brodie took a breath and said it quickly. 'I am to put myself at the mercy of Bishop de Kininmund and request a release from my vows.'

Fordun sat back. He let out a small, surprised grunt.

'Though I fear such a notion may be sinful,' added Brodie.

'Explain yourself.'

Brodie had prepared for this moment. 'I have made the discovery that I was never truly professed as a religious – an indenture says I was six on admission to the priory at Restenneth.'

Fordun appeared less than convinced. 'Go on.'

'The Augustinian constitution from the year 1339 forbids childhood admissions,' continued Brodie. 'And I was never expressly professed after that date.'

'Profession could be made tomorrow.'

Brodie turned his gaze on the flickering fire. 'You should be told this – my family was accused of treachery during the wars and disinherited. Some of their lands can be restored but only if I leave my order and join the secular world. Believe me that any restoration would not be for vanity or pride or riches – the title would be transferred to a priory gateman who has been spurned by the church, along with his dying wife. My chief interest lies in restoring the good name of the Afflecks.'

'Is that so? And does anyone, other than you, say it is possible?'

'One does – True Thomas.'

A burning coal hissed and flared.

Fordun regarded Brodie. 'Then it must be so – the old man cannot tell a lie.' He ran his fingers through straggly hair that sprouted from his temples and the nape of his neck. 'Brother Brodie, if there was no land to inherit, would you then make express profession?'

Brodie found himself copying Fordun's combing action, as though his will was so near spent he had to borrow an amount from elsewhere. He stopped himself, scratching his crown instead. 'Dwelling in God's tent has provided me with all the necessities of life but I have come to question the loyalty I attach to my vows. Forgive me.' He bowed. 'I commend this confession to your prayers and my soul to Christ.'

'Lift your chin off the floor, brother.' As Fordun stood, he took a chewing stick from a bundle crammed into a small tin on his desk. He paced from one wall to the other, first using the stick to pick at his back teeth then flipping it round and gnawing the other end. When it became frayed, he threw the stick in the fire. 'You have served me well as a scribe and I can see that your intentions are founded in the observance of good works.' He took a sip of liquid from a pot on the desk, rinsed his mouth and spat noisily in the fireplace, away from the flames. 'Bishop de Kininmund was a friend of Prior Archibald and would have you brought back to obedience. And so, rather than you petitioning the Bishop of Aberdeen, I will petition the Supreme Pontiff, if my influence still stretches to the papal enclave since being confined so closely to my desk to write the history of a nation.' He smiled to himself.

Brimming with relief at receiving an encouragement when he had anticipated a chastisement, Brodie spluttered a reply. 'There is no need...Though, of course, if you would...'

Fordun waved away his fawning gratitude.

Recovering, Brodie recognised more that might prove beneficial in Fordun's words. He held his hands out to warm them at the fire, though they were hardly cold. 'You said Prior

Archibald *was* a friend of de Kininmund – is he no longer the bishop's man?'

Fordun arched his brows in surprise. 'I had thought you must know it – Prior Archibald joined a pilgrimage to Compostela, since the Feast of Saint James fell on the Christian Sabbath for the first time in eleven years, though he and the others were followed by a terrible sickness on their return through Galicia and France. Brother Brodie, the plague is back. Your Prior Archibald is dead.'

Chapter 13

"Why get ye your dispensations
to have it more easie?
Certes either it seemeth
that yee be unperfect,
or he that made it so hard,
that ye may not hold it."

Jacke Upland, unknown author (c 1400)

5th Day of October, 1361, until the 18th Day of April, 1362

A papal reply came with unexpected haste and in the hands of a nuncio rather than any common sent legate. The reason given for the nuncio's hurry was his eagerness to commemorate the feast day of Regulus in the land where the saint brought the remains of the blessed Apostle Andrew, though he later admitted to Fordun he had sought out an urgent commission to northernmost Christendom in the hope it would provide him with a refuge from the plague. Other than the veneration of Saint Regulus, the foremost purpose of Archdeacon Bertrand Cariti's legation was to oversee collection of the tenth of church income requested by King David. He made no direct accusations at ecclesiastical council but his careful words carried a warning that all church monies should go towards the king's ransom, none into the king's deposit.

The archdeacon carried out his common business at the mercat cross on the first day in October that no rain fell. Brodie gathered to learn his fate alongside the others: the white friars granted the collection of first fruits of void benefices; the canon of Saint Nicholas defended against envious whisperings; the burgess and his wife permitted to remain married despite being related in the fourth degree of kindred; the Dominicans denounced as heretics and ordered to be delivered up; the collector excommunicated for laying unlawful hands on church rents.

Archdeacon Cariti read on. "... To the lay brother with the name Brodie, who was received as an oblate orphan by the Augustinians at Restenneth but never truly professed, his confessor shall give him penance and absolution, and dispense and commute his religious vows until the day of death..."

The short sequence of words took Brodie from the beginning of his life to the end, offered to deliver him from the comforts and constraints of the religious world to the uncertainties and possibilities of the secular.

*

Expecting the papal process to take at least until the next year, and doubtful about its eventual outcome, Brodie had made little attempt to ready himself for secular life. And so, in the weeks that followed the announcement of his dispensation, he entered a kind of limbo, not of the infants or the patriarchs but of the still living, who awaited the opening of worldly rather than heavenly gates.

Brodie kept his bed at the red friary, but only for a limited time. The friar learned of the papal decision – from an unknown mouth – the day after the announcement. At evening collation, he declared that Brodie was restricted to the same three days' hospitality granted to any mariner in port or Hanseatic trader. Shunned by the brethren for two of those days, he left on the third with the promise of a place by Fordun's hearth. The cathedral clergy received him less severely, allowing him to pray by their sides and eat in the chaplains' court, provided that he closely guarded his mouth and eyes. Although Brodie had a notion of simply taking up a hoe and subsisting on whatever harvest he could eke from Fergus's rig, Fordun refused to perform the rite of absolution and dispensation until a more dependable solution was found. All the time, Brodie continued to pull an Augustinian tunic over his head, eat with a common

241

spoon, render his praise and share the sufferings of Christ.

An agreement was finally reached a week before the end of October. Fordun had firstly put it to the bishop that it would be necessary to retain Brodie as a secular scribe if his own national history and Brother Peter's chronicle were to be completed within the appointed time. However, Peter refused to allow a single penny to leave the treasury and find its way into Brodie's palm, whatever benefits it would bring. With Peter threatening to appeal against the papal dispensation and even seek Brodie's excommunication, Fordun proposed an alternative arrangement. Rather than a payment from the cathedral, Brodie would receive lodgings, a ladleful of every sack of victual and a small portion of Fordun's Philorth prebend in return for continuing to provide scribal services to all the canons, including Brother Peter. Seeing the personal advantages, Peter reluctantly agreed. And since Prior Archibald could not object from his burial chamber, the pact was sealed.

Closer to none than sext, when the church was at its most empty, Fordun led Brodie to the towering cathedral altar and ordered him to kneel. The priest began to read from Deuteronomy. "If you make a vow to the Lord your God, do not be slow to keep it. He will require it of you, and it will be counted against you as sin. But if you refrain from making a vow, it will not be counted against you as sin." He made the sign of the cross on Brodie's bowed head. "By the absolute power and authority of the sovereign pontiff, who holds the place of Christ throughout the church, you are dispensed from all vows. Once living to the supreme Lord alone, you are called back to human life. In the name of God and the most Holy Trinity, I absolve   you   from   your   sins   and   every   bond   of excommunication. May the Father of Mercies give you pardon and peace. Amen."

*

Brodie received his first penny-fee from Fordun on Martinmas, in advance of work carried out. During visits to burgh traders in the days that followed, a clothier provided him with a modest black mantle of the cheapest fustian – for wearing in the cathedral – in exchange for five shillings and two of the new silver groats. An upholder who dealt in clothes previously worn by others sold him a buttoned cote, grey hose and a felt hat at half the cost.

Back at Fordun's manse, Brodie neatly laid his cowl, surplice and both Augustinian tunics on a stool by his bed, his cloistered thoughts held in their folds.

*

Having a different purpose in mind for his Candlemas payment, Brodie kept the strings of his purse drawn tight until an opportunity arose to saddle the piebald.

After the Paschal Vigil and Mass, the whole of the cathedral chapter and congregation prepared for the feasting and prayers that would take place during the Octave of Easter. And they did so with the zeal of those who feared divine vengeance. Some said it openly, others whispered it: the plague had yet to travel north, but for how long?

Amid the early morning ado, Brodie entered the cathedral by the rear entrance that led directly into the passage beyond the presbytery. Moving with stealth, he stepped into the treasury, where he placed his folded religious garb on Brother Peter's chair. Next, he went to the library, slipping from the pages of an old breviary the accounts of consistory court proceedings he had copied for Mariota.

First, he would deliver the tonic of goat's milk and spotted lungwort he had bought at the Netherkirkgate for Alyth. Then, he would hie the piebald farther south – even if it meant breathing air corrupted by the plague – until he reached Mariota's door. He would go to her as a secular, just as True Thomas had advised, endowed with the expertise of a proctor and sufficient savings to pay her libel fee in the consistory court.

Chapter 14

*"Time with the season: only she doth carry
June in her eyes, in her heart January."*

Thomas Carew, *The Spring* (1640)

18th Day of April, 1362, until the 5th Day of May, 1363

The mainways and byways mostly carried northbound travellers seeking an escape from the plague. Against that tide, Brodie moved south at an easy pace. But while pestilential winds blew beyond Dundee and Perth, nothing fiercer than a seaborne gust touched Brodie's cheeks. And with each day that he drew closer to Restenneth, the breeze stilled; through a growth of stubble, the sun warmed his crown.

Turning onto the carse west of the priory, Brodie faced directly into the still rising sun. Such was the glare, he reached for his hood, groping behind his neck before arriving at the realisation that he no longer wore a monastic cowl. Muttering a cheerful rebuke at his own foolishness, he shaded his eyes instead with the felt hat from his saddlebag.

Even from that distance, he could see that the drawbridge was closed, an unusual safeguard since the abandonment of the priory.

Brodie dismounted to lead the piebald across an area of marshland, returning to the saddle when he reached firm ground. He shifted his attention to the watchtower. No smoke twisted up from Fergus's brazier and there were no signs of movement from behind the half-open shutters. Then, almost alongside the palisade, he heard the thud of footsteps on wooden flooring.

Brodie shouted up. 'You would shut the gate to a loyal friend? Do you spill pitch and tar on the heads of your enemies?'

In place of an answer, he heard the jolt of the rope drum beginning to turn. The drawbridge dropped with a thud.

The watchtower door opened just as Brodie reached the gatehouse. 'I would shut the gate to the loyal friend who shows himself to be a breaker of oaths – you never returned to Kilkerran, despite your promise.'

Dazed at the sight of Mariota rather than Fergus before him, Brodie managed only a shake of his head.

'A promise made four years ago.'

'But the delay...' Brodie slid clumsily off the piebald. 'The delay was because I could not be of any help to you, until now.' He began rummaging in his saddlebag and pulled out a sheaf of documents. 'Look, I have consistory court papers that will help your cause and...' He wagged his purse in the space between them. 'And money to pay your libel fee.'

Mariota took the reins of the piebald and turned away.

'Mariota...' Brodie ran in front of her. He slackened the strings of his purse and emptied his savings at her feet. The coins clattered to the ground, rolling in different directions across the uneven, stony surface. 'They are yours. To fund your annulment. I saved them. On your behalf.'

Mariota's stiff expression softened. 'Your intention was kind but I have no need of your coins.' She brushed past him.

Brodie called after her as he scrambled to pick up the coins. 'But the proceedings against your husband...I have knowledge of the courts now.' Only then, Brodie had a thought that unsettled him almost as much as Mariota's anger. 'Is your husband here, at Restenneth, with you?'

'My husband is dead – taken by the plague.' She swivelled round. 'And do not ask another word about it or, God forgive me, I might say an unkindness about him.'

Brodie followed her to the stables but said nothing. He loosened the leather girth and lifted off the saddle while she removed the bridle. Still in silence, Mariota brushed the piebald with a rough cloth; he went to fetch water in a pail. When he returned from the river, Mariota was checking the piebald's hooves for stones.

She finally spoke as they followed the short path from the stables to the tofthouse. 'Your clothes,' she said simply. 'Have they changed because of efforts to make your solemn word good?'

'And much more besides.'

Brodie pleaded his case, but not as a proctor acting for Mariota before the consistory court as he had expected. Instead, he petitioned the Wards – Alyth barely awake on a truckle bed, father and daughter sharing a stool, all in a swelter around a fireplace crammed with logs – to reach a judgement on the worth of the efforts he had made on their behalf.

In support of his petition: Brodie had sought the king's touch on a coin for Alyth, despite expecting, and receiving, a wrathful response; on each visit to Restenneth, he had carried a treatment for scrofula, including the tonic from the Netherkirkgate apothecary – he handed it to Mary, pale and slender, who took it through to the cooking area; there had been delays in acquiring title to the Affleck lands, though they were not of his making and would soon be overcome; in anticipation of the inheritance, Brodie had forsaken the religious life to allow a transfer of the lands to Fergus; throughout all the years, he had continued to consult records on ways to obtain an annulment of marriage; and, just three days ago, he had set out for Kilkerran with a determination to find Mariota an escape from her husband.

He glanced uneasily at Mariota due to mentioning her dead husband but could discern no reaction in her eyes.

Fergus whistled softly through his teeth. 'Brother...' he started, forgetting already that Brodie no longer used the fraternal form of address. 'You say it as though you owe an apology, yet you have paid more debts to us than would be possible to count on a tally stick. And for that, you have our everlasting gratitude.' His voice carried a rasp from his throat, like an unoiled chain rattling around a slow-moving cog.

Mariota sat quietly, looking between Brodie and her father. Alyth was falling restlessly into a slumber.

Isabel emerged from behind the wattle screen that divided the toft, carrying beakers on a tray.

The first he had seen of her in many years, Brodie was distracted by the similarity she bore to her mother. He studied her as she crossed the room. She must already have passed the age at which the plague took Mey. And in those years, she had grown taller and broader than her mother, with hair a shade darker, a length longer, features more distinct. 'It contains henbane, sire,' she explained, handing him a drink, her deference suggesting she had few memories of Brodie. 'But only the smallest quantity – to help her find peace in her sleep.' She gestured with the tray in her hands towards her grandmother.

Fergus took a sip of the brew and again shook his head. 'No longer wearing the habit...' He waved his flat palm in an up-and-down motion at Brodie's outfit. 'I cannot conceive it. Will you not face a punishment?'

'The dispensation was granted by the Holy Father and the ceremony conducted by Priest John – there can be no excommunication.'

'But your earthly and heavenly places were secure?'

'Secure, but at the end of Prior Archibald's rod and Brother Peter's harping tongue.' He drank from the beaker, the burnt, bitter taste of the henbane immediately apparent. 'I fear my devotion began to wither the day Master Robert was slain. And God allows only those with ever attentive ears to hear his voice.' He shrugged. 'It is as God wills it. I have the patronage and guidance of Priest John now. Travelling from one place to the next at his behest, I have become familiar with secular ways so there is little to become accustomed to, other than buying and owning meagre possessions.' He tugged at the thighs of his hose, grinning. 'And the tightness of these wretched garments.'

'Perhaps you will sustain yourself by collecting a tenth part of the Monikie lands that you say are due to pass to my father,' said Mariota, mischievous for the first time since Brodie's arrival, though her smile still contained reservations.

Fergus downed his brew. 'We should prepare to eat,' he declared. 'The Easter week is a single, joyful day – did your teachings not tell you that was so Brodie?'

'The great Lord's day,' agreed Brodie.

'Do we have meat?' Fergus called through to Mary and Isabel, who had both returned to the cooking area.

Isabel's head appeared around the screen. 'Only the last of the coney. Along with kale and cabbage.' She looked back to the cooking area. Brodie heard Mary talking quietly to her sister, though he could not make out any words. Isabel reappeared.

'And some of the new leeks. They could be put in a pot with almond milk.'

'Then we shall have an Easter feast of coney and almond milk, to receive our guest with honour.' Fergus stood and patted Brodie on the shoulder. With small, near-silent mutterings, he shuffled through to the cooking area.

The messes of green pottage served up were ample enough, though the portions dwindled with each luncheon: a broth of grey peas on Friday and thin, white oats mixed with curds and cream on Saturday.

Concerned about providing the Wards with Easter plenty – and equally eager to regain Mariota's favour – Brodie left for Forfar after scraping the last of the cream from his bowl.

Since it was the seventh day of Easter Week, no burgh traders had hinged open their shutters. However, they had adhered less strictly to other ordinances: the drain through the main street was blocked and overflowing, letting off a stench; broken barrels, crates and other debris had not been cleared in a week at least; the fire tubs contained as much rotting vegetable peel as water to douse flames. Brodie left the main street to the dogs and rats and followed a new odour, dull and sweet, north along the Fleshergate. Close to the head riggs, he heard the rhythmic thwack of a heavy blade. A dozen steps on, a butcher came into view, wielding a cleaver in his back yard.

Brodie bought the best meats available from the butcher's depleted stock, a leg of pork – overpriced by at least a penny – and six larks. He handed more of the money originally put aside for Mariota's libel fee through the open door of a victualler on East Wynd, receiving a loaf of white bread and basket of sweetmeats in return.

After presenting the purchases to a yet more grateful Fergus, Brodie went directly to the priory buildings – no longer maintained by Alyth in a condition suitable to receive guests – and swept out the chapel. With dusk concealing further layers of dust, he placed candles on the sills, decorated the bare altar with the standing cross from the tofthouse and invited the Wards to take part in an Easter vigil.

Brodie led the observance, though not in the manner of a priest directing his parishioners; they sat together among the pews closest to the unfinished nave, all their ears hearing the readings from the lectionary, all their voices chanting the Alleluia. At noon the following day, they gathered around a table, broke the white loaf – despite it not being divinely blessed – and shared their feast. Afterwards, they rested body and mind, avoiding any affairs or work that might hinder repose or worship.

Brodie completed Alyth's tasks in the priory following the Easter celebrations, diligently scouring the buildings that any guests would visit to eat, sleep and meet – the refectory, prior's quarters and chapter house – before cleaning the unseen rooms, admittedly with a degree less vigour. All that time and before, Mariota and Isabel tended the rig – protecting the sweetest celery from the first frosts, the gooseberry bushes from late chills – while Mary restored the garth with new plantings of parsley and summer savory.

In the days of May that led towards Ascension Thursday, Brodie returned his broom and cloth to the storeroom and, at Mariota's request, retrieved the rusting hand plough from the byre.

'Broken,' he said. Holding up the plough, he indicated to Mariota that the mouldboard had come loose from the frame.

'Can you make the repairs?'

Brodie examined the damage. 'It might mean a visit to a smith...'

'Ploughing would have to be finished by Whitsun.'

They both looked across the grassland that Mariota intended to cultivate, towards the bend in the river, their shadows cast back in the direction of the stables. Rather than respond directly to Mariota, Brodie voiced a disquiet. 'The church is harsh with those who breach its rules – we should seek permission to plough from the mother house at Jedburgh.' He fiddled with the plough irons rather than search out Mariota's gaze.

'The church is harsh with those who serve it loyally for many years,' Mariota snapped back. She sighed quietly, through her nose. 'Brodie, the land is no longer of use to the church – the brethren are long gone, as you know well, few others visit, even the goats that grazed on the grasses have left.'

'All you say is true, but an ecclesiastical court might reach a less merciful verdict.'

Mariota turned to face him. 'Brodie, my father can no longer scrape an existence and the yield from the rig is not sufficient since I arrived with Isabel and Mary. Your offer of title to your family's lands deserves our earnest gratitude but until the transfer is made we must find another way to put bread on the table.'

The signs of privation were there to see: most of the crops in the rig had been replanted by Mariota due to previous neglect; dampness seeped into the toft through threadbare turf and wattle; the sheets from Alyth's bed had been so often soiled that the stains remained even after washing.

'But I can put bread on your table. I said as much to your father some years ago and it is a promise I will keep. The money I earn from scribing is enough to meet your needs as well as mine.' Brodie considered placing a reassuring hand on her elbow or shoulder but the thought involved a calculation: could he hold the plough in one hand while he did so or would he have to lay it on the ground, carefully enough not to cause further breakages? And how would she react to his touch? He shuffled the plough between his hands. The moment lapsed.

'You are kind, Brodie. A breaker of oaths – but surely a kind one.' She combined a light tone with a young girl's smile; together, Brodie judged – relief taking the place of awkwardness – they amounted to an offer of forgiveness.

*

The mouldboard firmly affixed, the ploughing at Restenneth complete, Brodie returned to Aberdeen. In the months that followed, he earned three further term day fees from Fordun. The fourth payment due, he sat alone in the Saint Machar library, watching through the south window as a late morning gloom descended. And just as he could not know whether the storm began with the thickening of the clouds or the grumble of thunder from afar, or which was the first drop of rain to fall, he was unable to locate precisely when he happened on a decision. It might have been the day in September that the dispatch box arrived in Aberdeen in advance of the first full parliament for almost two years, Lindsay of Glenesk's brief disclaim of four oxgangs of land by the Broom Well – along with royal confirmation – among the documents contained within. Or the day in December that Fordun regretfully announced he neared completion of his great history and would no longer need Brodie's assistance. Perhaps the week in midwinter that Alyth died – itself a kindness of sorts – and was then buried below cold, hard turf. Or back when Brodie tilled the first furrow of Restenneth soil and Mariota rewarded him with a bannock and coulter wedge of cheese before streeking the recently repaired plough with new ale.

All of those days or none, his resolve was now firm.

The following springtide, he wrote his final entry for Fordun, an account of the conspiracy devised by disloyal magnates – Robert the Steward along with the earls Douglas and March – and thwarted soon after by lieges of the king mustered from the four corners. As a postscript to the document, Brodie added a message of indebtedness to Fordun for his generosity and begged that the priest accept a gift of turbot bought from the market.

They set off together the morning after a supper of flatfish in syrup, shared at Fordun's insistence and skillfully poached by his hand. Fordun's destination was the bishop of St Andrews' manor of Inchmurdoch in Fife, where the rebellious Steward and his sons would publicly swear fealty afresh to David prior to a grand ceremony to wed the king to his second wife, Margaret of Logie. No longer concerned with the king's affairs, Brodie rode alongside only as far as Restenneth. Once there, he would make a public declaration of his own.

Chapter 15

"What is better than gold? Jasper. What is
better than jasper? Wisdom. What is better than
wisdom? Woman. And what is better than a
good woman? Nothing."

Geoffrey Chaucer, *The Canterbury Tales* (1387-1400)

5th Day of May, 1363

'Hear these words!' Brodie stood with his back to the door of the Restenneth church porch, clutching a scroll in each hand. His audience watched from among the weeds and rubble of the half-built nave: Mary and Fergus sitting on a stone bench from the church, Mariota and Isabel leaning against the low south wall. A stormcock took its cue from the expectant hush, calling impatiently from above the church rooftop, as raucous as a ratchet.

At the bird call, Brodie instinctively looked north-east, beyond Pitscandly, for the approach of rain clouds, though none came; the sun bored through a high haze.

'I have here...' He held up the scroll in his left hand, 'the rightful inheritance of the Afflecks of Monikie, unjustly deprived of their holding on account of obediently serving their liege lords, even if history has made known the errant ways of those Umfraville lords.'

Mary clapped softly and let out a small exclamation of triumph.

Brodie resumed, pulling down the flaps of his cap to partially cover his face, as though wearing a mummer's mask. He affected the tones of a performer playing the role of Misfortune at a guild pageant. 'But, sire...damoiselles...' He doffed his cap at each of them in turn. 'That did not settle the fate of these troubled lands. No sooner had they had been restored than they were designated for new owners.'

Fergus jeered in response to Brodie's low, luckless tone.

'But despair not friends because this tale has a joyful ending – the lands at Monikie were destined for worthy ownership.' He paused for effect then flourished the scroll above his head. 'Do any in the crowd know of the Wards of Restenneth so that I might present them with these deeds?'

Amid the applause, Mariota called out. 'We are the Ward family but who is the player that makes this promise? Behind that mask you could as well be a fool as a prince.' She moved towards him and went to lift the flaps of his cap.

Brodie pushed the cap back himself. 'I will show you more than my face. Here, read my name on this parchment.' He unrolled the scroll in his right hand and held it flat against the church door, one hand at the top, the other at the bottom.

'If I could read…'

'You can read well enough,' encouraged Brodie.

Mariota peered closely at the document on the door. 'That seems to be my name.' She pointed at the text. 'And that might be yours,' she glanced up at Brodie before straightening. 'But I can read no more.'

'Then let me.' Brodie took the scroll from the door and read aloud, losing his gamesome tone. "In the face of this church, I Brodie Affleck offer four oxgangs at the Broom Well, for you to dig, work and take profit as surety against a solemn pledge." He raised his eyes from the page to regard first Fergus, then Mariota. 'Mariota of the Wards, I pledge thee my troth, as a husband does to a wife.' He let go of the bottom of the parchment, allowing it to spring back into a tight scroll. 'Do you consent?'

Chapter 16

"Come live with me and be my love,
And we will all the pleasures prove,
That hills and valleys, dales and fields,
Or woods or steepy mountain yields."

Christopher Marlowe, *The Passionate Shepherd to His Love*
(c 1588)

7th Day of May, 1363, until the 4th Day of June in the Same Year

Brodie asked the same question at the porch of the church for three consecutive Sundays and on the holy days of Ascension and Pentecost, Mariota his audience on each occasion.

On the fourth Sunday, which followed the second term day of the year, the land and property at the Broom Well passed into Ward hands.

Fergus insisted that they all remain at Restenneth to greet Priest John of Fordun, who arrived two days after the Feast of Corpus Christi, and then make the move from one home to the next with fitting ceremony.

And so, on the fourth morning of June, Brodie nailed the banns to the Restenneth church door and then set about weaving a garland of foxgloves and field flowers. Mary and Isabel scattered almond-scented bridewort in the porch and chapel.

As no objections or accusations had been made in the weeks since Brodie first stepped on the porch to proclaim the banns, he returned for a final time to the church door, now opposite Mariota, with Priest John facing the audience. Brodie placed the garland over Mariota's head, a band of wound rushes on her finger. Hands joined, they exchanged consent.

'To this, I too pledge my troth.'

'By the faith of my body, I will.'

'By these oaths, as is the law and custom of the holy church,' said Priest John. 'I betroth you in licit marriage as a man and a wife.'

*

On trussing-bed and chaff-filled mat in the roof space of the Broom Well farmstead, between sheets and blankets brought from the priory linen press, Mariota fixed him in a fastness. Crimson with the blush of modesty, she gripped him slight but tight inside her, as fingertips clutch a narrow ledge. The unstableness came and went, hands and lips moving with a restraint that would wake no others.

They curled on their sides, loosely facing one another, Mariota's head on Brodie's shoulder, tucked under his chin. Brodie marked the time it took for her to drift into sleep by finding places where her skin wrapped tightly around her bones. He brushed hair back from her brow, traced her spine, ribs, knuckles and the jutting angles of her shoulders, encircled her wrist between his thumb and middle finger.

In sleep, Mariota turned onto her other side.

Her back to him, Brodie strapped an arm over her shoulder, across her breastbone, as firm as a harness.

She twitched a leg, sighed.

Up so close, in the darkness, Brodie could see no more than blurred twists of her hair. He closed his eyes.

Mariota's breathing settled back into a rhythm, the tiny, frosty breaths she cast on his forearm carrying no more force than the slow beat of a songbird's wing.

Book V

"About this time, there was apprehended and taken, for a most abominable and cruel abuse, a brigand who haunted and dwelt, with his whole family and household, out of all men's company, in a place of Angus called the Fiend's Den. This mischievous man had an execrable fashion, to take all young men and children, that either he could steal quietly, or take away by any other means, without the knowledge of the people, and bring them home and eat them. And the more young they were, he held, the more tender and the greater delicate."

Robert Lindsay, *The Historie and Cronicles of Scotland* (c 1579)

Chapter 1

"A! Fredome is a noble thing!
Fredome mays man to haiff liking;
Fredome all solace to man giffis,
He levys at ese that freely levys!"

John Barbour, *The Brus* (c 1375)

Summer, 1363, until the 20th Day of July, 1370

Brodie hoarded the passing days, weeks and months as husband of Mariota and secular freeman, like a moneylender greedily counting and re-counting his pennies, shillings and merks.

But between sweet conjugal embraces, shared pleasures and Fergus's fireside tales, they laboured hard on the farm.

Brodie harvested timber, rebuilt the barn and repaired the roof of the farmstead. With the last of Brodie's earnings, Mariota stocked the farm: swine, geese and pullets for the yard, a cow in the byre. Mary and Isabel prepared the croplands around Scotfaulds and Fallaws – abandoned during the first outbreak of plague and since fallen into decay – sowing two great fields, leaving one fallow. Fergus shared the ploughman's duties with Brodie and spent his other days in the Downie woods, training coppice stools from the stumps of felled hornbeam and constructing enclosures to protect saplings from browsing beasts.

Together they endured the barley blight in their second year and shared the abundance of their third and fifth harvests, then later the bountiful wheat yield in the summer of 1370.

'Manuring only the wheat crop brought great rewards at the market in Dundee,' Brodie called out to Mariota as he crossed the trickling waterfall at Holemill. He took the right fork in the track, the cart juddering sharply on the more heavily rutted surface. 'There was no change in the price of the other winter crops, yet each bushel of wheat sold for two shillings more than last year. How could you know so much about such matters?'

Mariota waited until he drew alongside. She leaned on her rake, hand high on the handle. 'Marriage to a Carrick farmer taught me much about turds.'

Brodie jumped down from the cart. Mounds of raked hay were strung out behind Mariota. Beyond, other women also worked on patches of the common ground at Labothie. 'You have earned your bread today. Are you ready to load the hay onto the cart?'

She laid the rake on the ground and walked back along the mounds of hay, returning with a pitchfork. 'The hay is ready to be loaded, my swain. But not by me.' She handed him the fork. 'As well as earning my bread, I have earned the assistance of a husband who idles at market while his wife toils with a scythe and hay-rake. You load – I will watch the setting sun.' She sat on the ground, back and head against the wheel of the cart, eyes closed to the ripening sky.

He poked her outstretched leg gently with one of the prongs. 'Your rule is harsher than any prior or abbot.'

She opened one eye and stared back.

'But if the strength of a man is needed to complete the task, how could I withhold my charity?'

Mariota kicked the pitchfork away. 'Your charity is accepted, though it is well-earned rather than given freely.'

The sun was low behind Labothie Hill when Brodie loaded the last of the hay onto the cart. He hoisted himself up alongside Mariota, now in command of the reins. His shirt clung to his sweating back and chest. Using his sleeve, Brodie wiped his damp forehead. 'If you have earned your bread, I have earned the ale to sop it in.' He paused, coming to a thought. 'Or, better still...' The cart joined the smoother track and Brodie reached behind the wooden slat where they sat. He produced a sack, opening it for Mariota to inspect the contents. 'See here – most of a lamb. We can roast it over a fire, for supper.'

Mariota shook the reins. 'Is it wise to buy lamb when mutton costs half as much?'

'Mariota, there is no need to concern yourself. While the value of wheat goes up, the price of meat continues to fall. This sackful cost only two groats.'

Mariota's expression was equivocal, in equal parts impressed and unconvinced.

'And live beasts are little more – only a shilling a head for wool-bearing ewes. I have a notion that we could continue to make improvements on the farm, perhaps using some of the new methods from England, increase our profits and purchase a flock, to graze on the common ground here...' He waved an arm to his right, where Labothie Hill still loomed. 'And on the pasture by Monikie Burn.'

Mariota looked around, perhaps considering his suggestion, or assessing the fading daylight. 'I would not be sure we can afford such a notion.'

'But a shilling a head is cheaper than at any time since I have tended sheep. And yet the merchants and weavers of Bruges demand more sacks of wool and woolfells than the whole of the kingdoms of Scotland and England can produce, while paying a generous price. With a score and ten ewes, a ram to sire lambs and more furrows of wheat to harvest, we could afford to hire a cottar to gather the hay – rather than break your back – or grassmen to farm our acres. You could wear miniver instead of fox fur, and cloths of silk.' He put an arm around her waist, his hand settling on her hip. 'It could bring prosperity. And contentment.'

'That may or may not be so. But my reason for questioning the cost of such an enterprise lies elsewhere. Brodie, the money may be needed for another purpose. The mother of Lord Lindsay's hayward passed by on her rounds. It seems that her son, the comely Niall, will ask to take Isabel as his wife – providing a suitable dowry can be arranged.'

Brodie closed the sack and returned it to the cart behind. 'Then we should delay our roasted lamb until the appropriate feast day.'

Mariota turned her eyes from the track ahead towards her husband. 'Brodie, you left behind the need to follow the liturgical year so closely when you left behind the cloisters.'

'The day after next is the Feast of Anne, the mother of the

Blessed Virgin, patron saint of wives…' He put his arm back around her waist and squeezed her ribs. 'And brides-to-be. We will find the dowry – if that is what your father and Isabel choose.'

Chapter 2

"And after, as he growed in might and strength,
he laboured ever in hunting and in hawking…
And as the book saith, he began good measures of
blowing of beasts of venery and beasts of chase,
and all manner of vermin."

Sir Thomas Malory, *Le Morte d'Arthur* (c 1470)

15th Day of April, 1371

The mewling monk arrives as I prepare to leave my new Lochindorb stronghold, to hunt buck of the first head at Dulnain.

Displeased, I return the gyrfalcon to its perch and remove my hawking glove.

He makes obeisance before his presence is proclaimed, bowing and scraping.

In my impatience, I let his grovelling impertinence pass. 'Lord Alexander Stewart of Badenoch…' My groom keeper makes the announcement while ushering the monk forward. '…I bring to you the Augustinian Brother Peter Fenton, also a servant of Bishop de Kininmund at the Cathedral Church of Saint Machar.' The foot-licker now behaves with more courtesy, moving on command, kneeling three times and awaiting my permission to speak.

'You bring a message from my father, King Robert, from his coronation and council?' I remove the falcon's hood and stroke its soft head.

He straightens. 'I do, my lord.'

'I also attended coronation and council – why would my

father entrust this to you rather than deliver it to my own ear?'

He is close to the hearth and takes a step to the side because of the heat. 'After Holy Week, his merciful Highness King Robert reconvened an audit of legal judgements and grants awaiting affirmation, to examine the dispersal of territory and title under King David's royal command. I was appointed clerk of audit to that commission...'

'Ah, wretched King Davy – sick from an arrowhead in his skull, in thrall to the English and without a bairn to put on the throne at his death.' Momentarily, I feel pity, though it passes with the arrival of a more agreeable thought. 'Then Alleluia! – my father accedes in his place to become King rather than Steward. And light dispels the darkness of sin and death.' A second, even more pleasurable thought follows the first, as sweet follows savoury: my father has recognised the error of granting the earldom of Strathearn to my low-ranking half-brother and transferred it into my name, or perhaps – and this may be more likely – the vacant Caithness title is mine.

My groom keeper returns to the chamber. 'The boat is readied to leave the island, my lord,' he says.

My haste to lead a chase through Baddengorm Woods and along the river at Dulnain is rekindled, my eagerness to learn the nature of the message fortified. I dismiss the groom. 'The message from my father – deliver it,' I order the monk.

He gropes in a satchel, produces a book and opens it at a marked page. His fat lips tremble. 'As...as clerk of audit, I made a discovery that connects this book with the letter inside – a connection that concerns the blasphemous beast Christie of the Cleek.' He goes down on one knee and proffers the open book as though inviting me to pick from a platter.

I stare at it. 'That is all? You bring no more than a book and a letter from my father, damn him?'

The monk is bewildered, unsure how to respond to my incautious words. 'Your father bids only that you read these pages,' he says with neutrality.

'Give me the cursed book so that I can be gone from here all the sooner.' I snatch it from him. The open page is marked by a letter bearing the name of Lindsay of Glenesk in the top margin. I lift the letter to reveal the richly decorated pages of the book below. Illuminated miniatures show young hoopoes plucking the plumage of an adult bird, wild he-goats locking horns, a pyre of fire-bearing stones. The entries are from the year 1341: the besieging of Stirling Castle, the taking of Edinburgh, a brief account of King Davy's return from France. And this, from the month of August:

> *"Pity us! The kinbrother of Cleek the Butcher treads his diabolical feet on Restenneth's Holy soil. Pity us more! This Duncan of the abominable Christies fled before the most high and most excellent Robert the Steward could slit his nose and brain, out of reverence for the passion of our Lord."*

Then I read the letter.

> *"Lindsay, Lord of Glenesk, to all good men gathered together as a Commission of Audit, greetings. By testimony of this letter, let it be confirmed that four oxgangs north of the Broom Well, by Monikie, and the houses and enclosures there, were conferred on Brodie of the Afflecks and any other Afflecks of the same kin, to peaceably hold as freehold. This grant was made valid and sure in the year of the Lord 1363, so that those in possession could do with it whatever they deemed expedient, if acting legally and securely. At the same time and in sameways, lands from the Feugh to the A'an were given and granted to Duncan of the Christies of Finzean. Despite that benevolent consent and favour, claim to the territory was not pursued and so it remained stable and certain with the Lindsays of Glenesk by hereditary right.*
> *Our Lord have you in his keeping and grant you perpetual health. This is commended to writing and strengthened by the authority of my seal at Edzell on the twenty sixth day of the month of April in the year thirteen hundred and seventy less one."*

My impatience is beginning to turn to anger. 'So, Lindsay land at Finzean was granted to the fugitive Christie insect, but never claimed?'

'Of course, Lord Lindsay of Glenesk cannot have known Cleek's brother was the grantee's true identity but, yes, I believe so.'

'By the five wounds of Christ, how did you make such a discovery?'

He is unnerved by the change in my tone, which is mocking, though he cannot be sure of it. He answers earnestly. 'The letter was among papers collected when the commission was first formed two years ago. As clerk, it was my duty to give all previous correspondence proper consideration. Before even that – on the birth of your older brother – your father bid that I compile a genealogy of the Stewarts, from Ninus who built Nineveh until our present age. The book you hold is that work. Since it was put down by my own hand, I was able to make the connection with the letter.'

He picks his preening words with a precision that betrays previous use, or careful rehearsal. I discern this too: he imagines that receiving an appointment from my father, citing my ill-nurtured brother and putting sentences down on quires of parchment bring him closer to me in status.

'You delay my hunt for this?' I wrench the page from its binding and tear it into pieces, which fall to the ground.

He is close to uttering a complaint but instead stares open-mouthed, briefly pointing a weak finger at the scraps of parchment by my feet, gold leaf from a partial illustration glistening in the firelight. Then he returns to servility. 'Begging forgiveness, my lord, but your father has declared that his kingship requires justice to be served on the fugitive Christie and his kin – I believe the other name on the letter may provide a means to do just that. Brodie of the Afflecks was the faithless Augustinian brother who, before spurning his habit, granted sanctuary at Restenneth to the brother of Cleek. I proposed to your father – and he agreed – that it is unlikely their names would again come together so closely by chance alone. Finding Brodie Affleck may lead you to Duncan Christie. They could even be in league.'

The monk has the beginnings of a satisfied smile.

I think on it for a long moment. 'Do you know more about this Brodie Affleck?'

'Only that he dwells at the Broom Well lands with a wife, two of her Ward kinwomen and her eldfather.'

'Very well. You will make it known to me if you come upon these names again,' I tell him. 'You are the Lord of Badenoch's man now.'

He bows. His scalp gleams with sweat.

Hawking glove and falcon back on my hand and wrist, I leave my chamber. For the next while, I have more noble prey to pursue.

Chapter 3

"Ancient exalted seed-scatterer, whom time gave
no progenitor:
he knew no moment of creation in his
primordial foundation.
He is and will be all places in all time and all
ages,
with Christ his first-born, only-born and the
holy spirit-borne."

The hymn, *Altus Prosator*, ascribed to Saint Columba (c 6th century)

17th Day of December, 1374

Brodie was the first of the men to fall to prayer by Isabel's bedside. 'Praise be! God's ordinance has delivered a boy bairn.'

Heeding the cue, young Niall also kneeled. Fergus struggled to do likewise, finally lowering himself awkwardly onto one stiff knee.

Mariota and Mary, sitting on the bed either side of Isabel and the tightly swaddled newborn, bowed their heads. The midwife, already on the floor as she mopped a large smear of blood below the birthstool, had no distance to travel to take up a position of prayer.

Brodie continued. 'By all the virtues of the most Holy Trinity, by which he created everything. By the mystery of the Holy Incarnation and the merit of his most blessed Passion. By his most glorious resurrection and infinite power, God is alpha and omega, the beginning and the end. For of him, and through him, and to him, are all things – to whom be glory for ever. Amen.'

Fergus moved alongside the bed. 'Are you well?' he asked Isabel.

'And the child?' said Niall.

Isabel, damp hair brushed back from her brow, stroked the baby's fair head. She nodded slowly.

The midwife continued on her behalf. 'A preparation of juniper and ergot was needed to hasten the spasms. And blood had to be let from her feet.' Broad arms bare, the midwife finished mopping the floor. She stood – small, gimlet-eyed, severely shortened nails at her fingertips – and threw the blood-stained sheet among a pile of others by the fire. 'But mother and child are hearty enough.'

Niall scraped a chair across the room to sit by the bed. 'The boy is to be given the name Maol.' He looked between Isabel and his son, though the announcement was made to the others in the room. 'In the same manner as Malise – a servant of God.'

Even with the baby's eyes closed, Brodie could detect a resemblance between father and son. They shared the same fair hair, rawboned features, bright lips and – Brodie could not help but think it when the swaddling linen fell loose – feet too large for their slender limbs.

'Has there been a baptism?' Brodie asked the midwife.

'There was no need,' she answered. 'He is well enough to be taken to a priest.'

'Then we should not linger.' Brodie gestured towards the closed shutters to indicate the darkness that lay beyond. 'The priest at Kirkton will already be at the altar for evensong.'

The others murmured their agreement, though Mary insisted on first laying fresh heather on the floor. Mariota offered to remain behind with Isabel.

With the baby wrapped in blankets and furs, Niall led Mary and the midwife out of his small but stone-built tofthouse. Brodie and Fergus followed behind. Despite the cold, Brodie felt a relief at leaving the lying-in room, which was thick with the heat of the fire, steam from pots of simmering water and a multitude of breaths, level and laboured.

Due to Fergus's laggardly pace and his reliance on a stick for support, they were soon a distance behind the others. Fergus paused to rest at the top of the slope rising from Scotfaulds.

'Would you rather I fetched a horse from the stable?' offered Brodie.

'The stables are farther than the church,' replied Fergus, wheezing clouds of breath in the icy air. 'I will manage on two feet rather than four.'

His own hip and knee aching in the cold, Brodie had a notion he might saddle two horses and ride alongside Fergus to the Kirkton parish church. Instead, he guided Fergus across dark ground, ruts and grasses already firm with frost, to an outcrop beyond the path. 'You should at least sit for a moment,' he said.

Fergus spoke once they were both seated. 'It is surely the truth that fortune's wheel spins low and high, at once bringing sorrow and then turning to happiness.' He drew his hand up and down the smooth shaft of his stick. 'Alyth died twelve years ago on this same day – had you made the connection?'

'A week before Christmastide – I have named her in my prayers on that day ever since.' Brodie stared at his feet and shook his head. 'The course of God's will is inscrutable.'

Fergus hacked up a blockage from his throat and spat it out. 'Come – or we will miss the baptism rite.' He eased himself to his feet and rejoined the path.

Fergus kept his quiet until they reached Monikie's western boundary, entering a mixed grove of mostly bare trees but with heavy pine branches overhanging the verge. The wind eased and Fergus straightened his shoulders. 'Do you still try to get Mariota with child? Such a turn of the wheel would surely be a marvel.'

'A miracle more than a marvel – my age is no longer fresh and green enough for fatherhood.' Brodie laughed, though it lacked conviction. 'But we have a grandnephew, if not a son.'

'An heir to take on the land and the farm.' Fergus produced a hand from a sleeve, pointing at Brodie then himself. 'You and I – we will show him the ways of the flock and the fields, as we did Malise.'

'Even though we are bloodkin, we will be as the boy's godfathers,' agreed Brodie. 'I can teach him to read and write words. We can both instruct him in wisdom and morals.'

Beyond Monikie's dwelling houses, gusts veered around Catterthun's flanks, gathering pace as they skimmed the fields. Fergus hunched into the chill north-easterly. He raised his voice to be better heard over the buffeting wind. 'And faith,' he added. 'We must also instruct him in faith – Alyth would expect no less.'

Chapter 4

*"Wolves get their name from their rapacity: for
this reason we call whores, she-wolves, because
they strip their lovers of their wealth. The wolf is a
rapacious beast and craves blood. Its strength lies
in its chest or its jaws, least of all in its loins...It
is said to live sometimes on its prey, sometimes on
earth and sometimes, even, on the wind."*

The Aberdeen Bestiary (c 1200)

6th Day of December, 1376

"In the beginning, God created the heaven and the earth. And
the earth was without form, and void. And darkness was upon
the face of the deep..."

Maol snatched at the book in Brodie's hands.

He swatted the child's hand away. 'No, no, no.' Brodie found
a page with illustrations and thrust it towards the boy across the
hearth mat. 'See these – see the birds and fishes.'

Maol rocked backwards, appearing mollified.

Brodie continued reciting the creation narrative, though he
now did so from memory, preferring to hold the book so that
the page faced outward, hoping it would hold the boy's wavering
attention. "And God said, Let the waters bring forth abundantly
the moving creature that hath life, and fowl that may fly above
the earth under the firmament of heaven. And God created great
whales, and every living creature that moveth, which the waters
brought forth abundantly..."

Maol grabbed the book again, this time freeing it from
Brodie's grip. He raised it high over his head, giggling, and

dropped it with a flutter into a bucket by his side.

His patience dwindling, Brodie reached for the bucket, though that caused Maol's sniggers to give way to wails of protest.

Brodie leaned back: laughter.

He reached for the bucket: shrill, red-faced howls.

Finally, he sat still, moving neither back nor forth.

Maol extracted some mucus from a nostril and rolled it between his fingers. He opened and closed his thumb and forefinger, stretching and squashing the sticky mess.

Brodie's growing frustration was disturbed by a noisy rattle of the door latch, followed by a rush of cold air.

Niall's mother stepped inside and Brodie had the confusion of feeling relief at the arrival of a motherly figure yet disappointment that it was not Mariota or the sisters.

The eldmother quickly closed the door and removed her hooded cloak, shaking off flakes of snow.

Maol might also have been confused because he sat quietly, though in readiness for uproar: head twisted round to face his grandmother, mouth open, face frozen in a scowl.

She hung her cloak on a peg by the fireplace and placed a brown tweel bundle on a stool. 'A gift for the boy in the name of Saint Nicholas – a plaid for the winter days,' she explained.

Accustomed to a sense of discomfort in her presence, and always expecting that whatever he said would displease her in some way, Brodie offered a simple courtesy. 'Dame, God give you good day.'

'It is not so good – foul, even.' She picked up Maol and rested him on her hip. 'What troubles the child?' Dark despite her age and taller than most, she stared down at Brodie.

'He wants the book.' Brodie gestured at the book in the bucket. 'And will not allow me to take it back.' Uttered aloud, Brodie realised that his own words carried the tones of a bleating child.

'He is concerned about his bucket – it contains all his treasures, as you should know – not the book.'

Brodie peered into the bucket but saw only some common twigs, an onion sprouting shoots, a broken cup, a length of bark in the shape of a crude boat, a yarn spool and a painted stone.

Still holding Maol – silent but watchful – the eldmother bent down to take the book from the bucket. 'So, this is the bestiary you copied from Lord Lindsay's library as a Saint Nicholas gift? Niall tells me it contains great artistry.' She began to turn from page to page.

'The text came easily enough to my hand but I am no illustrator.'

She turned some more pages. 'I had not expected burnished gold and white filigree, but could you not have filled in some colours?' She snapped the book shut and handed it to Brodie. 'A child would better receive a gift that provided it with nourishment, or warmth, rather than sketches of beasts from other worlds. If you must fill the boy's head with the contents of these pages, you should at least restrict your lessons to repetition of the word of God.'

'The words I read praise the Lord and his creation.' He bowed, mostly to avoid his gaze colliding with hers.

'Then that is as it should be.' Only briefly satisfied, she shivered in an exaggerated way, lips aquiver as she exhaled. 'This house is overly cold. Why does the boy not wear hose below his tunic?'

Brodie stuttered a response. 'He had none on…he takes them off…'

'Then you should put them back on – he is in your care.' She took a step towards the hearth but stopped. 'And now I see there are no logs to replenish the fire.' She sighed heavily. 'I will fetch the firewood – if you tend to the boy. You are capable?'

Brodie ignored the taunt.

The eldmother put her cloak back on and bustled out the door.

Brodie found the hose in a small, crumpled pile by the beds. Despite a struggle, he fastened them to the boy's braies. Again sitting by the fireside, he continued reciting from the bestiary. "And God said let the earth bring forth the living creature after his kind. And it was so." He pointed at one of his better line drawings. 'Look – a horse.'

Maol traced the outline of the horse's head and back.

'And this is an ox.'

'Oc,' attempted Maol.

'And there is a bull standing alongside a cow.'

'Sheep!' Maol pointed excitedly at the opposite page.

'A sheep, yes. We will make a shepherd of you yet,' said Brodie before continuing. "And God made the beast of the earth after his kind, and cattle after their kind, and every thing that creepeth upon the earth…"

The eldmother clattered back in carrying an armful of logs. She kicked the door shut with her heel. 'Maol!' she shouted. Without Brodie noticing, he had wriggled one leg free of his hose. 'Back on!' she commanded.

The boy did as he was told. Then, with the scolding still close by, he kept his eyes on the book. 'What that?' he asked.

'Here begins the book of the nature of beasts – of lions, panthers, tigers, apes and dogs. And that…' Brodie tapped the page next to Maol's finger. '…is a lion.'

'I know that.'

Brodie pressed on. 'The lion is the mightiest of the beasts for he quails at the approach of none.'

Maol stared, fascinated.

Taking advantage of the boy's apparent interest, Brodie returned to the text. "All beasts vent their rage with tooth or claw. They are wild because they enjoy natural liberty and are borne along by their desires. Free of will, they wander now here, now there. And where their instinct takes them, there they are borne."

'Boy!' shouted the eldmother.

Brodie looked up from the bestiary; Maol was once again attempting to free himself from his hose.

His grandmother stood at the other end of the room, eyes bulging; she brandished a pestle menacingly, the way a duellist wields a smallsword. 'Do not dare.'

The boy yanked his hose back on, mouth turned down, lips twitching.

To stall any tears, Brodie offered a distraction. 'Listen to this. When a lioness gives birth to a cub, she produces him dead and watches over him for three days, until his father comes on the third day and breathes into his face, so that he will be revived as a whelp.'

Brodie stopped.

Whelp: reading the word, his eye was not drawn to the sketch of a young lion alongside, as might be expected. Nor did he conjure an image of a cub in his mind. Not of a lion, or a bear or a dog. Or even a wolf. Brodie did not see a picture of a whelp at all: he saw the word written on a page. But on a different page, in a different hand.

"From the seed, a whelp will crawl…From a whelp, the wolf will grow."

He saw it written twice, in the same flowing script, among lines of riddle on scraps of parchment; verses of riddle that had guided him to Christie and helped find salvation for the Affleck name; a quest that had brought him the land he now occupied and led him to take Mariota as his wedded wife. However unaccountable, the prophecies in the riddles had mostly come to pass. Yet since the upturn in his fortunes, Brodie had paid no heed to those lines of verse that still made no sense.

Maol's grandmother was still shouting in the background. 'I swear it – try to remove another stitch and a man-wolf will crawl through your window and eat you alive when next you close your eyes to sleep.'

"Packsaddle child, full grown foe."

Chapter 5

"The fact that the she-wolf gives birth when the
thunder first sounds in the month of May signifies
the Devil, who fell from heaven at the first display
of his pride…The wolf's eyes shine in the night like
lamps because the works of the Devil seem
beautiful and wholesome to blind and foolish men."

The Aberdeen Bestiary (c 1200)

16th Day of May, 1377, until the 18th Day of the Same Month

The wines improve with each new story-telling: sweet Spanish
while the minstrel recites a simpering romance by the
Englishman Chaucer; Rhenish to accompany John the
Barbour's recently completed poem recalling Brus's valiant
deeds; spiced hypocras as my father prepares to address his
guests before the third and final reading.

He takes a long drink as soon as his cup is filled, cocks his
head appreciatively and swills back some more.

I taste the hypocras: the wine is superior, though the
concoction of spices contains excessive cinnamon, insufficient
ginger.

My father stands unsteadily. He gives a nod to the Barbour,
who sits at the second-mess table to his left. 'A masterly
depiction of our lion-hearted king and his feats of high prowess.
A payment from the collectors of customs in Aberdeen will soon
be in your purse – which, as an auditor to the exchequer, you do
not need told.'

Some fawning fools laugh.

Turning to the throng, my father peers through eyes that are losing their sight. He leans forward, gripping the table board for support. 'The crown that Brus wore on his basinet now sits on my own head, though sad to say that other wearers, through misfortune and folly, have allowed their foes to be their judges...'

The words he utters are the beginnings of a song he sings when he adds drunkenness to thirst: hapless King Davy coupled suffering and wretchedness with foul thralldom; he put the sovereignty of the whole kingdom in peril to buy his own release from England's Edward; a noble heart can have no ease if freedom fails. '...and while thralldom is worse than death – for as long as thrall lives it mars a man, body and bones, while death troubles him but once – freedom is more prized than all the gold in the world. All of which is known and asserted by those who will take this inheritance – my eldest, John the Earl of Carrick...' He lays his hand on the shoulder of my senior brother, who sits directly to his right. 'So too, my other noble sons.' He waves a loose arm down the dais in our direction. 'So prized is my next son, the virtuous and learned Earl Robert of Fife, upright in heart and mind, that the final reading to fill your ears on this day of Brandan the Bold was commissioned in the days after his birth – a treatise on the flowering of the house of Stewart.'

There are some nods of approval.

I recall the occasion the book's monkly scribe arrived at Lochindorb claiming to have found a connection to the fugitive Cleek brother.

My father does not sit, as expected, after making the announcement. Rather, he looks to the ceiling of the Dundonald great hall, fresh with paint, as though picking out a bright new thought from among the rich colours. 'Lords and prelates, so worthy are these princes that a new earl is to come from among their ranks.' He glances at each of us in turn: my seniors, the Earls Carrick and Fife; my lesser half-brother, Earl David of Strathearn. Then his gaze rests on me: the only lord among us who is due – overdue – an earldom.

'Bow your heads low to the next Earl Palatine of Caithness...'

My rightful rank is to be conferred.

His gaze moves to my left. '...David, who has governed Strathearn with a sage head.'

I do this: I rise up from the table – forgetting to observe

courtesy and silence – walk along the dais behind each brotherly earl and bend to whisper in my father's ear. 'Sir, I am Alasdair Mor Mac an Righ – Great Alexander, the king's son – and I will have my rightful patrimony.' My face is scornful, his affronted, but he does and says nothing. Even though I have shown irreverence to my sovereign, I do no not take leave with my head lowly. As I pass the humble end of the hall, I gesture to mac Anndra and my groom to follow.

One of my brothers – the breathless, indignant tone tells me it is likely John of Carrick – rends the quiet with an indistinct threat.

My groom fetches a lantern and we are gone.

As we ride north through one short night, then a second, I tally my titles against theirs. I hold these titles: Lord of Badenoch, Lieutenant north of Moray and in all the sheriffdom of Inverness, Royal Justiciar in the Appin of Dull, Baron of Urquhart. My brothers hold: earldoms. Of Carrick; Fife; Strathearn and Caithness.

It is only on crossing the Almond River that I have a notion of obtaining another title: a vacant title that carries more righteous esteem even than an earldom, at least in the mind of my father; one that is earned rather than bestowed.

Mac Anndra musters a band of Clann Donnchaidh men at Dunkeld and we ride east across the Sidlaws, north around Dundee, through Pitairlie to Monike. We follow the wooded track described by a tounman. Half a league north of a place called the Broom Well we pass fertile fields and come to a farmstead.

In the light of a fading sun and a brightening moon, mac Anndra and the Donnchaidh fetch those from within the farmstead. They issue in just the way they were described – if I remember precisely – by the monk who attended Lochindorb in the days after my father's coronation: the man I take to be Brodie Affleck – slender, of middling years – a wife who cries after her husband, two kinswomen and an eldfather. The wife holds a bairn. All are pushed to their knees.

'Brodie Affleck?' I direct the question at the husbandman.

He bows, then raises his head. He glances around at the Donnchaidh men, weapons drawn. 'No, my lord. But...' He stops, fearing that each additional word may provoke a new danger.

'You are farmer here and these rustics are all of the Ward family?'

'I farm here and these are the Wards, but the land is not held in my name.'

'Then speak plainly – who holds the land?'

The old man bows. 'I hold title to these lands,' he says.

'Then you are Affleck?' I ask, though his age does not fit my presumptions.

'I am Fergus the Ward, once a soldier of lord Bishop de Lamberton and gateman at the Priory of Restenneth.'

I have come to know that an examination such as this, in the presence of men-at-arms who bear their weapons loosely, often prompts lies and evasions. I turn again to the younger man. 'Then I will ask a question you are better able to answer.' Still, mounted, I draw my own blade and point it at the woman who holds the child in tight arms. 'Is this your henwife?' She shuffles on her knees closer to the younger man.

He puts an arm around her shoulders and stares at me. He hopes the embrace is a sufficient answer.

'Answer,' I demand.

'It is…She is.'

My assessment is that this one is weak and might piss himself. Out of curiosity, I stare a while at where it would stain his tunic. He remains dry and I curse my minor misjudgement. 'Stand and move to me,' I tell the wife.

Her movements are hesitant but her eyes do not waver from mine.

'Your name?'

'Isabel, of Lord Lindsay's haywards at Monike and Labothie, my lord.'

'And the child you carry?'

'He has the name Maol – a servant of Christ.'

'So many names – none of them the one I seek.'

I am about to order the Donnchaidh men to wield their weapons with purpose – since a stiff blade is surest to cut through deceit – but have a whim. 'The boy would care to sit astride the warhorse of Lord Alexander Stewart, the king's great son, no? Bring him here.'

She is reluctant, though the choice does not belong to her.

I smile and pull my mail coif back, so it hangs loosely at my neck.

Her apprehension might ease a degree; perhaps she sees something fatherly in my gestures.

I reach down, take the child from her and rest him on the pommel at the front of my saddle. I let him touch the reins. He begins to bounce with pleasure, as though on a cockhorse. 'If these churls cannot speak the plain truth, you will do it for them. Boy, is Brodie Affleck among those before us? Is he your father? Point your finger at him.'

'Leave the boy be.' The eldest of the women, who kneels on the far right of the group, stares up at me defiantly. 'You say your business is with Brodie Affleck – I am his wife Mariota and can tell you that he does dwell here but is this week and next droving a flock of black faces from Melrose.'

The crop-wench has spoken without an invitation to do so.

And her words ignite a blaze.

It begins with a roar to my left. I turn and see the old man hastening towards me, a previously concealed blade in his hand. I laugh – I hear it inside and outside my head – the *old man*, the old soldier, is coming at *me*. I hear these sounds keenly, see these movements more slowly than they occur, in the way of a master huntsman during a pursuit. Two Donnchaidh are on the pathetic old fool. My horse throws back its head at the commotion. There is a lightness in its front hooves and a tightness in its shoulders so I lean forward and loosen the reins to prevent it rearing. The boy loses his balance and falls to the ground with less than a thud. The mother runs to him, whimpering, arms flailing. The old man is quickly dispatched. He snivels in the dirt. For an old soldier, he takes his death with little dignity, less so than the child, who at least is silent. The mother may or may not die but she too falls silent below the horse's hooves, wrapped around her child. It is wasteful; her features were fair, though it was her own choosing to crawl in the mud. The crop-wench who set this fire and the youngest woman have risen from their knees, which I did not sanction. The younger man remains on his knees, motionless and staring, as though engrossed by the antics of a performing dog or dancing bear. The crop-wench screams foul abuse and strikes together stones she is holding. I remember a passage from a book: *"Then we took stones in our hands and beat them one against the other, because we attract the attention of the saints of God."* I pull the right rein, into her din. '...violator of your own noble blood...the devil's tyrant...a hateful, craven beast...die the ill death of a wolf...' Both women back off as I approach, but the youngest one is not sufficiently fleet. I spur my horse to a canter. She crumples under its wheeling limbs. I hold the horse still, ensuring it settles a shod hoof on her neck. The crop-wench mumbles an invocation. 'Mary...have mercy...' She drops the stones and gathers up her skirts. Her bawdy mouth gasping for breath rather than curses, she runs east, towards the burn we crossed to arrive at the farmstead. Mac Anndra is awaiting my command. 'Slay her,' I tell him. 'And raise dragon however you choose.' It is just light enough to watch him hungrily give chase. Before she reaches the burnside brushwood, he slashes a blade at the backs of her ankles; the wounds will prevent further flight but allow him to take his pleasure from living flesh rather than a withering corpse. No moans or sobs are audible but the younger man might imagine otherwise because he presses his palms to his ears. He now lies face down, a Donnchaidh boot on his back.

'You still say you are not Brodie Affleck?' I ask.

He strains his neck upwards from the dirt and screams it. 'MY NAME IS NIALL – OF LORD LINDSAY'S HAYWARDS.' He begins to weep.

'Very well, I have been given reasons to believe that what you say is true. And since you speak the truth, I will allow you to live. In return, you will perform a task for me. When the one called Brodie Affleck returns from his droving, you will tell him that he is served with a writ of arrest by Alexander Stewart, Lord of Badenoch – for abetting the fugitive brother of Christie the Cleek.'

The Donnchaidh men gather spoil. I must wait some time longer for my prize, a title earned rather than bestowed: captor of Duncan Christie, brother of Cleek the flesh-eating savage.

Chapter 6

"But O the heavy change, now thou art gone,
Now thou art gone, and never must return."

John Milton, *Lycidas* (1638)

27th Day of May, 1377

Brodie laughed, disbelieving. It was too fanciful, too improbable. The Tay ferryman was fabricating or exaggerating. Or simply mistaken. Were any with the name Ward among the slain? The boatman could not say. He knew only that a hayward of Lord Lindsay had survived. One of Lindsay's many haywards. Yet he was certain the killings had taken place just north of the Broom Well. Brodie led the black faces off the ferry. The boatman called after him: 'The Lord of Badenoch's caterans – it is said they were in pursuit of the bogle-brother of Christie Cleek.' The brother of Cleek. Duncan Christie, whose whereabouts were known only to Brodie.

"Hear my prayer, O Lord, give ear to my supplications…"

Brodie hurried across the Carse of Gowrie, the sun warm, the air thick with insects and the nectar of flowers. The farmstead was deserted, but undisturbed. No, not undisturbed. Metal moveables, some of the child's possessions and the standing cross, all gone – he checked below the boards – and their savings. Also gone. So, a robbery. But no bloodstains. No signs of the killings described by the ferryman. The geese and pullets still pecked in the yard. Brodie penned the sheep, leashed the hound. He went to the barn, the byre, the cropfields, the woods at Downie. No-one. Clouds obscured the sun. Brodie heard the rustle of nearby trees, then felt the oncoming breeze. The bells of Kirkton church tolled. For the day of Augustine of Canterbury? Yesterday. Corpus Christi? Tomorrow. The bell continued to sound: a long, slow peal of mourning.

"Hear me speedily, O Lord, a faintness is upon my soul…"

Brodie ran. Up then down Catterthun's slopes, past the ruined fort. Parishioners processed from the church. Brodie saw only Niall's face. No Isabel by his side. Or young Maol tottering behind. No Mariota, Fergus, Mary.

"Hide not thy face from me, my God, lest I would be as those who go down into the pit…"

Niall dropped to the ground on sighting Brodie. He begged forgiveness, maundering. 'It is the ninth day of mourning…the number of months the Blessed Mother held Christ in her womb…death watches with all her might…' He waved his bony hands dementedly in front of his face. 'These eyes saw it all, these hands did nothing…other than fill their grave cuts with dirt.' Brodie left him at the church gate, sobbing.

"Grant them eternal rest, O Lord, and let perpetual light shine upon them…"

The graves in the cemetery: five mounds of turned earth, crammed close together, none yet marked. Brodie staggered backwards, as though dealt an unseen blow. He heard a distant cry, likely from his own throat. He took a handful of soil from one of the four larger mounds. Did Mariota lie beneath? Fergus? Or one of the sisters?

"Jesus said, I am the resurrection and the life. Those who believe in me, though they are dead, yet shall they live again…"

Niall ran alongside, still whelmed by grief, now also in a frenzy of fear. 'You must know this – they died at the hands of the Lord of Badenoch, a wolf as Mariota described before her death. He seeks you, Brodie Affleck. You, for abetting the fugitive brother of Christie the Cleek. He has served a writ for your arrest.' He clutched Brodie's sleeve. 'You must leave, or the next grave will be yours. I beg you.' Brodie scattered the soil he held on each of the graves.

"May their souls and the souls of all the faithful departed, through the mercy of God, rest in peace."

Chapter 7

"At this grief, my heart was utterly darkened;
and whatever I beheld was death."

Saint Augustine, *The Confessions of St Augustine* (c 397)

Summer, 1377

Brodie considered ways he might die by his own hand rather than live a life of death.

Most often, he imagined himself crossing the broad sands at Buddon Ness, a bright night sky overhead, a weighted sack strapped tightly to his back. He would enter the water and, briefly enlivened by the chill, take one step then another until the waves passed over his head. But in abandoning his body to the seas, he would lose his place in consecrated ground alongside Mariota, Fergus and the others. Any other means – hanging from a rope, perhaps, or cutting a hand or foot to drain the blood from his body – would lead to a finding of felonious self-killing and the certain denial of an eternity in heaven's bliss with his wife and family. The taking of a poison – he could easily obtain death cherries or water hemlock roots – might not be detected but amounted to so monstrous a sin that he dared not harbour such thoughts.

And so he lived.

And the decision to do so brought with it a slow return of sense and mind.

Still he wept for his losses and damned his decision to make the journey to Melrose. Still his flesh wasted, his raw skin flaked dry. But the trembling sickness in his gut eased and he found some moments of sleep that did not relive events never seen by his eyes or heard by his ears. Rather than move from one rude shelter to the next, gathering nuts and berries, cowering in fear of the Lord of Badenoch, Brodie took up habitation in a little used shepherd's shieling on the high slopes of Fothringham Hill, distant enough from the Broom Well to provide a refuge, sufficiently elevated to allow him to keep a vigil for the approach of cateran men-at-arms. He pilfered eggs, vegetables and a hen to roast. From the hilltop, he watched the shadows of huge clouds sweeping all the distance from Forfar to Monikie. The first yellow leaf of autumn appeared on the lower branches of a hornbeam in the clearing where he sat, at what he guessed was the end of July. Some days later, the beeches beginning to turn brown, he ate the last morsels of cabbage and apple and then descended the hill on its wooded southern side, collecting white-blossomed rosemary as he went. Night had fallen by the time he reached the Broom Well.

Niall stood at the farmstead threshold, gaping, as if Brodie bore the curse and mark of Cain. He explained his reaction as surprise at the unfamiliar thicket of beggarly hair on Brodie's chin and cheeks, though it was more recognisable as terror at his proximity to the outlaw sought by the wife-killing Lord of Badenoch. Disguising his fear as concern, he agreed to all that Brodie asked and more. Together they led a mule from the stable and – with the help of the brother and sister who now farmed the holding with Niall – filled panniers with loaves, bannocks, salted meat and lately harvested vegetables. As Brodie readied to leave, Niall hurried back into the farmstead and fetched out Mariota's few remaining possessions: the ring of rushes Brodie had given her as a bond of matrimony, a leather neck twine with small wooden cross attached, her basin and ewer, two blankets and a head covering that doubled as a shawl.

Before putting distance between himself and the Broom Well, as he had promised Niall, Brodie made the short journey east to the church at Kirkton. He removed the cross from Mariota's neck twine, clutched it tight in his fist and knelt to pray by the grave mounds, now less discernible due to a covering of weeds and grasses. He called out each of their names aloud and laid a sprig of rosemary on each grave, also burying Mariota's cross beside the fieldstone that carried her initials. Brodie attached her wedding band to the twine, which he tied around his neck. Then he took the mule's halter in his grip and turned south towards Kirkcudbright. If Duncan Christie and his family had not already fallen prey to the scent hounds, they should be warned that Alexander Stewart, the Wolf of Badenoch, was on their trail.

Chapter 8

"I gazed on the sight: my hands I clasped;
chill sorrow seized my heart;
wild grief made tumult in my breast,
though reason whispered 'peace'."

Pearl, unknown author (14th century)

13th Day of August, 1377

'Brother? Brodie?'

Hearing the long forgotten religious address, seeing an unfamiliar figure approach on horseback, Brodie slowed as he crossed the bridge over the River Dee. Orange and pink glowed through a tear in twilight clouds. The stench of the Kirkcudbright tannery carried across the water and caught in his throat.

The man continued on some paces, then dismounted. He wore the clothes of a prosperous merchant: beaver-fur hat and shortened cote, ample gut spilling over a thick belt and, judging by his heavy tread on the wooden planks, sturdy cordwainer's boots.

'Brother Brodie, is it you?'

Brodie recognised the heavy-hearted tone and stooping walk. He pulled his mule to a halt.

The man walked to within Brodie's reach.

Behind a beard that had grown as full and rounded as his belly, the man bore an unmistakable, rueful frown. 'So, you have returned.'

While anticipating that Duncan Christie was unlikely to receive him as an old friend, Brodie had expected a degree more civility. 'I can be gone soon enough – I only came to warn you of a dire danger.'

'A danger?' Christie quailed. 'Is it King Robert?'

'Not the king – the king's son. Alexander Stewart, Lord of Badenoch. He seeks my arrest. For abetting your flight from Restenneth those many years ago. No doubt a writ awaits you also.'

'Have you been questioned?'

'Only my wife and her family were asked the Wolf of Badenoch's questions. None survived his notion of a justice ayre.'

Christie crossed himself then pressed his hands together in prayer. 'Sincerely, I am more sorry than any tongue can tell.' He looked around in thought, upstream, downstream. 'Do any others know that David Maxwell, Kirkcudbright hide merchant, is in truth the ill-famed brother Christie?'

'No others know.'

His head lolled. He closed his eyes, screwed up his face and kneaded his scalp. 'Then we are both safe here.' The reassurance was intended as much for himself as Brodie. He put a hand on Brodie's shoulder. 'Come.'

Brodie turned his mule in the direction Christie was travelling, away from the Dee, towards the Merse on the opposite bank. They crossed the soft ground, the wind in their faces, the odour of the tannery ever more distant. Perhaps saving his words for another occasion, but also fearing that tears would wet his cheeks, Brodie gave only the briefest account of the fates that had befallen him since leaving the Augustinian order and claiming the Broom Well land from the Lindsays.

Other than murmuring sympathies, Christie remained in silence until after they had called at the stables. He drew Brodie to a halt before they reached a sturdy, newly built house. 'I will make you my welcome guest, just as you helped me find refuge. But for the safe-keeping of us all, you should follow these instructions.' A sureness in his voice, he proposed how they would account for Brodie's presence to his wife. No mention would be made of writs for arrest; Brodie would be described as a runaway religious, escaping a harsh rule, rather than a fugitive from the law; he would take on a new name and make some changes to his appearance; his true identity would be revealed to no others, including Christie's daughters, which now numbered three.

The lies seemed small alongside Christie's concealment of his past.

'He is to be the keeper of my ledgers,' Christie told his wife.

Agnes Maxwell bowed her head, smiling. 'As you say.'

She was shorter than Brodie recalled and some grey streaked her hair. But in her fleet smile, eyes as keen as a dart, she remained a reflection of Mariota. He detected his wife too in the way she sat at the loom, one leg wrapped around the other like a vine, slim fingers and thumbs working the warp and weft of the yarn.

Chapter 9

> *"(Alexander Stewart), whose wickedness had earned him universal hatred...joined by certain vile creatures...drove off all the bishop's cattle, and carried away his property, killing at the same time in the most high-handed way the peasants."*

Hector Boece, *Lives of the Bishops of Mortlach and Aberdeen* (1522)

August, 1377, until the 31st Day of May, 1383

Every night before sleep, Brodie wrapped himself in Mariota's shawl – which he swore kept her scent, even as years passed – and lit a rushlight for five ascending souls. Every day, he watched his wife grow old in the lines that formed around Agnes Maxwell's eyes.

He worked diligently for Christie, keeping the accounts, intromitting tax levies, copying notarial instruments, drafting correspondence and bonds, preparing orders for payments due, receipts for payments received. In moments Brodie preferred, he tutored Christie's youngest, Annabel, in words, numbers and the little science he knew. Half a woman when Brodie arrived, she took to learning with childish zeal. Full grown, she was better with rows and columns of figures than any man, Brodie and Christie included.

Other than to accompany Christie into the burgh, or visit a notary or proctor, Brodie left the tannery only once a year, on the sixteenth day of May, arriving at Saint Ninian's white stone chapel near Kilkerran two days later. Alone or among other pilgrims, he prayed and slept at the Culdee church where his search for Mariota had ended twenty years before, remaining there from the date of the killings until the anniversary of his matrimony – two novenas of mourning, one for each family he had lost – asking God for reasons why he had endured such suffering. No voice thundered from the heavens in response, though Brodie heard his own whispered thoughts often enough: God had awarded him what he deserved for spurning the Holy Mother Church.

The family of pilgrims – a husband, wife and shaveling boy of 15 years – arrived on the last Sunday in May. After making brief introductions, they went directly to the chapel for the evening hour. Lying prostrate, arms outstretched, they left little space for Brodie, who remained on his knees at the rear of the tiny church, in a space beside the door, alongside the place where all their travelling baggage was stacked. The murmur of the pilgrims' worship and the scent of their sweat drifted through the chapel.

Brodie had completed his psalms and was silently reciting the Magnificat when he heard the approach of voices outside. Fearing horse thieves, he eased open the door. In the clearing beyond, three men, then a fourth, came into view. They began making camp with the briskness of practised travellers, two collecting firewood, another hunched over a flint and tinder. The fourth dropped a sack of belongings and trudged towards the chapel.

Brodie resumed a position of prayer as the chapel door swung open, grazing his leg. He looked up to see a grimy face, thick with hair. The man peering in grunted and yanked the door shut, though it rattled in the frame and swung ajar.

Distracted from his devotions, Brodie watched through the gap as the men busied themselves. Each was as dishevelled and callused as the next. They built up the fire and added sparse ingredients to a pan of water from the burn, exchanging words in what Brodie recognised as the rough tongue of the uplands. Putting the words he had read in books together with those he had used on his travels with Fordun in the north, west and Outer Isles, Brodie gathered that the men were soldiers, bound for England. The one who issued most of the commands – the same one who had looked into the church – used the name

Mackintosh, two others seemed to be called Foulson. The fourth answered to the name Lauson. The younger Foulson tended the pottage. One by one, the others settled alongside him around the fire. Together, they boasted of victorious combats in Birse and Buchan against a foe that Brodie could not discern: the Quhele? The Kays or Camerons, Brodie guessed. Whatever the foe's name, the mention of the earldom of Buchan provoked a fury in Lauson. He stood, picked up a woodcutter's axe and started hacking at the nearest sapling. With alternate blows, he spat out a name and a curse: 'Great Alexander, the king's son...House of the bitch on you...Great Alexander, the king's son...House of the bitch...'

'Enough,' interrupted Mackintosh. 'Whatever ill fate Alexander Stewart has brought on us, he is Earl of Buchan and Lord of Badenoch – for that he retains our fealty.'

'But he stood us to law to be prosecuted for grave harm inflicted against Justiciar Lindsay of Glenesk's chamberlain – by *his* order and command!' Lauson threw up his arms in exasperation, the axe head waving heavily.

'Finding his name in a petition to the king from the interfering Earl of Carrick forced him to do so by royal authority. And he at least offered us his protection by ensuring we were exiled rather than suffered the loss of life and limb. Be grateful – we will earn our fortune fighting in King Richard's paid army against France.' Mackintosh prodded the fire with a stick.

Lauson returned to slashing at the tree. 'I say it still – house of the bitch...'

'Cease this commotion!' The father pilgrim barged past Brodie into the clearing, son and wife at his heels. 'This is a house of God – peace must reign.'

Lauson turned and stared. The three men around the fire got to their feet.

Lauson snorted and resumed felling the tree.

'Do as I say!' The pilgrim said it as though ordering a stubborn beast of burden to halt after travelling the length of a furlong.

Lauson uttered an indistinct obscenity and lunged at the pilgrim.

Without time to make a calculation, Brodie leapt to his feet and blocked the soldier's path, both palms outwards and upwards in a pacifying gesture.

Lauson stopped. He was markedly smaller than Brodie but as broad as a door.

Brodie spoke in the soldier's tongue, stumbling over a remembered phrase from scripture. 'The pilgrim says only that, whether you eat, or drink...' Brodie gestured at the pan on the fire. '...Or whatever you do, do all to the glory of God. Give no offence, neither to Jews, nor to Gentiles, nor to the church of God.' He waved backwards towards the chapel.

Such was the quiet and stillness that followed, Brodie wondered if he had faithfully translated the passage from Paul's letter to the Corinthians, or if his intervention had simply bewildered all those around the clearing. The pilgrim, gaunt and fearful, edged behind his son. He clutched the badges – among others, Brodie recognised a scallop shell from Compostela and the saltire of St Andrews – that were arrayed on his tunic like a livery collar.

Mackintosh stepped forward, tugged Lauson back by the shoulder and turned to Brodie. 'Tell him this.' He pointed at the pilgrim. 'He should guard his mouth in the company of warriors of Badenoch. Tell him this too – we are men of God and have no cause to harm those who follow the example of the saints.' Mackintosh screwed up his eyes, which were as dark as the dirt covering his face. 'The men of Lord Alexander Stewart of Badenoch – whether spurned or favoured – kill only rightful enemies, low-borns and whores.'

The words roused never-distant memories of Brodie's wife and family, and their slaughter by the Lord of Badenoch and his men. But within the recollection, Brodie was unable to form a reliable, living likeness of Mariota. He conjured up an image of Fergus easily enough, walking by his side in the priory grounds, in days before the plague. And the rest of the family: the sisters and Maol huddled around the fire at the Broom Well farmstead, drips breaching the thatch in a downpour, Niall playing at dice, all discernible despite the darkness. But Mariota was nowhere. Or her back was turned, sitting on the edge of the bed, wearing a chemise, brushing her long hair. Or she appeared at a distance, walking along the river at Restenneth or returning from the fields. The figure he saw at the loom or cooking over a fire bore as much resemblance to Agnes Maxwell as his own wife.

His ire bestirred but restrained, Brodie turned away from Mackintosh and went to the pilgrim. 'Go back into the chapel. And beseech Saint Ninian to protect you and your family from these men. Or leave.'

Moving with purpose, he fetched his saddle and panniers from the church and readied his horse.

The soldiers eyed him indifferently as they sat down at the fire to eat. The pilgrims returned meekly to the chapel.

Brodie mounted his horse and rode to where the men hunched over their bowls. He stopped alongside Mackintosh, who looked up briefly but then returned to his pottage. Speaking in his own lowland vernacular, fingers gripping the handle of his sheathed knife, Brodie addressed the back of Mackintosh's head. 'All those killed by Badenoch and his caterans are not rightful enemies and whores. And your liege lord will be held to account for his crimes, by God if no man will do so.'

Brodie spurred the horse through the woods. Rather than wait for a response from the soldiers – and so discover if they had even understood his harangue – he asked a question of God. In return for Brodie reopening his eyes to the deifying light and inclining the ear of his heart, would God help him find justice for the crimes committed against Mariota, Fergus and the others? Or could such a covenant do more, and entrust Brodie with exacting his own vengeance on the Wolf of Badenoch?

*

'You have made it your business to find a way to avenge the deaths of your wife and friends?' Christie spluttered a disbelieving laugh. 'And you seek redress from the king's son, a prince to the throne?'

'With God's indulgence.'

Christie seemed unable to summon any words. He stared up at the blackened beams and rafters of the square dwelling behind the tannery, once his own house, then a storehouse until Brodie's arrival. As Brodie's dwelling, it at least now contained a corded bedstead, storage chest and table with leather-backed chair. Christie had undertaken to build a fireplace and chimney into the wall, though the work had yet to be carried out. They sat on stools around the central hearth.

'Justiciar Lindsay's chamberlain was slain on Lord Alexander Stewart of Badenoch's orders – my ears heard his soldiers assert as much.'

Christie shook his head. 'Brodie Affleck, you have surely lost your wits. How could this testimony possibly assist your...your ill-conceived cause?'

'The Lindsays of Glenesk are well known to me. The Affleck freehold...' He saw the parcel of land from afar and aloft, as though he were standing at Labothie Hill's highest point. 'My family lands were restored by the Lindsay seal. I kept company with his household.'

Christie raised a tufted brow. 'And I once shared a lavender-scented bathhouse with the Earl of Galloway – it does not make me his skainsmate.'

'The Lord of Glenesk will be eager to know the truth of his chamberlain's death. He is just and fair-minded – and no friend of the Wolf of Badenoch.'

Christie picked up the pitcher by his stool. He walked around the fire and filled Brodie's beaker. 'The murder of the chamberlain caused much concern, even among those on the king's council – I have heard as much said at head court – but the case is closed. Those soldiers are the ones who suffered the penalty. No new testimony will allow Justiciar Lindsay to prosecute against Badenoch according to the law – he is safeguarded by his father the king.'

Brodie searched for a challenge to reasoning so plainly put. Finding none – and aware that he had formed doubts of his own – he took a long drink. He swirled his beer and then drained the dregs. 'The last time I was here, you told me that your mind saw pictures of your brother whichever way you turned. Is that not so?'

Christie remained where he stood, pitcher in hand. He nodded slowly.

'Then you were fortunate – I am losing sight of my wife and her family. Their likenesses are slipping from my mind.'

Christie filled his own beaker.

Brodie continued. 'I have made it my task to obtain justice

and I will find a way to do so.'

Christie sat back down and stared into his beaker of beer. He let out a long, slow breath and then shuddered, as though measuring the final approach of a long-awaited defeat. 'Less favour would be shown to Alexander Stewart if he was not the king's true son.'

Brodie furrowed his brow in bafflement.

'If you seek disgrace for Alexander Stewart of Badenoch, you could make it known that he is not the king's son at all.'

Brodie straightened on his stool. 'Go on.'

'You were once a scribe for the king, and sat in the Aberdeen cathedral library, yet I ask you – have you ever read a word about the birth of Alexander Stewart?'

Brodie shrugged. 'I could not say with certainty, I have read many...'

'But think on it – announcements were made at mercat crosses around the kingdom at the birth of Carrick, sickly Walter and the younger Robert. Even the arrival of daughters has been greeted with some fanfare.'

Brodie was reminded of Brother Peter's Stewartis chronicle, which was commissioned on the birth of young Robert and, he was sure, contained extracts about the birth of the other elder Stewart brothers. Yet it was true that he could recall nothing in its pages about Alexander's earliest years. 'That may be so but such an omission need not have the meaning you suggest.'

Christie leaned towards Brodie, into the smoke of the fire, one conspirator to another. 'It is not widely known but King Robert's first wife, Lady Elizabeth Mure, took up residence not far from here, at her father's Rowallan keep, in the days after the boy-child Alexander's birth. Why would she do that?'

'Again, I could not say – perhaps to be in her mother's care?'

He sighed. 'More likely it was out of shame. Once there, she took a pilgrimage, along with her son, visiting the well formed from Saint Winning's tears, praying to the relics held at Mauchline and Glenluce, lying a day and night at Saint Ninian's Cave and arriving at the Shining Place on a date that would fit precisely with the boy reaching the age of one year. It was recorded in the abbey cartulary. She believed the child to be tormented by demons – the Glenluce monks who taught me literacy affirmed as much.'

'A son of the king can be demon-possessed. Even the house of Saul was troubled by evil spirits.'

Christie got to his feet and turned away from Brodie. 'But the seed of a defiler would more likely fall under the power of the devil, no?'

Brodie drained his beaker. 'You ask many questions and provide no answers that bring me any closer to finding justice.'

Christie hunched down beside Brodie. 'I am the cause of your miseries,' he blurted, his eyes wide. 'And for that I offer you a lifetime of remorse, and this hidden truth – the never-ending shame and disgrace belongs to me, and my brother, not Lady Elizabeth. I am certain that Alexander Stewart is not the king's son because his mother was ravished while our hostage in the caves of Maskeldie – a vile crime, and doubtless the reason he now seeks my arrest. And yours also, for assisting my escape. Far from a true prince, Badenoch is the spawn of that violation – the bastard son of Christie Cleek.'

Chapter 10

"Alexander Stewart, son of the king...was
accused at various other times before the king and
council of being negligent in the execution of his
office...and was useless to the community...and
ought to be removed from his office."

Roll of Parliament (1388)

14th Day of June, 1383

Brodie regarded the apparent truth of Alexander Stewart's
origins as an unearthed treasure, a jewelled votive offering
washed up on the shore: its value was obvious, but what
precisely to do with the discovery? Could he turn it to profit –
or at least the Wolf of Badenoch's loss – without facing an
accusation of crime? Was there a way to obtain further
confirmation of its authenticity? Who might he tell of the find?
Was there anyone that would know ways of putting it to use,
while also offering trusted counsel?

Brodie peered past the Saint Machar rood screen to the choir
stalls beyond, his ageing eyes straining in the low light. He picked
out Brother Peter Fenton – jowls noticeably more fleshy than
before – but not Priest John of Fordun. Brodie made his way
back through the public throng standing in the nave. He left the
cathedral through the south door, the pulse of the canons'
prayers fading as he walked east along the chanonry towards
Fordun's manse.

Priest John called Brodie through the closed door rather than
open it with his own hand.

Inside, a change in the arrangement of the room caused

Brodie to glance around in momentary confusion. Fordun sat upright in the bed, which had been shifted from the south to the north end of the manse. Crumpled in a thick layer of blankets, he was reading from a small book – the pages cut as quartos, perhaps a book of hours – which lay open on his lap. Although late evening, he had no candles burning due to the midsummer sun still casting light through a tiny window to his right. He peered over his book at Brodie but said nothing.

'Not at Mass – the bishop will call you to his chambers for a scolding.'

Fordun's sullen reply stripped the cheer from Brodie's tone. 'Lately, the bishop has less cause to call me into his presence.' He put his book down and held his hands out, as if for inspection, turning them this way and that.

Brodie moved closer, still an arm's length away but close enough to see crooked fingers and blistered skin. Looking up, his gaze snared on the broken features of a leper.

He took a step backwards.

'Leave if you would prefer,' said Fordun.

Brodie had known many infirmarians who, like Saint Francis, tended lepers; some had fallen to the malady, most had survived untouched. He took a step farther from Fordun's leprous breath but remained in the room. 'There are worthy physicians in Aberdeen…'

Fordun broke in. 'Physicians, barber-surgeons, herbalists… none can devise a treatment for living death.'

Unable to locate a fitting response, Brodie shifted his attention to his own feet.

'But I am gladdened that you are here,' continued Fordun. He patted a withered hand on his chest to show that what he said was heartfelt. 'Not many last as long inside my door as you have done. What brings you here?'

'Your counsel,' said Brodie, relieved to be able to turn to the purpose of his visit.

'Go ahead – this affliction has yet to corrupt my judgement.'

'Very well.' He twisted a loose sleeve button. 'Alexander Stewart of Badenoch has perpetrated murders and herschips, harrying and slaying,' said Brodie, judging it kindly not to augment Fordun's grief with a full account of his own sorrows. 'And I believe I have found a way to bring the punishment he is due – he is not a rightful prince and that truth should be made known.'

Fordun's stare lingered, as though he were assessing Brodie's sincerity. He chuckled and smiled dimly. 'The whole of the king's council, and many others besides, know the truth about the Lord of Badenoch – he cruelly oppresses the peaceable subjects of his own brothers, Carrick and Strathearn. Bishop de Tyninghame here in Aberdeen has beseeched the king in letters patent over fire raising and plundering in Birse. So too the Bishop of Moray due to threats and terrors in Rothiemurchus. Understand this, Badenoch is malign and arrogant – and dishonourable to his wife, Countess Ross – the whole kingdom knows as much. Yet he goes unpunished, why? Because he enjoys the protection of his father. And his father is the king.'

Brodie had readied himself for such a response. 'And if the whole kingdom learned that his true father was not the king – what then?' Before Fordun could raise a query, Brodie asked another question. 'Do you keep a copy of Peter Fenton's Stewartis chronicle?'

'In the chest.' Fordun aimed a buckled finger at a chest by the foot of his bed. 'Tell me…' He trailed off as Brodie left his bedside.

Bending to open the chest, Brodie was reminded of the words in the Mass of Separation that cautioned against touching anything used by a leper. He could not help but wonder if the clasp, or the lid, or the papers inside might carry a contagion. Despite his fears, Brodie opened the chest – releasing a waft of stale air – and leafed through documents until he found Brother Peter's chronicle. He settled on his knees and turned to the pages that recorded events after Lady Elizabeth Mure's release from captivity.

As suggested by Christie, there was no direct reference to young Alexander's birth. Only a brief, vague mention in early 1343 of two births: *"Two times in the same number of years, the Steward's gentlewoman, Lady Elizabeth of Rowallan, has had births."* The infants were unnamed though one was identified as a boy, presumably Alexander, the other a girl, likely Princess Katherine. Nothing in the subsequent pages detailed Alexander's early boyhood.

Brodie got to his feet and took the book to Fordun. 'Do you think it an oddity that a chronicle of the house of Stewart does not name Robert Steward's fourth-born son, an heir to the throne, or describe his earliest years? Could it be out of shame at his parentage?'

'Perhaps.'

Brodie had expected some measure of surprise at the announcement of his discovery.

Impassive, Fordun laid the open chronicle on top of the prayer book in his lap. 'Let me show you a curiosity about this book.' He turned forward several pages and tapped his finger first on a passage of text, then an armorial crest in the margin alongside. 'What do you see?'

Brodie took the book, again mindful of the peril of infection. Due to having copied the entire text for Brother Peter in the Saint Machar library and also using the book as a source of reference, the passage about Pope Clement endorsing the legitimacy of Lady Elizabeth's offspring as potential heirs to the throne – described as necessary due to King David's indefinite captivity in England at the time – was not unfamiliar.

'The crest,' prompted Fordun. 'Look closely.'

Brodie saw that a number of illustrations in Fordun's manuscript differed from those in other copies of the book: a picture of the Normandy plague ship, carried along on a black cloud, decorated the margins; so too an image of Robert, as Steward, sitting among the kingdom's magnates, an eagle supporting his insignia. Several heraldic signs had also been added, though Brodie's eyes remained only on the one indicated by Fordun. Smaller than the others, its colours were bolder than most: the distinctive azure and argent chequered band of Stewart against a gold shield, a black wildcat arising from a red crown.

Brodie shook his head, unsure of Fordun's meaning.

'I have seen it in no other copies of Brother Peter's chronicle, or any other books,' continued Fordun. 'The arms of Alexander Stewart of Badenoch, no doubt added by a mischievous monk who shares your doubts about his paternity.'

Brodie still did not comprehend. 'But it carries the proper mark of Stewart.'

'Look closely,' Fordun repeated.

Brodie edged closer. At that proximity, caught in the dimming sunlight, he saw that Fordun had shed much of his once wayward hair, revealing a reddened, peeling scalp. His cracked skin had darkened in colour so that the fiery mark on his cheek could no longer be distinguished.

'See the diagonal band…' Fordun traced the red strip down and across the shield. 'It runs from the upper right to the lower left.'

Brodie continued to stare at the page. Belatedly, it seemed, he grasped Fordun's meaning. 'Is it a sinister mark? One that denotes bastardy?'

'You put my teachings to some use.'

'Then this is further proof that Badenoch is not a rightful prince.'

'The scribble of one monk is unlikely to bring disgrace on the Lord of Badenoch, Earl of Buchan.'

Brodie took a step back. 'I have more – the testimony of one who has knowledge of his true father. Would that be compelling enough to bring him disgrace?'

Fordun's smoke-bleary eyes flickered, rekindling a once familiar expression of keen curiosity. 'That might depend on the identity of the true father.'

Brodie walked away from Fordun's bed, picked a log from a stack at the side of the fire and threw it on the flames. He stared across the room. 'The father is Andrew Christie, the one every nursemaid calls the bogle-man. Such a truth would surely force even the king to turn against Alexander Stewart of Badenoch.'

Fordun closed his eyes and rested his head on his bedstock.

When the priest reopened his eyes, Brodie saw a look of mild pity on his face.

'Brodie, you must be muddle-headed…'

'It is the truth.' Brodie stiffened. 'Many years ago, I prevented Christie's brother from being turned over to Lord Robert and put to the mob. I abetted his flight from Restenneth and for five, six years he has repaid me with a sanctuary of my own. I heard the truth about Alexander Stewart's origins from his mouth – his brother defiled Lady Elizabeth Mure while she was held hostage in their cave. She lived apart from her husband in the days that followed and the infant Alexander was born the precise number of expectant weeks after her captivity. He is the misbegotten spawn of that foul coupling, I have no doubt.'

A clear drop formed and then dangled at the end of Fordun's flattened, misshaped nose.

Brodie fished a rag from his own pocket and offered it to Fordun, arm stretched towards the bed. 'Your nose,' he said. 'It leaks.'

Fordun used a corner of his blanket to wipe his nose. 'What you say about Alexander Stewart may or not be true. Either way, making it known while his father sits on the throne would only cause you to lose your seditious head.'

'But history must contain truth, not the courtly fictions of John the Barbour and Peter Fenton – that was always your teaching. And if this is the truth about Alexander Stewart, it should be known.'

'Hold your hasty tongue.' Fordun held up a hand to silence Brodie. 'Just so. But not while his father reigns. Hear this proposition.' He pulled the blankets tight around him. 'Since you left your desk at the library, I have resolved that my history should take the same form as Higden's Polychronicon, a masterly work that catalogues events from the earliest times. But in compiling the chapters on the origins of the Scots, I have only found time to loosely assemble the latter years in a collection of annals, which include your additions. And now these useless claws...' He lifted his hands. 'These are no longer able to complete the task. You could gather together the annals with accounts of the most recent events, including the truth about Alexander Stewart of Badenoch. No courtly fictions – you could finish the task that you and I both began.' His nose dripped again. 'It is said that King Robert is already ailing and so you could distribute our continuous history once Carrick has taken the throne. Such a work would find considerable sympathy during his kingship. And you would be less likely to lose your head. What do you say, Brodie Affleck?'

Book VI

*"Christiecleek! Christiecleek! became instantly
the national nursery bugbear. No child would cry
after the charmed name escaped from the lips of
the nurse; and even old people shuddered at the
mention of a term which produced ideas so
revolting to human nature."*

Alexander Leighton, *Wilson's Tales of the Borders and of
Scotland* (1857)

Chapter 1

"Bury me therefore, I beg you, in a midden and write for my epitaph: 'Here lies the worst of kings and the most wretched of men in the whole kingdom.'"

King Robert III, to his wife on his deathbed (1406)

19th Day of April, 1390, until the 9th Day of May in the Same Year

The passing of King Robert the Second gave Brodie little cause to sorrow and none to bewail, though out of Christian piety he offered up a prayer for the departed. But if the king's life had brought mostly discord, some goodness might arrive after his death: Carrick would take the throne, hopefully curbing the Wolf of Badenoch's wickedness, and Brodie could seek justice of his own by bringing public disgrace on Alexander Stewart. So, in accordance with Fordun's instructions, Brodie gathered together the papers for their history – the annals from most of the past century, with only some recent accounts to add – and hauled his limbs, ever heavier with age, onto one of Christie's horses to return again to Aberdeen, thankful at least that the coldest days of winter were past, the time for his annual pilgrimage to Kilkerran not yet upon him.

A bloom of green copper-salts had formed on the padlock that secured John of Fordun's manse. Rot was beginning to creep upwards from where the wooden door met the ground. Brodie banged on the door with a flat hand. 'Priest John?' He went to the window but the shutters were closed. 'Priest John?'

The turns in the track to the cathedral church were familiar, the damp dirt below his soles the same, but all else that Brodie perceived was out of alignment, like the slight differences apparent in the copy of a copy of a manuscript. The canons' quarters were in poorer repair than he remembered, the bishop's palace grander. The precinct wall seemed to have lost some height and – lit up by an early, easterly sun – taken on a lighter shade. When he left Kirkcudbright, most trees were bare. Here, now, the dark branches in the orchard were brindled with a multitude of tiny leaves and blossom buds.

In contrast to the changes outside the Cathedral of Saint Machar, the interior remained as before. The new steeple was still incomplete – building materials lay around, though the work appeared to have stalled – and a thick coating of dust on the cherrywood reredos behind the high altar gave the carved figure of Christ a grey glow, more earthly than heavenly, just as it had on the day Brodie left Aberdeen.

He kneeled in the nave among a scattering of Monday morning worshippers, though his purpose was not to praise the Creator aloud. His opportunity came when a priest left a chantry chapel at the rear of the nave and made his way through the church. Brodie hurried over. 'Forgive me, Father – may I ask a question?'

The priest, elderly but not known to Brodie, kept his lips tight and gestured with his hand that they should leave the church to speak. Brodie followed him until they both stood outside the south porch.

'In speaking, you will not escape sin. And so you should set a guard to your mouth in the presence of God,' said the priest, explaining why he had asked Brodie to leave the church. He smiled with satisfaction, as though he might also feel contentment simply at standing outside in the spring sunshine. 'But allowance to speak is also granted, even to perfect disciples.' He nodded his permission to proceed.

'I am looking for John of Fordun, priest and historian – do you know where I might find him?'

'Him and all the other faithful with a marked grave – Priest John died more years ago than I know.'

Even in asking the question, Brodie was aware of the likely answer. But death had visited him so often that he regarded it as less of a stranger, more of an unannounced guest. 'Then he will have relief from his afflictions.' He took a moment. 'And his history – has it yet been made public?'

The old priest chuckled. 'Ah yes, has so much been said and yet so little read of any other book?'

'So it is not public?'

The priest sniffed the air. 'And who is it that asks so many questions about John of Fordun?'

Brodie hesitated, weighing up how to respond. 'Brodie of the Afflecks...' After living with an assumed name for so many years, he heard the strangeness of uttering his own. '...I scribed for Priest John – here in the Saint Machar library. Some of the history is put down by my hand.'

'Then you should be made aware of the instructions that are contained in his legacy. If I recall, it makes reference to the history, and perhaps also to you. I will put a request to Dean Fenton at chapter in the morning and...'

'Brother Peter Fenton?'

'...Is the Dean of the cathedral chapter, yes. So, is the executor of Priest John's will and legacy.'

*

Observing the terms of his covenant with God, Brodie worshipped devoutly at Mass the next morning. Afterwards, he took up a place by the Saint Machar chantry chapel to wait for the old priest, and made a start on his noonday psalms.

'Brodie Affleck...'

Brodie recognised the slow, disdainful roll of the 'r', the forename and surname uttered as though they were the inbreath and outbreath of a sigh.

'A wonder it is to see...' Brother Peter was already beyond the choir chapel, moving through the nave. Held in the frame of the rood screen archway, he looked to have put on more bulk, though he walked with an upright gait rather than stoop with the added weight. 'So, you return to the vineyard of the Lord when there is a harvest to reap. I am told you are here to claim your bequest from Fordun – yes?'

Brodie eased himself to his feet, his back stiff. 'I am here on Fordun's living instructions – to finish the history he started.'

Long since sapped of patience with Brother Peter's rancorous ways, Brodie put the question he had travelled a distance to ask. 'Do you have his papers?'

'The cathedral library holds the papers he prepared. As a priest, all the moveables in his manse remained possessions of the church on his death.'

Peter did not need to say it, Brodie understood: Fordun's papers would not be permitted to leave the precincts of the cathedral. 'The old priest said Priest John's last settlement made reference to his history. Is that so?'

Peter shifted his hands from behind his back to clasped over his gut. Brodie saw that he held folded parchment between his fingers. 'The departed Priest John of Fordun determined that his history should only be made public at a time when it could celebrate Carrick's coronation.' He shifted his weight from one foot to the other. 'And then only after the inclusion of additions by a continuer. As executor, I am obliged to say that he names the continuer as you.' He held out a limp arm. 'This was among the letters he left to be read after his death.'

Brodie took the parchment and straightened its folds. His name was written on one side of the letter in Fordun's familiar, bold hand; the other carried the priest's seal, with its unmistakable image of an all-seeing peafowl and the simple motto *"Praise to God"*. Brodie looked more closely; the seal did not appear to have been broken and then attached afresh to conceal tampering. He opened the letter.

> *"John of Fordun, by divine permission priest at the Cathedral Church of Saint Machar, to his faithful and devoted clerk, Brodie Affleck, to whom this letter comes, greetings and apostolic benediction. Give yourself no cause to mourn my death – I know only relief that this cankered body is loosening its grip on my soul – but since my life will end before my work, the task of continuing our national history until the enthronement of Carrick falls solely to you. It is laid down in my disposition and settlement that access be granted to the cathedral archive so that your writings can be joined to mine.*

> But just as flowers of different colours are gathered
> from various fields..."

A brief list of documents that Brodie should consult to complete the history followed, along with the religious houses where they were held. He scanned the works – the chronicles of Paisley and Saint Colmes Inche, the Black Book of Scone, the Old Chronicle of Cambuskenneth, a newly discovered version of the Synchronisms of Flann Mainistrech – though his eye hurried to reach a name in the text that concluded the letter.

> "...To learn more from foemen of Alexander Stewart, call upon the Bishop of Moray. Since the malign Lord of Badenoch not only excels in sloth and guile, but also disobeys the teachings of the church, to the great danger of his soul, Bishop Bur considers that a warning of interdict should be sought when he loses the protection of his father, King Robert. And if he continues to divide church lands as he pleases and do injuries to its servants, in open contempt of the laws of the realm, he should be constrained by incurring sentence of excommunication, to instruct and command him in the virtue of obedience..."

Brodie read the letter again, as if for confirmation that a mandate might truly be obtained to sanction the Wolf of Badenoch's excommunication.

'You have Priest John's instructions – now return the letter.' Peter's tone was insistent. He had moved a step closer, his hand outstretched.

Brodie hesitated before handing it over, not knowing if the contents were intended to be shared with others. He briefly considered holding the letter to a prayer candle in the votive stand. Instead, he asked a question of his companion and counsel, Mariota, who remained with him, as light as the parchment in his hand. She appeared on being called, her location indistinct but apparently sitting, ready to smile. Receiving her response, Brodie cast Fordun's letter to the floor.

'A bishop awaits my visit, though I will return soon enough to access Priest John's writings.' He turned to leave, discarding Peter's affronted glare with no need to confer.

Brodie's stride out of the cathedral took on a rhythm, his steps counting out the number of years he had made the pilgrimage to Kilkerran to pray for Mariota's soul. Ten steps: he entered the cathedral porch. Eleven, twelve: he passed through the door and out into the church grounds. An unruly wind breached the otherwise still morning, buffeting Brodie as he stood in the shadow of the doorway.

He waited until the flurry eased before replacing his hat. Rather than pilgrimage to Kilkerran for a thirteenth year, he would visit Fordun's graveside and then give hot trod to the cathedral at Elgin. The Lantern of the North contained a chapel and altar dedicated to Saint Ninian. He would offer his prayers to Mariota and Fergus there, and then seek an audience with the bishop of Moray, new-found adversary of the Lord of Badenoch.

Chapter 2

*"The game becomes thereby more the image of
human life, and particularly of war; in which, if
you have incautiously put yourself into a bad and
dangerous position…you must abide all the
consequences of your rashness."*

Benjamin Franklin, *The Morals of Chess* (1786)

22nd Day of May, 1390

Already, I have the centre ground, footmen flanked by knights.

Mac Anndra stares at the arrayed forces, his white, mine red. He leans forward, elbows on his knees, chin resting on two closed fists, brow creased. His wit is slowing with age; he cannot find a suitable response to my shrewd manoeuvres.

My next movements devised, a capture imminent – certainly a bishop, possibly a warder – I can afford to take my attention from the game board. I tilt my head back, into the sun, the brightness forcing me to close my eyes. My father is dead, but summer has still arrived, heedless of even a king's mortality. And despite Carrick's lame efforts, I remain – in all but name – the King of the North.

I turn my thoughts from mac Anndra's creaking notions of a counter-strike, and hear – what? – the groan of the rope hauling water from the well, the drawn-out yawl of a buzzard. Cracking open my eyes, I see the bird circling high overhead. I become aware of preparations being made for this night's Feast of Corpus Christi: the aroma of bread rising in the bakehouse ovens; knives cutting through vegetables onto boards; the clerk of the kitchen shouting instructions to saucerers; a meat roasting.

Best carcass of mutton? Suckling pig? Or brawn, stewing with mustard and spices?

Mac Anndra moves his warder to safety. I capture his bishop and look to inflict greater damage.

A shout beyond the bailey and then the grating of a wooden hull on shingle announce the arrival of a boat at the east gateway, likely bearing a load for the feast.

I boldly push a knight forward, enticing mac Anndra into an ill-considered capture. He resists, opting instead to meekly nudge a footman forward. I consider the advantages of opening up a new front for attack down his king's flank, stroking smooth walrus ivory between my thumb and forefinger. But my calculations are interrupted by movement to my left. Lifting my eyes from the chequered board, I watch the approach of a group from the direction of the east gateway. My constable leads ten or twelve boys and men, three of whom drag large, wheeled crates, which I take it contain costumes and stage decorations for the miracle pageant.

'Forgive me, my lord.' My constable draws closer and kneels. 'This one requests an audience.' He beckons forward a monk. Or a player dressed as a monk. The monk/player takes a step towards me then drops to his knees.

Mac Anndra seeks to keep his lines closed. We trade knights. He moves the last of the four warders from its starting position.

Engrossed in the game, I forget about the monk/player until I again look up some moments later. He is still kneeling, head bowed. 'Are you a monk or a player?'

'Good greetings, most high and most excellent. I am an Augustinian brother, Dean at the Cathedral of Saint Machar and until recently a devoted subject of King Robert – by the mercy of God, may his faithful soul rest in peace – and his royal Stewart kin. Some years before this one, at this same stronghold, I pledged that Peter Fenton would serve you loyally, my lord.'

The name Peter Fenton, a distant pledge, this fat scut: I have no recollection of these trivialities.

He is still talking. '...boarded the ferryboat with these players to bring tidings of utmost urgency.'

The board is almost clear of footmen. And now one of my warders is removed. 'Not so!' The monk is diverting my attention from the game.

'Then speak! But do not disturb my peace any longer than you must.'

'Of course, my lord. There are two matters...' He fills then empties his lungs. 'I know the whereabouts of a fugitive you have long sought – Brodie Affleck, abettor of the brother of Christie Cleek.'

Two other distant names, though these ones I have not forgotten. 'And the other matter?'

'And I have read a missive letter that sets forth intrigues against you. Bishop Bur of Moray considers constraining you by ecclesiastical censure. My lord, it is proposed that you appear before commissioners for the correction of your soul, under pain of excommunication from the life-giving mother church.'

'Ha!' Mac Anndra exclaims in triumph, taking no notice of the words the monk has delivered. He lifts my queen from her square with a flourish.

My king is bared.

Mac Anndra picks up the purse from beside our feet. He throws it high into the air, cackling like a sea mew.

My anger swelling, I get to my feet, catch the purse of coins before it falls to the ground and pitch it into the darkness of the well. 'Make thee not a master in the house of Alexander Stewart,' I cite, reminding mac Anndra of his rank. 'In taking the prize, be humble and boast not overmuch. For by boasting, men know fools.' I overturn the table board and trestle with my boot. 'Gather the pieces,' I command.

The leader of the Donnchaidh abased and groping in the mud, I advance on the monk, imagining he is a combatant in an unruly tournament mêlée, measuring my strides so that the kick I aim at his throat carries the most force possible. My foot connects neatly – neither at the ankle nor the toes, but precisely between – and his head lurches. He clutches his throat with both hands, croaking for breath, then topples backwards, over his own heels, onto his back.

I bend over him. 'You dare enter through Alexander Stewart's gate and issue threats of excommunication?'

Now he tries to speak as well as breathe, though he is unable. His face turns as red as a winter berry.

I take a firm grip of his cowl and drag him from where we are gathered, below my chamber between the north and east walls, across the courtyard. Despite my vigour, I move with difficulty due to his bulk. I yank him up so that he is able to scramble on his knees. Once we reach the south-west tower, he has regained some ability to speak.

'The threats are not mine...I bring only a warning...for my lord...from a loyal liegeman.'

I do not give ear to his pleadings.

His wild eyes skirr the tower room, hoping to alight on a feature that indicates my intentions are less than malign; all he sees is a wheel stair leading upwards and an iron grate in the centre of the floor.

I open the grate, revealing a trapdoor beneath. 'Where is this Brodie Affleck?' I ask.

'He...he was in Aberdeen in the days before the Solemnity of the Ascension, at the cathedral where I hold senior office, though he let it be known that he intended to go to Bishop Bur – I believe, in connection with your proposed exclusion from communion. My lord, you should know that Archdeacon Barbour, that good friend of your father, knows of my presence here...'

I cut short his timid mitigations. 'As dean, you are faithful to the mother church, yes?'

'I walk in God's path by the guidance of the Gospels.' Momentarily, his chest puffs up.

'The church that seeks to condemn me with bell, book and quenched candle to eternal fire and the toils of the devil?' I open the trapdoor and wrap my knuckles around a tussock of his hair.

He squeals.

I pull him until he stares over the edge of the trapdoor into the water pit.

'I beg you! Merciful prince!'

'Let us learn the strength of your prayers. If the church withdraws the threat of banishment, I will send down a rope ladder. If not...' If not, his fate is of no concern to me.

'No, no, no...It is the depth of three men, at least...I will be injured. Or drown.' His legs kick out like a wounded doe, though I hold him fast.

'The water reaches only your waist. You can stand, if not sit – just as though you were in the choir stalls.'

He tries to get to his feet.

Once again, he is an opponent in a mêlée. I throw my weight at him behind my shield arm.

His balance upset, he tumbles into the pit, falling silently, though landing with a heavy splash closely followed by a thick thud. I close the trapdoor and bolt the grate.

Mac Anndra is waiting outside the tower.

'Muster the Donnchaidh,' I tell him.

Chapter 3

"Alexander Stewart, degenerating from the morality of his forefathers...was a bastard not born of the king's lawful marriage, surrounded by a large rabble of robbers and villains."

Hector Boece, *History of Scotland* (1527)

26th Day of May, 1390

After morning prayers on the last day of his novena of mourning, Brodie submitted a request for an audience with the bishop of Moray. Before evensong, permission was granted.

Brodie nodded his thanks to the boy chorister for delivering the message and passed beyond the oak screen that separated Saint Ninian's Chapel from the altar dedicated to Saint Duthac, emerging on the north side of the Elgin Cathedral nave. One by one, he paused at the huge piers supporting the high timber roof, making the sign of the cross at each of the instruments of the Passion carved in the stonework: crown of thorns, holy lance, reed with hyssop, seamless robe, nails, dice. Although the sun had settled below the western perimeter wall, Brodie blinked as he stepped from the gloom of the church into the cathedral grounds. He took the track that led past the west towers and the grandest of the manses – precentor, treasurer, dean, chancellor – before reaching the north gate. Through the gate, he crossed the Lossie at the bishop's mill and continued north for half a league, all the way wondering if God had chosen this occasion to grant him the means to bring justice to the Wolf of Badenoch.

'You are Brodie Affleck and your business here concerns Lord Alexander of Badenoch and Buchan, I am told?'

Brodie was still breathing heavily due to the climb up the Hill of Spynie but his toils were as nothing alongside the bishop's infirmity. Two attendants – one attentive, the other wearing a look of impatience – helped the old man out of a private chapel, into the hall of the bishop's palace where Brodie waited. Bishop Bur waved them away and edged his way across the room with the help of a stick. He paused midway to allow Brodie to kiss his ring, and perhaps also to catch a breath. Brodie had expected the prelate to be of a stature that matched his status. But he had an urge to take the elbow of the old fellow who struggled to climb the two steps onto his dais. Could this frail figure truly offer the best prospect of standing against the Wolf of Badenoch, said to be two heads taller than most and with the strength of a bear? The old man eased himself into his seat. Like his cathedral throne, it glittered with silver inlay and had a covering of crimson damask but was otherwise plain and modest.

'Speak then,' he said.

'Your Excellency, it is true that my business concerns the Lord of Badenoch.'

The bishop steadied his crozier between his knees and rested a palm on the crook. 'And you are here to explain why he harries churches in Strathnairn and now gathers caterans together at Forres, just a day's ride from these walls? He intends to seize lands from the abbey at Kinloss, is that it?' He thudded his staff on the floor by his feet.

'I…I could not say, lord bishop.' The bishop's misjudgement momentarily confounded Brodie. 'I know only that I was advised to beg your ear by the historian John of Fordun, priest at the Cathedral Church of Saint Machar in Aberdeen.'

Bishop Bur grunted in a way that might have amounted to disappointment at receiving an unexpected reply. 'If Badenoch has left Lochindorb bearing arms, his purpose will be to claim church fermes as his own, nothing is more certain,' he mumbled to himself. He remained in thought for a time, head tilted upwards, before finally lowering his eyes to Brodie. 'You have my ear – say what must be said.'

'Priest John believed we could share common cause in executing justice against Lord Alexander Stewart – you, lord bishop, in seeking his excommunication; I in recording his banishment in a book that celebrates the coronation of a new king.'

'Priest John…' His eyes elsewhere, the bishop seemed to be leafing through recollections. 'Yes…John of Fordun. And this book forms part of his great chronicle of the nation, which contains favourable accounts of the de Moravia churchmen?' He looked to Brodie for confirmation.

'It is, lord bishop,' answered Brodie. He had no recollection of passages about de Moravia churchmen, though they must surely exist among Fordun's many words.

The old man leaned forward in his chair. 'And what else do you propose to say about Alexander Stewart of Badenoch and Buchan in this book?'

'If I am given access to your papers and permitted a desk and writing tools – only the truth. That he is an unfit heir who deserves to be damned and separated from the society of Christians. That he is guilty of ordering the murder of Lindsay of Glenesk's chamberlain and has slaughtered many innocents.' Brodie straightened his shoulders, unsure how the bishop would react to his next revelation. 'And that he is not only a bastard son – which is avowed by others – but that his bastard father is Andrew Christie, the one-time cannibal known as Christie Cleek.'

'Sacred Heart! But…' His mouth hung open. 'But this could not be so. You must surely be mistaken?'

'I swear it to be so – I have it from the mouth of Christie's living brother, who witnessed the defilement.'

'By the sweet saints…' The bishop sat back and closed his eyes, long enough for Brodie to consider that he may have fallen asleep. 'Is this book endorsed by the new king?' he asked at last.

'I know only that Priest John made provision for it to be completed and circulated when Carrick is crowned king…when Lord Alexander no longer enjoys the protection of his father.'

Bishop Bur snorted disdainfully. 'You will wait long enough for Carrick's investiture – crippled by a kick from Douglas of Dalkeith's horse and a lax grip on kinghood before even taking the crown in his hands.' He briefly closed his eyes again. 'The prelates in Aberdeen have little interest in assisting with a text that shows no favour to Robert the Steward or denounces his bastard son, despite his depredations in Birse – is that so?'

'I believe some at least of the dignitaries at Saint Machar remain loyal to the Steward and Lord Alexander.'

The bishop leaned forward. 'Then I will give you what you ask.' He screwed up his face and peered at Brodie through folds of loose skin. 'And you can give history the truth about Alexander Stewart of Badenoch.'

Chapter 4

"Alexander Stewart, son of the deceased king...burned the church of Forres, and the choir of the church of St Lawrence, also the manor of the archdeacon, near the town."

Moray Chartulary (c 1390)

17th Day of June, 1390

The Lantern of the North is empty but for eddies of candlelight and the melody of a score and ten booted steps: on the stone floor of the nave; across the wooden platform supporting the choir; with heels brought together in the vestry outside the chapter house.

Bishop Bur must hear the tread of our feet on consecrated ground because the chapter house doors swing open.

I walk into the room, which is filled with churchmen, and take a place before the central pillar, mac Anndra and his son by my side.

The bishop rises from the bench opposite. For support, he grips the stone frame that surrounds his seat. 'This is no place for a rabble.' He starts in a low tone, which ascends to a shout. 'Be gone!'

I hear his words but I am occupied by the craftsmanship of the structure: eight sides to the wall, in the English style; horseshoe windows that reach the vaults; richly coloured wall-hangings depicting the crucifixion – on the west side – and the Day of Judgement, on the east.

'Your business in this fine meeting place concerns me, does it not?' Last evening, I left a scorched mark where the Church of Saint Lawrence once stood in Forres – to give notice of my displeasure at Bur's threats of excommunication – so this is not an improbable assumption.

'Our business is to arrive at a fitting response to those who lay violent hands on church lands.'

'Then you must hear my petition, since I am protector in these parts.'

The bishop, who until now has shown a hardihood that belies his stalwart years, regards the Donnchaidh assembled beyond the open door. He sits back down. 'Deliver it. Then be gone.'

'You are so gracious, Father.' I withhold his episcopal title, causing canons around the room to lift their heads and gape at each other in dismay. 'Withdraw the threat of my banishment from communion and, in return, I will continue to render to the church the multiple benefits, aids and assistances provided by the protection of the lord of estates in Badenoch, Buchan and Moray.'

The bishop is staring at the floor by his feet.

My offer will only be put once so I ignore his contrariness and continue. 'And I charitably acknowledge as your possessions the territories of Laggan, Insh and the lands of the chapels of Raitts and Dunachton.' I nod rather than bow, in sham imitation of deference.

'You acknowledge territories…and offer protection…' He raises his eyes, which have a firmness absent from many of fewer years and more bodily strength. 'And will you also submit proceeds due from justiciary and sheriff courts in your jurisdiction? Or pay rents owing for the lease of six davochs in the Rothiemurchus estate? Will you desist from further trespasses against the liberties of the bishopric of Moray?' He tries to stand but barely lifts his hoary arse off the dignitaries' bench. 'And will you affirm before God, as written in letters patent and agreed by king and council, that all such lands are held by the ecclesiastical potentate directly of the Crown?' He stabs his chest with a brittle finger. 'Those are my lands, Lord Alexander – and if you are to make satisfaction for your many sins, you will declare as much as an inviolable truth.'

Once his words have reached the floor, I look again around the room. This time I discern the carvings in the stonework: owls among leaves, Christ in majesty, gowned dwarves, demons and jesters. 'Advise me – how much is due on the Rothiemurchus lease?'

The unforeseen question discomposes him. He mutters something incoherent before recovering his bearing. 'Treasurer…' The churchman two places to his left gets to his feet. 'What monies are due to your coffers from Rothiemurchus?'

'I do not have the ledgers, your Excellency. Though I know it to be seventy two pounds at least.'

'And to what purpose must the Rothiemurchus teinds be put?' My enquiry prevents the treasurer sitting back down.

He glances between the bishop and me. 'It is laid down, my lord…my lords…that they are to provide for the lighting of the cathedral.' Now he returns to the bench.

'Then I should settle that debt without delay.' I turn and leave the chapter house, the Donnchaidh following me into the chancel. I go directly to the high altar and take the linen coverlet in my grip. 'And to do so I must illuminate the Lantern of the North.' I seize a candle from the altar and put the coverlet to the flame. There are several layers of cloth and they burn slowly at first. Churchmen hurry out of the chapter house, uttering cries and gasps. The flames burn evenly across the top surface of the altar – I am reminded of being told as a young student that the undermost cloth is treated with wax – though not with sufficient intensity to engulf the altar candles, which are mounted on prickets as tall as a child. I point to a Donnchaidh who leans on a pollaxe. 'You.' I beckon him forward as I step down from the sanctuary. Together, we heave the bishop's throne onto its side; the Donnchaidh understands my meaning and hacks at the wooden chair, which shatters with each blow. We load the fragments – seat, legs and arms, rails and spindles – onto the altar. The bishop has made his way through the crowd of canons and is standing just behind me. He is defiant, issuing threats through the crackle of burning wood and linen. I lean towards him. 'More than church moveables will be given to the flames if the threat of banishment is not removed.' The full extent of my grievance made plain, I turn to lead the Donnchaidh through the nave and out of the cathedral church.

'You will be brought to account!' the bishop shouts after me. 'The truth will be known – if not for your sins, then because of your baseborn origins.'

The force of this affront, which I have only previously heard issue from the lips of my father, draws me to a stop.

'Alexander Stewart is no son of a dead king…' He cackles loudly. I look over my shoulder and see him sharing his laughter with the other churchmen. Then he points at me, his countenance grave. 'You…are the by-blown spawn of a monster!'

I halt the withdrawal of the Donnchaidh and step back into the sanctuary, where I unsheathe my sword and lay it on the burning altar. The heat of the fire is building. I go over to the bishop, who backs into a huddle of canons. 'You will be punished,' he stutters.

I seize him by the heavy cord around his neck and thrust him to the ground. He squirms when I bend over. I gesture to the sword on the altar. 'Repeat those lies about my origins as you lie there and I will melt your deceitful tongue with forged steel. Do so later, and I will return to cut it out.'

He flinches. 'I repeat only what is sworn to me as the truth.'

'Then deliver the name of the slanderer and I will cut out his tongue rather than yours.'

'I could not say a name…' I read deceit in his eyes.

'A name,' I repeat. 'And I will leave you in peace.'

He tries to sit up, though I force him back down. 'I refuse to play a part in your villainy,' he spits.

I contemplate dispatching him as he sprawls on the church tiles. Before doing so, I assess the positions of the Donnchaidh lest the churchmen are foolish enough to mount a resistance. Mac Anndra, his son and three others stand behind me; the rest are gathered by the rood screen. Hundreds of gold stars glitter on the wooden screen, clustering around a holy cross. A notion arrives. 'The screen…' I say to mac Anndra. 'Strike it down. Fuel the fire.'

The rood screen cracks and splinters under heavy Donnchaidh blades. In no time, the fire in the sanctuary stretches towards the roof timbers.

Other than to impel his dignitaries and canons to pray for deliverance, the bishop refuses to speak a word. His silence causes the Lantern of the North to burn brighter.

'Brodie Affleck!' The shout comes from an unseen mouth amid the group of canons. 'He scribes in this cathedral's library.

And sleeps in a bed in the town. Put your questions to Brodie Affleck – and spare this sacred place any more flames.'

I had not anticipated any name in particular, though I am struck by how little surprise it causes me to hear this one.

Unbowed, the bishop continues to do no more than hold my stare. Before releasing my grip on his collar, I remove his bishop's ring – which is loose on his bony finger – and pitch it into the flames. The staff by his side follows. He resists when I try to wrench the cross from his neck, clasping it in a scrawny fist. I gather the slack of the cord and twist it around his neck until he chokes. 'Lord...give me strength and protection...' he gasps.

The churchmen begin to scatter.

'Against...evil and enemies...'

The cord snaps.

The bishop slumps backwards. 'Not the cross,' he croaks. 'It is cut from the beams on which Andrew the Apostle was martyred.' He puts his hands together in supplication. 'It must be passed to my successor. I beseech you.'

'Without doubt, it is a venerable relic,' I muse. The wood has worn smooth against many a cassock and warped slightly where the crosspieces meet. 'Such ancient wood will surely produce a bright flare.' I toss it into the fire, though it barely flickers. 'Consider it your contribution to my Rothiemurchus account,' I say.

He finds some strength to respond as I leave. 'You are a blasphemer, Alexander Stewart,' he yells.

I do not look round, but imagine him on his knees, grasping a bruised throat.

'And the son of the chiefest monster of all. Know this – your true father is the butcher called Andrew Christie. You are the seed of Christie Cleek, Lord Alexander. And that is a truth you cannot destroy in the fiery flames.'

I do not pause – the defamatory words associating me with the insect creature are quickly gone, drifting like smoke among the rafters – though I do turn to mac Anndra, the only one likely to have heard the bishop's taunt. 'Put the place to the torch,' I say. 'The boards on the floor, the joists in the tall towers. And any who remain within.'

Chapter 5

"The men of lord Alexander Stewart, son of the late king…in the presence of the said Lord Alexander, burned the whole town of Elgin and the Church of St Giles in it, the hospice beside Elgin, eighteen noble and beautiful mansions of canons and chaplains, and – what gives most bitter pain – the noble and beautiful church of Moray, the beacon of the countryside and ornament of the kingdom, with all the books, charters and other goods of the countryside preserved there."

Register of the Bishopric of Moray (c 1390)

17th Day of June, 1390, until the 19th Day of the Same Month

'Sire…Sire!'

Only in beginning to wake was Brodie aware of having previously fallen asleep. Before opening his eyes, he assembled his most recent waking moments: considering whether the destruction of Lochmaben Castle in the year 1385 was of sufficient historical significance to merit inclusion in Fordun's chronicle; experiencing a weary reluctance to return to a shared guest bed with torn sheets at the hospital of Maison Dieu; resting his head on the writing slope.

'Sire!' The canon shook Brodie's shoulder.

Raising his eyes, Brodie saw that saliva had crept from his open mouth onto the arm supporting his head, the candle on his desk had burned close to its holder.

And a young canon stood by his side, breathless.

Brodie recognised him as the attendant who had paid close heed to the bishop's needs in the throne room three weeks earlier.

'Your life is in great danger,' said the canon. 'You must leave.'

Brodie's vision was blurred in the eye that had been pressed against his arm. But the canon's warning matched the description provided by his other rousing senses. His ears heard the sound of distant shouts; his eyes discerned a shifting darkness beyond the library shutters. He recognised a faint odour of drifting smoke, appreciated the fearful urgency in the canon's tone.

'Lord Stewart of Badenoch is here,' continued the canon.

A surge passed through Brodie. Confusion: the Wolf, here, now? Guilt: despite imagining for ten years and more all the ways he might arm himself and take revenge, he understood in an instant that he lacked the strength and courage to do so. Fear: mostly he was filled with the simple urge to flee.

'But how…?'

'He is here to challenge the bishop over his excommunication.'

'But…'

'But he also seeks you – the one who describes him as packsaddle born, the seed of a monster.'

Packsaddle child. The seed of a monster. In the words, Brodie's fear was momentarily put aside by his recollection of the mysterious riddles folded in his knife sheath. *'From the seed, a whelp will crawl…Stewarts, Christies; damnation all…From a whelp, the wolf will grow…Packsaddle child, full grown foe.'* The lines of verse, which previously made no sense, took on an unmistakable meaning: they concerned the origins and rise of the Wolf of Badenoch, along with the threat he posed to Brodie and Duncan Christie.

'Lay bare the truth about Lord Stewart's depredations, just as you promised the bishop.'

'Depredations?'

'You will see for yourself when you leave here. Find a place of sanctuary, or better, go to those who stand against Stewart of Badenoch – the Earl of Moray, who has a stronghold at Darnaway, or find your way to Lindsay of Glenesk's keep at Daviot in Strathnairn.' The canon looked around in agitation. The shouts outside were close enough to make out the rustic tongue of Badenoch's brigands. 'Caterans approach – you must make haste.' He spoke in a low voice.

The thud from the adjoining room told Brodie that the main door had been thrust open with sufficient force to crash into the wall that held its hinges.

The canon reduced his voice to a whisper. 'Leave through the shutters. I will hinder them.'

Brodie put his hands together in prayer and bowed his silent gratitude.

The canon took a long breath in through his nose, in a way that made him stand taller, and then pushed open the curtain that divided the library from rest of the chancellor's manse. His sudden presence must have surprised the caterans because there was a lull before they let forth a clamour of commands and questions.

Moving with as little sound as his haste permitted, Brodie gathered his papers in a satchel. His footsteps drowned by the disturbance in the room beyond – the canon spoke the caterans' tongue with facility and so Brodie understood only snatches of the exchange – he moved to the window.

One of the caterans in the next room raised his voice higher than the rest. '...more fierce than any evil in hell...'

Brodie gently loosened the latch and eased open the shutters, at once relieved to discover that no glass had been fitted – unlike the bishop's palace and precentor's manse – and troubled that the window opening was considerably smaller than the shutters.

As he assessed the likelihood of making a successful escape, a hush fell on the next room. A moment later, a new voice spoke, this time in the lowland vernacular. 'If this is a library, where are the books?'

The canon hesitated. 'Through the curtain, my lord.'

'Burn every slanderous word.'

Abandoning caution, Brodie yanked open the shutters and tossed his satchel through the gap. Directly across the main north-south track, a group of three or four caterans with torches approached the door of the dean's manse. The cacophonous hiss and spit of an established fire came from behind, in the direction of the church. Brodie struggled to push one shoulder then the other through the window. But after doing so, he slithered out with some ease, landing awkwardly on one elbow. He gagged a yelp behind clenched teeth. Amid the confusion of canons, chaplains and church servitors running to and fro with water tankards and fire hooks, Brodie hurriedly made his way to the north-east corner of the cathedral precincts, where the shadows were at their most dense. With each weakening step, he imagined the dark figure of the Wolf of Badenoch, thick, black hair trailing from his head and chin, straining after him through the small library window, bellowing murderous instructions to his men. Brodie only chanced a backward glance once he had passed the fishpond and moved behind the bee yard: no caterans were in pursuit. He leaned against the perimeter wall, labouring for breath. No longer of few enough years to run with ease, a cramp stiffened his right hip. His elbow ached. He inspected his trembling hands, holding them to his face. Beyond his place of refuge, above the cathedral grounds, the late midsummer dusk was ablaze.

The fire was at its fiercest where the transepts and central tower crossed the nave and within the walls of the chapter house, which had already lost its roof. Flames jagged through the rose window on the west front and between broken buttresses on the north tower. Among the other buildings within Brodie's view, the chancellor's manse and library – so recently his place of slumber – were beginning to burn brightly. Smoke churned from the manses of the canons of Inverkeithny and Unthank along with those occupied by the dean, sub-dean, treasurer and precentor.

All Brodie could hear over the din of destruction was the swift flow of the Lossie directly behind the perimeter wall. He squatted down. Such was the infernal scene before him, he doubted that every last trickle of water from the riverbed could douse the unquenchable fire set alight by the Wolf of Badenoch.

*

Brodie made his escape from Elgin Cathedral to the scurrying rhythm of the river and his riddles.

His feet followed the gush of the Lossie, through the small arched gate used by the launderers, briefly north and west along the riverbank, then south out of the burgh. The words of the riddles marked the beat of his steps: four steps for every line of verse. *"From...whelp...wolf...will grow. Packsaddle...child...full grown...foe."*

But his wayguides took him only so far.

The riddles led him from the day he arrived at Restenneth Priory towards the fall of the Christies, and then onwards, past the rehabilitation of the Afflecks to the rise of Alexander Stewart. But no farther; however many times he recited the words, they offered no promise that he would find a way to prevail against the Wolf of Badenoch.

The course of the River Lossie took him through the short summer night to safety, but still a distance from the protection of either the Earl of Moray or Lindsay of Glenesk.

The sky behind his back aglow – despite the passing of dawn – Brodie crossed the bridge over the Lossie at the steep side of the Hill of Wangie. He reached Darnaway before a new night began to fall. The castellan provided him with salted pork broth and a woollen mattress. But due to the Earl of Moray's absence, only a valet of the chamber and a valet of the stables remained in residence with the castellan. Since such a meagre household could not assure Brodie's protection against cateran marauders, he accepted instead the offer of a mule. At cock-crow, he directed its rein towards whatever defences Lindsay of Glenesk's Daviot keep could provide.

Brodie's approach to Daviot told him that Glenesk's castle was as well garrisoned as Darnaway had been lightly manned. A crowd watched squires running the tilt in a tourney field on the west side of the keep, cheering when a young warrior in a high saddle successfully hooked the rope ring. Foot soldiers carried out other displays of military prowess; a small group of archers practised with their warbows, spearmen their javelins. Noblemen mounted on barded chargers watched the exercises from a hillock to the north. From a distance, Brodie discerned that several of the horses were clothed in caparisons of Lindsay red and azure. Closer, he saw that the largest, a destrier of at least sixteen hands, also bore Glenesk's seven-pointed, silver star.

A squire, his charger undressed, rode down from the hillock and drew alongside Brodie. 'You have business with the tenantin-chief and his lordships?'

'God speed, I am delivered here on the advice of a canon at the Cathedral Church of the Holy Trinity by Elgin, to ask for Lord Lindsay of Glenesk's protection from Alexander Stewart of Badenoch.'

The squire sat up in his saddle, keen and alert. 'You were at the burning?' Due to an oversize coif hooding his lean, beardless face, it was difficult to determine the squire's age.

'Word has reached you here?'

'Word of Badenoch's atrocities has reached farther than Strathnairn, and long before now. On hearing of the rough treatment of churchmen here at Daviot and also at Cawdor, Lord Lindsay ordered that we safeguard these walls and withdraw from the court of Richard of England – the day before the grand tournament of all sixty knights and the feast of the challengers at the Bishop of London's palace.' The adoption of a petulant tone placed the squire closer to boyhood than manhood.

'So, may I beg your lord's permission to retreat behind his defences?'

The squire replied with a haughty sneer. 'Retreat? Only for shame! We prepare for an assault on Stewart of Badenoch, not a retreat.' He slid the coif back from his brow and scratched behind a jutting ear. 'But Lord Lindsay would no doubt allow even an old man to take up arms in his cause.'

The squire's coif pulled back, Brodie could better judge his age: at least fifty, perhaps as many as sixty, years lay between them. 'In the time before your birth, I made fealty to Lord Lindsay, and owed him service for holdings near Monikie. The only blades I wielded in his vassalage were a ploughshare and sickle head, though I also cut pens to a sharpened point in his library. That could now be my weapon in your war with Badenoch.'

The squire looked puzzled.

'Will you put my proposition to your lord?'

The boy shrugged, replaced his coif and waved for Brodie to follow him towards the hillock.

Chapter 6

*"I humbly implore your Majesty to compel the
incendiaries to give suitable satisfaction for proper
re-edification, and the other damage which they
have occasioned."*

Bishop Bur, in a letter to the king seeking reparation for
the damage at Elgin (1392)

*19th Day of June, 1390, until the 24th Day of November in the Same
Year*

Such was Lord Lindsay's eagerness to assist with an enterprise
likely to bring disgrace to Alexander Stewart, he ordered that
Brodie be lodged in a chamber with garderobe until the disused
brewhouse by the river could be converted into quarters suitable
for a scribe.

Once in his quarters – scents of sawn pine from his newly
constructed desk, shelves and bed box still fresh – Brodie
completed his accounts of the Wolf of Badenoch's foul descent
and violent misdeeds. In the weeks following midsummer, he
wrote too of the offensive against the lawless royal heir, whose
excommunication was confirmed by the papacy in Avignon
before the month's end. Having established peace in the south
due to ratification of a truce with England on the Feast of Saint
Mary the Penitent, the king turned his forces north. The Lord of
the Isles was enlisted to maintain security in the west, the Earl
of Fife in the south-east. Lord Lindsay prevented disturbance in
Inverness, Strathnairn and northern Angus, while also reclaiming
territories in Atholl and Ross from Stewart's possession. Only
Mar and the Mounth in the undefended north-east remained

disorderly, as the continued arrival of those seeking refuge at Daviot testified. The numbers taking shelter in the great hall – and also on Brodie's floor – dwindled during harvest, though increased again when full grain stores provided the Wolf's raiders with added bounty.

One of the castle serjeants pushed open the door to Brodie's quarters. 'Newcomers,' he announced. A stiff autumn gust yanked the rope handle taut in his hand. Beyond, the wind pulled the falling rain hither and thither. Fat drops ran off the roof and splashed in a puddle at the serjeant's feet. 'And they have accounts for your pages.'

Brodie remained bent over the hearth, but closed his eyes against the flurry of ashes thrown up by the swirling draught. He stood, poker in hand. 'If any are young enough to rake this fire and fetch water for an old man, they are welcome to a bed here.'

The serjeant wiped his dripping brow with a gloved hand. 'Your luck is out – these sanctuary seekers are more elderly even than you. An old woman led by an old man.'

'They have travelled far?'

'The old dame shares a name with the Christies from the Howe of Alford.'

Christie?

'And the other is a churchman from the priory at Monymusk.'

Monymusk: the most northerly Augustinian house, small but with a noteworthy collection of ancient texts.

'Was the priory put to the flame?'

The serjeant struggled to haul the door shut against the unseasonable westerly. 'He says little, to me or any others – you should ask him for yourself.'

*

Allowing the sanctuary seekers a full two days and one night to rest, Brodie only made an approach to hear accounts of their misfortunes after supper on the third day.

Advised by the marshal of the hall that the old woman was detained in the infirmary but the churchman was close by, Brodie sought out the dark robes of an Augustinian among the throng. He found the churchman by the wall farthest from the

330

main doors, a distance from the fireplace and close to no others.

'It would be warmer by the fire,' Brodie suggested.

Hunched over, head almost between his knees, only a tangle of the churchman's thinning brown hair and a mound of woollen tunic were discernible. He offered no reply.

'Have you eaten?'

He shook his bowed head.

'You have come from the Church of Saint Mary and priory at Monymusk?'

He lifted a foot bound in thick, grimy bandages in silent response.

'You have suffered at the hands of Alexander Stewart of Badenoch?'

'Three score years a smith…' Finally, he spoke. The muffled voice was familiar, but only as a memory mostly forgotten. He removed a hand from his sleeve and slashed the air with an imaginary blade. 'And I could not swing one of a hundred tools in defiance.'

The demonstrative gesture, the self-mocking tone, both belonging to a Monymusk Augustinian skilled in shaping metals: Brodie recognised enough to make an estimation. 'Brother? Brother Finlay?'

He looked up, his features withered but still bold and gaunt. Forty years ago, he had tossed Brodie a farewell glance, casual. Now his stare was intense, if broken by emphatic, repeated blinking. Despite the passage of so many years, he showed no signs of surprise at laying eyes on a long past brother – now a secular – in such unexpected circumstances. Instead, he gave a single nod of acknowledgement. 'You are safe.'

'As are you,' offered Brodie, uncertain how else to respond. 'And the old woman who travelled alongside you – she is also safe, God be thanked, and receiving treatments.'

Chin resting on his chest, Brother Finlay again said nothing.

'Do you sleep by the fire?' All around, droplets of rain were falling where the roof was in need of repair. 'I have private quarters, if you would prefer?'

'You are kind,' he said, still not providing a direct answer to Brodie's questions.

'Brother, the old woman who arrived with you uses the name

Christie, is that so? And your priory is set in lands held by Christies, yes?'

'Christies and Farquharsons.'

'So Badenoch and his caterans have moved east – to seize the territories of those families?'

'Brother Brodie...' His use of the fraternal address suggested he had taken no heed of Brodie's return to the world. 'Badenoch no longer seizes property, he lays it to waste – Alford, Pitfichie, Lumphanan, the Hill of Fare, Crathes, Finzean – all lands belonging to Christies and their Farquharson kin. Since being driven back by the king and his barons, he pursues a new purpose, one within his grasp – finding the fugitive Christie brother and executing a writ of arrest.' Brother Finlay's fixed expression stirred due to the arrival of perplexity, eyes narrow, missing a blink. 'But surely that is the same reason you take refuge here – because you abetted Christie in his escape from Restenneth?'

Only in being directed to its start point could Brodie clearly see the route he had taken.

Assisting Duncan Christie's flight from the priory half a century before.

The Wolf issuing writs for their arrest.

The slaughter of Mariota, Fergus and the others.

Brodie's search for vengeance.

Learning the truth about the Wolf's misbegotten origins.

Describing those origins to Bishop Bur.

The Elgin canon's warning: "He also seeks you – the one who describes him as packsaddle born, the seed of a monster."

The destruction at Elgin and brutish execution of Duncan Christie's writ of arrest.

Yet Brodie saw too that following those waymarks had failed to bring him closer to justice. Rather, it seemed likely that he had done no more than provoke the Wolf's villainous wrath. 'Have any been harmed among the Christies and Farquharsons?' he asked.

'More have lost their homes, or their winter supplies.'

'And the priory – was it put to the flame?'

'Only the gatehouse.'

Brodie experienced a relief that the library, with its rare books, had been spared.

'Though some brothers fell not to rise again.'

Brodie's relief turned to guilt. He lowered his head. 'God have mercy on their faithful souls.'

Finlay again cast his eyes downward. He stared at his own hands and began distractedly rubbing his thumbs along the tips of his fingers, as though crumbling a mixture in a baking bowl. 'Brother Hugh was beaten due only to declaring that he once lived among the Restenneth brothers who allowed the Christie fugitive to enter their priory and take sanctuary.'

Prompted by mention of the name, Brodie's failing memory belatedly recalled that Brothers Hugh and Finlay had left for Monymusk together in the days after the plague. 'Did he escape their blows?'

'Beaten with sticks until his arms and legs were broken, his body dumped in the mill lade alongside the fraterer, almoner, some number of brothers.' Finlay rolled up the hem of his tunic, then sleeves, to show his own ripe, spreading bruises. 'There was murmuring from one of the others for a short time – I think the old fraterer – but I lay still among the bodies until after darkness.' He lifted his gaze, unblinking, until it drew level with Brodie's, in what might have been a weary plea for forgiveness. 'And then I ran – like a hare from a hound.'

Chapter 7

*"[It] has been the cause of wars, plundering,
arson, murders, and many other damages and
scandals."*

Pope Clement VII, in a letter to Scottish bishops about
Badenoch's marriage to Euphemia, Countess of Ross
(1392)

Winter, 1390, until the 23rd Day of November, 1391

The chill northerly ushered in by Advent brought a frost that set
the floods of November hard. Brodie huddled by the hearth,
unable to follow an urge to pass swiftly out through Daviot's
gates and journey to the south-west, to warn Duncan Christie
that the Wolf of Badenoch had executed a blood-stained writ of
arrest containing his name. But as the winter lengthened –
curbing even cateran forays in Mar and the Mounth – Brodie
turned to the realisation that his inclination to leave Daviot was
due in equal measure to a wish to put himself beyond the reach
of the Wolf. Like most ice-bound inhabitants north of the
Scottish Sea, he shivered as the snow falls continued into
Ascensiontide; but during some waking nights, Brodie also
trembled at the prospect of a flaming cateran bolt arcing over
the outer bailey in the direction of his quarters.

As it was, no oil-soaked arrow lodged in his roof timbers,
before or after the thaw. Nevertheless, he compiled his accounts
of the raids on Christie and Farquharson territory with a new
caution. If the few words Brodie uttered to Bishop Bur had
found their way to the Wolf's sharp ears, and stirred such anger,
how might he react when the full truth of his bastardy was made

public in Fordun's great history?

Brodie chose to make his approach when Lord Lindsay was commonly at his most content, after the monthly show of weapons by the garrison soldiers and men of means from Craggie, Scatraig and Mains of Faillie. He waited in the barbican between the inner and outer gates until he heard the approach of footfalls heavy under burnished armour, the signal that Lord Lindsay returned from an inspection of the stables and gatehouse. 'My lord, I beg to make a request.' Brodie doffed his hat.

One old man to another, but still Lindsay pushed out his chest and lengthened his stride in a display of youthfulness. 'Ah! My learned advocate against Alexander Stewart of Badenoch.'

Brodie experienced a mild qualm at conspiring with Lindsay to use the written word against the Wolf, and so straying from Fordun's teaching that history put down by a partial hand was no history at all.

'We have hand cannons from France to burn up any caterans who stand against us,' Lindsay went on. 'Did you hear their blasts?'

'Their smoke and fire will bring justice.' Brodie shifted his hat in his hands. 'As will the history to which I contribute,' he added, returning to his purpose. 'My descriptions of Badenoch's evil doing have been completed in just these past days. With your leave, I will now follow Priest John of Fordun's final instructions and consult documents held in religious houses in the south to conclude his remaining pages.' And, with good fortune, also visit Duncan Christie and his family at the tannery by Kirkcudbright.

'Defeat is close for the ignoble prince,' continued Lord Lindsay, as though deaf to Brodie's petition. 'It is said he may be ready to make satisfaction for his sins in order to find peace with the king and have his excommunication lifted by the church. Perhaps as soon as the next council held by the king. His submission, if forthcoming, must be recorded, alongside his disgrace.'

Brodie had an answer of sorts: neither his writings about the Wolf were complete, nor his inhabitance at Daviot.

*

Pennoned spears and braided banners raised high, Lord Lindsay's armed company joined the track that led to Perth. Caught in a low, mid-morning sun, the bare trees on the east bank of the River Nairn cast huge, monstrous shadows, across the dark water to where the horses and mules picked their muddy steps.

The council of the king convened in the library of the Dominican Church of the Friars Preachers after morning prayers a week before the day of Saint Andrew. The friars had pushed the library desks to one side, along the north wall, and set up tables from the refectory in the centre of the upper storey room, the settings for the king and those of first rank perpendicular to the others. The notaries and clerks, Brodie included, occupied the open carrels along the south wall, facing into the room rather than towards the small, square windows that overlooked the South Inch and the damp dwellings of Perth. Squires and retainers stood by the doorway.

Lindsay sat almost at the head of the lords' table, alongside some others Brodie recognised from latter years: Alexander Leslie, Thomas Dunbar, Bishop Bur, the fathers in Christ from Aberdeen, Ross and St Andrews. Less recent faces, ageing gradations of once striding youths, also appeared through the door: the Earl of Fife, Sir Archibald Douglas, John the Barbour. No Brother Peter Fenton, Brodie observed. And no Alexander Stewart of Badenoch, a face he had yet to see in any of his years.

Since Badenoch had still not arrived by the time the king took his place – and so his expected submission could neither be made nor received – the gathered prelates and nobles turned to other matters awaiting the great seal. The abbot at Cambuskenneth complained that some Linlithgow bailies had unjustly compelled the lands of Kettlestoun – leading to agreement that a precept be drafted forbidding such encroachment – and the appointment of Ingram de Lindsay as archdeacon of Dunkeld was confirmed, to Lord Lindsay's obvious satisfaction. The queen consort's private secretary began to set out the many reasons why she required an allocation that matched her new status when proceedings were interrupted by a single thud on the door.

The principal usher to the council entered the room alone and bowed. 'Your Highness, lords, prelates – Lord Alexander Stewart of Badenoch, Earl of Buchan and Ross.'

Brodie stiffened on hearing the name, and at the promise of close proximity to a long-standing foe of such fearsome reputation. Yet the figure that followed the usher into the room was not wholly as expected. Tall and dark, but neither as tall nor as dark as described. His hair fell in heavy, dank twists but reached only his shoulders rather than the length of his arms, and none grew from his chin and cheeks. Head bare, weapons surrendered and accompanied by a soldier girded with the belt of knighthood rather than a boorish cateran, his demeanour was at least courteous, even peaceable. His tow-haired knight, who held a distinctive kettle hat that put Brodie in mind of Thomas of Ersildoune for the first time in many years, stood among the other attendants. The Wolf, in gleaming cuirass and tabard, strode the length of the long table, close enough to the carrels for Brodie to feel a disturbance in the air as he passed. He went down on one knee before his regal brother. 'My lord the king. I am prepared to make satisfaction.' He spoke in a surprisingly soft, if simmering, hybrid of lowland and upland tones.

'You are prepared to do so?'

'On the wise counsel of my confessor and keeper of arms, John de Coutts – to avoid eternal punishment. And please my king.'

'You kneel before me, a man of respected and distinguished lifestyle, sending down sweet showers of flattery. And yet you have repeatedly shown yourself to be a violator of your own pledges, who twists away from his intentions. Why should I provide you with any forgiveness?'

'Your forgiveness would be a prize worth winning, most gracious king. Though you need no reminder that only a minister of Christ's mercy may pronounce absolution from the bonds of suspension and interdict.'

Brodie studied the Wolf's features: eyes that appeared small below thick, black brows, his nose buckled at its bridge. Somewhere beneath his steady countenance, he might have concealed a further expression. A taut sneer? A smirk at his own conceit?

'No man, even priest or bishop, can pardon an unpardonable

sin,' countered the king.

'I beg pardon and peace only from the Father of mercies, whose grace has no limit. And since, as you say, my communion with Christ has been gravely impaired, the reparations I make should be as generous...' he dwelled on the word. '...as my sins were grievous.'

Bishop Bur sat impassively, his eyes averted. Alongside him, Bishop Walter Trail of St Andrews – not as old as Bur but almost as enfeebled – raised his hand to intervene. The king nodded his permission, then fixed a sullen stare on an upper corner of the room, lips tight in the way of a child left to sulk.

'The Lantern of the North,' said Bishop Trail. 'Famed for its pious worship of God. The delight of strangers, praise of guests and boast among foreign nations. Lately, the glory of the realm. No longer. What reparation, however generous, could possibly restore its lofty towers and venerable utensils?'

'Only a firm purpose of amendment, true contrition – and an annual defrayal of twenty pounds for the whole period of Bishop Bur's mortal life.'

Bur put two flat palms on the table and hoisted himself into a standing position. 'And will you truly pay this twenty pounds? Or will you pay it in the same way you settled your Rothiemurchus account?'

Keeping his eyes only on the king, the Wolf ignored the taunt. 'Twenty pounds is a fee worth paying for the renewal of fervour and progress along the road of virtue.'

'But how could you make such a payment?' Lord Lindsay also got to his feet.

The Wolf rose from his knee and spun around. His knuckles tightened. 'Asks a lord of an earl?'

Lindsay marched down his side of the table, turned at the far end and made directly for the Wolf, finishing little more than a stride past where Brodie sat. He thrust out a finger. 'An earl by right of his countess wife in Ross and Buchan – a wife he treats worse than a hedge-pig – and master of stolen lands in Mar and the Mounth.'

The Wolf gave a single, slow shake of his head and then turned to again face the king. 'Heed not this defamer, brother king. His unmannerly words are not worthy of a yeoman let alone a lord. The payments will be made, just as I say. For salvation is found in redemption from sin.'

The king considered the Wolf of Badenoch for a length of time. Eventually, he sighed, despairing, and returned his gaze to the rafters. 'To secure lasting peace in this kingdom, is there one among us willing to offer absolution, supposing satisfaction is given?'

Bishop Bur sat back down.

Bishop Trail wheezily cleared his throat. Before he could speak, Lindsay lunged at the monk in the carrel next to Brodie, the only scribe whose nib still busily scratched on parchment. 'You are recording these proceedings?' He snatched the top page from the black friar's writing slope.

The monk leaned away. 'I am required by the king to make a public instrument, my lord.'

Lindsay scanned the document – his head as well as his eyes moving across the lines of notations – before swatting it with the back of his hand. 'The wrongful lord is not to be trusted.' He reached towards the monk, as though handing the page back, but instead held it over the desk candle. As the parchment flickered, he twisted his head to face the Wolf. 'Just as you burned the Lantern of the North,' he declared. 'Your words in this hall are no more than lies and false promises.' Lindsay dropped the flaming parchment to the ground.

The black friar jumped up to stamp out the flames.

'But be assured that the truth will be told about Alexander Stewart. My own scribe prepares just such an account.' He waved an arm vaguely in Brodie's direction. The gesture was inexact enough to indicate any one of the scribes in their carrels, or even a place beyond the south wall where they all sat. Yet the Wolf of Badenoch showed no such imprecision in where to direct his gaze, the weight of it causing Brodie's eyes to sink.

He loaded his pen with ink and feigned adding a gloss in the margins.

'Your scribe...' the Wolf drawled. Then, leaning close so that his words were a whisper in only Brodie's ear: 'And an abettor of Christie insects.'

A soft spray of spit settled on Brodie's cheek with the last word uttered.

He leaned away, still addressing Brodie but in a tone that reached every ear. 'Then put down this truth, scribe – the payments will be made.'

'And if they are not,' said Lindsay, 'you will answer to me in the list field. No earl could refuse such a challenge from a mere lord, is that not so?'

*

On Bishop Bur's commission, the Wolf of Badenoch was led to the door of the Church of the Friars Preachers and absolved from the bonds of excommunication, on condition that he make satisfaction of twenty pounds every year to the cathedral at Elgin and cast himself before the black friars' altar at the first and last hour of every Lord's day for seven weeks. He would fast on the three Ember days of Advent, Bur decreed, and remain excluded when Lord Lindsay and the others of the king's council feasted for eight days during the Octave of Epiphany.

Chapter 8

"He who does not know the evils of war will not reap advantage thereby. He who is skilful in war does not make a second levy, does not load his supply waggons thrice."

Sun Tzu, *The Art of War* (c 490 BC)

26th Day of November, 1391, until the 18th Day of January, 1392

For six Sabbaths, a shirt of raw goat's hair rather them camlet woven through with silk grazes the skin on my back and chest. For six Sabbaths, the Bishops Bur and Trail watch from the sedilla in the choir, Lindsay and his scribe from their gallery in the nave, as I bare my knees to bend before the high altar.

My churchly penance almost complete, I summon de Coutts. 'You have readied the Donnchaidh?' I ask.

'Awaiting your command, my lord.'

'Those whose names are most commonly uttered alongside mine – mac Anndra, his sons, de Atholl, the Duncansons – must remain in the shadows. As my confessor, you know more than any the depth of my penitence for damages at Elgin. But God is vengeful as well as merciful, is that not what your teachings advise?'

'He speaks as thunder from the sky when enraged.'

'Then Lindsay should hear that fury – for his insolent words in the Church of the Friars Preachers. His scribe, too, for writing deceits in the presence of the body of Christ. But since I am serving a sentence of ecclesiastical censure, others must be seen wearing this breastplate of righteousness. Raise the Donnchaidh septs – Mathieson, MacNair of Lennox, Slurach and his brothers. And take this message to Lachlan Mackintosh of Chattan, who also has been disadvantaged by Lord Lindsay's overbearing rule – great spoils are to be had if he makes alliance with Lord Stewart of Badenoch.'

I prostrate myself before the altar for the seventh and final occasion.

Unlike the other lords of council, the bishops do not linger once the spectacle of my penance is over, leaving Perth to prepare their churches for the Lenten season. Before the last baggage carrier has crossed the North Inch, de Coutts stands before me once again. 'You have Mackintosh's response?'

'He would take the Clan Chattan to the place where Christ himself suffered to obtain a herd of winter cattle the size you describe.'

A pact agreed, de Coutts returns north with word of the manoeuvres I have devised.

I wait, mimicking further, self-imposed penance by venerating the relics at the monastery on the hill at Scone, though laying eyes on the severed head of Saint Fergus for such a time simply brings to mind the certain outcome of any contest between flesh and steel.

I pray for one day and more while Lindsay makes ready to return north. When he announces that he will depart the following morning for the investiture of his kinsman, Ingram de Lindsay, as archdeacon of Dunkeld, I take my leave. Under whip and spurs, I reach a good trot on the road out of Perth while Lindsay's stableboys brush and braid like milk-coddled chamber maidens.

Clan Chattan men are encamped in every clearing as we pass through the woods at Birnam and Tomgarrow. The Donnchaidh and their kin are gathered by the river and in the mouths of the shallow caves on the north bank. Those of senior rank tryst at the most northerly of the falls of Braan: mac Anndra and his sons, John de Coutts, the Duncansons, de Atholl, the Mackintosh chieftain and his lieutenants. Our agreement is confirmed: Mackintosh and the Clan Chattan will lead the march into Angus; the Donnchaidh and I will take the rear, visors on close helms lowered, all armorial bearings and identifying livery removed. The spoils will be shared two to one in favour of the

Chattan men.

Three hundred in all, we follow the River Tay east by the last of the daylight. When we cross at the point where it meets the Isla, we have entered Lindsay territory. And so our work begins. The farms at Balgersho and Caddam are relieved of their stock – and their dwellings, where resistance is offered – during the dark hours. We reach the main prize, the rich farmland around the Cistercian abbey, as the new day slowly approaches. By the third hour, more cattle than men turn along the flagged road that leads north-west.

After skirting Blairgowrie, in the cold, still air of Drumlochy Muir, the gallop of a messenger from the south, our rearmost position, gives me cause for a moment's dislocation: since the strategy is to lure Lindsay into a combat along the main route from Perth to Strathnairn, I had judged any alert most likely to arrive from the advance guard in the north-west.

He draws to a halt. 'The Angus sheriff, Ogilvie, spurs towards us, Lord Alexander – at the head of a knightly troop.'

The teachings of others have done little to instruct my mind, but every general heeds the lessons of those who have previously made the choice between peace and peril. One such lesson comes unbidden: any manoeuvre that takes a leader of forces by surprise immediately becomes an attack on which his attention is fixed, like two sides of the same circle.

From my position – a slight elevation, covered to the west by pine woodland – I have a clear aspect in most directions. With a single, studied sweep of my head, I see this: north, the trail tilts upward, exposed on all sides; east, Mackintosh and the Clan Chattan on the flat ground of the heavy Cochrage mosses, leading the plundered cattle along the drove road; south, farm dwellings and the Glasclune round tower.

I give the messenger instructions to carry to Mackintosh: the Chattan men are to turn about; the herd and a fourth part of the body of troops – the oldest and least able – should be placed on the far side of the Glasclune Burn, at the threshold of the marshland, where they can be seen drawing water as though suffering from thirst; the remainder will take harbour in the outbuildings by the Glasclune tower.

I lead the Donnchaidh to the tower itself. No farmhand or

servant stands in our way, or even comes into sight, as we pass through the open Glasclune gate. A cateran broadaxe promptly persuades the old laird – as well as his dame and three ill-armed squires – to unbolt the round tower door. Along with mac Anndra and my close advisers, I occupy the topmost storey; the Donnchaidh take the lower tiers, three floors and a cellar.

From my stance at the garret window, I watch as those Chattan men not positioned by the burn hurry the last distance to places of concealment among the outbuildings. Before they are at a standstill, Ogilvie's approach is announced by the thud of hooves on damp turf. He follows the route of the herd, south of Glasclune. Staring into the low sun, through stunted burnside rowans, I catch a glimpse of shimmering steel as they pass by: at least a score, perhaps ten more, all sturdily armed and active. They slow their pace to cross a beam bridge – so preventing a great noise – before falling from sight on the far slopes of a hillock directly to the east. Emerging at the crown, Ogilvie draws rein, doubtlessly espying the herd grazing by the muir. He tarries, perhaps taking counsel, but for only a short interval.

Armed with righteous madness, assisted by the downslope, they are on the Chattan herdsmen in only moments. As instructed, the herdsmen abandon the cattle and scatter as if in disarray. Some lose their feet, and their lives. I count Ogilvie's mail-clad horse – a score and half-dozen, the colours of Sir Patrick de Gray among them – as they are drawn farther into the marsh. Unable to form an assault with lances lowered, they draw their swords and slash at fleeing Chattan men. But with each step and slash, hooves sink deeper into the mire, knights are unhorsed.

And a once united force becomes scattered.

I give the signal, blowing two long moots on my hunting horn.

And the Chattan hounds are let loose. A hundred warriors and more issue from the round tower gate, some taking the drove road, just as many others following the path of the Glasclune Burn. With no slope to climb and descend, those going by the banks of the burn arrive at the muir first. Before the last of the other group comes into sight, the rout is complete. As contrived, those not slain – including Sheriff Ogilvie and Sir Patrick de Gray – are permitted to escape in haste to the east. With some small assistance from Fortune, they will unite with

Lindsay at Dunkeld or elsewhere on the Perth mainway. As arranged, no pursuit is given.

The Clan Chattan load their dead onto a cart – it is not piled high – and halter the knightly horses that remain with legs intact. Then they continue north along the drove road and past the Blackcraig Forest; the Donnchaidh follow, under cover, on their flank.

We pass unhindered through Strathardle until the grey walls of Glen Brerachan steepen. At the glen's narrowest – beyond Tarvie, close to Dalnacarn – the first arrows fall on Chattan heads. From my position, leading the Donnchaidh along the southern bank of the Brerachan Water, I hear the cries of Chattan men, but see no attackers drawing back bow strings.

I halt the Donnchaidh, keeping a vigilant eye on those places that might conceal bowmen.

Another volley of arrows falls like a shower of hail. In the same moment, directly across the glen, a small flock of choughs suddenly changes direction, letting forth a series of grating screeches as they veer off. And I have the enemy's precise position.

"There is nothing more difficult than battle tactics – their difficulty lies in the calculation of time and distance, and the reversal of misfortune."

I detach the MacNair and Mathieson septs from the main body of Donnchaidh and lead them down to the floor of the glen. We cross the river where it slows and twists west, but find the rise to be sheer at the place of the ambush.

"The leader who changes his tactics in accordance with his adversary, and thereby controls the issue, may be called the God of war."

Rather than scale the rocks – as some Chattan men are attempting to do – we move away from the attack until arriving at shallow-sloping ground. Once there, we climb higher than the assailants and follow a ridge behind their position. Close by, it is clear they are little more than a rabble. One man is horsed but not in grand style. A local laird: Kindrogan, perhaps, or Edradour? His footmen throw as many rocks with their hands as loosen arrows from bows. The MacNairs and Mathiesons fall on them, mercilessly dashing out blood and brains.

"Ability to estimate the enemy, and plan the victory; an eye for steepness, command and distances: these are the qualities of the good general.

Whosoever knows these things, conquers; he who understands them not, is defeated."

The skirmishes won, Donnchaidh and Chattan marshal on the carse by the river. We travel the final distance through Glen Brerachan together – horses at a canter, herdsmen on our heels – to lay the fatal snare for Lord Lindsay. And where the master goes, so follow the servants, his deceitful scribe included.

Chapter 9

"Woe unto him who, when he falls, has no man to raise him up."

Proverb ascribed to King Solomon

18th Day of January, 1392, until the 19th Day of the Same Month

"Just as Saint Stephen – full of the Holy Ghost, replete with wisdom – was appointed the first of the seven deacons, so Ingram de Lindsay..."

The Dunkeld Cathedral doors clattered open, and then shut. The bishop paused his sermon.

Brodie turned his head; a knight, garments muddied and bloodied, appeared through the porch.

Bishop Sinclair resumed the installation ceremony, now watchful. "So it is that Ingram de Lindsay, who stands by this altar, is made a deacon in lofty degree, higher than the others..."

Rather than take his place at the rear of the church, the knight marched to the front of the nave, soles striking slabbed stone.

Bishop Sinclair fell silent. Occupying the stall to the bishop's right, Archdeacon Ingram de Lindsay looked up from the book of gospels – symbol of his new office – that sat open in the palms of both hands. Faithful to his new rank, he scanned the church for any who neared the precipice of sin, as though he were the eye of the bishop.

The knight stopped at the choir and went down on one knee, bowing low. 'My lords, forgive me.'

'Why interrupt this holy investiture, sheriff? Explain your purpose,' demanded Bishop Sinclair.

'I interrupt, lord bishop, due to a great urgency.' Sheriff

Ogilvie stood and swivelled to face Lindsay of Glenesk, who sat on the frontmost bench. 'Your estates are overrun, Lord Lindsay. This morning, I led a troop to arrest the lawbreakers but a great force was lying in wait among the marshes. Our horses could not…'

'Overrun?' Lord Lindsay rose slowly to his feet. 'Which estates?'

'The winter herd is taken – some hundreds of head of cattle. All from around Coupar Angus.'

'And the reivers – what was their kin?'

'They were Gaels, my lord, though I could not say more with any certainty.'

'Clann Donnchaidh? Fergusons or Shaws from the Chattan Confederation? Was Lord Alexander Stewart of Badenoch among the commanders?'

'Perhaps some, or all, of those tribes. More likely Chattan. But I saw nothing of Lord Stewart.'

Bishop Sinclair stepped forward. The new Archdeacon de Lindsay shifted his dalmatic where it had slipped off his left shoulder.

'This…this struggle that led to your flight…' The bishop did little to conceal his scorn at the failure of the sheriff's resistance. 'If it occurred earlier this same day, as you say – then where are the brigands now?'

The sheriff lowered his head. 'Though I escaped through guile and prowess, I was held for a time by one I believe to be a chieftain since he boasted in our own civilized tongue that his intention was to seize the entirety of Lord Lindsay's herd, next wending north to take those in Strathnairn.'

'Only Lord Lindsay's stock?' asked the bishop.

Sheriff Ogilvie looked to Lord Lindsay. 'Begging forgiveness, but the bragging chieftain said that, unlike others, your lordship had no cause to slaughter stock for sustenance through the famine months due to being favoured with excessive plenty and cursed by an arrogant invulnerability.'

Lord Lindsay puffed up his chest and took two long strides forward, to where the sheriff stood. 'Did any others escape unslain?'

'The stalwart knight Sir Patrick de Gray. My own brother in

near degree, Lychton of Ulishaven. Though before your arrival here, I also rallied the lairds of Cairncross and Guthrie. Ochterlony will reach us by morning, along with a band of knights.'

Lord Lindsay stepped up into the chancel. He turned to face the congregation, nostrils flared, jaw tight, the secular lord now officiating in place of the religious. 'Then these savages will be made to know that a prize disgracefully won does not bring favourable results. Before tomorrow's end, their heads will submit to Lindsay swords.'

*

In preparation for the rigours of conflict, Lord Lindsay's combined force broke fast with white loaves, salted bacon collops and blood pudding. They left Dunkeld with darkness still in place, three score horse and men, a mist of their breathing rising into the otherwise cloudless early morning sky. Brodie, the keeper of Lindsay's seal, his cofferer, the retainers and baggage carriers formed in close rank between two companies of knights and squires, Lord Lindsay in the vanguard, Sheriff Ogilvie and the Angus lairds at the rear.

The horses, well strawed and newly shod, made good ground, slowing only when they entered a thick, drifting fog at the carse where the Tummel met the Tay. The mounted party reduced its pace, travelling with a new alertness. Brodie tightened his grip on his reins. Moving through the fog – which at once provided concealment and near blindness – he returned to the Wolf's whispered, bodeful words. "Your scribe...abettor of Christie insects."

Past an age to relish the looming conflict, a weight shifted, eased, as first one packman, then another wayfarer, failed to provide Lindsay with any reliable sightings of the raiders' movements.

'Kindrogan?' The shout came from behind Brodie, just as Lindsay was calling the company to a halt at the Port na Craig ferry crossing. 'Kay of Kindrogan?' Sheriff Ogilvie added, riding past Brodie and the other attendants. He drew rein alongside a mounted knight at the head of the steep quayside. The sheriff clapped the knight's shoulder, exchanged words, and then called Lord Lindsay to join them both.

Brodie shuffled his mare closer, though could make out only parts of the discussion that followed. For certain, the mounted knight at the crossing point – the Laird of Kindrogan, just as Ogilvie supposed – had engaged in hard battle with the plunderers, suffering, it seemed, grievous losses. Brodie could not be sure, but the combat appeared to have taken place the day before, some hours after the battle near the Glasclune round tower. The plunderers, Kindrogan judged, might since have reached Dalreoch, or perhaps he gave the place name as Dalnacardoch? Lord Lindsay tossed his head back, then forward – mail collar rattling on shoulder plates – in irritation, or impatience. He dismounted, pushed through the crowd and spoke briefly to the ferryman, who Brodie recognised from the earlier southward journey. Lindsay remounted to address his followers. 'The moment to deliver our attack draws near.' He framed the declaration with silence: the battle-hardy general emboldening his troops.

Head and heart, Brodie slumped.

'The thieves passed close to here before nightfall, following the droveway north. But they are mostly footing it, while we have the fleetness of good horse. And since their way is to travel by night and lie among the heathers by day, they can be no more than ten leagues from where we stand, likely a distance less. Our horses will rest while we take provender with the Laird of Kindrogan's kin at the Black Castle across the river.' He punched a gloved fist first in the laird's direction, then at the opposite riverbank. 'But only until the sun rises above the roof of the Church of Saint Colm at Moulin. Then we spur fast, outdistancing the outlaws while they slumber, to set a trap at the Pass of Drumochter, which they must cross to find a way north.'

Cramming onto the ferry, alighting at the inlet on the north bank, passing the reedbed that showed signs of marl digging, at each place Brodie considered with dread the day that lay ahead. The respite would be brief: warm hearth, bowl of pottage, pitcher of ale. Then: an arduous ride north; the numbing chill of a clear, January sky; bearing witness to the slaughter of a band of uplandish rogues.

Brodie's brooding was disturbed by a clamour, incongruent, its source difficult to place.

He stopped, as did others around him, midway between the woodland fringing Moulin's lowly dwellings and the Black Castle walls.

'To the north,' one shouted, pointing. 'On the low slopes of Ben Vrackie.'

Heads turned.

And their ears were met by a din of harsh roars and steel blades clattering on wooden shields. At the same moment, a disorderly multitude of footmen issued from a winter-brown hillside copse, like a swarm of bees roused from its hive.

Lord Lindsay glanced this way and that, assessing options.

'My lord, your orders?' asked Sheriff Ogilvie. 'Should we counter?'

Lindsay sat up in his saddle. 'We know their stratagem from your battle at Glasclune – they wish to draw our horse onto soft ground, either in retreat the way we have travelled or on the wetland that lies between us. We will do neither. Are they the same strength as before?' he asked Sheriff Ogilvie.

'I would judge so.' The sheriff looked intently at the onrushing horde. His lingering gaze and furrowed brow betrayed a disquiet. 'Perhaps more.'

'Then we will make south for the castle gate, with no need to maintain rank and order.'

'But we cannot shrink from this mob behind stone walls, my lord, whatever their number.'

'It is no more than the appearance of a retreat. We will form a battle array on that field...' He pointed his drawn sword at a fallow parcel of land to the west of the castle. 'They will be forced to continue their charge longer than they would choose, and our horse will find firmer ground – then we will strike.'

Feigning confusion, the troop formed neither head nor tail as it moved along the track towards the castle. With no need to feign confusion at the tumbling course of events, Brodie simply followed the flanks of the charger ahead.

'We must show more urgency!' Kay of Kindrogan rode past at a gallop, yelling at Lord Lindsay. 'They are almost upon us!'

Lindsay slowed rather quickened his gait. He peered over his shoulder at the assailants.

Brodie followed Lord Lindsay's stare. The advancing marauders – ragged in appearance, most clutching round targes and brandishing close blades – were as near as the flight of an arrow, and still running on full tilt.

'Take positions at the far boundary of the field – Ogilvie, Sir Patrick and Ulishaven on the right flank; Ochterlony, Cairncross and Guthrie the left; I will take the centre along with Kindrogan. Retainers and clerks…' he nodded directly at Brodie, 'seek refuge in the castle, and behold the spectacle that will surely follow.'

Brodie and the others not armed head and hand crossed the field towards the castle's eastern gate. His mare sank some way into the dirt as it moved, though no deeper than its shod-iron hooves. The soil, still dusty with frost, was firm enough to withstand the pounding to follow, he judged. But if the ground underfoot would not hinder Lindsay's horsemen, the weather above may yet do so; Brodie watched as lumbering grey clouds curdled low in the eastern sky.

But more than just clouds stirred on the horizon. Brodie continued on his way, though his eyes remained fixed in just one place, the crest of a squat, spreading hillock beyond the castle. And the sight he beheld there was joined by a new noise – barely discernible over all the others – a long, low rumble. 'Can it be?' he muttered. Then louder, for others to heed, his breath coming fast: 'A herd is loose – and approaching our path!' He heard his own disbelieving tone.

But all saw the truth of it: great numbers of cattle – a hundred, two hundred, more – overflowing the nearby hillock at a tumultuous rush. And drifting above the charging herd, what Brodie at first took to be plumes of dust – unlikely given the frozen soil – revealed itself as smoke. Some of the beasts were alight. Or at least torches hung from their tails, causing them to hurtle and bellow in a frenzy of pain. The recognition that tows and resin had been attached to the beasts brought with it an understanding that the headlong charge was the work of man rather than God. Sure enough, a detachment of mounted horse followed a short interval after the last of the herd surmounted the hillock, driving them forward.

Brodie was ahead of even the keeper of Lindsay's seal, who rode a swift hunting courser, in the dash for the castle gate. A shift in the pitch of the commotion on the field – steel on steel rather than wood, high wails among the war cries – told him that the main bodies of men had come together in hard combat. Brodie stared only ahead, assessing distance and time. He urged his mare on with a jab of his heels. Lindsay's seal keeper, cofferer and two others were now ahead. A baggage carrier alongside cursed his rouncie for twisting its neck and ducking its head. All were forced to slow when the ground close to a trickling burn turned to a soft silt. But after passing it by, the castle's east wall as well as its sheer northern aspect came into view: gate open, drawbridge edging down. The herd was close, the mounted escort closer. But the shorter distance was with Brodie and the retainers. Brodie clenched his legs, kicked, slapped his mare's neck, its ribs, the point of its hip. He yanked the reins to the right. And crossed the boards of the drawbridge to safety.

Inside, Brodie cast around for a stableboy or place to tether his mare.

'Leave it!' shouted a castle warden. 'Follow this way.' He stood at the bottom of a spiral stair, one foot on the first step. The warden wafted his hand here and there, in a way that beckoned not just Brodie, but all the retainers, to follow his steps.

They reached the battlements, each finding a place at a crenel, as the herd bore down on the combatants in the field. And they looked on as the marauders, one moment hacking with mad ferocity, scattered as sheep without a shepherd at the blast of four short notes on an unseen horn. Lord Lindsay and his knights had maintained good drill and discipline following their opening charge, and so might have believed the enemy to be fleeing in fear. For certain – at least from Brodie's view-point – they appeared not to have noticed the herd approaching at their backs.

One of the squires was first to lose his seat. A knightly horse bore back but was brought under control. Another bolted. Others stamped and pawed the ground. Wheeling his huge destrier in a tight circle to prevent it rearing, Lord Lindsay turned south towards the source of the horses' distress. He let out an urgent command, inaudible from the Black Castle parapet boards, and the knights and squires attempted to rally. But before they could do so, the cattle were among them, still driven at speed by the mounted herdsmen. Most evaded the beasts, but could less easily control their own mounts. Amid the broil, the marauders who had recently withdrawn now returned to the field. Guthrie's gold and red standard fell as his horse bucked, so too the bright blue of Cairncross. One squire followed by another was hewn down, ravaged by swords. Ochterlony plunged into the crush and was transfixed with a spear, still strapped to his charger. Only a small group led by Lindsay and including Sir Patrick Gray – sagging on his horse and so perhaps also dead – Kindrogan, Sheriff Ogilvie and Lychton of Ulishaven kept their saddles, sweeping out their blades and giving such dints that the enemy made way wherever they moved. Breaking through the ranks of marauders, they hastened towards the castle.

Seeing the manoeuvre, the mounted drovers left the herd – beginning to calm as the torches were removed from their tails – and made chase.

By hard endeavour, Lindsay's depleted troop came to the castle without further loss. A boy poked his head uncertainly from a narrow embrasure high in the gatehouse. 'Open the cursed gate, child!' demanded Kindrogan. 'Can you not see it – I am Kay of Moulin's kin?' A small look of horror and the boy disappeared.

The mounted herdsmen rounded the north wall as the drawbridge lowered. One of their leaders raised a shout; they beset Lindsay's men before the drawbridge had reached its midpoint.

'Raise it! Or you will yield the castle!' shouted the warden, now atop the battlements over the gatehouse. The drawbridge jerked, stopped and began once again to close. The warden looked on in dismay at his young charge: frustration at the boy's failure to let down the drawbridge before the arrival of the assailants, swollen to exasperation that he then came so close to inviting them inside to occupy the castle. 'Idle-headed, witless bantling.' The warden leaned and spat over the parapet wall, as if ridding himself of a bitter taste. His ire come and gone, he returned to urgency, seeking out a timid creature by the north-east tower.

'My lord…' Brodie took the figure – slender and unnaturally tall, but still a youth – to be Kay of Moulin. 'Your kinsman does not have the force to make a defence – we must assist…On your directive.' He dipped his head to one side, brows arched, deference with a practised reminder of the need for decisiveness.

The young lord straightened his mail vest. His hands remained tightly clutching its hem. 'Of course…Make all effort.'

'Then hear me!' The warden shouted it, to all those gathered on the battlements. He nodded at two footmen, sturdy in thick-padded arming shirts. 'My own serjeants will lead the defence, by my side. Along with this stronghold's smiths and wrights.' He raised his chin to indicate he was next addressing Lindsay's retainers at the rear of the grouping. 'All of you will also aid your lordship by drawing blades in his cause.'

Brodie caught himself resting, then removing, a hand from his knife sheath.

'Our strategy is this,' continued the warden. 'When we are at the ready, the drawbridge will be lowered…'

'But we will surely be overrun,' protested Kay of Moulin.

The warden ignored his young master. 'We call on Kindrogan and Lindsay to join us on the bridge, where our combined force can be attacked on all but one side, by only a limited number of horsemen. In joining the fray, we deal strokes savage and swift – swordsmen swinging at riders; those with short blades pricking the underside of their mounts.'

Brodie again felt for his belt knife, puny in a thicket of barbed arrows, broad blades and heavy hooves.

'Once all Kindrogan and Lindsay men are with us on the bridge, we draw back, making double haste, allowing our bowmen to loose their arrows. As the foemen shelter beneath a protective mantlet of sling shields, the bridge is raised, taking any adversaries still on it into the moat.'

The warden squinted over the parapet wall. Below, a number on both sides had been brought to ground by the coming together. The assailants – who outnumbered Lindsay's men by two to one – were mostly upland herdsmen, but certainly no rabble. As many as five were armed head to foot, none bearing coloured livery, but all with near unblemished coat-armour and finely crafted helms, peaked Milanese sallets and kettle hats.

'With God as our help, we will make an end to what they have begun,' declared the warden. 'Make ready to fight!'

So bleak was Brodie's spirit as he waited for the drawbridge to slowly open, he could as easily have been sitting in a sinking boat, or crouching in a burning house. The warden had formed a sizeable force from within the castle walls, though they were armed with an ill-array of weapons: as many hammers, cudgels and cleavers as swords, pikes and well-ground axes.

When the bridge was little more than half lowered, the warden began the advance. Brodie shielded his eyes against the creeping sun. He edged forward, unable to move more hurriedly through the press. The warden took a spiked mace on his cheek, lifting him off his feet. Brodie heard phantom echoes of his bellow-grunt even after he had fallen. A flaying sword was lighted up by sunlight. The serjeants reached the length of the bridge and jumped down onto the moat embankment. Brodie's foot skidded, on scale moss, or bloody splashes. The bridge settled into its groove with a judder. He stumbled. Fighting men stepped off and onto the wooden boards, making attack and defence. Over their heads, Lord Lindsay's countenance was distracted; bewildered; buoyed. He exhorted his men to move towards the drawbridge. A tan warhorse loomed, its hooves causing the wooden planks to shudder more vigorously. A castle smith, still in leather apron, beat its knees with a splintered shaft. Brodie lunged at its neck, catching its brisket. 'The scribe!' shouted the rider. Clearly those words. 'I have him!' The knife stilled in Brodie's hand. The horse-soldier was one of the knights he had observed from the battlement: armed cap-a-pie in steel plate, red spurs on his heels. Although a ventail covered his chin, his expression was visible – eyes clenched as though guarding against smoke and smoulder – due to wearing a kettle hat rather than helm with visor. Brodie made the connection without the need for further thought, as though instinctively parrying a blow: two months previously, in the library of the Church of the Friars Preachers, the same kettle hat, held together with distinctive brass rivets, had called Thomas of Ersildoune to Brodie's mind. Then as now, it belonged to a knight with straw-blond hair that fell over his ears, below its rim; one of those leading the unidentified band of marauders appeared to match the appearance of the Wolf of

Badenoch's confessor and keeper of arms, John de Coutts. The drawbridge creaked, lifting a fraction but then stalling under the weight of all those crowded onto its boards. One of the serjeants called out: 'Retreat – in good order!' Some turned and ran to the castle gate. Others appeared not to hear the command. Arrows hissed through the air and thudded into targets and hard ground. A riderless horse scrambled on the bank beyond, then slid thrashing into the moat. Brodie stabbed again at the tan horse before him, this time causing a seeping wound. Backing off, he groped for its bridle in an attempt to haul it off balance. The knight – some doubt had arrived, could it be de Coutts? – switched his sword from one hand to the other and slashed down. Brodie withdrew his fingers before they were removed. The bridge crept upwards, causing not a few to stagger. 'Lindsay is the chief trophy!' The yell came from the embankment, causing the blond knight to sit upright, as though it was intended for his ears. 'But so too the abettor!'

Your scribe…abettor of Christie insects.

Eyes now level, the blond knight stood in his stirrups. He raised his broadsword with both hands, high over his head. And was flung from his saddle by the arrival of a long-lance through his mouth. Lord Lindsay, upright on his destrier, gripped the handle of the lance. 'Go, go, go!' He urged Brodie towards the castle gate. Brodie gaped. The kettle hat rolled from the prone knight's head. He staggered to his feet, hands cupped around his bloodied face. Seeing the knight's distress, a roughly clothed footman ran some short steps at Lindsay, who twisted his shoulders to come firmly on once again. He pinned the assailant back with whetted lance tip. The footman gasped but showed no other signs of discomfiture. Pulling himself forward on the shaft of the lance, he roared like a rending lion and swiped his sword at Lindsay's ankle, shearing leather boot and saddle straps. Lindsay let out a wretched howl and released his hold of the lance; his foot swung loosely from his leg. The bridge tilted, swayed. Brodie looked around; fighting men were jumping off one end and the other, the man Brodie believed to be de Coutts at a crawl. The bridge rose more freely. Lindsay's horse lost some grip. The folds of the footman's clothing, and perhaps also his flesh, remained pressed to the boards by the lance. The bridge jolted up, no longer any effort being made to raise it circumspectly. Lindsay sat unsteadily on his horse, his head lolling, as though he may at any moment slide to the ground. Brodie grabbed his bridle and, voices beckoning from the gateway, stumbled down the steepening drawbridge.

Shuttered behind the castle's defences, someone took the bridle from Brodie's hand. A number of others joined in easing Lindsay from his saddle and carrying him into the courtyard. Two castle wives left the side of a wounded soldier – sitting upright, arm held out stiffly – and ran over to tend the lord. 'His leg took a sword,' Brodie explained. 'The bone is broken and should be set. He would benefit from henbane, or mandrake. And a paternoster.'

As with the others not receiving treatment for wounds, Brodie hurried to the battlements to watch the next movements of the assailants. Reaching the top of the spiral stair, he tallied the scatheless: one of the serjeants, most of the castle craftsmen, only Kay of Kindrogan from among the knights. Although those within the castle were scant in number, they could take some relief that the force beyond the walls, on the far side of the moat and with the herd on the field, produced no siege hooks or pots of Greek fire. More than Brodie would expect had dismounted and were kneeling in prayer. Some others made a great show of their victory, waving drenched arms and baring their breeches amid a babble of jeers. One made to piss on Ogilvie's splayed remains, another rolled the corpse of his half-brother, Ulishaven, into the moat. A distance on, one of their knights stood apart, close to the burn on the east side, his back to the castle. After a glance around, he removed his helmet and stepped down the shallow bank. He leaned over and ducked his head under the water, then turned, dripping, back to the bank. Through the sparse shadows of withering shrubs, Brodie distinguished black hair, heavy with water and sweat, which reached beyond the knight's shoulders. He saw too dark features against pale, beardless skin; features that, at least from afar, closely resembled those he had regarded for seven weeks as the Wolf of Badenoch cast himself before the black friars' altar in penance for sins many and grave.

Chapter 10

"We should take steps to ensure that notorious wrongdoers dwelling in the highland parts of the kingdom, who have inflicted and continually inflict without cease slaughters and burnings and other great harms and injuries on our faithful subjects already for a considerable period of time, are restrained and curbed from committing such evil deeds."

King Robert III, in a letter to the sheriff and bailies of Aberdeen (1392)

25th Day of March, 1392, until the 25th Day of September, 1396

Deliberations of the three estates adjudged adherents of the Clan Chattan to be chiefly responsible for the wrongdoings at Glasclune, Dalnacarn and Moulin, with fifty or more publicly proclaimed and denounced at market places. Some Donnchaidh followers – John and Michael Mathieson, the Slurach brothers – were also put to the king's horn. But none of standing were strictly punished due to an insufficiency of identifying evidence. Brodie's insubstantial testimony before the assize provided the Wolf of Badenoch with a new grudge to place upon significant others, but achieved no more than that alone. Lachlan Mackintosh of Chattan withdrew to his distant seat at Loch Arkaig, beyond the reach of the king's ayre but close enough to Kay of Kindrogan to allow a feud to simmer and boil.

Lord Lindsay continued to wage war against Badenoch but, perceiving a greater weakness, he did so through court and council rather than with steel and fire. On behalf of Countess

Euphemia Ross, supported by Bishop Bur, he petitioned the papacy with accusations of the Wolf's cruelty, adultery and concubinage. Pope Clement the Seventh's grant of a separation of marriage bed and board restored the countess's belongings, and deprived the Wolf of any claim to lands in the earldom of Ross. But despite the loss of further rents – from the baronies of Urquhart and Bona, as instigated by Lindsay and confirmed by the king's seal – the Wolf continued to make satisfaction for damages caused at Elgin, promptly submitting reparation payments of five pounds before every successive term day.

And on each term day, Lord Lindsay and Brodie arrived at Elgin Cathedral to confirm notification of payment.

'Here!' Since two winters past, Bishop Bur had received Brodie and Lindsay in his chambers, lying on his stand-bed, propped by a bolster. This Lammas Day, despite his ill health, he sat upright in a chair in the cathedral grounds, just through the south gate. He waved an arm and shouted again. 'Here!' His voice was sharp enough, and impatient, even if his body had all but submitted to death.

Leaving the north-south track, they moved closer, slowly due to Lindsay's infirmity. Brodie saw that the bishop sat on a litter rather than a simple chair, canopy overhead, cushioned covering the colour of dyer's rocket, wooden footstool attached. He was alone, though two canons worked with cropmen closely behind, preparing ground for planting where the Unthank manse once stood. The bishop was so slight a figure that Brodie wondered if any bones existed beneath his fulsome blankets and robes. He seemed to read Brodie's expression. 'The sun helps my condition,' he said.

A warm breeze shifted the long grasses around their feet but – Brodie looked to the sky – the sun was held securely behind a slab of marbled clouds.

'The loaf…' reminded Lindsay.

Recalling his duty, Brodie kneeled to offer the bishop the Lammas loaf.

'And sitting here, I can better watch for the arrival of Badenoch's courier,' the bishop added, taking the bread.

'He has not yet arrived?' asked Lindsay, instantly attentive. 'The Lammas payment has not been made?'

'Just as you say, no payment has been made.' The bishop's smile barely nudged his cheeks, though his narrow, eager eyes disappeared in pleats of loose skin, betraying his glee. 'And if it has still to be made by the end of this day, the Lord of Badenoch must be held to account – just as you vouched in the Dominican church when he was given absolution.' He cast a glance at Lindsay's lame leg. 'But if the flower of chivalry, conqueror of England's Lord Welles, has a buckled stalk – who will now meet him in a joust?'

Lindsay followed the glance, his eyes coming to rest on his own bent ankle. He stiffened the arm that rested on his cripple's stick but showed no other hesitation in replying. 'In anticipation of this day – though I admit I expected its arrival sooner – I have put my mind to just that question.' He met Bishop Bur's sly smile with one of his own. 'And in so doing, I have devised a way to bring dishonour, not just to Lord Stewart of Badenoch, but also to his accomplice, Mackintosh of Chattan. A number on each side – Donnchaidh and Chattan boors arrayed against my bold champions and the finest who owe allegiance to Kay of Kindrogan. In judicial combat before our lord king, the nobles of the realm and the whole community.'

'The victors to be crowned with laurels, the vanquished to accept defeat as final...' The bishop tilted his head sideways, nodding in approval. He clicked his tongue with each forward movement.

'The iniquity of men brings them to justice,' Lindsay concurred.

The bell tolled – not the great bell that Brodie recalled, but some other, less lofty instrument altogether – and all three looked up.

'For now, we are called to bless the Lammas loaf,' continued the bishop.

Lammas, it occurred to Brodie: the final day of the wolf-hunting season.

*

The combat approved by the king without demur, Brodie documented the preparations. Missive letters with the royal seal

361

were dispatched to Badenoch and Lachlan Mackintosh of Chattan. The judicial battle was to be held on the Monday before the Feast of Saint Michael the Archangel, in the gardens of the same Dominican monastery where the Wolf declared his repentance. The royal exchequer contributed fourteen pounds – and, as some weeks passed, a further three shillings – towards the cost of the contest. Iron barriers were erected around a deep ditch on three sides of a level square at the Inch north of Perth, the Tay in spate forming the fourth boundary of the combat area. A timber gallery for the king and his nobles was constructed around the friary's gilded arbour summerhouse, with benches laid out for burghers and merchants.

And with every hammer blow that transformed the carse into a grand arena, Brodie edged closer to the day he would once again come within range of the Wolf of Badenoch's harsh gaze.

September winds arrived on the day of the contest, carrying tattered clouds quickly by and causing flurries of tree spores, as tiny and cold as droplets in mist, to drift and swirl from branches.

Since the numbers of influential witnesses invited were so great, Brodie sat near the door of the friary church at morning prayers – a good distance from the place he had watched the Wolf make satisfaction – leaving sharply to ensure he found a seat that would support his bowed and aching back. The lower ranks – craftsmen and apprentices, rustics who had left behind their husbandry – were already gathered in a great multitude. Due to it being the first morning without rain since before the autumnal fast, the earliest of them had recognised an opportunity in the occasion and set up stalls to sell victuals and wares. On seeing the church begin to empty, some drifted from the vendors' stalls to find a position on one of the frontmost benches or barriers. The seats around Brodie also started to fill: the friary brothers; canons from the churches and monasteries of Perth and Scone. A good number wore Augustinian robes: Andrew de Wyntoun, Prior of Loch Leven and makar since Barbour's death a year before, conspicuously took a place in the summerhouse; to Brodie's left, a novice – sturdy for his years, ruddy-cheeked, calm and courteous – introduced himself as an Inchcolm Abbey apprentice's hand with the name Brother Walter, from the noted family of Haddington bowmakers. A party of knightly French visitors, all wearing bone-coloured tabards woven with gold and silver threads, was ushered onto the North Inch to the sound of trumpets and clarions, their purpose to carry accounts of Lindsay's triumph across the Northern Ocean to King Charles the Beloved. The lords and earls entered the summerhouse in procession, then the Dukes of Albany and Rothesay. A great noise commenced again when Lord Lindsay, Kay of Kindrogan and Alexander Stewart of Badenoch appeared through the gate that led to the friary nave followed by queen consort and king, all mounted on fully dressed warhorses. None who emerged matched the description of Mackintosh of Chattan: no taller than a stripling, but broader than two.

Distant notes, a throb over the trumpet blasts, grew to a loud pummelling of drums and the screech of warpipes as the two bands of combatants ended their march through the town by rounding the high wall where the friary stables backed onto the Balhousie Castle bailey on the west side of the North Inch. The party that led the way wore russet tunics, Brodie guessed, to represent the red in Lindsay's heraldic arms. The others were clothed in sundry garments, of different shades. Instruments still blaring, they lined up on the field, opposite one another in the way of two great armies.

No sooner had the fighting-lines formed – thirty on each side, stripped naked but for under-garments – than the innumerable pronouncements and proclamations began, superficially drawing the spectators' attention while diverting their interest. Brodie allowed himself to settle a look on the south-facing gallery to his right. The Wolf of Badenoch stared haughtily upwards, leaning vaguely to the side and barely dipping his chin when addressed by those alongside. Some rows down, de Coutts – face disfeatured by Lindsay's lance, blond hair shorter than before – shaded his face when the sun appeared through a chink in the clouds.

Such was Brodie's distraction, he barely heard the cry from the herald that signalled the commencement of hostilities. With hoarse shrieks, the sixty, each armed with a knife or sword and a double-axe, rushed headlong and struck, their onset like bulls. The battle joined, they swung weapons with equal ferocity, disregarding their own defence if they could strike out at an enemy. For a while, the encounter was maintained with the same fury on both sides, but the groan of Lindsay and Kay men became more frequent. And when four, five of them fell in succession, the weight of victory inclined to Chattan and Donnchaidh, who were soon two men to one. And just as a torrent flows from a trickle, until it carries along boulders as well as pebbles, the course of the contest was fixed. All around lay the dead and maimed, skin slashed, heads cleft. Only a dozen remained on their feet, some clutching wide wounds and loosed limbs. One, small and crook-legged but thickset, backed away from the others. The only left alive from Kay and Lindsay's side, he looked over his shoulder – to the area where Brodie sat – and elsewhere: in the direction of the gilded summerhouse; along the length of his own shadow; past the spectators crowded close to the friary walls. The combatant made a calculation; but no part of it involved surrender to a noble ending. He dropped his short sword and targe, turned from his enemies and took off at a smart run – seemingly free from injury – directly towards the river. Three of the closest Chattan and Donnchaidh gave chase but before they were on him, the fleeing warrior barged through the thin crowd on the fringe of the Tay and, losing his footing, slid down the steep banking into the tumbling brown water. From all sides of the arena, onlookers surged to the crest of the embankment, some of rank even leaving the summerhouse for a better vantage. Brodie eased himself to his feet and stood on his own seat. Fingers pointed and some shouted out on believing they sighted a thrashing arm or head bobbing in the swift current, but none did so with any certainty. Even the children who briefly followed the river downstream could not confirm the man's fate. Standing unevenly, his weight supported by a staff, Lord Lindsay simply stared in apparent disbelief.

The trance was broken when Badenoch leaned across queen consort and king, both still sitting, and spoke in Lindsay's ear.

Reading the indignation on Lindsay's face, Brodie left his seat to better hear his lord's response.

'...then it must be settled by chivalric combat, my war lance couched against yours.'

The Wolf of Badenoch threw back his head and let out a

boisterous cackle. 'Your finest champions are humbled and yet you imagine that you – a cripple from a previous defeat – can redeem even a scrap of honour?' He laughed again, a series of disdainful grunts intended to attract the attention of those around, like slowly and deliberately knocking on a door. 'Lindsay of Glenesk, the most righteous of lords, defies the terms of a judicial proof before his sovereign king.' He shook his head dramatically to emphasise the hypocrisy of it. 'But if further evidence of final defeat is needed, then I am willing to provide it, in chivalric combat – provided you are able to raise yourself in your stirrups.'

Lindsay thrust his face forward. 'If I am still able to maintain the saddle with the most noble game, I can do so easily enough with vermin of the chase.'

'Then the utmost ignominy and dismay will be yours…'

The king stood, separating the men, a pacifying hand held out towards each. 'As the law demands, the claim is settled in favour of Lord Stewart and Mackintosh of Chattan. None of their kin will suffer punishments for past wrongs, and those held at Stirling Castle are to be released from their irons.' From looking between the two nobles, he turned to face only Lord Lindsay. He stroked his abundant white beard. 'Proper judicial procedure has been observed, my good lord – there will be no more combat this day.'

Lindsay bowed. 'If this realm's notion of justice is rewarding wickedness with glory…' Though his bearing remained obedient, his tone brimmed with defiance. 'I will take my leave and pray for its sorry soul.'

*

Lord Lindsay was first to return to the monastery after the trial by combat, moving at a hurried hobble to pray at the chapel and altar dedicated to Saint John. But others soon followed behind: wounded fighting men laid out in the infirmary and warming room; black friars tending injuries; Brodie transcribing notations in the library along with a justice clerk and two monks, Dominicans or Benedictines, hunched beneath dark tunics.

'Brothers…sires…'

The address, which carried the beginnings of a question, had a softness that caused Brodie to squint out of the window for its source before twisting to look over his shoulder.

The Inchcolm apprentice who had sat alongside Brodie at the arena stood in the open doorway. 'Am I permitted to take a desk?' He bowed, his bald crown as ruddy as his cheeks.

The others in the library also looked around. 'You are permitted to observe the keeping of silence!' one of the monks hissed, his voice dry and brittle.

His question still unanswered, the apprentice scribe remained where he stood, running his thumb up and down behind the strap of the satchel slung over his shoulder and chest.

Recognising his discomfort, Brodie summoned the young Augustinian forward, showing him into the adjacent carrel.

'May I speak?' he asked.

Quietly, Brodie mouthed.

'It came to me when you followed Lord Lindsay from the arena…' whispered the apprentice, the partitions of the carrel keeping his words close by. 'Are you the same Brodie Affleck who continued the work of the great historian John of Fordun, and also scribes for Lord Lindsay?'

Brodie was commonly identified as Lindsay's scribe; as one year passed another, however, his name was less frequently put alongside Fordun's. 'I have been fortunate to receive the patronage of bold and wise men,' he answered, also in a hushed voice.

'Priest John of Fordun believed that our race descended from the Egyptian pharaoh's daughter, Scota, and King Gaythelos of Greece, in the days of Moses, is that not so?'

'As do many others.' Confounded by the wayward turn in the conversation, Brodie put his finger to his lips. 'We must maintain a silence,' he reminded the apprentice.

'But the venerable priest sought to establish the origins of the Scots with more zeal than any others. And I have a genealogy that traces every king since Gaythelos, from the Chronicle of Saint Colmes Inche,' the apprentice added eagerly. 'Is such a complete line of descent, which confirms the highest antiquity, included in Fordun's history?'

Mention of the book held at Inchcolm reminded Brodie of

his continued failure to complete the history by consulting the documents listed in Fordun's will and legacy. 'The annals are not yet complete…though Priest John described the Chronicle of Saint Colmes Inche as a worthy text to browse.'

'But sire, you have no need to browse the text – I can provide you with the genealogy. I have copied it once already. For the Great Register of St Andrews. And can do so again. The task practises my hand.' He spoke more quickly, and loudly, in a way that fitted his young years. Breaking off, he delved a hand into his satchel. 'I illustrate, too – see.' He recovered a scrap of material and thrust it close to Brodie's face.

The drawing of a small, cog-built ship crammed with passengers and crew had been put down by a heavy but diligent hand, on paper, rather than parchment or vellum, Brodie noted, as he took the scrap; Scota, in silver-blue gown, occupied the vessel's stern castle, an aspect of dignity attempted but not quite captured in the penwork. Below the illustration, the apprentice had scrawled his name.

"…*Brother Walter…Walter of the Bowmakers…Walter Bower…*"

'This is only a sketch, I could…' He switched from one estimation of Brodie's studied expression to another. 'Oh, the name is not written out of boastful vanity…it was also practice – at those initials.'

Each "*B*" and "*W*" was over-sized and decorated with a pattern of simple hatching.

Vanity or not, seeing the words returned Brodie to the day he had scratched his own name on a page that recorded Master Robert's death: his first stumbling step towards compiling the Annals of Egglespether.

'My purpose is to compose a book that will please every Scot, just as…'

'Let there be the greatest silence!' One of the monks – old and tousled, a Benedictine, Brodie now saw – had moved from his seat to deliver the scolding to young Bower. 'So that not a whisper is heard!'

Brodie bowed in apology, silently.

When the Benedictine shuffled away, muttering, Brodie patted the air in a gesture that bid young Bower sit down. But just as the apprentice quieted – satchel emptied, nib sharpened

– urgent footsteps entered the library, the steady beat on the boards provoking an exaggerated sigh from the Benedictine. Before Brodie turned, Lord Lindsay was at his shoulder.

'Not a word of that mockery of justice is to be included in your history, I command it!' Lindsay glared at the others – who were all looking on – a warning that he considered the injunction extending to them, and then marched towards the library door. 'We leave for Daviot at next light,' he called back to Brodie.

'But my lord…' Brodie got up to follow Lindsay, directing a weary shake of his head at young Bower. He flexed a stiff knee, grimaced and hurried on, catching up with Lindsay near the foot of the broad wooden staircase. 'My lord…you should know…'

Lindsay continued, down the last few steps and through the double doors at the bottom. Once outside, he followed the south wall through the monastery grounds, the clatter of preparations for the night's feast discernible from the kitchens and refectory. As they approached the prior's quarters – overlooking the river, as grand as a lesser palace – he stopped to offer Brodie an explanation. 'I will pray with the community at evensong and then pray alone while they take repast. For now, I will inform the prior, and his majesty, that hospitality is no longer required.'

'My lord, the outcome of the combat will be known whatever is written by my hand. The justice clerk was one of those in the library, making a record of proceedings at the king's behest, and the makar Wyntoun, who is favourably disposed to the royal Stewart line, sat with the earls and barons in the summerhouse gallery.' And though Brodie did not say it, Fordun's memory necessitated including an account in their history regardless of Lindsay's command.

'Then I will implore the king to decree that no final judgement is recorded until an opportunity for restitution is provided. He will surely grant such a request – it is his…' Lindsay trailed off. He puffed out his cheeks, his shoulders dropped. He stared across the main bridge over the Tay to the partially flooded Stanners Island and east bank beyond, perhaps recognising for the first time the futility of his cause and finality of his defeat.

A brief, heavy shower had mostly cleared the North Inch, though some buyers and sellers remained at stalls. A tethered mastiff barked a relentless beat. On the edge of the woods, children played hare and hounds, the hare leaving behind a short-lived trail of fluttering, reddened leaves for the others to follow. Closer by, a group of hunters walked along the western riverbank south towards the monastery, one idly swinging a falconer's lure above his head. A bird perched on an arm fluttered its wings, causing another on a different arm to do likewise. Two men ambled behind the falconers, both wearing full-length noblemen's robes – collar and belt high, sleeves trailing – one beardless with long black hair, the other strikingly blond.

Lindsay's features set tight. He shifted his weight between his stick and his healthy leg. Then, as if drawn forward by his own stare, he lurched towards the hunters, at a gait that belied his age and infirmity.

Again, Brodie found himself scurrying at Lord Lindsay's heels, along the ridge of the riverbank, through dense pine trees and down a slanting path towards the shore. At the foot of the path, amid shades of darkness – thick shadows cast by dusk, the muck-brown river, flattened dirt below their feet – they came to within twenty strides of the Lord of Badenoch's oncoming hunting party: the Wolf and de Coutts walking behind three falconers, two with hunting birds perched on their arms, the third swinging the lure, now more sedately by his side.

Badenoch did not immediately react to his rival's presence, taking several steps before he pushed past the falconers. Despite the gloom, Brodie imagined that he detected a smile.

'Ah, the righteous lord!' the Wolf taunted. He stopped close to Lindsay. 'And his drooling lickspittle.' He cast a sneer aside. 'What could possibly bring my bested opponent to the riverside? An audience with his conqueror, perhaps?'

Lord Lindsay put his hand on his hilt.

'Or for a lesson in how to capture and kill?' The Wolf swept a look behind, enlisting his men in Lindsay's belittlement. He snatched a string of dead fowl from the belt of one of the falconers and gestured at the smaller of the two hooded birds, a young peregrine with dark plumage, on the gauntlet of another. 'This nestling does not tower so well, but she took these prey better than any short-winged hawk available to a lesser lord. You should not end the day with your hands entirely empty.' He tossed the limp fowl at Lindsay's feet.

Lindsay drew his sword. 'You offered to banish our quarrel in chivalric combat.'

Brodie took a staggering step backwards.

The Wolf pointed at the string of fowl on the path between them, ignoring Lindsay's challenge. 'You refuse a gift from an earl's table?' He shrugged and kneeled to pick up the game birds.

Then sprang to his feet and, arm straight, swung a clenched hand that arced from the ground to Lindsay's temple.

Lindsay fell like a stem before a scythe.

Despite the evidence of his eyes – and because he had heard no blow – Brodie considered the possibility that Lindsay had simply slipped. Yet he lay still, legs rigid. The string of fowl had been kicked to the side; one of the birds' wings fanned out in the dirt: brown, muddied white, band of green, a sheldrake. Someone laughed – not the Wolf, Brodie judged – though mostly he heard the river, as close and clear as though he were stretched flat on the bank guddling for trout. An instant of blackness. And Brodie was hurled to the side. He put out a hand, fell onto his knees. The Wolf stood over him.

"Punishment is justice for the unjust."

Brodie recognised the words of Saint Augustine. He raised himself onto one knee and waved a beseeching hand; his lips moved, letting out an indistinct sound but no words.

The Wolf poked a toe at Lindsay's lifeless body. 'In the river,' he ordered.

De Coutts took the two falcons, along with their jesses and twine leashes, allowing the three falconers to roll Lindsay's body down the narrow, rocky shoreline and into the water. His legs drifted with the current but his chest caught in the shallows. One of the falconers waded in and heaved him into deeper water, as though assisting with the launch of a rowboat.

The Wolf leaned over Brodie, the rock that felled Lindsay still in his hand. 'Justice has been served on the puffed-up lord…'

To Brodie's left, Lindsay's body had already disappeared downstream.

'And without his protection, an outstanding writ of arrest can now be executed on his slandering scribe.' The Wolf took a fistful of Brodie's collar, then hauled him towards the river. 'And also on the insect brother of Christie the Cleek.'

Brodie's head was rammed below the water. He struggled to break free but the weight on the back of his head increased, as though more hands had fallen on him. The noises of the river were at once quieter and louder in his ears. He attempted to close off his breathing, though water seeped up his nose and trickled down the back of his throat.

The Wolf pulled him clear. 'So, where is the insect?'

'I…I could not say,' Brodie panted.

Again, his head was under. He remained still this time. He screwed his eyes shut, his sole purpose to keep his breath.

Yanked out of the water, his eyes burst open, he snatched quick breaths.

'Is the insect alive?'

Brodie said nothing.

Under, without seizing a breath, he gulped water. Briefly fretful, his neck and arms tensed as he pushed up. His chest heaved. His thoughts surged and swam, then settled. He let the one knee that held him up give, so that he slid flat on the bank. No shock of cold – rather, his throat burning, his chest warming – he opened his eyes. Mites and motes, tiny tree fruits floated past, like yeast disturbed in ale. He lifted one of his hands from the riverbed, held it close and stared through the giddy water at the crease on his palm, the joints of his fingers, the dilating lentil spots. A hand at prayer, in embrace, sharpening a pen, guiding a pen, lifting a beaker, smoothing parchment, blistered, clutching a shovel. He closed his eyes; behind them, bright flashes glistered, like so many stars. He parted his lips. The water seeped in.

And then he gasped air.

Still prostrate in the water, his head wrenched up and back by coarse fingers, straining neck thrust forward, Brodie coughed, unable to dislodge the water caught in his throat.

'Is the Christie brother alive?' Leaning over, the Wolf's face was close enough for Brodie to gulp down a quantity of his curdled breath.

Brodie snorted out a rheumy string of mucus. 'God, help me find justice…'

'You seek justice? Then we are in accord.'

At an unseen, unheard signal, those holding Brodie down

released their grip; hands lifted from his arms, a knee from the small of his back and a foot pinning down his legs. He raised himself onto all fours, spitting out grit and fine-grained silt. Before he could straighten, the Wolf took him by tufts of sparse hair at his temples and dragged him backwards until he toppled and lay on his back, head on the bank.

'Hold him down,' the Wolf directed.

The falconers did as instructed, one with leaden knees on Brodie's shoulders.

Staring upwards at a garland of dim light between tall trees on each bank, the highest branches swaying heaviest, a new dread began to form.

The Wolf picked up the sheldrake he had offered Lindsay, unsheathed a knife and tore at the dead bird where nut-brown feathers met white. He murmured to de Coutts – '…remove the hood…' – and disappeared from view. Brodie heard slicing, a knife through meagre flesh onto stone.

The Wolf reappeared, standing over Brodie's head, the larger of the two hunting birds, a gyrfalcon, perched on his arm. 'You slander my name because you are in league with the Christie brother, yes?'

Wedged between the legs of one of his captors, Brodie was barely able to shake his head.

The Wolf continued. 'I have made it my business to exterminate the loathsome Christie swarm – chief among them the brother of the flesh-eating savage. And I believe that slanderous lies have passed from his mouth to your ears.' He squatted down and fed a scrap of drake meat to the gyrfalcon, its broad, dappled back and tail towards Brodie. 'You seek justice? Then you will lead me to that beast's door.' He laid another piece of meat across the top of his gauntlet, allowing the falcon to devour the food. 'So, I ask again – where is the brother of Christie Cleek?'

Merciful Lord of life, lover of souls, make my heart courageous.

The Wolf took a slice of meat and smeared Brodie's cheek with blood. He turned his arm so that the perching gyrfalcon faced Brodie. 'Have you nothing to say?'

Grant me the grace to bear my suffering.

He squeezed his lips and eyes shut, drew in his neck and chin, as though pulling every facial thew tight with a drawstring.

'Take it...' whispered the Wolf.

Brodie was braced for greater torment: the falcon picked at the blood on his cheek, piercing, but with the acute jab of a sharpened pin pricking the outline of an illustration on parchment rather than the force of a sticking knife in living flesh. Despite his continued peril, Brodie felt the merest flush of relief. Relief that, in blunting death's sting, he could perhaps now endure whatever the Wolf might inflict.

A thumb pressed open Brodie's right eyelid. De Coutts stooped over him, lip peeled to the gum and pinned in place by a taut scar, one unmoving eye opaque, lichen-blue. The knight held his tongue between his teeth, a broad notch from its tip, his attention on reaching to the ground by Brodie's side.

Brodie tried to blink his eye shut; his lid quivered under de Coutts's grip but remained open. He glimpsed dark green sheldrake feathers between the knight's fingers; and a gobbet of the fowl's cold flesh was jammed into his eye socket, de Coutts holding it firmly in place. The truth of what would follow arrived as fast as a fall.

The falcon fixed a claw on his cheek and snatched at the duck meat. Shades and shapes moved. Brodie squirmed beneath his shackles. An arm broke free and he swatted the bird, though caught only an outstretched, brittle wing. The bird clenched its talons in his skin. Brodie opened his left eye; the Wolf rather than de Coutts leered down. 'You will lead me to him.' Since the meat was held tightly, the falcon gouged deeper. Over whatever cries and pleadings he uttered, Brodie heard a crackle within his head, felt a fibre pulled tight, slacken, sensed a space diminished, air escaping.

The Wolf jerked him into a sitting position. His arms again free, Brodie reached up to his eye: bloodied but intact.

'Fail to speak once more and, for certain, you will lose one of the eyes that reads your defamatory words.' He held his hunting knife to Brodie's wrist. 'If I must ask a second time, you will also lose the hand that writes them. A third time, the other eye. A fourth time...I can whittle until darkness, and then begin again when light returns.'

Brodie made the decision to remain alive, at least long enough to contrive a means of escape, or a death free of torment, offering the Wolf a lie that contained mostly truth. 'I could not lead you to him. But he was alive. Many years before now.'

'And lo!' The Wolf leaned back on his haunches. 'But if he remains alive, why could you not lead me to him?'

'I…I could not know with any certainty if he remains alive. Or where to find him.'

'You do not know with certainty – but you have a notion?' The Wolf put his knife hard against Brodie's knuckles.

In picking his next words, Brodie strayed further from the truth. 'I was on an errand in the south and saw him only from a distance in the marketplace at Roxburgh.'

The Wolf's blade pressed firmly enough to draw a ragged thread of blood.

Brodie tried to pull his hand away, slithering backwards on his backside.

And an arrow spat past between Brodie's face and where the Wolf crouched, spluttering into thick undergrowth behind where they were gathered.

For a moment there was little movement – eight or ten martins roused and flew south; one of the falconers tottered and sank down dizzily; heads turned towards him – then all was astir. 'The peregrine!' wailed the falconer on his knees. 'She is struck.' He stared dumbly at the place on his wrist, still outstretched, where the bird had so recently perched. The two other falconers helped him to his feet. De Coutts stood and hurried over to the huntsmen.

The Wolf followed. 'The peregrine is struck?' he asked, disbelieving.

'By an arrow.' The huntsman raised both hands, palms skyward in incredulity.

The incomprehension that Brodie briefly shared with the others turned to recognition of an opportunity. Digging his heels into the riverbed and raising himself off the gravel bank with his hands, he slowly dragged himself farther into the water, the bending and straightening of his legs unseen below the surface. Preferring to listen to the distracted exchange on the path than watch for turned heads and keen eyes, Brodie stared straight upwards at the sky, an ill-defined smudge of dark cloud cover and near nightfall. His shoulders caught on a hump of underwater rock, a thigh scraped a jagged edge. He continued to push and pull with hands and heels. The benumbing water touched the wounds inflicted by the falcon, cheek and clamped-shut eye, inducing a shock, and a kind of relief. He slipped deeper into the river, until he felt only water and no hard ground below. Resisting the temptation to attempt to swim – and therefore likely drown – he lay flat and still, just as though at play in the Fithie River. Water filled his ears, lapped his face, his legs sank. But, otherwise, he floated like a felled tree. He might have heard raised voices and the splash of a chase, but remained motionless, even when given cause to gulp down mouthfuls of swirling river water.

Brodie only opened his eyes when the current eased and silky strands of riverweed gently grasped his bared lower leg. He had drifted into a slow-moving slough that passed by the narrow east side of Stanners Island. Above, the dim figure of a child strained to peer over the handrail of the bridge over the Tay, longbow clearly visible between hands held together in prayer. Fair and stocky for his height, even when shrouded in religious robes – young Bower? – the figure seemed to nod his head.

Brodie passed below the bridge and his feet found a mudbank between Stanners Island and the eastern shore of the river. After scrabbling onto the island and crouching among thick ferns, he looked up. The boy had disappeared; nothing moved on the bridge.

But a disturbance on the far shore suggested the beginnings of a pursuit.

Clothes sodden, water warm between heavy folds, bones chilled, he scuttled across the shallow channel to the east riverbank. Once there, he settled on a simple purpose: skirt the North Inch and reach the monastery stables unseen, then select a courser – by theft if necessary – brawny but lean, vigorous enough to outrun a hunting pack and reach Kirkcudbright in four days or less.

Chapter 11

September, 1396, until the 26th Day of February, 1397

Brodie's flight from Perth put distance between himself and the Wolf of Badenoch, though it also took him closer to death. The courser he led furtively from the monastery stables carried him to Kirkcudbright by Saint Michael's Day, just as he had hoped. But by the Feast of Thomas de Cantilupe, he had fallen into a sore illness, a sweating sickness due to his dousing in the Tay, followed by an unnatural heat. And despite Duncan Christie's charity and succour, a continuous fever endured from the earliest frost of winter until the first shoots of spring.

'You lie in a bed beyond a tannery and yet the air is more corrupt inside than out.' Christie dumped a bundle of logs by Brodie's hearth. He kneeled and began to bank up the fire. 'The odour in this place...' He shook his head rather than continue.

Brodie roused some way but remained on the threshold of wakefulness. Louder than Christie's carping, he heard the groans of his own swelling veins and joints. A tremor in his guts suggested the coming of a bloody flux. His tongue was thick and dry. 'The odour of death, is that what you would say?' He spoke through cluttered breaths. 'Or the odour of sin? Sin at making known your survival – and proximity to Roxburgh – to the Lord of Badenoch?'

Christie tapped his forehead with his knuckles. 'Brodie Affleck, if you did not give my name as David Maxwell, Kirkcudbright tanner and merchant, then there is no threat – I have repeated as much many times.' He returned to replenishing the fire. 'But if it is safety you want – let alone convalescence – you should leave this place and cross the river, where Agnes and Annabel can better attend to you.'

Brodie moved his eyes right and left. Hardly able to rise from his bed, use of a name that was not his own, deprived of the miserly comfort of Mariota's shawl and other possessions, the papers for Fordun's history scattered in far-off libraries: the dwelling behind the tannery was as adequate a place to die as any. 'Melancholy from my liver will fill my spleen wherever I lie,' he croaked.

Christie stood. 'Your spleen can be purged.'

'It is doubtful I have any blood left to let.'

'Purged with medicine, not a lancet. Borage syrup. Or a fortifying drink, to dissolve your sickness as the sun melts a covering of ice. The Candlemas Fair continues this week in the toun, and from tomorrow it will include the first market day since lambing began. Vendors and stallengers will come from all parts – including those offering the most potent remedies concocted in these isles and beyond.' He shuffled to the door, wagging a finger. 'I will find that cure, old man Affleck, and return before the month is ended. Until then, stir the matter in your spleen by moving your arm like this...' – he yanked his fist up and down – '...as though ringing the church bell at the Priory of Restenneth.'

*

If not Christie's grunted greeting, Brodie was mostly woken by Annabel's touch. Or the scent of the bathing water that moistened the linen cloth in her grip; neither rosewater and resin, nor syrup with honey, she had insisted on her last two visits.

'Pulped green apple?' he wheezed.

As with her mother in younger years, Annabel bore something of a resemblance to Mariota, though with firmer features and, when required, a firmer disposition. 'And you too are bid a good morning, sire.' Her reprimand, playful but stern, could have come from the lips of either woman.

And it gave him cause to open his eyes to a new morning. 'God give you good day,' he responded.

As always, she sponged his brow lightly and then, with more vigour, scrubbed his face, hands, feet and lower legs. Through half-shut eyes, he watched her work: childless, widowed in the lesser plague outbreak of 1392 and now the only daughter still in Christie's care, yet she retained sufficient brightness for Brodie to recognise the pupil he once taught how to balance a debit against a credit in a ledger. 'Lift yourself,' she said, hitching him up by the armpits until he was propped against his bolster. She brushed crumbs from his sheets and stood, hands on hips. 'There…'

Whether cause or coincidence, Brodie's condition had improved in close correspondence to Annabel's visits, more frequent since her father's departure for the Candlemas Fair.

'So…apple pulp?' he asked again, a plain attempt to detain her longer.

'Too few apples remain from winter storage to put in bathing water.'

'The water…' He pointed at the basin by Annabel's feet. 'Could you bring it to me one more time?'

Conceding to his wiles, she held the basin by his cheek. He leaned over and took a long breath. 'You have obtained…oil of laurel?' he asked.

'Oil of laurel?' she exclaimed. 'Such a rarity is more precious than even the winter apples.' She took the basin away. 'This is no more than a coction of scented mayweed in salt water – to clean out your pores.'

'A meal of mutton and mustard might better bring me to health.'

'Ah, so your appetite is…' Annabel was interrupted by the door swinging slowly open, and an ancient figure stepping inside the dwelling.

Annabel's distraction could not match Brodie's astonishment. He sat upright, in a single moment filled with life. 'Thomas? Of Ersildoune?'

The eldfather before him was in all parts different to Thomas of Ersildoune – a whole head shorter, bald rather than grey-haired, patchy stubble in place of a beard, the waxed apron of a physician instead of a justice clerk's russet robes – yet indefinably the same. Certainly, he possessed the same mildewed appearance and crumpled skin. Yet the old man he last met below the Eildon Tree would be a hundred years or more. And this figure seemed to have aged only near ten years in the space of closer to forty.

'Thomas of Ersildoune?'

Although Brodie had whispered it, the old man seemed to hear the words. 'True, True Thomas…' he chuckled.

Duncan Christie stepped from behind the old man. 'He gives himself the name Thomas but will disclose no more, whatever questions I ask.' Christie shrugged. 'Other than that he is a physician of sufficient skill to cure whatever ails you.'

Brodie must have looked unconvinced – in truth, still stunned – because Christie continued.

'At the Fair, he eased the swelling of a merchant's wife suffering the dropsy. And soothed distemper in others with his remedies.'

Taking Christie's testimony as sanction to begin work, Thomas moved to Brodie's bedside.

'But the cost of treatment…?'

Christie waved away Brodie's remonstrance.

Thomas sat down on Brodie's bed. He closed his eyes and turned his blank face to Brodie. 'Aches in all places, sickness in the chest, spitting of blood, spasms and shivers, dimness of senses – yes?'

'And guts that purge…'

Thomas opened his eyes. 'Then you suffer windiness of the spleen and melancholic humours have dropped onto your stomach.'

The old man was close enough for Brodie to conduct an examination of his own: the foggy eyes matched those of Ersildoune, so too the tussocks of white hair sprouting from his ears.

Thomas grasped tight fingers around Brodie's midriff. 'It is likely you also have some dryness in the kidneys.'

He wore the same listing grin as True Thomas. But, Brodie belatedly observed, no battered kettle hat.

Thomas stood. 'Has your pot been emptied?'

'No…' answered Brodie.

'Have you shit in it?'

Brodie and Annabel looked between each other. 'Again, no.'

'Good – pass it to me.'

With a look of puzzlement, Annabel reached beneath the low-slung cords of the bed and handed Thomas the pot.

The old man swirled the contents and poured a dribble into his cupped hand. He examined the overnight urine closely, then sniffed. '…a shade green…excess froth…' He tipped the liquid back into the pot and wiped his palm on his apron. 'But you have some time left. Years, likely. Seven at least.' He muttered the last part of the prognosis to himself, as though dwelling on the soundness and precision of his own professional judgement. 'But to live even one more month you must do this – take seven fat bats, cut off their wings, flay them well, draw out the entrails, boil in water with wormwood and sage and add to a tub. Then cover your head, wrap your chest in the skin of a goat or calf and soak in the healing water for as long as it takes the sun to travel a quarter of its arc from sunrise to sunset.'

Christie was the first to speak. 'Bats?'

'The fattest you can trap. But hold still – I have an aid for you…' He rummaged in his saddlebag.

The others exchanged doubting glances.

Thomas drew out a stiff scrap of paper or parchment the size of a playing card. He folded it in half once, twice, three times and handed the tiny, tight parcel to Brodie. 'It is no more than a reminder of what you must do,' he said, head cocked.

Brodie went to unfold the scrap.

'Read it once I am gone,' instructed Thomas. Steady on his feet, he moved across the room with small, slow steps. He stopped at the door. 'You have few possessions left after your flight, yes?'

'My flight?' Brodie and Christie cast fearful gazes in each other's direction.

Thomas took no heed. 'Only a sheathed knife that is your own?' He jutted his bony chin at the knife by the bedside, giving Brodie momentary cause to think him simply observant rather than possessing an inner eye. 'The instructions will fit neatly in the sheath.'

Brodie might have detected a lingering hiss in Thomas's voice; but, if so, softer than before.

And then the old man was gone, in a single stride, as fallen blossom scatters in a flurry of wind.

Still reflecting on the improbability of Thomas's reappearance, Brodie fingered the parcel of parchment. Slowly, he opened the folds. The fragment was instantly familiar. Two torn edges, two straight, it was adorned more plainly than the other three scraps in his knife sheath. Yet the vine that twisted down the right margin would perfectly graft onto the tiny scroll Christie had flattened on the dirt of the tannery drying shed two score years before.

Christie stepped closer. Brodie shifted his attention from the illustration to the verse alongside.

> *"A scribe, a merchant, an earl, of late;*
> *A fiery star summons their fate.*
> *The mother hag will swear, forsooth:*
> *A half-blind man will see the truth.*
> *A bogle-man, a Wolf begetter,*
> *Slay a son to save a daughter."*

Book VII

"The love blinks of that bogill, fra his bleary eyes,
As Belzebub had on me blent, abased my spirit."

William Dunbar, *The Tretis Of The Tua Mariit Wemen And The Wedo* (1505)

Chapter 1

"When shall we three meet again
In thunder, lightning, or in rain?
When the hurlyburly's done,
When the battle's lost and won."

William Shakespeare, *Macbeth* (c 1605)

*11th Day of February, 1402, until the 29th Day of March in the Same
Year*

The blazing star, tail like the flame of a torch, appears to the
north of west after Mars enters Aries, just as the witch foretold.

When it moves directly north of the sun and shakes down its
flaming hair, longer by half again than before, I dispatch a party
to deliver the sorceress back to Lochindorb. She arrives when
star and tail are near set, only several hairs visible in the east
before sunrise, a single strand in the west after sunset.

I watch from my chamber as the boat carries her across the
water. Rather than allow her to lay a foul foot inside my walls, I
meet the boat on the foreshore beyond the east gate. Although
an emissary of the Cailleach mother hag – Queen of Winter and
raiser of windstorms – she brings no roaring tempest. The day
is bright and clear, more summer than spring, the water still.
Since her touch is feared, she steps from the boat unaided by
attendants. As before, she is swathed in dark under and over
gowns. Her head is covered by a hood, a black veil drawn across
her unearthly face. Yet she neither bears the horns of a boar nor
carries a staff to freeze the ground.

The sorceress bows her head and then remains in the same
position, unmoving.

'You advised that I retrieve you here to seek counsel when an apparition showed itself. The star with the tail of a dragon was that apparition?'

Despite my question, she does not speak.

'Answer, shrew!' I demand.

'The star lights up one prophecy with another.' Her voice is almost a whisper, not pitched high or low, neither coarse nor alluring.

'And this second foretelling concerns the whereabouts of the brother of Christie Cleek and Brodie Affleck, the scribe?'

Still downcast, she replies after a hesitation. 'Just as the fiery star rises and falls, so Christies flourished once, and will flourish again.'

I look around to gather reactions before responding: mac Anndra shrugs; de Coutts is wide-eyed, credulous; the boatmen dare not lift their eyes from the ground. 'Is that all you say, shrew – that the insect kin will prosper?'

'You should go south I say, the tail of the star shows the way.'

My tolerance lapses. 'The mother hag can shape mountains and wreath them in snow, yet her sorceress cannot give the location of a common runagate with any exactitude? Half the world is south of here!'

The ungodly witch is dismissed with a payment of grain and venison – precautionary protection against the visitation of a crop failure – and I retire to devise an earthly means of taking myself to within a blade's reach of Christie and Affleck.

Again, I look from my chamber window, now as the boat turns and leaves the east shore to cross the loch. It gives me some contentment that the winds have changed with the passing of noon; the boat pitches in north-blown waves when it leaves the shelter of the island; the witch who professes to conjure storms is huddled in the stern, her worthless words adrift in the gusts.

'Lord Alexander…' My groom keeper stands in the doorway. 'Confessor John de Coutts requests a hearing.'

I turn from the shutters. 'Then my ears await – eager to learn why a confessor in faith heeds the ramblings of a heathen prophetess on the foreshore when, before her arrival, he urged against taking her counsel at all.' I say it as a reminder that his master observes all.

He kneels, moves forward, and kneels again. 'My lord, it is true I gave attention to the witch's words but for a reason you may not suppose.'

I gesture for him to explain.

'I ask to be heard not as confessor, but as keeper of arms.'

'Then speak as a keeper of arms.'

'The witch used the words "flourished once, and will flourish again" — both parts of which are close to those contained on heraldic arms.' He slavers without control as he speaks, rousing an urge in me to cut out his mutilated tongue and make his disablement complete. He continues, still drivelling. 'It could be no more than a meaningless concurrence, but the first part is connected to the Christie name, the second resembles words on the seal that belongs to the chief of the Maxwells, a family that has numerous seats in the south. I need not say it, but the witch directed us go south in our pursuit — perhaps there is a connection between Cleek's brother and the Maxwell household. A search for Christie could be limited to that family's southern territories.'

My interest is stirred.

'Lord Robert Maxwell of Caerlaverock and Renfrew is loyal,' he adds. 'So too the kinmen who have keeps and towers in Dumfries and Annandale. They would likely assist in any search.'

'Are there other branches?'

'I believe others have lands at Kirkcudbright, Melrose and perhaps also Roxburgh — the place revealed by the scribe Affleck when we seized him after the great North Inch victory.'

Oddly, his stare is all the more intense due to issuing from only one eye.

'Fetch mac Anndra,' I command. 'And send a messenger for Angus MacNair of Lennox — he knows the southern families and lands well enough to guide a hunting party.'

Chapter 2

*"Behold the young foal, and the snail on the flag
so slow;
Without food being tasted, judge the year will not
prosperously go."*

Medieval rhyme

Springtide, 1402, until the 30th Day of September, 1403

Despite an almost full restoration of his health – his senses remained dimmed on recovery, and deteriorated with each passing year – Brodie moved out of the dwelling by the tannery and into the main Christie house during the winter that followed the appearance of the dread sign in the northern sky.

As feared, the comet proved a harbinger of ill fate: the harshest winter yet of the king's reign. Yet the subsequent spring and summer were as temperate as any since his predecessor took the throne: sufficient sun to warm their winter-chilled bones, enough rain to fill the rivers and sustain the crops.

When harvest came, the yield was so plentiful that the autumn festival was extended, beginning early – on the Feast of Saint Matthew – and continuing until the day and night of the Harvest Moon.

Early on Michaelmas, with Christie and Agnes in the front of the hide cart, Brodie and Annabel behind, they crossed the bridge by the tannery to the foot of the hill on the east bank, where Jean waited with her husband, younger son of the Laird of Twynholm, and a brood that spanned all ages. First down from the cart, Christie hurried over to embrace his eldest daughter. The others followed. Greetings offered and received, they boarded Twynholm's four-wheeled wagon, which bore smirches of muddied boots but not, gratefully, the odour and vestiges of flesh from flayed hides. Together, they rode past the backlands, one field in morning sunlight, another in shadow, and climbed the hill to the Church of Saint Cuthbert for Michaelmas prayers. After Mass and then repast of boiled pork, apples and the last of the blackberries, only Christie and Twynholm journeyed on to the Long Acre. Both promised to return after the horse races and wrestling contests, though it was more likely they would remain absent for one night or two.

A sighing wind woke Brodie on the morning of the Harvest Moon festival. From his bed in the upper east chamber, he listened for other sounds in the Christie house. He heard steady, slow breaths from the bedchamber alongside, where Annabel and Jean slept, but no heavy snores from Christie's mattress by the hearth downstairs. Occasional gusts squeezed between the shingles or dashed light rain against the glazed window. He drifted back towards sleep, rain pattering on the roof like seed scattered on firm ground.

He was awoken abruptly: the bang of a metal pot and Agnes's voice raised defiantly. 'You have no fields to reap — how did it come to be in your hand?'

'...threw my sickle...nearest the last sheaf...' The response, conciliatory in tone, was muffled but distinctly Christie.

Brodie eased himself out from under the blankets and coverlet, splashed his face with water from the basin and pulled on his breeches. Due to its steepness, he picked his way carefully down the east gable staircase, emerging into the kitchen.

Brodie may have been first to wake, but he was last to rise. Christie stood just through the door that led outside, brows arched high, a ragged straw figure in his upturned palm; Agnes and Jean faced him stiffly, awaiting a further response. Alongside Brodie, Annabel rested her fingers on the handle of the door to the undercroft, delaying her descent down the steps while she took in the exchange. Margaret, who must have arrived while Brodie slept, sorted apples in a bowl. She turned from regarding her father over one shoulder to watching Brodie's entrance over the other.

Brodie greeted her with a nod and a blink still heavy with sleep.

'Sire.'

The interruption seemed to bring Agnes back to the source of her ire. 'Believe this – keeping the Cailleach for a year will bring the dearth of the farm to this house.'

'The last sheaf was cut before Hallowmas – the doll is the Maiden not the Old Witch,' implored Christie, holding up the tuft of plaited corn by one of its grey ribbons. 'If such fables are to be believed, she will bring good fortune not ill.'

'That idol is not remaining in this house.'

Christie turned to Brodie, exaggerating his vexation with a shake of the head. 'Will an erstwhile brother in religion accept an apology for my wife's godless ways?'

The question awoke Brodie more fully, causing him to recognise the purpose of the bustling activity in the kitchen. He light-heartedly put his hands together in prayer and inclined his head. 'The apostate will accept your kind apology – but only if he is permitted to assist with preparations for tonight's godless Harvest Moon festival.'

A high-pitched noise between a shriek and a giggle came from the doorway through to the main room; Matthew – grandson to Jean and first great-grandson for Christie and Agnes – had toddled through unnoticed and held a raw, unpeeled onion poised at his open mouth.

'Matthew...' Jean hurried over.

The boy took a bite, immediately let the onion drop from his mouth and scuttled back through to the main room, face contorted, spitting.

Agnes narrowed her eyes and gave a small laugh. 'The idol can hang in the barn with the mice.' She said it with finality and returned to stirring a brass pot. 'But only until Yule morning or when the mare foals, whichever comes first.'

The disagreement over, Margaret returned to her apples.

'You could assist with my preparation of the Saint Michael bannocks...' Annabel – jug in hand, three bowls one inside the other under her arm – nodded at a candle-holder in a recess by the door. '...by lighting a candle and leading me down to the pantry.'

Brodie gave a small bow and lit the candle on the brazier. Once in the undercroft, they passed first through the buttery –

where Annabel filled the jug with sheep's milk – and then into the pantry.

Annabel separated the bowls. 'Equal quantities of rolled oats, wheat flour and barley meal in each,' she instructed.

Brodie found a sack of rolled oats and began scooping the fine flakes into one of the bowls.

Annabel opened bags of wheat and barley and did likewise. 'You say little of your time in the cloisters – was it harsh?'

The unexpected question caused Brodie to pause and consider a fitting response. 'Much changed after the arrival of the plague,' he said vaguely.

'But you are not an apostate, as you described in the kitchen?'

'Be assured, I am no apostate.' He continued scooping the oats.

'How can that be, if you removed your religious habit?'

Annabel had previously sought to learn about his past but not with such persistence. 'Let me just say that I was never rightfully professed and so had no need to abandon my faith.' The bowl of rolled oats full, he stood.

'And does that faith allow you – or any of us – to venerate, or fear, the spirits of corn dolls?' She jerked a disapproving head in the direction of the steps leading up to the kitchen.

Brodie smiled comfortingly. 'Your mother and father quarrel mostly for amusement – their faith is with God and the saints.'

'Mostly…though my mother recites the Pater Noster devoutly at Mass – then burns juniper in the byre and decks the house with mountain ash.' Annabel also got to her feet. 'And she describes the corn doll as the Cailleach…' Annabel quieted, but expectantly, as though those words were sufficient in themselves to provoke a response.

His failing sight adapted to the gloom, Brodie lowered the candle between them. He shook his head, uncomprehending.

'The Cailleach…known also as the mother hag.' Annabel nodded, small, brisk movements that urged him to grasp her meaning. 'The riddle from the physician,' she declared finally, losing patience with his slow-wittedness.

The riddle that had troubled her ever since Thomas delivered it to Brodie's bedside. He attempted reassurance. 'Cailleach or carlin, mother hag or mother corn – the last sheaf is known by many names, in many places. But it is a story, an ancient custom – no more. And the riddle was mistakenly delivered instead of a list of ingredients, by an old man losing his senses.'

Yet the same riddle confirmed that the fates of a scribe, a merchant and a one-time earl were bound together – surely, Brodie, Christie and Alexander Stewart, the former Earl of Ross – and rightly forecast the appearance of a great comet.

'The riddle also made mention of a daughter in peril – you believe that too has no meaning?' asked Annabel.

'It is no more than a rhyme, likely lines from an old carolling song…' Brodie's reassurance stalled as he rehearsed the riddle to himself, his thoughts snagging once, then again, on the middle lines. *"The mother hag will swear, forsooth…A half-blind man will see the truth."*

Chapter 3

"[He was] another Apollo, a prophet of truth,
[possessed of] hidden secrets."

The poet Henry of Avranches on Michael Scot (c 1235)

All Hallows, 1404, until the 27th Day of February, 1405

The boy messenger awaited as they returned from All Saints Mass, appearing on the path that led to the cluster of pear trees at the rear of the Christie house. He wiped his mouth with his sleeve, as though he might already have collected a helping of ripe fruit as a down payment on his full delivery fee. Some years fewer than ten and so barely tall enough to reach even the lowest sagging branch, he nevertheless maintained a bold swagger as he neared. He picked up a bulky saddlebag from the doorstep and held it out with both hands.

Christie stepped forward to take it, grumbling. '…a holy day, for rest of mind and body…abstain from the sending of packages…'

'I am to put it only in the hands of the merchant's clerk,' said the boy. His tone was rehearsed, an echo of instructions given earlier. 'And cannot say the name of the sender.'

Christie slowed, showing surprise, but did not stop. He handed the boy a cut coin and led his family into the house.

Brodie took the bag, but with some hesitancy. He received few enough messages – a debtor's petition, a note of uncollected taxes from the chamberlain – and, once a year, the package of writing materials that Christie collected from Glenluce Abbey. He weighed the unfamiliarity of the saddlebag in his hands and head – its dimensions, the rub of leather, the odd timing of the delivery – and loosed its bindings.

Brodie stared at the papers he pulled out, mostly bewildered, some part of him not at all surprised: Fordun's history.

Unfastening the twine that held the gatherings together, he briefly considered that it might be a copy of the original manuscript stored at the Saint Machar library. Yet the endpaper was the same – no markings other than Fordun's peafowl seal on the bottom half of the page – and the flyleaf as he recalled, an untidy list of chapter headings with text scored out and additions scrawled where space allowed. He quickly flicked to the period when he began his own annals – the plundering raid on Restenneth and murder of Master Robert – and then the year he put down the last account, the Steward's conspiracy against King David. All was precisely as he remembered; even his farewell postscript expressing gratitude for Fordun's generosity had yet to be cut through. He reached again into the bag: the sender had retrieved documents not only from Saint Machar's Cathedral, but also from the shelves of his own Daviot quarters. He lifted out a batch of papers – his later writings about the Wolf's changing fortunes, and three books, instantly recognisable as Michael Scot's trilogy of works. He opened the first of the books, Physionomia, and picked at the tear in the cover that had concealed one of the verses of riddle; the second, Liber Particularis, carried the familiar illustration of a four-fingered man, which had led him to Glenluce Abbey, and on to Duncan Christie. Only Liber Introductorius appeared different, bulkier. It fell open in his hands. A bifolia had been inserted between the centre leaves, each side blank, and a bone-handled magnifying lens was fastened to the top of the left-hand page by two small hemp loops, one at either end. Brodie untied the loops. Not a single magnifying lens, he found, but a pair of scissor eyeglasses, which swivelled open by means of a rivet in the handle.

He balanced them on his nose and held the metal frame in place with one hand; his eyes swam, then cleared.

And not blank parchment in front of him: a single line of text on the page, beneath where the eyeglasses had been.

Brodie clenched his eyes shut and blinked them wide open due to a slight dizziness. He picked up the book and moved it back and forth until finding the most favourable distance for reading.

> *"God is the father who presents a child with an unused parchment for him to write down his teacher's utterances, for good or ill."*

Through the mirk of the years, Brodie recalled it with clarity, the passage that Thomas of Ersildoune recited on their first meeting. And he remembered with more clarity still, alongside the quotation, the advice given to a newly appointed Restenneth Priory scribe: once started, the blank page must be filled, whatever dangers and accusations that might provoke. Guided by the wording of Thomas's riddle, Brodie could conceive it no other way. The eyeglasses were a gift from a nameless patron – surely none other than the enigmatic True Thomas could access a cathedral archive and breach a castle's high walls? – for a half-blind man who must see, and write, the truth about the Wolf of Badenoch.

*

His half-sight bettered by the eyeglasses, Brodie gave himself the task of reading Fordun's history from the first word to the last, making alterations and corrections where they were needed to complete the work.

Due to a new ache in the knuckles of his right hand accompanying the abiding stiffness in his left, Annabel assisted with scribal duties, transcribing longer passages of text and sewing Brodie's pages from Daviot into gatherings.

And the great chronicle near concluded, the decision was made: when the winter was fully passed, Brodie would leave his desk and, escorted by Annabel, journey to the religious houses that held the documents listed in Fordun's will and testament.

The first appearance since autumn of a swelling mid-morning sky gave them cause to make preparations to leave. Agnes oversaw the loading of the hide cart, while Brodie gathered together his writing materials and Annabel filled a trunk. Laden with sufficient victuals for a pilgrimage the whole length of the

Way of Saint James, they crossed the bridge and joined the road that led north, to follow Fordun's itinerary.

With Annabel at the reins, Brodie sat back on the bench seat, allowing the hardness of the wooden slats to jolt against his back as well as his backside. He lifted his chin into a thin breeze, reduced by a straining sun. Despite the discomfort of their travel, he measured his satisfaction at both moving closer to fulfilling a long-held purpose, and also approaching a new springtide. The carse ground below their turning wheels was soft and slow, but at least neither sodden nor frozen and hard-rutted. Where the track again met the river, mill boys splashed in the shallows, shrieking at the cold but grateful for an opportunity to rid themselves of winter fleas and lice. A barge carrying windblown timber, likely from Clatteringshaws, drifted by. Annabel guided the cart beyond the crashing waterwheel. A line of boats was beginning to form farther upstream, waiting to pass individually through the narrow channel on the far side of the waulk mill lade. Judging by the odour caught on a gust, at least one transported pike and bream from the Glenken Waters to the marketplace in Kirkcudbright. Just about to manoeuvre through the channel was the grandest of the vessels: fit for seagoing, a barge more than twenty cubits in length, with a single mast, sail gathered, and a cabin that occupied half the hull. Three boatman steered the barge: one on the far shore, gripping a rope fixed to the stern, another at the tiller and a third wielding a pole that reached the riverbed. A fourth, apparently a passenger, leaned against the cabin bulkhead, in haughty profile. His straggling hair was as white as the water churning on the mill wheel and, when he turned his gaze from the boatmen to the trundling hide cart, Brodie recognised other aspects: a leering grin, slow to spread, scored cheek, sightless left eye.

By degrees, the Wolf's confessor, John de Coutts, aimed a forefinger at Brodie, raised his other arm, plucked an imaginary bow string close to his seeing eye, and released an imaginary arrow.

*

'A return so soon?' Christie sat on a milking stool – too small for his bulk – outside the main door of the house. He rattled hazard dice in one hand. Leaning forward, elbows on knees, his eyes squinted against the rheumy sunlight. 'Did Agnes forget to load two pallet beds and a roof to cover your heads?' His joviality lasted only until he shaded his eyes and saw more of Brodie's expression. 'Some ill has befallen you already on your journey?'

Brodie jumped down. He shook his head solemnly at Christie. Without giving an instruction, he held the horse's bridle in an outstretched arm, in anticipation of Annabel stabling the cart.

'Say it – what troubles you?' Christie asked.

Her frown revealing disquiet, Annabel took the bridle, while Brodie ushered Christie farther from the door. 'We are found by Alexander Stewart of Badenoch.'

Christie glanced east and west along the track, as though expecting an army of caterans to appear on the bridge across the Dee or descend from Sour Hill. He turned briefly to the house. 'Here?'

'His man, his confessor, de Coutts sighted me riding the cart.'

'Could you be mistaken?'

'No mistake. He was aboard a boat upriver, at the waulk mill. The current will since have brought him closer still.'

'Perhaps it was not Badenoch's man…or he did not see you in the cart.'

'God preserve us all, but I swear he saw not only my features – but also those of your youngest daughter.'

Christie's head fell forward. He took on the appearance of a man who had been told he must endure two deaths rather than one.

'We must leave, you know that?' continued Brodie. 'And soon – or de Coutts will certainly come upon us.'

Christie allowed his head to loll back and rest on his shoulders awhile. He let out a stuttering sigh and beckoned Brodie with a wave. 'And you, my dear,' he said to Annabel. 'But first fetch your mother – she has left for the Cumstoun Pool.'

'There is no need to fetch me, I am not yet gone.' Agnes appeared from behind the house, a hefty wickerwork basket strapped to her back. 'Is a wheel on the cart broke? Or even the axle? I said as much – no journey of such a length should be made until day is longer than night.'

'It is not the cart. Come. Inside the house.'

Agnes stopped on the path. 'But I have undershirts and shifts to wash and mend.' She tapped one of the straps of the wicker basket.

'Leave the linens and come inside.'

Agnes was about to speak further but, perhaps due to the heaviness in her husband's voice, she stopped, instead removing the basket from her back and following him into the house.

Christie bid the others sit at the table, though he remained on his feet, striding the length of the main room, one way and back again, shaking his head in the direction of the floorboards.

'Tell me – why have you returned?' asked Agnes. Unsure whether to direct the questions at her husband, daughter or Brodie, she looked between all three.

Christie decisively chopped the air with one hand, drew in a long breath and sat at the table. He steadied himself, arms stiff on his knees like props. 'I have a confession that should have been made long ago.' He tapped the tabletop nervously with bunched fingers. 'Do you remember that I could never endure it when you quelled our daughters by uttering the name of the bogle-man Christie Cleek?' he asked Agnes.

His wife sat back, arms folded. 'I remember that you hid a shame from your past, and do so still – is that why you would now make confession?'

'There is a reason I could not thole that name,' he continued.

'You chose wrongdoing over virtue during the famine years, just like the brigand Cleek – is that your sin?'

'I did not choose it!' he shouted, standing and bringing his palm down on the table with a thud.

Annabel placed a hand on his elbow. 'Sit, father...' She lowered him back down to his seat.

Lips taut, jaw grinding, he bowed his head, cradling it in the crook of his arm. 'What choice for a mere boy...?' he mumbled.

'So, a boy brigand?' replied Agnes.

'No common brigand.' He raised his head enough to observe the response of those around the table.

Agnes's eyes and mouth widened on comprehension of his meaning. 'You were associated with the monster Christie Cleek?'

His face had changed in almost every characteristic – more soft flesh than hard bone, reddened hair thinner on his head, thicker on his chin – but the eyes set in the face were a reflection of those belonging to the young fugitive who begged Brodie for sanctuary at Restenneth Priory those many years before.

Once more, Brodie heard his plea. 'A boy cannot escape association from his own kin – his true name is not David Maxwell but Duncan Christie, brother of Andrew Christie.'

Before Brodie could establish the effect of his declaration on Agnes and Annabel, Christie spoke again. 'My confession is for you also, old friend. I am no brother of Andrew Christie. I am Andrew Christie.'

Chapter 4

*"Such creatures of the night are hated by the rest
and hate them in return. The wolf hates the
sheep, and birds the owl. This last is of use in
fowling when they use a night-hawk."*

Michael Scot, *Liber Introductorius* (c early 13th century)

*27th Day of February, 1405, until the 24th Day of March in the Same
Year*

'I am the bogle-man.'

In saying the words, I move beyond a long-endured dread.

And I cannot be certain what I find in its place. The shame that Agnes described, but more than that alone. A lightness? An easing? More closely, a respite.

The lull allows me to deliver my confession. I am Andrew Christie, of the Christies of Finzean, who were disinherited of their lands during the wars for the throne. Only my younger brother Duncan and I escaped the slaughter, though we were driven to wickedness through need and want: theft of livestock and victuals; the killing of a Restenneth churchman, in defence, during a skirmish; the blasphemous taking of the churchman's dead flesh – Annabel hurries away when I begin to relate this, though returns to hover by the door through to the kitchen; holding Lady Rowallan for a ransom; defiling the same captive while wild with madness.

Agnes sits, mostly silent. She has me fixed in a stare that simmers with contempt.

I explain that, although the lesser sinner, my brother received the greater punishment. Weakened by injury and illness, he was captured by the Steward's men while I hid. In my absence, and answering to my name, he was hanged, drawn and cut apart for two men's transgressions while I cowered at the Gallowden.

Old man Affleck interrupts to say that lies must have been told at the trial because a second Restenneth churchman – Denton? Fenton? – who was present during the skirmish, identified my brother as Cleek to those present at the legal proceedings.

I raise a hand to quiet him. Perhaps the churchman sought the glory of being the one to point an accusing finger at the notorious cannibal; perhaps he suffered a confusion during the disarray of the skirmish. The lies and mistakes of the past are no longer my concern. I return instead to my confession, the final part of which tells how I have brought dire peril to those in this house, to Jean and Margaret, their sons and daughters, even young Matthew.

'My vile coupling produced a spawn to match. The bastard son of Lady Rowallan is Lord Alexander Stewart of Badenoch, an unworthy prince, who is guilty of many more hateful crimes than two orphan brothers. And now his man has come upon us – assuredly, to serve a writ of arrest for the trespasses I have recounted.'

At this, Agnes stands. Wordless, she collects together belongings – some garments from the wicker basket, a patchwork, her soft shoes – covers her head, puts on a gown and wraps a shawl around her shoulder. She opens the door latch. 'Annabel, all that you will need for a stay at Twynholm is on the cart already. We should go to Jean without delay.'

In a swither, between sobs, Annabel repeatedly offers me her forgiveness. Since she owes me nothing, I refuse.

And they are gone.

I almost laugh – this outcome was surely as inevitable as high tide following low – but I do not dwell. If de Coutts asks sufficient numbers of tounmen the same question, he will soon enough know the identity of the old man and younger woman who were travelling north in the worn-out cart. Before deciding where to go, and to what purpose, I cross the bridge and give the master tanner a false account of the whole family making a pilgrimage to Whithorn to receive a dusting of Lent ashes.

Affleck is in the stables when I return, fastening the girth below the mule's belly.

'Badenoch's man will be further delayed by asking for the whereabouts of Duncan Christie and Brodie Affleck rather than David Maxwell and his clerk,' I say.

Affleck is having difficulty fitting the mule's bit; one thumb is thrust into the corner of its mouth, the other hand struggles to hold the bridle over its head. I go over and take the bridle. As we work, it occurs that he is due an explanation, in likeways to my wife and daughter. 'I say it in mitigation and not as evidence of innocence, as it was deceit disguised as truth…' He looks up, thumb still between the mule's teeth. 'But when seeking sanctuary at Restenneth, you asked me to give the name of the brother of Cleek for the priory records and I gave that answer straightly – Duncan Christie. Only in desperation, and then remorse at causing a kindly brother such misery, did I never correct the falsehood that the name was not mine to give.' I put my spare hand on his shoulder. 'Any words of apology are meagre against the many sufferings that wrongful judgement has caused you.'

'You have made apologies before – there is no benefit in doing so again.' The mule widens its mouth, allowing him to put the bit in place.

'And if I were to ask for your favour one final time – would that need an apology?'

He gestures for me to continue.

'You witnessed the murder of Lord Lindsay by Badenoch's hand, yes?'

'The only witness, other than his own company.'

'Then would you travel north with me and give that testimony to his son, the Earl of Crawford?'

He stops while buckling the throat latch. 'Why so?'

'To and from the tannery, I formed a notion. Two old men do not have the might to challenge de Coutts and his armed guard. But a troop of Lindsay knights who have learned the name of Glenesk's killer would have the means and the purpose to assist in a confrontation with Badenoch himself.'

'You would take the fight not to the lieutenant, but to the general?'

'It is the general who seeks revenge on the one he believes to be Christie Cleek's closest living relation. And going to him in the north will draw the threat from my family here in the south. I will invite him to combat to settle our account. The tannery will provide for my wife and daughters, whether I live or die.'

Affleck shakes his head. 'Earl Lindsay might offer support, as you say, and others who suffered losses at Glasclune and Moulin. But you are too old for such adventures, and no match for the knightly Lord Stewart of Badenoch, even if he agreed to meet a lowly merchant in combat.'

'Perhaps not from a lowly merchant – but almost certainly from his own bastard father.'

Grasping my logic, Affleck recites the lines of riddle aloud. *"A bogle-man, a Wolf begetter – slay a son to save a daughter."*

*

The younger Lindsay, Earl of Crawford, receives us in ways I have come to expect from great men: seated in a high chair; a display of anguish – in equal degrees theatrical and sincere – on hearing grievous tidings; swift recognition of how to turn adversity to opportunity. He dispatches messengers to petition the king to enforce the arrest of de Coutts for his part in Glenesk's killing and orders that missive letters are sent from Daviot seeking to form soldierly alliance with Kay of Kindrogan and the house of the Ogilvie sheriffs. I offer the earl my drawn sword, however aged the hand that holds it, but say nothing of my intention to bring it together with a blade belonging to the bastard Lord of Badenoch. In response, he instructs that we do no more than take a place by the hearth until Affleck's old quarters are cleared. I sheath my sword.

Chapter 5

*"Here endeth the book of Michael Scot, astrologer
to the Lord Frederick, Emperor of Rome, and
ever august; which book he composed in simple
style at the desire of the aforesaid emperor. And
this he did, not so much considering his own
reputation, as desiring to be serviceable and useful
to young scholars."*

Michael Scot, *Liber Particularis* (c early 13th century)

April, 1405, until the 20th Day of July in the Same Year

Ever guileful, mac Anndra succeeds in outpacing the same king's justices who seized de Coutts. Three of his sons follow closely behind from Roxburgh. The fourth and youngest arrives at Lochindorb after receiving custody and protection from MacNair of Lennox for some number of weeks.

In the great hall, between messes of cheeses and wafers with sweetmeats, I stand to salute the return of the younger son. But since my cup is not brimming, I beckon the marshal. 'The cellar is empty of hypocras?'

He hesitates, knowing he will lose his own allowance of wine if his response is not to my satisfaction. 'Although the returning lords have accepted your generous hospitality with an eagerness that matches their devotion to their master, I have ensured supplies are sufficient, my lord.'

'Then why is this cup not filled?'

'Forgive my presumption, Lord Stewart, but I bid the servers fill no more cups with wine only because superior supplies arrived while you ate – the new kind of aqua vitae from Lindores

Abbey, the captured spirit of barley beer. The trader warrants that it is finer than any distillate from all of Italy. And to prove as much, he offers three skins to your lordship for no payment, while asking only that you consider purchasing the two full casks loaded on his boat.'

This new aqua vitae has never passed my own lips, though I have heard it described as an elixir that slows age and quickens the heart.

The skins of barley spirit fetched by the marshal are emptied before they reach the reward table.

I summon the trader.

Whatever the merits of the drink, which is more ardent than sherry but not as sweet, it has done nothing to slow the years of the whitebeard brought before me. Seeing his wasted frame draw near, I suspect that he brings his trade to my gate mostly in the expectation of receiving the nourishing charity only a lord can provide. Hearing his feeble-minded prattle, I come to believe that I will soon extract due payment for that same hospitality; the old fool is prepared to determine ownership of the barley spirit by means of an ill-advised wager. By his terms, if he loses a simple game of chess, the casks are mine; should he win, I pay full price, and give a gold coin more. As an additional stake, a piece of silver will be awarded for every chessman taken.

Since I am expert in the art of chess – though he cannot know as much – and for the humour of it, I accept, though I have a mind to simply relieve him of his cargo and set him afloat without a boat below his feet.

He soon learns that he has been outwitted. When I lose my first footman, I call a leatherwright, who removes a nail from my boot. I pass it to the old trader: the piece of silver he is due under our agreement. He mumbles, irked, but withholds any further protest.

The silver coins he surrenders to my palm stack ever higher.

The worthless boot nails I relinquish to him form no more than a scatter on the tabletop.

The contest almost over – both his warders are taken – the old man speaks. 'Your sole is near loosed,' he says of my boot, neither a question nor a declaration but somewhere between both.

I recognise the remark for what it is: an attempt at distraction by the near defeated.

I say nothing.

'My buttocks are ready to burst,' he tries. 'May I pause for the latrine?'

I wave him away. He takes a torch and shuffles towards the servants' quarters. He cannot abscond without passing the constable at the gate. The casks of barley spirit are mine.

He returns to the game with a new purpose – even taking sufficient of my pieces to claim the last nail from the sole of one boot and the first two from the other – though the eventual outcome is not in doubt.

*

The rowboats and currachs take to the water when the signal light is waved by the Lindsay man inside the Lochindorb stronghold. The moon has moved into its last quarter and so there is more dark than light but still we advance slowly to remain unseen and unheard. The first boat reaches the island by the north-east tower at the fourth hour of the night, the time when phantoms and demons go abroad as winds and shadows, by the word of the same Lindsay infiltrator.

Swathed in dark clothing, and concealed by the gloom of gathering clouds, Lindsay, Kay and Ogilvie men-at-arms draw their small craft onto the shore. Close to the rear of the armed fleet, Affleck and I do likewise, along with the grooms and retainers. Together, we press close to the castle wall to await the opening of the east gateway.

*

I turn advantage to account, advancing a footman to the eighth rank.

The old trader stares at the chequered board, straining to detect an end-game that does not exist. Finally, he topples his king.

'You will need assistance to unload the casks?' I ask.

He bows in submission. 'Your strongest men.'

I raise my cup and drain the dregs of aqua vitae.

*

Judging by the voices we hear approaching the gatehouse from within – several in number, raised neither in wrath nor in alarm – the Lindsay man guising as a trader has lured a detachment of Badenoch's guards to the foreshore.

Three different voices? Four?

Earl Lindsay and Ogilvie of Carcary exchange nods and whispers.

The gate, narrow for a keep, swings open.

And at least four issue, all stout and firmly made, perhaps five. But only a glint of protecting armour among them.

Twice as many leap from the nearby grasses, led by Ogilvie. A Lindsay soldier close to Affleck also stirs but grabs only the slightest of the figures. Although the caterans are soon overcome, they fight with more than common fierceness and the noise of the onset is likely to rouse others inside the garrison. Earl Lindsay hauls at one of the fallen. He orders others to do the same: the dead and wounded must be pulled into the shadows by the bailey wall, out of sight. Once there, he assembles our force into a tight circle. The most lightly armed are instructed to secure the gateway and tend the few wounded, then prepare the boats in readiness for a hasty withdrawal. The main body of troops will enter the gate to pursue Badenoch. The earl casts around the huddled circle and begins to briskly examine one among the company. The lord is in residence? Then where within the walls? How many fighting men are present? What is the placement of those men? An eldfather wearing a steel kettle hat – the frail figure pulled aside in the affray – steps into the circle to give his answers. From the questions asked, I gather him to be the Lindsay man who gained entry to the castle by feigning to offer goods for trade.

'Can it be?' Alongside me, Affleck interrupts the old man to say it, in a voice that approaches astonishment, and is far from a hush. 'The one who uses trickery to join in bringing about the fall of the Lord of Badenoch is Thomas of Ersildoune?'

I strain my eyes. But it is dark and I cannot share in Affleck's certainty. While the old man is of sufficient years to tally with the physician who attended Affleck's bedside, he is surely of too few to be the same justice clerk who advised that disinherited lands would be returned to both our families following King David's return from exile in France.

Affleck is given no opportunity to establish the truth of it: Earl Lindsay quietens him with a glower and a slash of his hand.

The old man laughs softly, first facing Affleck, then turning to me. 'True Thomas? A deceiver?'

'He is a loyal Lindsay of Ersildoune and Wauchopedale,' interrupts the earl. 'And must lead us without delay to the ignoble Lord Badenoch.' He looks to the old man. 'Say again – the entryways to the great hall are how many?'

The force is divided into three groups, one to enter by each door to the great hall, as described by the old man: Ogilvie through the kitchens, Kay of Kindrogan by the servants' quarters and Lindsay from the courtyard. Since we are given no particular instructions, Affleck and I choose to join the rear of the Lindsay party, which we judge most likely to come upon Badenoch first.

By the covenant we established at Daviot while awaiting the formation of the combined force, Affleck will seek to bring Badenoch to justice by picking him out from whatever mêlée follows, and then bearing witness to his fate; I will wield a blade against my son in an attempt to save my daughters. He unsheathes his knife; I draw my sword. My blood quickens. Dead since the day I last saw my wife and youngest daughter, I am roused by a spark of life.

Old man Lindsay of Ersildoune and Wauchopedale leads the way, through the gateway to a greensward that shifts with the noises of livestock at night. Kindrogan and the Kay men break off to enter the servants' quarters. The rest of us pass through a low archway into the courtyard. A northerly wind buffets us as we enter the open space. It swirls around the courtyard, bringing rain that slants one way then another. There is a stirring from the servants' quarters, but no great turmoil. We remain pressed to the wall that leads north, then west. No resistance is offered. At the double doors to the great hall, we pause. The old man directs Ogilvie to the kitchen block but remains with the Lindsay party. Shouts come from within the hall. Ogilvie disappears from view; in the same moment, we force our way through the doors, which are bolted but cannot withstand our numbers. Inside, our sudden, boisterous arrival stalls Kindrogan's advance towards the lord's table, though his men continue to emerge through the servants' door a distance to our right, assembling behind their master. Badenoch's caterans are more than might be expected for such a late hour, most already with arms drawn. Two of rank stand on the dais to our left. The taller of them, dark and barefaced – and so meeting Badenoch's description – is screaming the same indistinct words over and over. The shorter of the senior men jumps onto the table board. He snatches up a silver candlestick and draws a dagger. Plates, trenchers, messes of food, game boards, mazers, all tumble to the ground. The lull caused by Earl Lindsay's appearance provides the caterans with an opportunity to counter our thrust. Without exchanging words, all at one throw, they rush on our positions in two formations. Kindrogan is quickly driven backwards but Lindsay swords defend dauntlessly. I duck Affleck down until he is crouched close to the floor: we must eschew the hard battle; our struggle is with the devil not his demons. 'The taller one is Badenoch?' I ask Affleck. But before he answers, a new commotion arrives: a cluster of men, bare-chested or clothed in loose linens – I presume them to be servants latterly at work in the heat of the kitchens – stumble backwards through the door at the far end of the lord's table, harried by soldiers who tread on the bodies below their feet in their haste. Ogilvie himself pushes through the doorway, threatening cruel perils to any who stand in his way. Almost immediately, he disregards the servants and comes on without check to assail the caterans beyond, apparently in recognition of Kindrogan's plight. A black and yellow wall-hanging behind us has caught alight. We move away from the flames, closer to the dais. 'That is Badenoch.' Affleck nods at the tall, beardless one, who is still calling out, it seems demanding that a groom arm him with boots and a blade so that he might be attired and armed as a prince to defy the intruders.

Until now, I have been regretful but at ease with the task I must carry out. But learning that Badenoch is unarmed, and with Earl Lindsay's fighting force moving closer to its prey, the moment has come sooner than I expected. Hunched behind a board that has slipped from its support, I am close enough to make him out in more detail: black hair greying beyond its roots, wine's tawny glow in his cheeks, blood-reddened eyes. Some of his features may reflect mine – a crook nose, the same heavy brow? – but his face is so rent in fury I discern little with certitude. Perhaps only that he is less the son unseen in three score years, more the ageing, thwarted prince who must have vengeance on the blood relation of Christie Cleek.

Slay a son to save a daughter.

Before rising, I offer myself, and accept, the gift of a brief hesitation: fewer than a hundred breaths, before I take my son's life or lose my own. I look around. Affleck is leaning close, a hand on my shoulder. His words are audible but I do not hear them; his tone is urgent, agitated. The fire has spread from one wall-hanging to the next. A bench behind us is ablaze. Although the ceiling is stone-vaulted, the flames are beginning to crawl along the wood-panelled ribs, flaking paintwork that depicts the shining heavens. The combat is surging to the far end of the hall, Earl Lindsay dealing ghastly strokes with his distinctive two-handed sword. The caterans are mostly in one corner, reeling to and fro, but still raging like she-bears robbed of their young. Amidst it all, old man Lindsay of Ersildoune and Wauchopedale takes a place directly in front of the lord's table, apart from the fray. Inexplicably, he removes his kettle hat, tilts back his head and begins to sing, a high, sweet wail. Confounded by the spectacle, Badenoch finally silences; he barely takes heed as I get to my feet and slowly step forward, weighing the sword in my grip. Between lyrics, the old man whistles like a skylark in flight.

I step onto the dais and call along the length of the table. 'I bring an offer.'

Badenoch turns and regards me through a billow of smoke. 'Earl Lindsay expects me to treat of peace with a low-bred?'

'I offer peace of a sort, but not at the earl's behest. I offer the life of Duncan Christie – if you pledge to spare his kin from harm.'

Mention of his archfoe's name distracts him from the tumult; his eyes are on me alone. 'Mac Anndra...' Still staring, he gestures for his liegeman, now back down from the tabletop, to approach me. 'The Christie insect is here?' asks Badenoch, following behind. 'And you expect riches for delivering him into my custody?'

'No riches. Only the pledge.'

'Then become my man, help defeat the trespassing foe and deliver the insect – you will know my mercy.'

'By my word, Christie will be delivered. But I will pay no homage.'

He appears to consider this, half turning away. As he does so, I catch just enough of his expression to detect – what? – compassion? Esteem for an honourable adversary? He dips his head at mac Anndra. 'On the low-bred!' he snaps.

Mac Anndra swipes at my midriff; smoke clings to his blade, following the stroke. I feel, or imagine, a ripple in the air and stagger backwards, off the dais. I am unscathed but on my arse, my sword lost. Mac Anndra jumps down and pins me to the floor with his dagger, the point on my gut, between the taut fastenings of my arming shirt.

Badenoch squats next to me. 'The Lord of Badenoch will neither spare the loathsome Christie swarm nor parley with ill-bred churls. These are my terms – describe which among the invaders is the Christie brother and you will be permitted to become my man. Or else you will breathe out your life.'

And so, in accordance with nature's design, the father will be laid in dirt before his son. I glance over my shoulder in the hope that I catch sight of Affleck refreshing my soul with redeeming last prayers. The threads of the wall-hanging have mostly turned to ashes; flames curl around the pole from which it is suspended. No-one is close to where we both hid behind the fallen table board. Mac Anndra slashes at the fastenings of my doublet and digs a boot into my hip. Before he removes me from human affairs, I am obliged to make payment for debts accrued. I try to sit upright but he forces me back down, his foot on my chest, until I lean on one elbow. I switch my attention to Badenoch. 'The noble lord reaches heaven along the paths of mercy and truth,' I stammer.

He sighs, as though a tutor disappointed at a pupil's failure to grasp a simple teaching.

'Dispatch him.' He is facing me as he gives mac Anndra the command.

I close my eyes and make silent confession.

But rather than press tighter against my gut, the liegeman's dagger slackens, his arm twitches. I open my eyes. Affleck has an arm over his shoulder and is holding him securely by the chin, head yanked back. The old scribe has bored a blade into his neck, behind his jaw, and is slicing through his flesh with firm, even strokes, from back to front, in the way a herdsman wields a sticking knife. The blood, and life spirit, flow freely. Badenoch is grappling Affleck from behind, attempting to seize his knife arm, his hair, an ear or collar. The liegeman's head lolls, his face sallows. Affleck keeps his grip, despite Badenoch's attentions. I grope around for my misplaced weapon and, stretching, lay a hand on metal heated by nearby flames, a hilt with a familiar twist of loose leather strapping. I grab the sword and get to my feet as the liegeman falls to the ground alongside where I sprawled. Badenoch scoops up a chunk of masonry and clubs Affleck on the side of the head. Affleck grunts, a knee buckles. Badenoch cocks his arm to strike again. I straighten my blade. And rest the point in the soft hollow of the Lord of Badenoch's throat.

He stiffens, benumbed.

'If you do not choose mercy, then I will show you truth,' I say. 'It was Andrew Christie, violator of your mother, not his brother Duncan who escaped the parties sent out by the king in search of Christie Cleek. I know it because I am Andrew Christie.'

His eyes flare.

'I know this also – you are the seed of that defilement, the bastard son of the execrable Christie Cleek.'

His lips part but he says nothing; a bubble of saliva forms and pops.

'And I am your wretched father.' I lean on the pommel of my hilt with a flat palm, then lean again with added weight. Whatever words he is considering in response – mocking disbelief, a sneering rebuke – are caught on the sharpened edges of the blade as it passes steadily through neck and nape.

'Come!' Affleck is tugging at my arm. 'The day is won – we must leave now!'

I turn, giddy, and look about the room. The blaze is brightest along the south wall, by the doorway where we entered. The flames have reached the highest point of the ceiling. Bodies are strewn, some also burning, mostly caterans.

'It is done. They are safe.' Between coughs and curses, Affleck is saying it again and again: 'They are safe now...your wife and daughters...' He lets go of my sleeve and runs for the door that leads to the kitchens, along with others.

Only old man Lindsay of Ersildoune and Wauchopedale is still. And now silent, his harmony complete. He holds my gaze and bows extravagantly – one leg extended out behind, a tumbling wave of his hand – just as though the great hall were filled with onlookers and he the minstrel savouring the acclaim at the end of a well-received performance.

A stone of a certain size and weight falls from the crumbling ceiling and lands on the back of his bare head. He topples over in a single motion, brow dashing against flagstones, blood bursting through.

A thunderous crack sounds directly above.

I look up. A huge block of plasterwork has broken free, painted stars glittering in the firelight.

Chapter 6

"We go, go, go. All are perishing, but to love God."

Michael Scot, *Physionomia* (c early 13th century)

24th Day of July, 1405

> *"In the blessed name of God, I David Maxwell,
> burgess of Kirkcudbright, hide merchant, sinner,
> being in good mind and safe memory, make this
> testament. I pray that the Lord my creator rescues
> my unclean soul to His mercy, my body being where
> His grace disposes of it. Land and buildings at the
> tannery by Kirkcudbright will pass to my wife,
> Agnes, and heirs in tail. I bequeath my moveable
> goods – silver fittings, utensils of brass and wood,
> leaden vessels, instruments of the household,
> featherbed with mattress, blankets and linen sheets
> – to my wife and daughters, in whatever parts they
> are chosen to be divided. All gowns, robes, hoods
> and shoes are to be sold and what is received for
> them, as far as it will extend, is to provide for poor
> men and women, according to their conditions, in the
> toun of Kirkcudbright. To amend previous
> trespasses, I bequeath 30 shillings for any canons
> and clerks that belong to Kirkton church in the
> parish of Monikie, to sing and say 500 masses for
> the good of the soul of Prior Bernard of Restenneth,
> who was murdered by the one called Christie the
> Cleek. Solemn services are to be read, with torches
> of wax lit at the altar, for my own soul, and for all*

> *Christian souls, while the world shall last. I make my executor Brodie Affleck, also my clerk. I ordain that he be rewarded for performing the administration of this testament with seven pounds taken from the profits of the tannery at Kirkcudbright, for the construction of a simple dwelling at or near the aforesaid Kirkton church, with a life pension of two pounds to be paid half-yearly so that he will act as keeper of that graveyard, where his own family lies buried. This is my whole and last will, set to my seal on the fifteenth day of July, in the year of God 1405."*

Brodie turned the will over and began writing on the dorse.

> *"On this twenty fourth day of the month of July, the present testament was accepted as rightly proved before David Lindsay, Earl of Crawford, his chaplain at Daviot and other trusty persons from the bishopric of Moray, whose seals are appended. I, Brodie Affleck, have sworn in form of law to take upon myself the burden of execution of this testament, and also to deliver a copy of it to the deceased's wife, Agnes Maxwell, for her advancement, for evermore."*

Brodie removed his eyeglasses and tipped back his head. He closed his eyes to give better ear to the sounds beyond his Daviot desk. A cart creaked by outside, shod hooves treading heavily on the courtyard slabs. A soughing wind veered down the wall chimney. But no rain rattled the roof, despite the summer months knowing more wet days than dry. If the south-westerly continued to gust, he could make Kirkcudbright before Assumption Day, the abbey at Inchcolm in half that time.

He laid the will aside and lifted Fordun's history from his book-rest. Brodie thumbed the thick bundle of pages he would soon entrust to the younger, more nimble hand of Brother Walter Bower, no longer callow apprentice scribe, now chief copyist at Inchcolm Abbey, tasked with making a dated record of all noteworthy events in the kingdom and neighbourhood. Brodie arrived at the blank endsheet and smoothed the bulky book on his writing slope, as flat as he could manage. He held his eyeglasses to his face and, in the bleary light, leaned close to the parchment.

> *"Two days before the Feast of Saint Mary Magdalene – patron of tanners, who was cleansed of seven demons – the lurking-place called Lochindorb was overcome by a terrible storm and then the greatest silence. And in the quiet, the bodies of Lord Alexander Stewart and a whole number of caterans were found lying around, all blackened as if scorched by lightning, dead as ash. It is spoken for truth that the pernicious lord was visited by demons warring in mutual slaughter over the souls of those who fell by his hand and now live in everlasting glory: beloved wives, innocents at the breast, high-born nobles. As I myself, who writes these lines, beheld with my own eyes, he gaped over his slain like a black beast. Let him be remembered in this history and others as the evil one, the Wolf of Badenoch."*

Author's Note

Evidence linking the bogeyman legend to fourteenth century Scotland is found in the chronicles and poems of the day.

The earliest written use of the words 'bogill' or 'bogle', which is believed to have produced the derivatives 'bogey' and 'bogeyman', appeared in the work of Scottish poet William Dunbar in 1505. Dunbar and other Scottish writers who used the term in the years that followed were influenced by Lothian chronicler Walter Bower and his contemporaries. In 1447, Bower's *Scotichronicon*, which relied heavily on the work of John of Fordun and an unknown continuator, contained the tale of Christie Cleek, also associating the cannibal with a wolf.

The nineteenth century folk tales that updated the medieval story described Christie Cleek as a 'nursery bugbear' since the 1300s. The folk tale, *Christie of the Cleek*, was written 30 years before it was vouched that the word 'bogey' appeared in more modern nursery stories.

The present Queen Elizabeth is descended from Robert the Steward and Elizabeth Mure. The present heir apparent to the throne, Prince Charles, holds the title Great Steward of Scotland.

Acknowledgements

My biggest thanks go to Shirley and Maisie: both of them for their support and encouragement, Shirley in particular for her spot-on analysis throughout, Maisie for the easy way she makes me smile. Thanks also to Alison and Peter for their helpful feedback when it was most needed, Kenny for his wise advice and Marzanna for the pictures. And, of course, there would be no book at all without the backing of Seonaid and Huw at ThunderPoint – their decision to take on the book is much appreciated.

Originally setting off in a completely different direction, the plot only really began to take shape after I read the folk tale, *Christie of the Cleek*, in *Wilson's Tales of the Borders and of Scotland*. As such, a debt is owed to John Mackay Wilson, Alexander Leighton, who revised the original work, and the other collectors of our folk tales and legends. Likewise, the chroniclers who recorded the events of their time – particularly John of Fordun, Walter Bower and Andrew of Wyntoun – provided much historical detail, as well as a sense of the rich language used in medieval Scotland. The modern editions of John Barbour's, *The Bruce*, and Blind Harry's, *The Wallace*, were also invaluable, as were the academic studies of the reigns of David II, Robert II and Robert III by Michael Penman and Stephen Boardman, and the colourful social histories of Ian Mortimer.

Special acknowledgment also goes to the many excellent online religious and biblical sources, including www.biblegateway.com, and to the poet Keith Douglas for his powerful insights into the damaging effects of war on combatants.

Thanks are due to the following for permission to use quotes from the titles listed:

University of St Andrews for *Scotichronicon* by Walter Bower, edited by D.E.R. Watt with Alan Borthwick (1998)

Birlinn Limited for *The Early Stewart Kings: Robert II and Robert III, 1371-1406* by Stephen I. Boardman (2007) © Birlinn Limited, reproduced with permission of Birlinn Limited via PLSclear, and for *David II, 1329-71* by Michael A. Penman (2004) © Birlinn Limited, reproduced with permission of Birlinn Limited via PLSclear

Pan Macmillan for *Cannibal: The History of the People-Eaters* by Daniel Korn, Mark Radice & Charlie Hawes (2001) © Pan Macmillan, reproduced with permission of Pan Macmillan via PLSclear

Conan Doyle Estate Ltd for *The White Company* by Arthur Conan Doyle (1891)

Cambridge University Press for *Runaway Religious in Medieval England, c.1240-1540* by F. Donald Logan (1996), with text from *Memorials of St Dunstan, Archbishop of Canterbury*, edited by William Stubbs (1874) and *The Register of Thomas de Cobham, bishop of Worcester, 1317-1327*, edited by E. H. Pearce (1930)

HarperCollins for *The Pursuit of the Millennium* by Norman Cohn (1970)

David Burr for his translation of *Bernard of Clairvaux, Apology*, at Internet History Sourcebook

Peters Fraser & Dunlop for the extract from *The Canterbury Tales* by Geoffrey Chaucer, translation and notes by David Wright (1986), reprinted by permission of Peters Fraser & Dunlop on behalf of The Estate of David Wright

Oxford University Press for *The Oxford Book of English Verse 1250-1918* by Sir Arthur Quiller-Couch (9780191970221, 1992), and for *The Oxford Handbook of Victorian Poetry*, edited by Matthew Bevis (9780199576463, 2013), by permission of Oxford University Press

Saint Andrew Press for *Scottish Religious Poetry from the Sixth Century to the Present: An Anthology*, edited by Meg Bateman, Robert Crawford, James McGonigal (2000)

University of Aberdeen for *The Aberdeen Bestiary*,
www.abdn.ac.uk/bestiary

Hodder and Stoughton Limited, Maria Boulding and New City
Press of the Focolare for *The Confessions of St Augustine* by Maria
Boulding (1997) © Hodder and Stoughton Limited, reproduced by
permission of Hodder and Stoughton Limited

Scottish Parliament Project based at the University of St Andrews
for *The Records of the Parliaments of Scotland to 1707*, K.M. Brown et al
eds (St Andrews, 2007-2016), 1392/3/1, and RPS 1388/12/3

University of Birmingham for *Scotorum Historia* by Hector Boece,
translated by Dana F. Sutton (2010), © University of Birmingham,
at The Philological Museum

Scottish History Society for the *Calendar of Papal Letters to Scotland of
Clement VII of Avignon (1976)*

Llewellyn Worldwide for *Scottish Witchcraft: The History and Magick of
the Picts* by Raymond Buckland © 1991 Llewellyn Worldwide, Ltd.
2143 Wooddale Drive, Woodbury, MN 55125. All rights reserved,
used by permission

Thanks also for the responses from the Stationery Office, Boydell
& Brewer, John Wiley & Sons, and Faber & Faber.

About the Author

Craig Watson

Craig Watson is the author of the non-fiction book, *The Battle for Hearts and Minds*. The Bogeyman Chronicles is his first novel.

He is an established journalist who has written extensively for the UK and Scottish national press and won a number of awards.

In 2002, he set up the Scotnews agency, providing media consultancy and writing services.

Before moving into journalism, he studied Scottish history at Aberdeen University.

More Books from ThunderPoint Publishing Ltd.

Mule Train
by Huw Francis
ISBN: 978-0-9575689-0-7 (eBook)
ISBN: 978-0-9575689-1-4 (Paperback)

Four lives come together in the remote and spectacular mountains bordering Afghanistan and explode in a deadly cocktail of treachery, betrayal and violence.

Written with a deep love of Pakistan and the Pakistani people, Mule Train will sweep you from Karachi in the south to the Shandur Pass in the north, through the dangerous borderland alongside Afghanistan, in an adventure that will keep you gripped throughout.

'Stunningly captures the feel of Pakistan, from Karachi to the hills' – tripfiction.com

QueerBashing

By Tim Morriosn

ISBN: 978-1-910946-06-0 (eBook)
ISBN: 978-0-9929768-9-7 (Paperback)

The first queerbasher McGillivray ever met was in the mirror.

From the revivalist churches of Orkney in the 1970s, to the gay bars of London and Northern England in the 90s, via the divinity school at Aberdeen, this is the story of McGillivray, a self-centred, promiscuous hypocrite, failed Church of Scotland minister, and his own worst enemy.

Determined to live life on his own terms, McGillivray's grasp on reality slides into psychosis and a sense of his own invulnerability, resulting in a brutal attack ending life as he knows it.

Raw and uncompromising, this is a viciously funny but ultimately moving account of one man's desire to come to terms with himself and live his life as he sees fit.

'...an arresting novel of pain and self-discovery' – Alastair Mabbott (The Herald)

Changed Times

By Ethyl Smith

ISBN: 978-1-910946-09-1 (eBook)
ISBN: 978-1-910946-08-4 (Paperback)

1679 – The Killing Times: Charles II is on the throne, the Episcopacy has been restored, and southern Scotland is in ferment.

The King is demanding superiority over all things spiritual and temporal and rebellious Ministers are being ousted from their parishes for refusing to bend the knee.

When John Steel steps in to help one such Minister in his home village of Lesmahagow he finds himself caught up in events that reverberate not just through the parish, but throughout the whole of southern Scotland.

From the Battle of Drumclog to the Battle of Bothwell Bridge, John's platoon of farmers and villagers find themselves in the heart of the action over that fateful summer where the people fight the King for their religion, their freedom, and their lives.

Set amid the tumult and intrigue of Scotland's Killing Times, John Steele's story powerfully reflects the changes that took place across 17th century Scotland, and stunningly brings this period of history to life.

'Smith writes with a fine ear for Scots speech, and with a sensitive awareness to the different ways in which history intrudes upon the lives of men and women, soldiers and civilians, adults and children'
- James Robertson

A Good Death

by Helen Davis

ISBN: 978-0-9575689-7-6 (eBook)
ISBN: 978-0-9575689-6-9 (Paperback)

'A good death is better than a bad conscience,' said Sophie.

1983 – Georgie, Theo, Sophie and Helena, four disparate young Cambridge undergraduates, set out to scale Ausangate, one of the highest and most sacred peaks in the Andes.

Seduced into employing the handsome and enigmatic Wamani as a guide, the four women are initiated into the mystically dangerous side of Peru, Wamani and themselves as they travel from Cuzco to the mountain, a journey that will shape their lives forever.

2013 – though the women are still close, the secrets and betrayals of Ausangate chafe at the friendship.

A girls' weekend at a lonely Fenland farmhouse descends into conflict with the insensitive inclusion of an overbearing young academic toyboy brought along by Theo. Sparked by his unexpected presence, pent up petty jealousies, recriminations and bitterness finally explode the truth of Ausangate, setting the women on a new and dangerous path.

Sharply observant and darkly comic, Helen Davis's début novel is an elegant tale of murder, seduction, vengeance, and the value of a good friendship.

'The prose is crisp, adept, and emotionally evocative' – Lesbrary.com

The Birds That Never Flew

by Margot McCuaig

Shortlisted for the Dundee International Book Prize 2012

Longlisted for the Polari First Book Prize 2014

ISBN: 978-0-9929768-5-9 (eBook)

ISBN: 978-0-9929768-4-2 (Paperback)

'Have you got a light hen? I'm totally gaspin.'

Battered and bruised, Elizabeth has taken her daughter and left her abusive husband Patrick. Again. In the bleak and impersonal Glasgow housing office Elizabeth meets the provocatively intriguing drug addict Sadie, who is desperate to get her own life back on track.

The two women forge a fierce and interdependent relationship as they try to rebuild their shattered lives, but despite their bold, and sometimes illegal attempts it seems impossible to escape from the abuse they have always known, and tragedy strikes.

More than a decade later Elizabeth has started to implement her perfect revenge – until a surreal Glaswegian Virgin Mary steps in with imperfect timing and a less than divine attitude to stick a spoke in the wheel of retribution.

Tragic, darkly funny and irreverent, *The Birds That Never Flew* ushers in a new and vibrant voice in Scottish literature.

'...dark, beautiful and moving, I wholeheartedly recommend' scanoir.co.uk

Toxic

by Jackie McLean
Shortlisted for the Yeovil Book Prize 2011
ISBN: 978-0-9575689-8-3 (eBook)
ISBN: 978-0-9575689-9-0 (Paperback)

The recklessly brilliant DI Donna Davenport, struggling to hide a secret from police colleagues and get over the break-up with her partner, has been suspended from duty for a fiery and inappropriate outburst to the press.

DI Evanton, an old-fashioned, hard-living misogynistic copper has been newly demoted for thumping a suspect, and transferred to Dundee with a final warning ringing in his ears and a reputation that precedes him.

And in the peaceful, rolling Tayside farmland a deadly store of MIC, the toxin that devastated Bhopal, is being illegally stored by a criminal gang smuggling the valuable substance necessary for making cheap pesticides.

An anonymous tip-off starts a desperate search for the MIC that is complicated by the uneasy partnership between Davenport and Evanton and their growing mistrust of each others actions.

Compelling and authentic, Toxic is a tense and fast paced crime thriller.

'...a humdinger of a plot that is as realistic as it is frightening' – crimefictionlover.com

In The Shadow Of The Hill

by Helen Forbes

ISBN: 978-0-9929768-1-1 (eBook)

ISBN: 978-0-9929768-0-4 (Paperback)

An elderly woman is found battered to death in the common stairwell of an Inverness block of flats.

Detective Sergeant Joe Galbraith starts what seems like one more depressing investigation of the untimely death of a poor unfortunate who was in the wrong place, at the wrong time.

As the investigation spreads across Scotland it reaches into a past that Joe has tried to forget, and takes him back to the Hebridean island of Harris, where he spent his childhood.

Among the mountains and the stunning landscape of religiously conservative Harris, in the shadow of Ceapabhal, long buried events and a tragic story are slowly uncovered, and the investigation takes on an altogether more sinister aspect.

In The Shadow Of The Hill skilfully captures the intricacies and malevolence of the underbelly of Highland and Island life, bringing tragedy and vengeance to the magical beauty of the Outer Hebrides.

'...our first real home-grown sample of modern Highland noir' – Roger Hutchison; West Highland Free Press

Over Here

by Jane Taylor

ISBN: 978-0-9929768-3-5 (eBook)

ISBN: 978-0-9929768-2-8 (Paperback)

It's coming up to twenty-four hours since the boy stepped down from the big passenger liner – it must be, he reckons foggily – because morning has come around once more with the awful irrevocability of time destined to lead nowhere in this worrying new situation. His temporary minder on board – last spotted heading for the bar some while before the lumbering process of docking got underway – seems to have vanished for good. Where does that leave him now? All on his own in a new country: that's where it leaves him. He is just nine years old.

An eloquently written novel tracing the social transformations of a century where possibilities were opened up by two world wars that saw millions of men move around the world to fight, and mass migration to the new worlds of Canada and Australia by tens of thousands of people looking for a better life.

Through the eyes of three generations of women, the tragic story of the nine year old boy on Liverpool docks is brought to life in saddeningly evocative prose.

'...a sweeping haunting first novel that spans four generations and two continents...' Cristina Odone/Catholic Herald

The Bonnie Road

by Suzanne d'Corsey

ISBN: 978-1-910946-01-5 (eBook)

ISBN: 978-0-9929768-6-6 (Paperback)

My grandmother passed me in transit. She was leaving, I was coming into this world, our spirits meeting at the door to my mother's womb, as she bent over the bed to close the thin crinkled lids of her own mother's eyes.

The women of Morag's family have been the keepers of tradition for generations, their skills and knowledge passed down from woman to woman, kept close and hidden from public view, official condemnation and religious suppression.

In late 1970s St. Andrews, demand for Morag's services are still there, but requested as stealthily as ever, for even in 20th century Scotland witchcraft is a dangerous Art to practise.

When newly widowed Rosalind arrives from California to tend her ailing uncle, she is drawn unsuspecting into a new world she never knew existed, one in which everyone seems to have a secret, but that offers greater opportunities than she dreamt of – if she only has the courage to open her heart to it.

Richly detailed, dark and compelling, d'Corsey magically transposes the old ways of Scotland into the 20th Century and brings to life the ancient traditions and beliefs that still dance just below the surface of the modern world.

'...successfully portrays rich characters in compelling plots, interwoven with atmospheric Scottish settings & history and coloured with witchcraft & romance' – poppypeacockpens.com

The House with the Lilac Shutters: and other stories

by Gabrielle Barnby

ISBN: 978-1-910946-02-2 (eBook)

ISBN: 978-0-9929768-8-0 (Paperback)

Irma Lagrasse has taught piano to three generations of villagers, whilst slowly twisting the knife of vengeance; Nico knows a secret; and M. Lenoir has discovered a suppressed and dangerous passion.

Revolving around the Café Rose, opposite The House with the Lilac Shutters, this collection of contemporary short stories links a small town in France with a small town in England, traces the unexpected connections between the people of both places and explores the unpredictable influences that the past can have on the present.

Characters weave in and out of each other's stories, secrets are concealed and new connections are made.

With a keenly observant eye, Barnby illustrates the everyday tragedies, sorrows, hopes and joys of ordinary people in this vividly understated and unsentimental collection.

'The more I read, and the more descriptions I encountered, the more I was put in mind of one of my all time favourite texts – Dylan Thomas' *Under Milk Wood*' **– lindasbookbag.com**

9 781910 946107